Norman Invasions

E-Rights/E-Reads, Ltd. Publishers
171 East 74th Street, New York, NY 10021

www.ereads.com

Norman Invasions

by John Norman

E-Reads®

Contents

The Calpa

I AM spelling this the way it sounds, though I suppose, too, it might, in English, be spelled with a 'K'. The particular expression, above, which I have chosen to refer to the phenomenon, antedates English, at least as we know it. It derives from some other language, I think a very old language, perhaps from some predecessor of Danish, or from Jutish, or Saxon, or, perhaps more likely, from one of the older Celtic tongues. It seems clear that its original language is no longer spoken, but the word has lingered, or survived, threading its way toward us through various languages, most recently a Scottish Gaelic, until it nestles now in English, at least locally, almost as though hiding, a word never forgotten, occasionally recalled, and appearing now and again, though commonly only in whispers, as among my current neighbors, who are simple, ignorant, seafaring village folk. So, you see, we do not know where the word came from, that is, in the beginning. It may have been coined hundreds of years ago, perhaps thousands of years ago, perhaps from a time when Stonehenge lay in the distant future, by shell peoples, or by the paddlers of round, leather boats, the latter gathering and fishing near the shores of what we now think of as the western North Atlantic, but it is heard, too, interestingly, but as one would suppose from linguistic affinities, in this case old Gaelic, to the west, at the edges of the Irish Sea, again, of course, among seafaring village folk. It seems to be known in various places elsewhere in northern Europe, in the Wirral in Wales, for example, and perhaps anywhere here in the north, anywhere where there are simple folk, ignorance, superstition, and dark caves, washed by tidal floods, narrow waterways, cold waters, unseen, treacherous currents, lonely pebbled beaches, extended rocky shores, cruel, shadowed inlets. So it is an old word and seems to have been used, and is occasionally still used, though seldom before outsiders, to refer to the phenomenon. There are some more modern equivalents, too, but it seems to me more appropriate to use the older word, as do the villagers. The older word is more darkly reverent, I think; it is perhaps thus closer to the phenomenon.

So that is the word we will use. *Calpa.*

In English I do not think we have another word as well suited to the phenomenon. So we shall use it.

Too, I think it may prefer that word.

I find that I prefer it.

It is the case, however, or so it seems to me, that there is another word, if one may use that expression, in some language, a language quite unlike those with which you are likely to be familiar, for the phenomenon, a word in its own tongue, so to speak. In that language, in some sound, or something analogous to a sound, possibly even in some alphabet or syllabary, or in something analogous to such things, it occurs.

I have heard it, so to speak.

How might stars, or hurricanes, or stones, or tornadoes, or storms, or swift currents of water, lurking beneath a placid surface, speak? Such things do not, of course, speak, but, if they could, how might they speak? Could we hear them? Not the fury, not the inert passivity, not the incandescent tumult, but the words, the meaning? Could we hear it? These are analogies, of course, and doubtless not all that helpful. I am sorry. There seems to be little help for that. Still, suppose that there were things quite unlike ourselves, dark things, hard to touch, which could come and go, and were not much like things with which we were familiar, not like stones, and storms, and stars, but things distant from us, things alien to us, and that they could speak to one another, though we could not hear them. Does the ant hear the declamations of the market, do the flies understand the noises of the abattoir, or merely dumbly rejoice in the welcome, red feasting?

Who knows in what worlds we live?

Sometimes it seems to me I have access to that language, but only in dreams. To be sure, this could be madness. Surely I remember the hoofprints on the beach. They were real enough. Surely I remember what happened to the room. That was real enough, too. Certainly, at best, these hints, or recollections, or songs, or cries, are remote. More interestingly the sounds do not seem to be those natural to a human throat. Too, which mostly puzzles me, is that they do not seem to resemble the sounds of birds, or animals, either, with which I might be familiar.

Sometimes I think these things, the whispers, to be of the nature of the footfalls of spiders, but, of course, one cannot hear such things. Though doubtless they make a sound. Loud enough to the spider. Loud enough doubtless to the entangled fly, its senses strained, listening. At other times I think perhaps it sounds like darkness, but darkness makes no sound, not in any normal sense, not as we think of it. But if it could make a sound, as it encroaches, as it comes closer and closer, perhaps it would be like that. Sometimes it is easier to understand, like the tiny crackle of leaves in a forest, as though stirred by the movement of something near us, unseen, or like wind, as it moves about among cliffs, or prowls in caves, near the shore.

Those things are easier to understand.

I suppose I cannot make this clear. I do not think there is any help for that.

It is said that one cannot imagine anything an acquaintance with which one has not had first. One can imagine the golden mountain, of course, though one had never seen a golden mountain, but that idea, allegedly, is the combination of the ideas of gold and mountain, with both of which we are familiar. There is, of course, Hume's missing shade of blue, that shade, though not hitherto encountered, whose appearance might be conjectured from those of previously experienced contiguous shades. But even that is controversial. It seems plausible that, in the sensory modality at least, one could not imagine a sensory continuum unlike any hitherto experienced. The child who is blind from birth may become a physicist and understand better than many of the sighted the causes of color, the properties of surfaces, the agitation of atmospheres, the physics of illumination, familiarizing himself with abstractions, befriending equations, and such, but he will never see the blue of the sky, the red of the rose.

But I think I have seen this thing, or heard it, so to speak, this different thing, this dark thing, which is hard to touch, which can come and go. How this can be I have no idea.

The villagers, of course, at least some of them, usually the very old ones, insist that it can be sensed, at least at times, though what it is they sense they do not know. "It is here," they will whisper. Or they will say, "It is there, now, down on the beach." And then the villagers will hurry home, close the shutters, and bolt the doors.

One man had claimed to see it, last year, at night, in the moonlight on the beach, a fisherman, but his description made little sense. Perhaps one sees it as only one can see it, not perhaps as it is, but as it appears within one's own categories, textured, colored and shaped, tamed, enculturated, to reside within comforting fences, those of a required, quotidian familiarity. The man died at sea.

Let me tell you about the phenomenon, or, better perhaps, about the legends.

We will call it the *calpa*, as that word has been used, and, I think, for that of which I would speak.

It is a strange feeling, rather perhaps as though the ant suddenly understood the speech rushing over him, like clouds on a suddenly intelligible, stormy morning, or the flies suddenly grasping the meaning of the squeals and the blood.

The thing could understand itself, of course. But how

could one of us, you, or me, understand it, we a strutting mammal vain in our costume of bones and blood, dragging our murderous past behind us, like a shadow, denied, not looked at. One does not look back. Why should the phenomenon seek us out, if it does? Does it sense an affinity there? Does it need us? And, if so, for what? Or is it a vengeful, malicious, tormented thing? Or is it innocent, carelessly, unwittingly, destroying things in its passage? Is it to be blamed, any more than an avalanche, or deep, chill water? Any more than a force of nature? For I am not like the villagers. I am not superstitious. I do not think it is evil, or a demon or a devil, a preternatural being of some sort. I am sure that it is a part of nature, a nature unfamiliar to us perhaps, but doubtless with its own conditions and laws. Nature generates only her own. But how much of nature do we know? We reach out, apprehensive and curious within our cabinet of sensations, and extend our fingertips, and touch nature, but what part of it, how much of it? I think only a small part. And the phenomenon, too, I think, restless, raging, within its lair, sometimes puts out its paw, and touches nature, too, but perhaps another part. But sometimes I think that the fingertips and the paw, occasionally, perhaps at a doorway, at a narrow place, touch one another. I have felt it touch my shoulder. Heavy, and cold. And I cried out. Too, it must, for a single moment, have felt my fingers, reaching past the paw, or hand, in its flowing, freezing, cold, salty mane. For it drew back, and was gone.

Why had I reached toward it?

Why had I not recoiled, and shrunk away?

And had it reached out, to touch me?

Had it thought to announce its presence?

Its space is doubtless as real to it as ours is to us. And perhaps it shares our space, but we do not, entirely, share its.

Its space may enclose ours, as the sea encloses the land.

My grandfather spent time in this village, on holiday, coming up from London, and my father, too. I suppose it is a family tradition, or such. It seemed the thing to do, to come here.

They, my grandfather, my father, never told me the stories, if they knew them. I think they did. I heard them only here, and in the third time I came, last fall.

The villagers, you see, though kindly enough, and friendly enough, at least on the whole, tend to be a close lot, and reticent. I suppose this is not unlike villagers in many places. They are hard to get to know at first. Typically, they tend to put aside, or resist, questions. Sometimes it seems they are suspicious of outsiders. They know their own, keep to their own, fend against the outside, and keep their secrets.

Will the ant go about its business, as usual, will the fly continue to feed? Yes, after a time, for the ant is an ant, and the fly a fly.

And so, too, we, in the village, will continue about our business. It is not clear there is anything else to do.

It comes from the waters, it is said, and reenters them. Normally, it does little harm.

I am sure it bears you no ill will.

The owl bears the mouse no hostility. Perhaps it is even benevolently disposed toward it, or, at the least, regards it with a benign moral neutrality. The lion does not begrudge the antelope its grass. The wolf does not bestir itself to agitate against the lamb. In nature each has its own place.

Some think the calpa is evil. But it is not evil. I can assure you of that. But then neither is the owl evil, nor the lion or the wolf. Nature is not evil, but it is itself. That is its reality. It is merely that its moral categories, if it has them, are not yours.

The calpa bears you no ill will. It is, however, territorial, and will kill to conceal its presence.

It would be well for you to understand that.

No one knows where lies the house of the calpa.

Also it must breed, and seeks shallower spaces, waters where first, perhaps, it was spawned.

Coming back, one supposes, in each generation, from unimaginable journeys in alien seas.

I think men project their own fears on the calpa, that they tend to see it, or understand it, in terms of their own categories. But their categories, I fear, are not those of the calpa..

I remember the raving, the incoherence of the fisherman, drunken, ranting in the pub, crying "fishlike and human," who later drowned.

But there are many descriptions of the calpa. Crustacean like, the bird with human eyes, the cat, the subtle serpent.

Let the ant and the fly understand men as best they can, but they can do so only as they can.

They can have only the ant's and the fly's understanding of man. How adequate can that be? Adequate enough perhaps, for the ant and the fly.

It was four weeks ago, early in the morning, well before breakfast, come down from the house, that I was wandering on the beach, considering an article on the difficulties of economic calculation in guild socialism, when, bemused, the tide recently ebbed, I noted a set of unusual marks in the sand. It was not clear how they might have been formed, if not as some sort of hoax. More than anything they resembled the prints of a gigantic animal, hoofed, a horse or something horselike. I traced them back to where they seemed to emerge actually from the waters. That seemed to me puzzling. I supposed that the horse, for such it seemed to be, must have raced along the beach, and, here and there, entered into shallow water, run there, and then come back on the beach, this accounting for its seeming emergence from the water. I tried to confirm this line of reasoning by walking along the beach, and locating an entry point from the shore, but, in the time I was willing to give it, I found no such sign of entering the water. But, as hunger began to tell on me, I retraced my steps, to return to the house where I was staying, the same, incidentally, where my grandfather, and my father, long ago, had stayed. Even to the same room, with the single, large window. The hoofprints, for such I supposed they must be, if not a hoax, were those of an animal, unshod. The few horses in the village, except for colts, were, as far as I knew, shod. The prints, as I have said, were large, and, to speak honestly, seemingly much too large for a horse, as we understand such animals, too large even for one of the gigantic beasts bred for heavy haulage. They were also deep, very deep, the beach gouged. I wondered at how weighty the beast, and how swift, sharp and terrible must have been the hoofs which could have made such marks. Could sand have bled, the beach would have been covered with blood.

It seemed as though a gigantic beast, a horse, or some hoofed, horselike thing, had raced along the beach in the night.

Looking more closely, I discerned, then with amusement and chagrin, that the putative stride of the beast was incongruous, the distances between prints, and this convinced me of the joke some prankster, doubtless one of the village boys, had seen fit to play on the well-dressed, formal Londoner, the naive stranger, come here again, uninvited, on holiday. The prints were so far separated that it seemed the beast, between its gougelike strikings of the earth, must almost have flown across the beach, so far apart were the impacts of those mighty hoofs.

Surely the hoax might have been more cleverly perpetrated.

What a fool I had been!

I looked about, and called out, but no one answered. It seemed likely to me that the lad, or fellow, responsible for this hoax would have enjoyed witnessing my concern.

I clapped my hands, and laughed, saluting whoever might be watching. I had been gullible for a moment.

But no one revealed his presence.

No one stood up, and waved.

A small scuttling thing concealed within its carapace, disturbed, moved backward toward the water. It avoided one of the deep, dark marks. I continued to look about, but saw no one. Sometimes the cat from Hill House, where I had my room, followed me. She was a golden-haired Persian, odd for the area, a stray, come in from somewhere. She had, as cats will, settled in at Hill House, adopting it as her own, apparently recently, a few days before I arrived. I was fond of her. Guilelessly ruthless, affectionate, innocently merciless, loving, agile, graceful, furtive, stealthy, beautiful, watchful, she had all the sinuous charm, the patience and cunning, the moral freedom, of her breed. I sometimes bought fish in the market, putting it in a pan near the house for her. But I did not see her among the rocks, or on the nearest, graveled path, that which I had descended to the beach. A bird flew by, skimming the waters. Some cattle would be grazing, above, I supposed, somewhere. I supposed, too, high above, in its hole in the turf would be one or more waiting, coiled serpents, harmless things, waiting for the heat of the day.

It was a peaceful morning.

I shivered a little, as a cold wind swept by.

I was preparing to go back up the beach, and climb to the house, when I noticed two of the fishermen, nets over their shoulders, coming down to the shore. Two small boats were on the beach, drawn above the tide line.

I waved to them but they did not see me. I then returned to Hill House for breakfast. Later I began work on the article. Interestingly enough I saw the two fishermen returning to the village, carrying the nets. They were hurrying. It seemed, after all, they had not gone out on the waters.

February 2nd. *At the pub last night. Wild stories. New tracks found on the beach. Fifth time now, I think. First time some weeks ago. Villagers fearful. No boats putting out again. Paid for ale. Willing to speak before me. Raining, drenched by the time of getting back to Hill House. Dream recurs.*

It seems clear the prankster, whatever might have been his original intent, perhaps to discomfit a visitor, has decided to expand the scope of his hoax. His object, it seems, is to frighten the village. I do wish he would stop, as the men are losing workdays. I think perhaps the culprit here is young Gavin, a bold, outspoken, rather flairful lad, who is rather close to my own age. He seems a cut or two above the local folk, and has more schooling, at least a year at Edinburgh.

I once challenged him on this matter outside the pub, but he was very firm in his denials, even when I promised to keep his secret, if he saw fit to share it with me. After all, I, too, could see the sport of this, though I think it had gone too far, and told him so. "It is not my doing," he said. "But there must be a fooler in the village! Who could it be?" Well I certainly had no idea, if he did not. Most of the younger folk, when they came of age, either left the village, or drove, or, going to the highway, bused to work in one of the nearby towns. A diligent, sober crew they were, none of whom seemed a likely source of a hoax. The older people we rather automatically excluded. To my amusement, Gavin informed me that he suspected the prankster was none other than myself, and he, too, promised to hold the secret, if I should choose to impart it to him. This seemed to me a delightful turnabout.

We concluded our conversation under the eaves of the pub, as it began to pour.

I returned to Hill House, drenched, and shaking with cold, and certainly much the worse for a pint too much at the pub.

The cat was inside, the night so miserable. She came up the stairs, after a few minutes, and made her presence known outside the door. I admitted her, as I would, and she was soon curled at the foot of the bed, asleep.

It seemed I should have fallen asleep almost immediately but I was unable to do so. The night at the pub was still muchly in my mind. There had been much wild talk about the prints, which were attributed, as ignorance and superstition would have it, to no ordinary cause, of course not, but to any number of uncanny, preternatural visitations, presumably all ill-omened, foreboding, and demonic. You know how superstitious simple folk can be. Old Duncan insisted they marked the calpa's return, after almost a generation. That seemed then to be the consensus, at least among the older fellows. How tiresome is superstition!

Gavin and I did our best to soothe these wretched, brittle fears, and bring the light of at least a little rationality into the evening's discourse, but I fear we were largely unsuccessful. "There are the prints!" would say a fellow. "Put there," we said. "A hoax!" "By who, then?" asked another. "We don't know," I said. "There are the prints," would reiterate another, shuddering, and so it went.

Although the calpa takes many forms, or, perhaps, more accurately, is given many forms by those who see it, the most common seems to be that of a gigantic, horselike being, with massive hoofs, a long, flowing mane, and huge, wild, burning eyes. Sometimes it is thought to be seen under the water, abeam, or gliding in the cold darkness beneath the keel, or rising toward the bulwarks, then descending again. Sometimes it is claimed to have broken the surface, only to submerge again. This has led some to speculate that it is some sort of sea creature, reptilian, long thought extinct. Other speculations have supposed a small whale, or other aquatic mammal. Some see it, too, sometimes, it seems, as having arms and a human head. Surely the imposition of some sort of discipline would be appropriate for sailors found drunk on their watch. I have wondered if that form was not, perhaps subconsciously, suggested by the image of a centaur. But that seems an unlikely image for mariners. To be sure, the image of the centaur may have been founded, long ago, not on Scythian horsemen, but on that of the calpa. Many were the galleys which brought tin from England to the Mediterranean. Some think that to see the calpa is itself a sentence of death, a forewarning of doom, but this is inaccurate. There is no reason why seeing the calpa, if one could actually do so, would, in itself, be a sign of impending death. Of what interest or concern are we to the calpa? Is this not vanity on our part? Are we so important that denizens of metaphysical realms would find it incumbent upon themselves to oblige us with such unsolicited, unwelcome notices? Let us dismiss the fanciful, self-regarding vanity of that thought. On the other hand, there would perhaps be dangers in bearing this dreadful witness, perhaps rather as in meeting a dangerous animal unexpectedly, eye to eye, within a critical charging distance.

Seeing a lion is not in itself a sign of impending death, but it is quite true that these events are not always unassociated. It is true, however, that the calpa is territorial, and that it will protect itself. One does not enter certain cold, tidal caves, one does not swim in certain waters. As the legends have it, the calpa will kill, usually by drowning. Presumably it does not like to seen. Like the cat, it likes to conceal its presence. That is not uncommon with many forms of life. On the other hand, there are some legends, too, though admittedly rare, that the calpa has carried some to safety.

Who knows the nature of those it might save?

Why would it do so?

But I am speaking now as though there might be such a beast.

As the storm beat on the roof, and the wind whirled about Hill House, and lightning flashed beyond the window, off seaward, my mind, from the ale, wandered as it would.

Suppose, I thought, there might be such a thing as the calpa. If it is so secretive, so withdrawn, so jealous of its privacy, why would it mark a beach with its hoofs? So here, surely, was some sort of inconsistency.

Then I smiled, so silly was the thought, as if there might be such a thing.

I wondered how the prints came there. They would now, in the storm, be muchly washed away. Too, the tide would take most of them. They would be gone by morning.

Suppose there were such a thing, I thought. You can see how drunk I was, how tired, so disordered, lying there, pulling up the blankets, listening to the storm. The cat stirred when I pulled at the blankets, but did not, as far as I could tell, awaken.

Lightning flashed outside the window. The framing of the window, in its partitions, suddenly became a terrible shadow on the wall, one that looked for a moment, in the swiftly following crash of thunder, like the gigantic thrown-back head of a rearing horse.

So distraught was my fancy!

At the same time the cat, startled, awakened with a

screech, and stood at the foot of the bed for a tense, wicked instant, ears back, back arched, hair erected like bristling wire, a forepaw lifted, claws exposed, fangs bared, hissing, spitting, toward the window. Then she turned as suddenly and leapt from the bed, and fled out the door, which I had left ajar for her passage.

She had been frightened by the storm, the noise.

There had been the prints on the beach. What if it were not a joke, not a hoax, even a stupid, cruel hoax.

What if the old men, and old Duncan, were right.

But the calpa, I thought, no more than ghosts, or devils, or demons, or angels, or such things, would leave prints, nor stir pebbles, nor mark beaches.

Thus such marks must have some natural, explicable origin.

But there may be diverse natures, of which we are familiar with only one.

And suddenly I wondered, the thought chilling me, if such a beast, if such there were, in its passage, had even needed to leave such prints, now doubtless muchly washed away. Any more than fog, swift and zealous, need leave marks. And I had the odd sensation that it might have chosen to leave them. But, if so, why? Could fog, if it so chose, take on might and form, and weight, and speed, and a hungry ferocity, what might be its tracks? Could even the hoofs of an eager fog, massive, palpitating and alive, luring, blinding mariners, so torment the earth? Might its claws scour beaches, furrow stone? But if it, or, better, some such thing, could take on equine form, donning a foreign coat and metaphysical mask, perhaps one even incongruous to its nature, might it not leave such marks? There had been prints on the beach, dark, deep prints. I had seen them, and so had others, coming down to the beach in the light. This was no fancy private to me. Something had passed there. That seemed clear. Need such marks have been put here? If not, why had they been put here? Could they be curiously annunciatory? Was this a signal, a knell, from a far-off place, betokening something, a visitor, a presence? I thought of a scratch on a sidewalk, a mark on a wall, scrawled in colored chalk. Was this a flag, or cairn?

Or perhaps it was only an exuberance of movement, of a creature of great power, bursting into an unfamiliar reality, testing itself in a new space, excited by a new body, trying it out, exulting like a horse racing its phantom fellow in the midnight darkness, in the cold, between the cliffs and sea, the wind stinging its eyes, whipping in its mane.

I have come home, I thought. But I must soon leave.

Or could this be its announcement, this racing, reflective of its power, its joy? Is this the way it claims its territory, I wondered. Thusly marking it? Against whom? But why would it claim territory? Why does an animal do that? The antelope has all the grass of the plains, I thought. Why does it stop in one place, and put down its horns, and stamp its hoofs?

I am not sure, but I think I then fell asleep.

I had the sense of rising from the bed once, but I do not know if this occurred, or if it was part of a dream.

I went to the window, or seemed to do so, which was cold, and streaked with rain. It felt chilled to my fingertips. In another flash of lightning, I looked down into the yard and, for an instant, it seemed to me that below, looking up at me, was a girl, illuminated, streaming with rain, unclothed save for long, bedraggled, soaked yellow hair clinging about her body like seaweed. She looked up, indifferently, unmindful of the storm, and then turned away. When lightning flashed again, the yard below was empty, save for some debris, a barrel, some puddles into which the fierce rain pelted, the drenched, smitten grass, the glistening stones of the walk. It must have been in a dream, as otherwise the poor thing, naked, and exposed to the elements, would have been half frozen. I had seen her before, I was sure, but only in dreams. In my earlier dreams, perhaps oddly enough, as they were the dreams of a young man, she, unlike the accommodating, sensuous maidens of many other dreams, had always been fully clothed, indeed, decorously, primly so, in Victorian propriety, in a starched, white shirtwaist, with a cameo brooch, with a long, black skirt to her ankles, with her yellow hair bound back behind her head. Her image in these recurring dreams was that of an upper-class scion from another era, one rather removed from ours, one more refined than our own, the image of a self-assured, self-possessed, proudly prudish, deliberately reserved, exquisitely formed, exquisitely feminine, exquisitely beautiful young lady, a lady as if of another time and place, a young lady well-bred, elegant, fashionable, proper, and genteel, very much so, aristocratic, self-satisfied, priggish, frosty and distant. She had always, in these dreams, had a look of smug, sheltered Victorian innocence, almost affectedly so, and of an almost contrivedly demure purity, and chastity, mingled with an expression of coldness and disdain. Sometimes this had excited my fury. How she regarded me. For something told me, in the dream you understand, that she, though this was unknown to her, belonged to me, that she, though at the time quite ignorant of the fact, was mine, *literally.* Sometimes, behind her, I had seen, briefly, the image of a great horse.

I was awakened once later, in the night, by the return of the cat. Her fur was wet, so I conjectured she had left the house through the kitchen, where there was a cat flap. I toweled her down a bit, and soon, again, curled about herself, her tail wrapped neatly, delicately, about her small, golden body, she had purred herself asleep.

In the meantime the rain had abated.

I lay there for a time, and then, as I could not get back to sleep, rose, drew on boots, and some clothes, and, taking my torch, went downstairs. I left the house through the kitchen, quietly, in order not to awaken Mrs. Fraser, or any of her roomers. In the yard, under the window, I shone the light about.

The grass had been muchly depressed by the night's rain. The stones were wet, and reflected the light of the torch. There were puddles here and there, and, in places, narrow, arrested trickles of rain, like stilled, small rivers, arrested in their passage, shored by mud and pebbles. Though I had come down with trepidation, I soon felt a fool in the darkness, blazing the light about on the sodden grass, the stones, the bordering gravel. I am sure that, by then, I had slept off the fumes of alcohol, but I was undeniably agitated, even trembling. I was muchly unsettled in my thinking. Work on the article, too, had not been going well. I might well return to London, I thought, perhaps as soon as the morrow. Given the obscurities, the troubling oddities, of recent days, the hoax of the prints, the rumors, the uneasiness of villagers, I now found myself less loath than I would have been earlier to exchange the tranquility of the village, supposedly ideal for gathering together one's thoughts, for the distractive bustle of Mayfair.

I shall return to London, I thought.

I have wondered, sometimes, if that would have been possible.

I was about to return to the room when the beam of light fell upon a small patch of bare, damp ground, some feet within the wall, at the end of the yard. I focused the light on the ground. I looked up. I could see the window. The cat must have awakened, and noted my absence, for I could see her. She sat on the sill, within the panes, looking down at me. How silly she must think humans, I thought, to be prowling about so late, in a muddy yard, when they might be snug abed in a warm, dry room. I put the beam down again. The mark was not absolutely clear, because of the rain, as it had softened the earth, but what I saw, at least if casually observed, might have easily been taken as the print of a small, delicate, well-formed foot; there was the print of the heel, and of the sole, and of the toes; it seemed, clearly, the print of girl's foot, of a small, delicate, feminine, naked foot.

Some village girl must have left it, I thought. Perhaps one of those who helps Mrs. Fraser with her cleaning. But this seemed absurd, given the time of year.

I would not return to London on the morrow.

I returned to the room and sat up for a time, bent over, my head in my hands. Then, as it was still quite early, I went back to bed. Happily I slept. When I awakened my first thought was that my trip to the yard, of last night, might have been in a dream, as well, but the mud of my boots, and the dampness, and disarray, of my clothing, thrown to a chair, convinced me that I had, indeed, left the room that night. After breakfast I reconnoitered the yard again, returning to the place under the window. I saw nothing, then, that was clearly a print. It had rained again, in the early morning, while I had slept. If the print had been there, it must have been washed away.

The most rational interpretation of the night's business was that I had walked in my sleep, as some do, and dreamed, in so walking, of strange things. This was the most rational interpretation, so it was the one I accepted.

I returned then to some research pertinent to the article, utilizing some of the relevant books and journals I had brought with me, in a small, wooden crate, to the village.

What occurred three nights later I could not dismiss so easily.

February 5th. *Back late. Another visit to the pub. More conversation with Gavin. Prints not on beach now. Duncan apprehensive, strangely quiet. Cronies subdued. New ale. Things return to normal. Or nearly so. Foolish to have been disturbed. Fear is like contagion, transmitted from one person to another. Some sort of animal communication probably, on some atavistic level. Must resist. Am now above such things. Article going well.*

I was not really back so late that night, as I remember it now. The behavior of the cat was surprising. She fled from me. I read a little, until after midnight, and then retired. I did leave the door ajar so that she might return, if so inclined.

The villagers are good fellows, but some of them are becoming a bit irritating. Wherever I go in the village, one or another seems to be about, and not just about, but about watching, pretending not to be watching. If I did not know better, I would suppose they were spying. I find this oppressive, and intrusive. Perhaps I am merely becoming excessively sensitive, or even paranoid. Perhaps I should speak to some of them about it. But that might cause unpleasantness. It is not my fault if I do not share their archaic attitudes, nor choose to sympathetically credit their superstitions. That they have no right to expect. And surely Gavin, one of their own, does not, either. I saw old Duncan today at the end of the village, near the road leading to the highway, talking to a constable. When he saw me, he walked away. I would really resent it if he, or others, were spreading rumors, or making irresponsible allegations, particularly to the law. Perhaps about the prints. But they are gone now. Hopefully that business is over and done with. I trust that the constable, who bikes down now and then to the village, has at least a modicum of common sense. I have met him once or twice, and he seems to be a decent, sensible fellow. If old Duncan's conversation had anything to do with me, I trust the constable bore his remarks in good humor. But enough of this. I have work to do.

That night the dream was different.

She seemed to see me for the first time, that prim, exquisite, coveted thing, and seemed know herself, perhaps for the first time in her life, this astonishing her, and frightening her, coveted. Coveted, *as a mere object.* Something that could be possessed, that could be seized as a prize, like a jewel, something that could be owned, literally owned, with no rights whatsoever, owned uncompromisingly, totally, callously, without quarter.

She regarded me.

Did she then understand that she was seen as a mere object? Did she then understand why she was so seen, and the rightness of it, why she was seen so, that she was seen so because that was what she then was, in that moment, a mere object? An *object.* How frightening for her, to understand herself as that. Oh, yes, of course, no simple or common object. But a precious, beautiful, living object, wondrous, deep, sentient, and alive—a masterpiece of foresight, preparation and training—but an object nonetheless. Beneath the whiteness, the crispness, the starch, the severity, the formalities and protocols, the conventions, the inculcated restrictions, the rigidities, the enmeshing, conditioned coldnesses and inhibitions, she was a slim, lithe, sleek, well-formed little beast, attractively bred, an appealing animal, an attractive little animal, an extremely desirable little *animal.*

Ready in the courtyard of nature for appropriation.

Ready for snaring, for capture and use.

Did she then understand, in the dream, of course, if only for a terrifying moment, the meaning of her slightness, her fragility, her vulnerability, the destiny and meaning of her excruciatingly, tantalizingly alluring slim curves, of her remarkable, unmistakable, considerable beauty?

In the dream, you see, I had suddenly grasped something which she had not, that she was the product of a long line of calculated, supervised breedings, a line, perhaps one of several similarly selected stocks, which had been supervised and tended for thousands of years.

She had been bred for me.

Her eyes were wide, straining to see and understand, to comprehend. Her lower lip trembling, her small hand at her palpitating breast, so delicate and appropriate a gesture, she backed away from me, and, in an instant, frightened, turned and, fleeing, vanished, and did she think there was an escape for her, and there was suddenly then a vast snorting noise, a roar, or neighing, like thunder, and a mighty form rose up before me, dark and gigantic, rearing on its hind legs, its hoofs flailing, slashing at the air, and I crouched down before it, and covered my head, and screamed.

I am rather sure I remember the sounds of shattering wood and glass, and voices, solicitous, first in the dark, calling up to me. Then, in a bit, I heard steps on the stairs, hurrying. A moment later Mrs. Fraser, followed by two of her roomers, entered the room. She was carrying a candle. I had seen its flickering light approaching, through the opening I had left, as I usually did, for the cat. She looked about, at me, and then the room, and cried out in dismay. In a moment or two the other roomers appeared.

"Are you all right, sir?" said Mrs. Fraser.

"Yes," I said. "I must have been sleeping. I must have cried out. I'm sorry."

"What happened here?" asked a man.

I looked about, wildly. The room was in disarray. It might have been the stall of a powerful, maddened animal.

"I don't know," I said. I didn't.

The window was shattered, its wooden partitions splintered away, scattered with a shower of glass into the yard below. The sill was broken. The side of the window on the right, as one looked out, had been forced from the wall, enlarging the opening. Indeed, though the window was a large one for the structure, part of the wall was gone. Some planking, and several slats of ruptured lath, plaster clinging to it, projected outward from the room. It was as though something quite large, some huge animal, like a bear, a bull or stallion, had somehow inadvertently found its way into the room, and had then, in terror or fury, perhaps sensing itself confined or trapped, bolted, rushing blindly toward the window, shattering it, and leaping to the outside.

I staggered to my feet. "I must have been walking in my sleep," I said. "I must have done this, somehow. I don't know how, but I must have done this. I'll pay for the damage, surely. I'm sorry. I'm terribly sorry!"

"This is not your doing, sir," said one of the roomers.

"Never," said another, grimly.

"Is anything missing?" asked another, looking about.

"There must have been a thief, a prowler," said one of the men.

"Sir is not of the village," said a fellow. "Someone thought he had money."

"Do you have money?" asked another.

"Not really," I said. "Nothing much."

"A thief would not know that," pointed out another.

"The gentleman awakened, and the fellow went for the window," said a man.

"Such things do not happen in my house," said Mrs. Fraser.

"This must be reported to the constable," said a man.

"If you like," I said. "But I think I am all right. I do not think anything is missing. I may have done this myself, somehow."

"Never," said a fellow.

"I am sure this was not done by local folk," said a man.

"No, we have no thieves here," added another.

"It would be an outsider," said another.

"Aye," said another.

"Yes," I said. "Yes." Yes, I thought, it would be an outsider, an outsider.

"I'll have some repairs begun tomorrow," said Mrs. Fraser.

"Keep the outside door locked," said one of the roomers, uneasily.

"I have never seen the need, but I shall do so," she said. "It is a lamentable thing, that one should have to lock the doors of one's own house."

"Aye," agreed a fellow.

Mrs. Fraser and the others then left the room.

I sat on the edge of the bed. Oddly, I now felt serene. In a few minutes I rose and lit the kerosene lamp and looked about. Indeed, nothing was missing. With a piece of toweling I wiped away a large, hooflike mark from the shattered sill. When I returned to the bed, I discovered, to my surprise, that the cat was there, curled at its foot. Earlier she had fled at my very appearance, an unusual behavior on her part, which had troubled me, which had made me muchly uneasy. I petted her for a bit, and then retired. It was probably something like three in the morning. I saw the moon through the shattered window, and the sea beyond. I could not see the beach because of the cliffs, to which, in places, the waters were closely adjacent. I awakened once, wondering if, below, on the beach, I heard the sound of hoof beats, racing through the sand. Then, the cat at my feet, I slept soundly.

February 15th. *I have had the sense, for some days, that I am waiting for something. I am not altogether clear what it is, but I sometimes think I know its general nature.*

How much is real, how much is madness, if any of it, I do not know. Went to the pub. Haven't been there for some time. Odd conversation with old Duncan. Gavin not about. Finished article. Think it all right. Full moon tonight. Mention this because old Duncan called it to my attention. Not clear why. Think he may be mad. Perhaps we all are.

When the dream recurs now I am no longer disturbed by it, the dream of the girl, so lofty, haughty, cold, prudish and smug, and the horse, or that which, in the dream, assumes that form.

The girl is mine. She does not know it, of course, but she is owned, and it is I, her master, who own her. She has been bred for me, and for the bearing of my son, who will one day return to this place.

There are other aspects of the dream, but I cannot explain them to you. At the least it would be difficult. I think the words are lacking. Actually, it is the experiences which are lacking. Suppose one could add the sense of sight to one congenitally blind. What a new world would open for him. Now conceive, if only as an abstraction, for that is only how you can conceive it, and only how I could have conceived it earlier, before the dreams, what it might be if you were given, or discovered you possessed, new senses, if you, so to speak, for the first time opened your eyes and could see, or lifted your head, and could hear.

Doubtless old Duncan is daft. The things he says, the way he says them. We had a pint together. Interestingly, it seems he remembers my father, when he was here, long ago. We spoke of him for a time. It seems they had been friends, of a sort. "Gavin is foolish, he does not believe," he said, rather pointlessly, I thought. I did not speak to him about his interview with the constable, which, from a distance, I had inadvertently observed. I suppose he had seen me, from the manner in which he had concluded his conversation, and went about his business. He made no mention of this to me, either. To be sure, this might have had nothing to do with me.

"I have seen it, and more than once," said old Duncan to me, leaning forward, across the table, whispering. "Long ago, and lately, too, indeed, twice within the fortnight."

"What?" I asked.

"It, the *calpa*," he whispered.

"Of course," I said.

"Twice on the beach, and last night in the village itself, amongst the houses."

"Dear Duncan," I said, "you are old, and it is your imagination."

"Why have you come to the village?" he asked.

"To work," I said.

"No," he said.

"I do not understand," I said.

"Do what you have to," he said. "And then go. It is best that way."

"I do not understand," I said.

"I bear you no ill will," he said.

"I am pleased to hear it," I replied.

"Nor it," he said.

"It?" I asked.

"Aye," he whispered, "it."

"The calpa?" I said.

"Aye," he said.

"I am sure that it, too, would be pleased to hear it," I said.

"Tonight," said Duncan, lighting his pipe, "it is the full moon."

"So?" I said.

There was a rumble of thunder outside, which did not please me. Once before I had been caught in a storm here, between the pub and Hill House. I made a mental note to cut short the evening's pubbing. I had no interest in being soaked and chilled a second time, at least not so soon again. Indeed, even before I had left Hill House, Mrs. Fraser had referred to the menacing, gathering clouds, and recommended caution, and an early return. It might be a terrible storm.

"It was the full moon, too, once, long ago, when your father was here," he said. "It seems to like the full moon, like some fish, like some animals."

"There won't be much of a moon tonight," I said. "Too many clouds. A storm is coming in. Listen. Hear the wind?" It was indeed beginning to whistle about the pub. "I'll walk you home."

"No," he said, quickly. "You go by yourself. I'll nurse another pint."

"As you will," I said. It was curious. I almost thought he might be afraid. Surely I could have seen him safely home, supporting him, even in the darkness, keeping him from falling. He was not young any longer.

"It likes the moon," he said, "like some fish, some animals."

"Oh?" I said.

"The moon," he said, "will lay a road on the sea, leading to the cliffs. You won't see it, but it will be there."

"You're mad, my dear Duncan," said I.

"The world is mad, laddie," said he, "only it does not know it."

"If you believe in the calpa, and have seen it," I asked, "how is it that you are still alive, that you were not killed, drowned?"

"I mean it no harm," said Duncan. "I think it knows that, as you know I mean you no harm. I do not threaten it. I let it be."

"But surely you believe it to be some unnatural, demonic, dangerous thing?"

"Too," said Duncan, "I knew your father."

I remembered the beast of the dream, rearing, snorting, with its wide, distended nostrils and burning eyes, its mane wild, whipped and torn as in the blasts of a hurricane, seeming to be in more than the room, the high, broad hoofs flailing above me, like hammers.

"What difference would that make?" I asked.

"I do not know what it is," said Duncan. "I do know that it is, for I have seen it."

"And you have lived to tell about it."

"If none lived to tell about it," said Duncan, "its existence would not be known, would it?"

"No," I laughed, "it would not be." It seemed to me that he made his point, or something like it, in his daft way. Certainly I granted it to him.

"Perhaps it does not know I have seen it," said Duncan.

It does now.

"What did you say?" asked Duncan.

How strange he was. I had not said anything.

I myself had seen the thing, or a form of it, only in dreams. I had, of course, seen prints. So had most in the village, I wager, those who, in the daylight, had gone down to the beach.

"The whole thing is a hoax," I said.

"Gavin is angry," he said.

"Where is Gavin?" I asked.

"Not here," said he.

"What is he angry about?" I asked.

"The whole business," he said. "I warned him not to interfere."

He will not interfere.

"What?" asked Duncan, looking up.

But I shook my head, again I had said nothing.

Sweet Duncan, sweet, superstitious old fool.

I waited until Duncan had finished his pipe, and then I finished my ale, I had limited myself to one, and took my leave.

I wished to avoid the storm.

I missed seeing Gavin, for I was fond of him. He was one of the few villagers of my own age, or nearly so, perhaps a year or two younger. He had had some education. Sometimes we had spoken, about the sea, the village, fishing, and about London, that great, mysterious, far-off, sparkling, bejeweled, wicked city to the south.

Some of the villagers were illiterate. I rather doubted that Duncan could read or write, but I never inquired into the matter.

When I left the pub, to return to Hill House, I glanced up at the moon, through the racing clouds. I felt a drop of rain. There was a flash of lighting, far out to sea. It was a full moon as far as I could tell, but I had not kept track of such things, maybe a little less, a little more, maybe full. The astronomy of natural satellites had little to do, as far as I could tell, with the economics of guild socialism.

It had started to rain when I came to Hill House, but I did not immediately enter. I thought I might have heard a small cry, far off, but it was the wind. I looked up at the window, and the adjoining wall, which had now been repaired, though not yet painted. I had rather expected to see the cat there, ensconced in one of her favorite coigns of vantage, but was disappointed. I trusted she would take shelter as the night threatened to be formidable. I was pleased I had left the pub as early as I had.

I turned toward the door when the clouds broke and the moon loomed over me, white and monstrous. Then the clouds closed again, obscuring it.

I would be very pleased to reach the shelter of my room. I entered and went up the stairs. The outside door had not yet been locked. I gathered it would be, later. At least one of Mrs. Fraser's roomers had suggested that precaution. The cat, of course, could come and go through the cat flap in the kitchen door.

I made a brief entry in my journal, and prepared to spend the rest of the evening reading. The storm, meanwhile, became angrily active.

Such storms can last for hours.

Muchly was I pleased that the repairs had been promptly and efficiently accomplished.

I think I fell asleep, over the book.

I remember awakening, rather suddenly. It must have been late. My first thought was one of annoyance, that I had fallen asleep.

I wondered if I had heard a noise, a whimpering cry, a plea as though for mercy, or help. That would have been in some dream.

I was angry that I had fallen asleep.

The storm was still raging. One could see flashes of lightning in the distance, out to sea, and then, several seconds later, hear the rumble of thunder, rolling inward, crashing ashore. The rain poured on the shingles. One could scarcely see through the window there was so much rain running on the panes, banking on the partitions, flowing over. The wind whipped the rain against the glass. The shutters, which I had not closed, rattled on their hinges.

I should have prepared for bed before reading, I suppose, but I had not planned on falling asleep in the chair.

The shutters, caught in the wind, suddenly banged open and shut.

It may have been that sound that had awakened me.

I went to the window to fasten the shutters, as I should have earlier, either back and latched, or closed, and latched, given the storm. I decided to close them. That way the slats would protect the window, and the unpainted partitions, and part of the sill. Too, that might make it a bit easier to sleep, as the room, abruptly, unpredictably, was, again and again, washed with white light, followed by roaring thunder. I could see lightning, too, far out to sea. It seemed to be coming closer.

It would not be a pleasant job, opening the window, to get at the shutters, but it needed to be done. Certainly one would not want them crashing back and forth all night. Too, they might disturb the other residents in the house. It would be embarrassing if Mrs. Fraser, or one of her roomers, came upstairs to see about it, perhaps offering to fasten them for me.

I raised the sash and, half closing my eyes against the ferocity of the storm, feeling the rain drenching my shirt, reached outward to grasp the shutters. I had actually begun to draw them inward, to fasten them closed, gratefully, when I stopped, startled, for below me, in the yard, in the driving rain, oddly illuminated in the moonlight, between bursts of lightning, was a small, white figure, she whom I had seen before. She had been running, it seemed, and had just fallen in the gravel and grass, and was on her hands and knees. She turned, and looked up, wildly, toward the window. She was gasping, and muddy. Frantic. She was naked, as before, absolutely so, starkly so, save for that wealth of long blond hair, feet in length, bedraggled, clinging thickly about her like golden, sopped slave cord. How terrified, how beautiful, she was! There, miserable, in the cold and rain. She might have been a delicate, high-born Medieval maiden, escaped perhaps for a moment from barbarians, who had loutishly removed her rings, her jewels, and then, doubtless enjoying her humiliation, mocking her tears, ignoring her protests, roaring with laughter at her unspeakable, unconscionable grief and shame, inappropriate in a thrall, however new to her bondage, her brocade, and lace, leaving not the kindness or grace, or mercy, of a single thread upon her, this preparatory doubtless to handing her about, man to man, victor to victor, she their prize, now belonging to them, rightfully taken from weaker men, theirs now, by the right of nature, putting her to their common pleasure. Barbarians, if they found her satisfactory, sufficiently helpless and gasping, I supposed, might take her with them, on a leash, bound, to their ship. Such do well in cleaning stables, in scrubbing the stone floors of rude halls, in laundering, in carrying water and cooking, in serving at a master's table, and in his bed.

"Come in!" I called to her, my words fighting the wind and rain. "Do not be afraid!"

From her hands and knees she looked up. I do not know if she could well see me, given her seemingly pathetic condition, her fear, the cold, the rain, the night, the storm. I must have seemed dark to her, perhaps frightening, doubtless silhouetted in the frame, the light of the lamp behind me. How did she see me? Could she not see that I was muchly concerned for her, that I was profoundly solicitous on her behalf?

"You will freeze!" I cried. "Come indoors!"

She scrambled to a position half kneeling, half crouching, one knee in the grass, looking up, terrified, trying to cover herself, drawing her rain-soaked, bedraggled, golden hair about her with her small hands, pathetically, as if it were a rich but muchly rent, tattered cloak.

Position, bitch.

She then, for no reason I understood, numbly, seemingly uncomprehendingly, fearfully, went to her knees in the wet grass. The rain poured down. Lightning flashed. She had flung her hair behind her, perhaps that it afford no impediment to one's vision, realizing perhaps that such was not permitted, in the least, and knelt back on her heels, with her back straight, and her head up. Her hands were on her thighs, palms down. Her knees were widely spread. How open, how vulnerable she seemed! Never had I had a woman kneel so before me, never had I known a woman could so kneel before a man. I dared not even conjecture what might be the meaning of such a posture, that of a woman before a man. She looked up at me, frightened, the rain streaming down her body.

She looked well, so before me.

She was not prompt, I thought, she will require training.

Then I dismissed such an improper thought. Though, too, I thought, it would be pleasant to train her, to make her something worthy of a man's needs.

"It's terribly cold out there," I called down to her. "The storm! The night! You'll freeze! It's miserable! Come in! Come in, out of the storm!"

She rose to her feet, unsteadily, shaking her head. She stood in the cold, wet grass, in the moonlight, in the rain, partly bent over. Again she covered herself, as she could, ineptly, with her tiny hands, and hair.

Has she not risen to her feet without permission, I thought. That should require discipline.

"Who are you?" I called down.

Do you not know, the thought came to me.

"Come in!" I called to her again. "Come in, warm yourself by the stove, I'll fetch blankets, I'll make tea."

She turned, looking wildly about.

I recalled, angrily, that, by now, the door to Hill House would doubtless be locked.

"Wait!" I called to her. "I'll come down. I'll bring a blanket!"

At this point she turned about and fled, as though blinded with fear, irrationally across the grass and gravel, toward the wall, across the yard, opposite the window. Her small, wet body was then at the wall, pressing against it, scratching at it, sobbing. She looked pathetically upward, toward its top.

"Wait!" I called.

She turned about, wildly, frightened, as though trapped, and looked up at me, in the window.

"Don't be afraid!" I called.

Her back was against the dark, wet wall, pressed back against the wet stones.

"Wait!" I said.

She looked wildly about, to the right and left, and then fled to her left, toward the gate. In an instant she had disappeared. I was angry, but could not leave her out on a night like this. I latched the shutters fiercely, brought down the sash, seized the blanket from my bed, and hurried downstairs, and, in a moment or two, was out in the yard, and through the gate. I did not know which way she had gone.

I must find her, and help her, I thought.

She will not escape, I thought.

How different she now was from the prim maiden of my dreams. that well-bred, high-born, elegant maiden, so prudish, so proper, so fashionable, reserved, haughty and formal. So aloof, so icy, so cold, so indifferent. Gone now were the stiff, crisp, white, high-collared shirtwaist, closed by a brooch at the throat, the severe, ankle-length black dress, the dark stockings, the high, soft, black shoes, coming above the ankle, buttoned closed. She was reduced now, fleeing in the storm, naked, her hair unbound, outside civilization, to her female essentials, whose nature she had refused to recognize, whose meaning she had striven to suppress, whose destiny she had denied.

"Hello!" I called. "Where are you?" Surely she was risking illness in such weather. "I mean you no harm!"

I wondered if she were mad, but I was somehow sure she was not. From where had she been brought? What was her purpose here?

"Hello!" I called.

There was no answer. Only the wind and the rain.

She has disobeyed, hasn't she, I thought. That will require discipline. Then I thought, no, it is appropriate, now, that she disobey. It is fitting, and expected. She can be taught later.

The switch, the riding crop, the whip, cords, suitable feedings, I thought, can reform, and make more precise, her behavior.

Then I dismissed such thoughts, for they were improper, and radically inappropriate. My heart went out to the shivering waif.

"Hello!" I called, again, loudly, into the darkness.

"Hello!" I heard, from several yards away, out toward the cliffs and beach. A man's voice.

I hurried toward the voice. "Gavin," I cried, "is that you?"

"Aye," he responded. He was carrying a lantern.

"Did you see her?" I cried.

"Aye!" he said. "She ran toward the cliffs."

We came within a few feet of one another.

"Who is she?" asked Gavin.

"I don't know," I said. "We must find her. What are you doing here, this late, in the storm?"

He looked away, angrily, confused.

"Did you want to talk to me?" I asked.

"No," he said, surlily.

"Why are you here, about Hill House?" I asked.

He did not respond.

"You were spying on me," I said. "Why?"

"I caught you now," he said. "Going out to the beach! To make more mischief. Who is the girl?"

"I don't know," I said, angrily. "And I assure you I am

not in the habit of busying myself with the making of idle mischief, nor of taking trips to the beach in the dark, in the middle of storms."

He, at least, had dressed for the weather.

"It is you, I note," I said, "whom I find here in the dark."

"You are not the fooler?" said Gavin.

"No," I said. "And if there is a fooler here, it is surely you, not I."

In a flash of lightning the heath toward us, between us, who were near Hill House, and the cliffs, was suddenly, brightly illuminated.

We saw no sign of the girl.

"No hard feelings?" asked Gavin.

"No," said I, and we clasped hands, warmly. I put the blanket over my head, to gain what protection I could from the weather. I pulled it out a bit, so my eyes were shielded. I tried to wipe the rain from my eyes with the back of a wet hand.

"She was running toward the cliffs," said Gavin.

"That is dangerous," I said.

"Let's find her," he said. The rain was pouring over the brim of his hat.

Stay back.

"Why?" asked Gavin.

"What?" I called.

"Why should I stay back?" he asked.

"I didn't say anything," I called to him.

"It was the wind then," said Gavin.

We then, separated by some twenty yards or so, in the downpour, the moon muchly obscured by clouds, Gavin holding up the lantern, the heath brightened intermittently by flashes of lighting, went toward the cliffs.

"There she is!" cried Gavin, pointing.

The small, white, pathetic figure was crouching near the edge of the cliffs, the waters roiling in the wind and tide below.

"Don't move!" I called to her. I was uncertain if she understood where she was. "Don't frighten her!" I called to Gavin. "She is close to the cliff's edge!" Then I called out to the girl. "Stay where you are," I called. "We are friends. We mean you no harm. Come back with us to the house. We will see that you get home safely. Have you been attacked? Have you been robbed? Are you frightened? Come back with us. You will be all right! Things will be all right. Don't run! Stay where you are! We'll make tea! Have you eaten? Please! I have a blanket!"

While I was trying to keep a distance from the girl, who crouched in the grass, coaxing her to trust us, doing my best to avoid alarming her, Gavin had been approaching more closely.

Go back, now. Leave us! Go! Now!

Gavin raised his lantern, and shook his head, negatively. I did not understand his gesture.

What is wrong with him, I wondered.

He took another step, tentatively, toward the girl, the lantern raised, his other hand extended out to her, as though she might grasp it, and be led to safety.

"Don't be afraid," I called to the girl.

Perhaps the wind drowned out my voice.

She backed away from Gavin, her hand held out, as though to fend him away.

It is not he, little fool.

She looked wildly about, as though she had heard something. Perhaps Gavin had spoken to her, though I saw no indication of that in the storm.

He reached quickly toward her, and she stepped backward, and I cried out "Beware!" and, with a scream, she had twisted backward in the storm, and plunged from the cliff toward the cold, violent waters and cruel rocks below.

Gavin cried out with misery and ran to the edge of the cliff, holding up the lantern. I stood transfixed where I was, with horror. Those were not waters in which things were likely to live.

Suddenly behind Gavin there materialized a mighty, angry shape, yards in height, as though created from lightning and the storm itself. The shape was that of a monstrous horse, or horselike beast, and its eyes blazed, and it reared, and Gavin was suddenly, the lantern cast aside, his arms raised, beneath those plunging, anvil-like hoofs. He slipped backward and, as had the girl, plunged downward, in that terrible descent to the sea.

I threw aside the blanket, and ran to the cliff's edge and looked down.

The beast had disappeared.

I tore off my shoes, and dove from the cliff. I am a strong swimmer, but I had few allusions about this place, and the dangers. It was not a place one chooses to swim, even in summer, in daylight, in the best of weather. The waters were cold, the currents treacherous. But the girl had fallen, and Gavin had fallen. If there was a possibility of saving them, or one of them, I would seize it. I had waited a moment for a flash of lightning to illuminate the sea below me, before diving, to avoid, as I could, the large, scattered rocks some hundred or so feet below. Then I dove. Some of the rocks, I knew, might be just below the surface, invisible from above, in the night, but this was a risk I elected to accept. There was no time to make my way back, by the path, down to the beach, to enter the water and return to the point where the girl and Gavin had disappeared. In a moment the cold waters had closed over my head. I had missed the rocks. I tried to stroke my way to the surface, to see if I might see any sign of the girl or Gavin. I broke the surface, gasping. I felt myself swept to the side, and then back, away from the cliff. I tried to fight against the current. But I was being swept outward, away from the cliffs. Then, to my horror, I felt myself being drawn beneath the surface, almost as though by hands. It was one of the undertows in the area that made swimming so hazardous. I struggled to come again to the surface, to get my head out of the black waves, to breathe. Then I was drawn deeper and deeper, downward. My action, I saw, had been irrational. Surely more impulsive than brave, more stupid than noble. I have lost the gamble, I thought, bitterly, lungs bursting, aching for air.

I am not clear what happened then.

I had thought I was drowning and then, oddly, it seemed, for an instant, that below the water I had somehow breathed, and just before I lost consciousness I had the sense of a mighty body beneath me, rising from somewhere below in the icy waters, and I was afraid, thinking Atlantic shark, come near the shore, or perhaps it was some large marine mammal, or some archaic, indomitable reptilian form of life, perhaps one of a handful of creatures, anachronisms, lingering past the prime of their species, and my hands clutched at the thing beneath me and I felt vertebrae, the articulations of a wide, massive, sinuous spine, and then what might have been kelp, but was somehow sensed as a rude, flowing, cold, salt-encrusted mass of coarse hair. I clung to this, and felt myself drawn upward, through the freezing waters, toward the shore.

I came to consciousness on the rocky beach, below the cliffs, perhaps a hundred yards from where I had entered the water. I lay there, on my stomach. I was cold, terribly cold. It was still raining, heavily. The storm showed little sign of abating. My clothing was torn away, save for some shreds. I must have discarded it in the water, probably in panic, to free myself of the impediment it constituted, to rid myself of its dangerous, sodden drag.

I became aware, lying there, from the whitish light on the wet, pitted sand, that the full moon shone on the beach. The clouds must have opened for a moment.

I then stood on the cold beach, in awe, for not yards away was the calpa. It chose then to show itself in a form congenial to me, one familiar to me from antique and classical studies, that of a mighty, broad-chested centaur. Surmounting the gigantic, monstrous, hoofed, stallionlike frame was the human torso, hairy and bared, it, too, gigantic, but in ideal proportion to the body that bore it, from which it majestically arose. The thing stamped its hoofs. Then it pawed with one hoof at the sand, scattering sand and pebbles behind it. Its head was mighty, with beard and flowing hair, a head wreathed with kelp, like laurel. Its head was turned toward me, and I trembled. Yet was I pleased that it had deigned to show itself in a form I could comprehend, one that would not hurl me in a moment into the throes of madness. I lifted my hand, in surprise. In the mighty arms of this monster, held, cradled, sheltered, helpless, was the girl, carried there as easily, as securely, as might have been a small, lovely, living doll, or pretty toy.

She cast me a piteous glance. She was small and naked. Her wrists were crossed before her, and I suddenly realized they were bound, bound with her own golden hair. What fate might lie now before her, my pure, chaste, prudish, haughty, cold, aloof Victorian maid, now that she was stripped and bound, and clasped in the arms of such a brute?

How pleased I was, and then I struggled to put aside such thoughts.

He will teach you the flames of passion, I thought. He will melt your ice, you vain, stinking little bitch. You will learn to scream with need, and beg, as the slut you are!

"Release her!" I cried. "Let her go, you mindless brute!"

She extended her bound wrists to me, piteously, pleading.

"Put her down!" I cried.

The centaur, or centaurlike creature, put back its head, and laughed, a laugh which was like the wind and rain, like a force of nature, and it reared on its hind legs, and its prisoner, lifted so high in the air, yards over the beach, cried out with fear, and I stepped back, lest I be destroyed by the descent of one of those mighty hoofs.

The creature turned then, and, not hurrying, began to move along the beach, parallel to the shore, a bit away from the village, sometimes wading, splashing, through small inlets, the water to its fetlocks. I staggered after him. He stopped not far from the place where I had dived into the water, where the beach, at that point, ended, before the violent interval of waves, the hurtling, crashing sea, the rocks.

A few yards behind, I fell into the sand. I was weary, my body ached, I was exhausted. I was shivering with cold.

I was on my hands and knees. I felt I could hardly rise. "Release her!" I whispered. "Let her go!"

There was at that point a large rock, rather boulderlike. It had been smoothed by centuries of tides, of rain and wind. Its lower portions were now washed by the sea.

"Let her go!" I whispered.

The centaurlike creature then, with callous indifference, threw the girl on her belly on the smooth rock, her small hands, bound with her own hair, over her head, before her. She cast me a look of misery and terror over her right arm. For a moment his mighty hands held her in place. Then she was pinioned. Then she was covered. She shrieked.

"Stop!" I begged.

It was a ghastly scene, as though mythology had suddenly leapt ferociously alive.

Have her. Take her. Own her. She is yours.

"No!" she wept, shaken, struck, rocked, held. "Please, no!" These were the first words I had heard her ever utter. Then it seemed she could only endure, like a rag or boot. I feared she might be destroyed.

I staggered to my feet, and, blind with rain and rage, threw myself on the hideous, dispossessing, expropriating creature. My hands dragged at its hair.

In that moment it seemed that the creature was gone, and I lay beside her, she, his victim, his pleasure, his toy. She was shuddering, and wet and slick. Her hands were still over her head, bound. I could not but note how well the turned strands of golden hair, twisted together into fine, smooth, thick cords, served to bind her tiny wrists. I was gasping, and sore, from my ordeal in the water, from my efforts in somehow managing to dislodge her assailant.

Soberly, I did not see how that had been possible.

But it was gone.

She was breathing heavily. I could see the sweet fullness of her breast against the rock. She seemed not to dare to move.

"It is gone," I assured her.

"No," she said, "it is not."

I looked about. There was no sign of it, of the calpa.

"What are you going to do?" she whispered.

"Free you, surely," I said. "We must get you home."

Strangely, though, I turned her to her back, rudely. She went to lower her hands, to bring them before her body, but I thrust them back, angrily, over her head. She kept them as I had placed them.

I have waited a long time to have you thusly.

She looked at me, her eyes wide, frightened. I did not understand this reaction.

"We will get you some warm blankets, some hot tea," I said.

"Thank you," she said.

Were you given permission to speak?

"No," she said. "Forgive me!"

"For what?" I asked.

"I—I do not understand," she stammered.

I knelt across her body, doubtless to lean forward and free her hands.

You may lift your mouth, and kiss me.

I was startled at the unexpected, timid, soft touch of her lips on my body.

You are mine.

She turned her head to the side, trembling. "Yes," she said. "Yes."

"Yes?" I asked.

"Yes, I know," she said.

"You know what?" I asked.

She looked at me, confused, miserable.

Then it seemed to me I heard her say, and clearly, "*If you are a true man, use me. Use me as is your right, in accord with your right, as a master!*"

"What?" I said.

"I said nothing," she whispered.

Then, oddly, I backed a little away from her, on my knees. I stroked the interior of her left thigh. It was soft, and there was golden hair. Then I touched her curiously, softly, intimately. She, to my amazement, squirmed, and lifted her body, piteously, to me. Clearly she was begging another touch. I did not give it to her. Tears sprang into her eyes, and she put her head to the side.

Why did I make her wait? Why had it amused me to deny her, to remind her of her place?

I had not touched her because I was a gentleman, of course. It would have been improper, bestial, to have so touched and dominated her.

"Be kind," she begged.

I assumed she pleaded for mercy, to be unbound, to be clothed, to be hurried to safety, and shelter.

I looked down upon her. She was indeed the Victorian maiden of the dreams, but removed now from the fortress of her society. She did not seem so prim now, so proper, proud, and prudish, so reserved, inert, formal, and cold. No. Gone now was the crisp white shirtwaist, the severe black skirt, the brooch, her civilization. She lay before me, arched over the rock, bared and bound.

She is mine, I thought, literally *mine.*

How is this happening, I asked myself. Why am I not unbinding her, and hurrying her to warmth and shelter? Why am I keeping her before me, as she is, naked, bound?

She might as well have been a female slave, no more than a rightless, meaningless slave.

She is a slave, I thought.

She had been bred, and raised, for me, I thought, and has now been given to me, as a lovely gift.

She is mine.

I am a slave, and I beg the touch of my master.

"What?" I said.

"I said nothing," she whispered, "*—Master.*"

"What did you say?" I said.

"*—Master—*," she whispered.

"I do not understand," I said.

"You must understand," she said.

"What?" I asked.

"That I am yours, your *slave.* I have had dreams. Have you not had dreams?"

"Yes," I said, "I have had dreams."

"I have been prepared for you," she said.

"How have you seen me, in your dreams?"

"As you are now, as my barbarian lord, as my barbarian master."

The waves crashed about the shore.

"How could I fail to recognize my master?" she asked. "Have I not knelt enough before him? But why has he never touched me, why has he never fulfilled me? Has he not found me pleasing?"

"I am sure he would find you pleasing," I said.

"And how has he seen me?" she asked.

"As something to be taken, and put to a man's feet," I said, coldly.

"Yes," she cried, "that is where I belong, that is what is fitting for me!"

"Surely," said I, "this is madness."

"No, it is not," she said, "Master."

"If I accept you as a slave," I said, "you will be kept under perfect discipline." I could not believe that I had said this. Could it be I who was speaking?

"She who is slave," she said, "would will it, were she permitted to will, no other way."

Then she looked up at me, pleading, helplessly. She squirmed a little, tears in her eyes, and lifted her body just a tiny bit, as though fearing that I might be angered by her unsolicited importunity.

"What are you doing?"

"I am pleading silently, without speaking, for I have not been given permission to speak, hopefully, timidly, for the touch of my master."

"I see," I said.

"Please," she said, "be kind—*Master.*"

Rain still assaulted the beach, and occasionally lightning illuminated it, and the rocks, and sea.

"Ignite me, Master. Make me burn! It is what I am for!" she cried.

I caressed her flanks, and her breasts, and shoulders

and throat. I did touch the interior of her thighs and she encouraged me with a tiny supplicatory moan. I did not, however, deign to touch her intimacies. I knew that if I did so, she would buck and go mad with pleasure.

Clearly she had the makings of a slave.

I did not reject this thought, but accepted it. I saw no need to reject her slave needs. Clearly that was what she was. I would not shame her for this, save insofar as it would serve to heighten her passion, and make her the more helpless.

"You are a miserable, worthless, pathetic, needful slut," I observed.

Tears sprang to her eyes.

"Your ice has melted, my dear," I informed her.

"Yes," she whispered.

My Victorian maiden, I saw, was now no more than a slave, and clearly one desperately needful.

I wondered how many women were such, or would find themselves such, did they encounter masters.

"Subject me to the attentions appropriate to my nature and condition, Master," she begged.

I then touched her, and she screamed with need, a surrendered, begging slave.

She looked up at me, wildly.

"Split your legs, bitch," I said.

She dared to look at me, reproachfully.

I slapped her with the flat of my hand once, sharply, and then, sharply, with the back of it. This left a bit of blood on her lip, where my blow had forced it against her small, fine teeth.

This may seem brutal, but one does not accept insubordination, or hesitancy, in a slave.

It is not done.

"Now," I said.

"Yes, Master!" she cried, joyfully, then instantly obedient, tears mixing with the rain on her face.

I did not think further discipline would be necessary in this instance. She had been a slave from birth, bred for me, destined for me, but only recently, I supposed, had she comprehended that she had now, suddenly, come into the active state of her bondage, a state which, once initiated, would not be revoked.

One who has tasted slave meat does not return to the stale crusts of pampered sluts; compared to the slave all other women are tepid, and mediocre. And boring. It is no wonder that the fearful slave, anxious to obey and please, finds herself prized, and determinedly sought, amongst the abundant, disappointing garbage of her inert, confused, petulant, neurotic sisters.

I then took her into my arms and placed the seal of my claimancy upon her.

✦

So, too, I now understand was my mother bred for my father, and perhaps my grandmother for my grandfather. They are thorough, I thought, those who care for such matters.

✦

When I awakened it was to voices on the beach. I was lying alone, freezing, half in the cold water, half on the rocky sand.

Men from Hill House brought me back from the beach. They had begun searching for me when it was discovered I was not in my room. I kept to my bed for four or five days, recovering from my ordeal, accepting two visits from a physician, from one of the nearby towns, and being coddled by diligent, concerned Mrs. Fraser, she and her wonderful pots of hot green tea. I suppose I was fortunate not to have contracted pneumonia.

It had turned out to have been a markedly dreadful, terrible night for the village, for young Gavin had gone missing, and old Duncan, drunk, stumbling from the pub, lost in the storm, had somehow wandered into the sea and drowned.

Perhaps, I thought, he had come too close.

A day or two after I emerged shakily from my bed Gavin's body was found in the sea, by a trawler, several miles to the south of the village. I did not care to look on it, but I was told he had not drowned, but, apparently, had fallen from the cliff, and been dashed on the rocks below. His lantern was found at a spot at the cliff's edge, oddly flattened. His body was so battered, and torn, that it might have been trampled, but a fall to rocks, and being cast again and again by angry waters against rocks, was surely sufficient to produce these hideous effects. I was very sorry, for had I liked old Duncan, and Gavin, too. Indeed, the latter had been, in effect, my one friend, or closest friend, in the village. I acceded to the constable's conjectures, in his inquiry, that I had seen Gavin's lantern and had left Hill House to investigate the light, that I must have come on the scene of Gavin's fall, and had then, too, fallen from the cliff, though more fortunately than he, for I had managed to miss the rocks below. I was not the last person who had spoken to old Duncan but some of the other villagers. He had been alive and well when last I had seen him. It was not clear why Gavin had been about that night, but the constable had conjectured, sensibly enough, at least from his point of view, that he had been up to no good, out on such a night, that he was the trickster who had been playing the village for a fool, and was up to further mischief, taking advantage of the storm to avoid surveillance. He had heard of the prints, and of the disturbance in my room, and such, for old Duncan had told him about these things one day when he had biked to the village. That, it turned out, was the day I had seen Duncan talking to the constable. Duncan, of course, I knew from personal acquaintance, would not have favored the "hoax theory" of the anomalies. Such an explanation, of course, would be that which would first occur to a sober outsider, one not from the village, one like the kindly, sensible constable. "What did he say?" I asked, curious. "Nothing, really," said the constable. "Only a lot of nonsense, superstitious nonsense. He was a decent, sweet, but daft old man. And, too, I think he may not be the only one in the village, the crazy things they say. I think it may be the wind, the never-stopping wind, the sea, too, always, slapping at the cliffs. After a while, I suppose, anyone could go mad here." As the constable was leaving, he turned and said to me, "One of the things old Duncan wanted me to do was to keep an eye on you." "Why?" I asked. "More nonsense," said the constable. "Good-day, sir!" "Good-day, officer." That, I supposed, was why Duncan had so apparently abruptly concluded his discussion with the constable, when I had appeared on the scene. I bore him no ill will, sweet old Duncan, with his ale, and his pipe. I think he meant well. He had apparently known my father. He claimed to have seen the calpa. I wondered if he had. If there is such a thing, perhaps he had come too close. Indeed, perhaps he, like Gavin, had been abroad that night, curious, reconnoitering, unwisely. If so, he, like Gavin, might have been well advised to leave well enough alone. He was a character in the village. The village would miss him. I would miss him.

In my convalescence in Hill House I had, of course, given a great deal of thought, sometimes even against my will or intent, to the seeming events of the past few days, and particularly to those of the night of the storm. I supposed that, somehow, after returning to Hill House that night, and having fallen asleep in my room, I had then, again, risen in my sleep, and walked about, and that the events which had seemed to occur had been no more than the troubling aberrations of an unusual dream. I was fortunate not to have been killed in a fall from the cliff, in the midst of this dangerous, wayward peregrination. I remembered the details of the dream, of course. It was not the sort of dream one would be likely to forget. It had to have been a dream, of course. I could not have behaved in so uncouth and deplorable a manner as the dream suggested. Such behavior would have been crudely and inappropriately atavistic, not to be countenanced, simply unthinkable. Such things hark back to realities and times so ancient, basic, and primitive that they are best precluded from civilized attention, from polite inquiry. Let us not remember what men and women were, for fear we might learn what they are. Not all curtains need be parted. Not all doors need be opened. Perhaps it is well not to search for the truth; there is always the danger that one might find it. The rivers of blood flow deep. Doubtless it is best that we remain masks and shadows to one another.

I discovered that one change had taken place in the residents of Hill House. The cat had disappeared on the night of the storm. No one knows where she went. No one has seen her since.

One other incident may be worth recording, which occurred on the day I left the village, to return to the city. I was wandering on the beach, and, drawn by what morbid curiosity I know not, found my steps taking me to the vicinity of the cliff and the terrible, sea-washed rocks where the tragedy of the stormy night had occurred. There were no hoofprints on the beach, I am pleased to report. It had come to seem likely to me, over the last few days, that Gavin had indeed been perpetrating a hoax, one which, grievously, tragically, had cost him his life. When I came to the place beneath the cliffs, where the morning waters were roiling amongst the rocks, I climbed up a short way, perhaps some ten or twelve feet. There was the fresh, keen odor of salt and kelp. I looked up. The top of the cliff was some one hundred feet or so above me. I could see it edged, dark, against the sky. Then I looked down, and to my right, at the rocks. They were large, abundant and jagged. They were bright with spray in the morning sun. I had been fortunate, indeed, to have passed harmlessly between them in my fall. Then I looked down, between the rocks, into the dark, wicked, churning, violent waters, the lashing foam. I shuddered. It was amazing that anything could have lived in such waters. I had indeed been fortunate. I then made my way, carefully, slipping a bit, back down the rocks to the beach. There, on the pebbled, rocky sand, I stood for a time, looking out to sea.

The calpa, I thought, is not evil. It bears you no ill will. It is, however, territorial, and will kill to conceal its presence.

No one knows where lies the house of the calpa.

Also, it must breed, and seeks shallower spaces, waters where first, perhaps, it was spawned.

Coming back, one supposes, in each generation, from unimaginable journeys in alien seas.

It is capable, it is said, of taking many forms.

I supposed it then might, if it wished, take the form of a human being.

I then put these thoughts from me, as they seemed alien to me. I turned about, to return to Hill House.

My attention, as I turned about, was taken by a large, rounded, boulderlike rock. It reminded me, in its form, and location, of the rock in the dream.

I went to the rock.

I put out my hand. Caught on the rock was a long strand of golden hair.

Unscheduled Stop

HE ran across the soft earth, sinking not much into it. He did not run toward the hill behind him, that on the far side of the highway, the large hill pointed out by the tour guide.

"Stop!" they called after him.

It was the other hill, the hill of the stand, where it had ended, that he climbed, knowing this, and not knowing it, I would suppose.

When the sun is right you can see your own reflection in the window of the bus. You can look out and see yourself, and when the sun is right, in that place, it seems you can see the other self, too; a face looked back at him, maybe. We really don't know. He was far ahead of us now, and we called to him to stop.

He had cried out "Stop the bus!" and had pounded on the window, leapt up, fled down the aisle.

"He's ill," said someone.

"Stop the bus," said the guide.

The driver drew the bus to one side of the road.

"Do not demean me," she said. "Remove your shirt. I will not be demeaned. Spread it here, on the soft grass, and let us lie upon it and sing a little, just a little."

He looked back. The bus was far behind. He began to run up the hill.

"It is base treachery," she said. "Run, run from here. The guests in your father's house, they are McCormick."

He gasped, climbing the hill.

Behind him he could see the smoke, rising from the sheds in the hill fort, then the fire.

"I will tell him his name another time," she said.

"Cursed thing!" he cried. "I might have watched. I might have known."

The sky was dark now and he could see the bus below, white with a red stripe. The guide was there. The driver had come out. Two of the passengers, too, who would smoke. But it was not a stop for such. The guide, the driver, waved for him to come back.

There was smoke and fire behind him, from the hill fort, from the house of his father.

He had sprung from her side, from the softness of her, and the smell, and the dampness of the touching.

"I will tell him his name," she called after him.

There had been a great four-legged beast, a horse. He had heard of these things. At the pommel of the saddle, tied there by the hair, he had seen his father's head.

For one instant the eyes had looked at him.

The luck of the house he had seized, and, with others, was seen.

It was then he, and others, had run.

"Come back," they called to him, from below, from the highway, leading to the city.

He could see the men following, descending from the hill fort. He had seen the horseman.

On the top of he hill, he had put it.

The men were coming, the horseman, the others on foot.

They came upon him at the top of the hill. He saw the horse clamber to the top, slipping, the rider lurching in the saddle

"Die, whelp," he heard, "last of the kin!"

How he, youngest of the kin of the clan Lachlin, so many, the last?

The hill fort was aflame.

"Where is it, where is the luck of Lachlin!" cried the horseman.

He had turned to flee and had heard the horse, hoofs striking hard in the dirt, behind him.

Then what he felt seemed no more than a sudden, sharp, cold wind at the back of his neck.

"I will tell him his name," she had called after him.

He had not even heard the man dismount, or the others, afoot, coming up, to stand beside him.

The tour guide, and some others, were following him, slowly, up the hill.

He fell to his knees in a given place, and, with his bare hands, began to tear at the ground.

"What is it?" they asked.

He tore at the earth.

"Come back to the bus," said the tour guide.

His fingers were bleeding.

Then he touched it, his fingers just touching the pommel, the knob, at the head of the hilt, and then the hilt, the blade wrapped in cloth, muddy, rotted, and torn, and he drew from the earth that great blade, with the long hilt, that blade to be wielded with two hands by a strong man.

"Aii, that cloth," said the guide, seeing the muddy, tattered shreds, "that is the banner of the Lachlins."

"The clan Lachlin disappeared more than four hundred years ago," said the driver.

"The blade," said the guide, "surely that is the luck of the Lachlins."

"How did you know where to find this?" asked the guide.

"I put it here," he heard himself say. "But it was long ago."

The Hairbrush

(An essay in paleocosmetology)

ONE hears a great deal these days about child abuse.

Indeed, one gathers that frustrating a child, for example, prohibiting him from playing with matches in a haystack, may have serious consequences later on, as his maturation may have been jeopardized. On the other hand, a parent's concern, or, at least, the possible concern of many parents, with the welfare of his offspring, may militate against permitting him to frolic unattended in the midst of flammable substances. The problem then is how to permit the child to grow, to enjoy, and profit from, a remarkable learning experience, to proceed to express himself as a miniature individual, and, at the same time, to keep him alive.

If the child is, say, seventeen or eighteen, one may reason with him, pointing out the personal hazards involved, and the attendant social hazards, how much he means to his parents, for example, and how his siblings, and cousins, and friends, and the community, and so on, would miss him, and how any funeral expenses would have to be taken from his allowance, and such, and thus, by shrewd ratiocination, appeal simultaneously to a variety of interests, for example, to his instinct for self-preservation, social and civic responsibility, and greed. But, what if the child is not yet at the age of reason, and is discovered sitting in the haystack, beaming up at you, holding his first lighted match?

In my day, a primitive and benighted era, we would promptly remove the child from the haystack and extinguish the match. Indeed, we might even speak crossly to child, and might even warm his little stern for him. To be sure, this behavior might today land one behind bars.

But even the modern parent is unwilling to see his moppet immolated.

Accordingly there are a number of alternatives at his disposal. The most obvious is to anticipate the situation and be prepared for it, outfitting the tyke with protective gear, for example, with fire-proof gloves, an enclosed helmet, and an asbestos suit. If one cannot afford an asbestos suit, and such, perhaps having spent the money on the legally required car seat for his eighteen-year-old sibling, one might remove the haystack from the child, which will be less traumatic, apparently, than removing the child from the haystack, stand ready with a fire hose, have the haystack placed beneath a water tank which can be drained at a moment's notice, lure the child away with a new puppy or ice cream, and so on.

Still there are dangers.

I leave these cheerfully, however, to our new generation of child psychologists and social workers.

This paper is addressed, rather, to a quite different, but, I think, interesting question.

How is it that the human race got to be the human race?

How did we get here without our child psychologists and social workers? How did the little tykes make it so far with so little help?

Interestingly enough a new study has appeared which bids fair to illuminate this knotty problem in evolutionary theory.

And it has to do with the simple hairbrush.

Many were the dangers which confronted our paleolithic

ancestors, for example, cave bears, saber-tooth tigers, rogue mammoths, careless mastodons, not watching where they were going, other paleolithic ancestors, and so on. The human race, for better or for worse, had taken its leave of other primate species, which probably did not mind its departure, and opted for cunning, grumpiness, and home-made equipment, stone knives, axes, and such, thus enabling it to have at its disposal the means whereby, if suitably employed, it might eventually produce its own extinction, an advancement generally eschewed by more survival-oriented life forms. One must understand that things in those days were nip and tuck, though perhaps less so than in our day. Would the human race survive? What would evolution have to say about us? And what might we say about evolution? Could the genetic lotteries be rigged?

But back to the hairbrush.

It is well known that baby guppies, newly born fruit flies, freshly hatched crocodiles, and such, arrive in this world well-equipped to fend for themselves. Not so, of course, the newly delivered human infant. Mostly it just lies about and makes a great deal of noise. At birth, and for a good while thereafter, it is unable to lift a stone club, track a rabbit, or pounce on squirrels, let alone spear mammoths or contest real estate with large animals. But the precariousness of the human infant is well known. It was never doubted by even medium-sized predators. We may suppose that those mothers who followed the example of, say, the maternal crocodile, either letting the infant shift for itself, or eating it, did not find their genes frequently replicated. Thus, certain sorts of mothers, nurturing mothers, say, would be favored by evolution. Still the child was at great risk, and thus, obviously, so, too, was the human race.

One danger to the race which has hitherto received little attention is the risk involved in socialization.

Socialization, you see, though this has been seldom noticed, is replete with its own perils.

Obviously the child must be socialized, taught to grunt, and such. Food is to be placed in the mouth and not the ear. One does not romp with tigers. One should treat others nicely, particularly if the others are enormous and ill-tempered. One should be careful where one throws one's spears and shoots one's arrows. And, if the group is sufficiently advanced, and has mastered fire, one should not set fire to one's fellow tribesmen, and so on.

But this socialization, which must be achieved for group flourishing, and perhaps even group survival, also, interestingly, poses a dire threat to the very existence of the group itself.

But more of this anon.

Let us appear to digress briefly now, before suddenly revealing a plethora of startling connections and relationships which will astonishingly reveal that a seeming digression actually betokened a subtle fact of such moment that the very survival of the human race was contingent upon it.

It is recognized that your average human being is relatively hairless, compared, for example, to your average baboon or orangutan. Whatever the advantages of bipedalian hairlessness might be, in, say, avoiding overheating in the pursuit of antelope, one may well imagine the horror of hirsute parents upon discovering that some of their offspring were, in effect, born naked. Imagine the misery of relatively hairless young females poignantly observing their troubling reflections in merciless, reproachful pools of still water. What self-respecting baboon or orangutan could take them seriously? Was this some tragic genetic drift, like the ever-larger canines of the saber-toothed tiger which might end up doing little more than allowing the poor, doomed beasts to lacerate their own jaws? Clearly such biologically short-changed maidens would be of little interest to your average hairy swain. They must watch sadly while their more hirsute sisters were caught in the bushes or dragged to the back of caves.

Accordingly, as your average male could not overcome his disgust at the very appearance of a hairless female, and could soon see through the artifices and subterfuges of false hair, feathers, and such, he routinely chose hanging out with the boys, leaping off cliffs, or devoting himself to the service of, say, the bear god, who preferred to keep down the number of human beings, thus reducing the competition for desirable caves. So human males, rather than mate with hideously hairless members of the opposite sex, in one way or another, opted for a smug, fastidious celibacy, that in preference to a life of connubial revulsion.

And thus the numbers of humankind began to dwindle alarmingly, at least from its own point of view if not from that of other life forms.

Return now to the dangers of socialization.

There are obvious fads or fashions in many human endeavors, and such was the case, as well, in the paleolithic times now under consideration. The standard theory at the time among the child psychologists and social workers of the day, as can be made out from rock carvings, cave paintings, and such, was, in effect, "Spare the club and spoil the child." Many is the carving or painting showing a tyke in mischief being approached by an adult bearing a large club. The club then descends rapidly and squarely, and the little tyke, we gather, from his prone position, has learned his lesson, and is certainly unlikely to repeat his behavior. Now, clearly, striking the small child heavily on the head with, say, a large rock or a stout club does tend to reduce the likelihood of the child's repeating the disapproved or unacceptable behavior, but, too, obviously, it reduces considerably the likelihood, as well, of his eventually replicating his genes.

It is here that two evolutionary currents converge, to postpone, at least for a time, the imminent extinction of the human race.

And the humble hairbrush is implicated in this fortuitous sociobiological confluence.

A wise old woman, one supposes, for such seem most likely to track such cultural currents, noted that the numbers of extant children tended to decrease from month to month. It then occurred to her that if the blows administered by the instrument of discipline, the rock or club, were suitably cushioned in some way the children, statistically, would be more likely to survive, and the tribe might then make use of them in their maturity, for, say, spearing mammoths and bringing the meat home. We do not know how she came to this insight, but one might suppose that she herself had once, in her hairless youth, perhaps in pursuing a fleeing male, been surprised by, and cuffed by, a cave bear. Perhaps she should have known better than to have pursued a devotee of, or priest of, the bear god. In any event, she survived, with little more than a severe headache and a few claw marks. Had she been struck by the fleeing male's club, on the other hand, she might have had to put aside forever her hopes of winning his favor. At her instigation, several of her tribesmen, fearing, perhaps because of the claw marks, that she might be a witch, began to wrap fur about their disciplinary rocks and clubs. This act was regarded as a concession to decadence by the child psychologists and social workers of the day, but, statistically, more and more children survived, and the innovation began to catch on.

A wise old man, then, one supposes, for such seem most likely to track such cultural currents, began to note that the surviving female children, particularly those who managed to make it past puberty, began to look better and better to him, for their hair, now, was no longer the unkempt brushy tangle of yesteryear, loaded with twigs, leaves and lice, but was now long, silken, and glossy, a veritable pelt. He pondered long on these things and the matter was decided for him when a number of baboons and orangutans surprised and began to accost, in a vulgar manner, a number of village maidens innocently bathing in a nearby pool. As in those days mature, healthy, sexually normal male baboons and orangutans served as the arbiters in such delicate matters it was made clear to the old man, and others, that the tribal maidens had passed a severe test. If they could be of interest to judges so discriminating and able what mere human being, particularly one without a great deal of hair, would have the temerity to challenge a verdict so perspicacious and authoritative? In any event, many of the young males began to reduce their time with the boys and the number who flung themselves from cliffs in despair also declined. Similarly, the bear god now began to languish for devotees and priests and had to look more closely to the protection of his caves.

And the tribe began to increase.

And not only, of course, were the young human females now redeemed by, and enhanced by, their long, glossy hair, which they tended to dress and care for with great attention and vanity, when not fighting off the advances of males of a variety of species, but many of the young males, as well, now appeared better groomed than hitherto, and this fact was not long left unnoted by the pursued and appetitious maidens, whose rate of speed now tended to be correlated with the attractiveness of the pursuer.

It was thus that two sociobiological currents converged, fortunately for the human race. First, socialization, or child training, no longer, in most cases, constituted a hazardous time for youth, and a shift in aesthetic tastes took place, as well, from the lumbering, shaggy female to the graceful, quickly moving, but no more quickly moving than necessary, sexy, shapely, largely hairless but nonetheless beautifully pelted female.

It might be noted in passing that the child psychologists and social workers of the day now began to recommend cushioned disciplinary devices to attentive, concerned parents. The motto was still "Spare the club and spoil the child," but it was now understood that the club would be cushioned.

This, then, is the story of the hairbrush, how it came to be, and how, interestingly, we owe to this small and humble artifact the very survival of the human race.

It is rumored, incidentally, that in certain backward homes, in primitive areas, the hairbrush is still used as a disciplinary device.

Bamohee

YES, *bamohee.*

That is the word, *bamohee.*

It may sound to you like a mere colligation of meaningless syllables, So, too, did it to me, once.

I first heard this word from my grandson, Thomas, who was verging on three at the time. That is, approximately, as I have later discovered, the bamohee time, that is, the time in which that unusual combination of syllables, the mighty, pregnant "bam," the arresting, startling "oh," hinting of awesome, infinite wonder, and the sudden, devastating "hee" of insight and revelation, in a sudden synergistic burst of cognitive fury and illumination unlock the meaning of a species, the mysteries of time and space, the secrets of the universe and the riddle of being itself, itself.

But allow me to begin at the beginning, as far as these things have a beginning.

First, as far as I know, no other animal species says *bamohee.* It seems idiosyncratic to the human species. There is no record of its utterance, at least insofar as I am aware, by any other mammal, the cat, the horse, the dog, the mongoose, and so on. It is true that it may be mindlessly repeated by certain unusual birds, most notably the gaudy, nut-savoring parrot, but, as far as we can tell, it carries no special significance for our avian friends. To them it seems a mere nonsense word, as far as we can determine. Certainly, when Polly beaks the syllables her beady eyes do not suddenly mist and glow, her claws do not clasp her perch with alarmed fervor, her feathers do not lift, ruffle, and shudder with ecstasy, no more than when she says 'kitchen sink' or 'vacuum cleaner', two of her favorites, though lagging far behind the communicative "I want a cracker, stupid."

At one time, shortly before his third birthday, Thomas began to say *bamohee* frequently. It seemed to be a universal word, which might have stood for almost anything, a cookie, the neighbor's dachshund, a soiled diaper, the binomial theorem, anything. How naive we were!

Thomas would approach his parents with all the love, trust, and sincerity of a child raised as he was, raised in such a manner as to expect the best and noblest of the world into which he would soon be precipitated, a world he would soon discover, alas, as do we all, not designed expressly for his benefit. But the bamohee time of youth precedes normally the period of being pelted and punctured with "the slings and arrows of outrageous fortune." The lacerations and bruises of existence, at the bamohee time, lie around the corner, far from the crib and that mysterious, inexplicable artifact in the parents' bathroom, the potty chair. Thomas would approach his parents, look at them earnestly, and say, "Bamohee." *Bamohee*, of course, is not the first word a child is likely to say. That word seems to be "No," at least in English and Spanish, "Non" in French, "Nein" in German, "Nyet" in Russian, and so on. To be sure, "No" is often followed by another word, for example, "No, Mama," "No, Dada," and so on. It seemed as though Thomas, in his innocence, with his fresh view of the world, was honestly interested in communicating something, in telling his parents something, something important, that he was benevolently interested in sharing something with them, something which they might find of great significance, but they, alas, representatives of the insouciant, careless generation, so unlike that of their own parents, depression children, that splendid generation, mine, honed to nobility by sacrifice, tutored in adversity, brought to greatness by paucity, took little note of Thomas' offer. Rather they tried to distract him from *bamohee*, and lure him into the groves of 'kitchen sink' and 'vacuum cleaner', countries which might be trod even by ill-tempered parrots. If they had only listened. You see, the bamohee time is brief. It seems to be a tide which comes but once in a child's life. Its gift might have been immeasurable.

All human children begin by making similar noises, rather like all puppies and kittens make noises of a similar sort, appropriate to their kind. For example, the puppy or kitten in Tokyo or Moscow, or Mombassa, or Scranton, New York, makes very similar sounds. It is only later that English dogs learn to say "bow-wow," German dogs "wow-wow," Polish dogs "hou, hou," and so on. Similarly, the Japanese baby, the Iroquois baby, the German baby, the Eskimo baby, the Scranton baby, and so on, make similar sounds. A bit later babies begin to babble, but now the babbles differ, as the babies begin to pick up phonemes from their environment, liberally provided by significant others, in this case, parents, nurses, guardians, etc. Now the Eskimo baby babbles in recognizable Eskimo phonemes, the German baby in good German, of one sort or another, and the Scranton baby in Scrantonese, so to speak. Later, of course, these babies learn to speak, and their troubles begin. The Eskimo baby speaks Eskimo, the Japanese baby Japanese, and so on, and soon, like an absorptive sponge, with a quickness and fluency that will impress, but dismay, generations of adults struggling to master a tongue not learned at this marvelous time, they become insolently adept native speakers. Thomas' Uncle John, for example, has no difficulty in teaching Thomas words such as "*Achtung*, baby," "*Bon jour*," "*Hola*," and other useful phrases which may prove of use in nursery school, and in later life.

But *bamohee*, obviously, is Thomas' own word. Certainly it is not yet carried in the Oxford English Dictionary, in Webster's Unabridged Dictionary, or other such familiar reference works.

Thomas Wolfe, another Thomas, a remarkable writer

sometimes alleged to have been in desperate need of an editor, spoke of the forgotten language, a leaf, a twig, a pebble, or some such. One might add, a shred of paper, a piece of glass, a scrap of tin, as more characteristic of the contemporary urban landscape much beloved by devotees of the outdoors. But with all due respect to Mr. Wolfe, his editor, *et al*, leaves, twigs, pebbles, and such, are not a language. They are, rather, leaves, twigs, and pebbles, and as such, vegetables, minerals, that sort of thing. This is, too, not to deny that there is much to be said for a living, enchanted world, a human-friendly habitat. When the sprites, nymphs, centaurs, and satyrs picked up stakes and moved out, the neighborhood was never again the same. It is not all that much fun living inside a big clock, an inexplicable, inscrutable, indifferent, alien, meaningless foreign country, not knowing its language, or if it has one, dodging moving parts, and such. It does not seem much of an improvement over a magic world. Of course, the trains run on time, except when they don't. The fact that the clock may not tick when expected, or might tock when not expected, is not much comfort. It is bad enough living in a clock, let alone one that can't keep time.

But this brings us back to *bamohee.*

Wordsworth seemed to believe that the infant enters the world trailing clouds of glory. One gathers from this that Wordsworth was never present at a birth, and that any midwife with normal vision would have been well ahead of him on this score. On the other hand, there is expressed a belief here that the young child, before it gets around, soon enough, to forgetting momentous truths of inordinate importance, does, for a time, have such things in mind. It comes from some place and, for a time, is in touch with that place. It lies there in its bassinet, it seems, recollecting vistas, truths, and treasures, which will soon vanish, diaper by diaper.

One of the greatest of the strange philosophers is doubtless Aristicles of Athens, descended on his mother's side from Poseidon, the god of the sea. This is the fellow we know as Plato, a nickname, which suggests width, though of what is not clear in the tradition. Perhaps there is a great contemporary philosopher who to future generations will be known as Red, Curly, Shorty, or such. In any event, Plato, like millions of others, believed in reincarnation. He also seemed to believe that knowledge was essentially recollection, and that one, under suitable conditions, remembered seeing forms in some sort of previous existence, probably while waiting between bodies for a new reincarnation. There was a form of man, and hopefully of woman, of shuttles and bridles, of beauty, of justice, and so on. Perhaps there were also forms for kitchen sink, vacuum cleaner, pocket watch, can opener, sport utility vehicle, lawnmower, and such, but, if so, they do not seem to have been recollected until later on.

I would not have thought much about *bamohee*, despite Thomas' earnestness in bringing it to our attention, in the family, had it not been for an international congress of linguists held in Belgrade, to which I had been invited to submit a paper. Late in the conference, late one evening, after we had refuted one another's papers to our mutual satisfaction, we had adjourned, as is the wont of linguists, to a local bar, and were exchanging gossip. Having recently attributed, to our satisfaction, Dr. Emily R.'s appointment to H. University's linguistics department not to her superb work on the affinities between Hebrew and Cree, but churlishly to her liaison with senior professor William B., chairman of the department, we smugly returned our attention to our beverages, nuts, and pretzels. The thought of Thomas crossed my mind, perhaps because I had not seen the little tike in several hours, something in the neighborhood, roughly, of 252 hours. You know how grandparents are. Doubtless Thomas, too, was counting the hours till we should meet again. You know how grandchildren are.

Well, thinking of Thomas, I said, absently, "bamohee."

To my amazement, my colleagues, from diverse backgrounds, immediately looked up, startled, and evinced intense interest.

"Did you say 'bamohee'?" asked Professor Stein, from Munich.

"He did," confirmed Professor Nagaso, from Yokohama.

"I heard him, as well," said Professor Red Feather, an authority on Late Middle Gothic.

A variety of races, classes, ethnic backgrounds, creeds, ideologies, sizes, shapes, tastes in automobiles, and such, were present. We were short on proclivities, as we were all grandfathers, but other than that I think it fair to say that our group was fairly diversified and representative, at least with respect to most of those groups which must needs appear in any group appropriately diversified and representative. (To achieve this diversity and representation, it had been necessary, at the last moment, to add to our group a poet and two sociologists.)

And the attention of all, inexplicably, from my point of view, seemed suddenly, bemusedly riveted on my normally, calculatedly low-profile persona.

"Where did you hear that word?" demanded Professor Ngumba.

"From my grandson, Thomas," I admitted, hoping I had not thereby risked too much. Professional reputations are fragile, precarious. One *faux pas* in the right place can be seriously damaging. One intelligent remark in the wrong place can undo the work of a lifetime.

"Your grandson is between two and one-half and three years old," said Professor Ngumba, regarding me intently.

"Yes," I said.

"Yes!" said Professor Igluk, our only polar attendee, a specialist in all five inscriptions in pre-Doric Greek.

"Your experience, as well?" asked Professor Ngumba of Professor Red Feather.

"*Ja*," said Professor Red Feather, lapsing in his consternation into Late Middle Gothic.

My colleagues regarded one another.

We soon began to compare notes, easy as we were all of a splendid generation, and grandfathers, and it turned out that *bamohee* was a word familiar to us all, though most of us had not realized it until that moment.

We soon discovered that our grandsons and granddaughters, regardless of the background languages of their area, and the cultural backgrounds of each, had, all of them, independently, inexplicably, apparently originally, come up with the mysterious utterance, *bamohee.*

"Interesting," said Professor Stein.

At a conservative estimate there were surely more than twenty articles in this.

Naturally the first question had to do with the geographical location, so to speak, of *bamohee* on the linguistic map. As nearly as we could determine it did not occur in any natural or artificial language, past or present, known to adult man at least, nor was it a technical term in any science, discipline or *Wissenschaft* with which we were familiar, ranging from Renaissance alchemy to advanced string theory, two disciplines which have much in common. It was, of course, possible that it was in an alien language, a lingering relic of extraterrestrial visitation, perhaps dropped in conversation on the banks of the Nile, while the extraterrestrials were inexplicably tutoring natives in architectural subtleties, or on the landing fields of Nasca several hundred years ago, perhaps while the extraterrestrials were attempting to discover where they were, but this seemed unlikely, given the cross-cultural prevalence of the expression, and its odd window of usage, generally being discovered betwixt the second and third year, and then, in a few weeks, mysteriously vanishing, as though it were a light from another reality flickering briefly, and then going out.

"It is clearly a word," said Professor Stein.

"Agreed," said Professor Nagaso, less inscrutably than was his wont.

"But in what language?" I asked.

"That we do not know," speculated Professor Igluk, helpfully.

"I once had a course in philosophy," said our poet, noted for his reindeer cycle, who had been added to the group because otherwise there would have been no representative from the indigenous native peoples of northern Europe.

His remark put us all on our guard.

"It has been speculated, though most commonly by physicists and lunatics," said the poet, "that there are other lands, other realms, other forms of existence, novel spaces, unusual times, strange dimensions, which may impinge upon ours. What if there are doors, or windows, or transoms, between these realities and ours, through which things might occasionally enter, crawl, or wriggle? What if the child, before sneaking into a fertilized ovum, thereby cleverly concealing his real point of origin, came from such a realm? Would he remember it? Or, perhaps better, perhaps the natural child, at a certain moment, or brief time in life, as his little brain develops, when he is open to so much, and so little critical, can see or touch these mysteries? Perhaps *bamohee* is a word from that world, overheard, so to speak, by a naively eavesdropping babe. Or perhaps, for a moment, the mystery, in its ironic benevolence, with jocular insouciance, offers the moppet a glimpse into the meaning of it all, the point of the pointlessness, an exquisite insight into the origin, the significance, the meaning of the meaninglessness, a chance which for us would be the chance to grasp the key to the universe, to learn the secret, the first name of being, but for the child is no more than gazing in awe at the stripe on a shirt, or smiling at a pretty bird perched on a window sill?"

Though doubtless the poet had had his course in philosophy long ago, it was easy to see that he had not yet recovered from its effects. Clearly he was still nuts, or, put more sensitively, was "marching to the tune of a distant drummer," one who was missing a drum.

"That makes a great deal of sense," said Professor Red Feather.

I revised my assessment of the poet's contribution, though I suspected he couldn't tell an infix from a fireplug.

"What the poet says is clearly nonsense," said one of

our sociologists, added to the group that we might have a Melanesian boatman in our midst.

"Yes," said our other sociologist, striking the floor with his cane, his presence in the group accounted for by his eligibility for a handicapped parking sticker.

The fact that the two sociologists firmly agreed that the poet was in error, if not certifiably insane, naturally reversed my opinion on the entire matter, immediately, categorically. Agreement among sociologists is commonly taken as a sufficient condition for falsity. Those familiar with the academic world will not find this surprising.

"There are many differences between poets and sociologists," said Professor Stein.

It struck me then, reassuringly, that Teutonic perceptiveness still throve amongst those from the land of poets and philosophers.

"Poets are inspired madmen," said Professor Ngumba, whose grudgingly accorded admiration for inspired madmen was commonly remarked in the scholarly community.

"Whereas sociologists are not inspired," said Professor Nagaso.

There was general assent to this in the group, with two exceptions.

"But," said Professor Igluk, "whereas poets may ascend ladders of higher truths, rung by enraptured rung, leaping from metaphor to metaphor, enveloped in clouds of radiant illumination, we, as humble scientists, must content ourselves with lower truths, such as how things are, and are they really that way, and this brings up questions of hypothesis and theory, of consequences thereof, of experimentation, of confirmation and disconfirmation, and such."

These things were doubtless clearer to some than others, but they were obviously clear to Professor Igluk, one who had spent much time in thought, who had spent long hours meditating upon them, on the pack ice during the long polar night.

"We are grateful to you," said Professor Red Feather, the early portion of whose professional life had been spent in trying to rid himself of insidiously lurking animistic suspicions. He had eventually come to see the universe in terms of inclined planes, screws, levers, and automobile engines. He had not been regarded as worthy of an academic post, despite his background, until he had made this breakthrough. He had succeeded in reconciling these conflicting world views by means of taking an eight-cylinder 1956 Chevrolet Impala engine as a spirit guide. "You have recalled us to our professional responsibilities."

"But there is no way to test this sort of hypothesis," I pointed out, thinking that some oblique deference to the voice of reason might be in order. "The child can't help us. He can just stand there, look earnestly at us, and say *bamohee*. But that's about it. And earlier he can't even say this much. And later, all too soon, he seems to forget about the nature of reality, the secret of existence, the meaning of it all, and gets down to serious business, wheedling toys, demanding bread sticks, testing various brands of cookies, coping with toilet training, being coy with vegetables, annoying younger siblings, and such."

"True," said Professor Red Feather, sadly.

"A white crane wades. A feather falls into the stream. It is swept away," said Professor Nagaso, a remark I took as expressing regret.

"Who knows what an elephant thinks?" asked Professor Ngumba, moodily.

"*Du hast recht*," said Professor Stein, cryptically.

"You are correct," said the sociologists, in unison, with firmness.

We linguists then looked at one another. Together, simultaneously, we realized we had been mistaken.

"There must be a way," I said.

"Agreed," said my gifted colleagues.

"But how?" I wept. "How!"

"Hypnotic regression," said the poet.

We thought that not a bad suggestion, and surprisingly good, for having come from someone without a degree in linguistics. Poets spend much of their time bumbling about in the closet of the subconscious, beset by metaphors, but occasionally they rise, wearied and gasping, to the plane of common sense. Or tumble from the ladder of dreams to strike heavily on the pavement of rationality. I have seen more than one remember to put a coin in a parking meter.

In the morning we communicated our experiment, its intent, and weightiness, to the conference as a whole and all lectures, panels, receptions, wine and cheese parties, and award ceremonies were immediately, unquestioningly canceled.

As I was the first who had broached the bamohee matter, it was decided that I would be the subject of this groundbreaking experiment. A hypnotist was brought in from a local night club of dubious reputation and, shortly, suitably regressed to a babbling toddler, I doubtless became the center of attention, and the object of anxious anticipation, on the part of the staff and attendees of the conference, and, too, of a number of caterers and diverse, but insufficiently diverse, members of the maintenance staff. It is hard to think of everything, and protect oneself from enraged charges of illegitimate exclusion.

As it is well known that many individuals who have become privy to the secrets of the universe in the entranced state often experience difficulties in communicating, recounting, or even remembering, the special and remarkable knowledge obtained in that state, I had been furnished with a large sheet of white drawing paper and, considering the target age of the regression experiment, a set of crayons. I was to write down on the paper what I learned, lest it slip away in my emergence into a more quotidian reality.

I have listened several times to the taped record of the experiment, copies of which are available for a nominal fee from the conference organizers. I shall describe, briefly, certain highlights.

Apparently the regression was going well, age by age. Several of my comments are irrelevant to the experiment *per se*, such as the politically deplorable, but enraptured, one pertaining to Sally Krupnik in high school, and the uncomplimentary reference to Biff McGurk in grade school. Soon I was in the vicinity of the target age because we had recently left behind the bitterness of my third birthday party, in which I had received primarily socks and underwear.

"How will I know when to stop?" asked the hypnotist, his question clearly recorded on the tape.

Suddenly I gurgled out, in a voice scarcely recognizable as my own, "Bamohee!"

"That is it!" said Professor Stein, who was, by general consent, guiding the willing, if puzzled, hypnotist.

I can recall clearly, even now, trembling, my eyes moist with tears, that incredible instant of illumination, the bamohee moment. The clouds seemed to open up, the sky to rejoice, the wind to sing, and reality itself, like an inverted glove, suddenly turned itself inside out, and I saw the other side of being, where it was and how it had been, and a great white crane, wading, lost a single feather, and watched it, as it was swept away, becoming a universe. And behind the other side of being was another side, and another, like dazzling mirrors, and I saw that one universe was a mouse, and another a butterfly, and that there were more spaces and dimensions, and worlds, and truths, than buckets of equations could hope to guess at, and that the name of reality was not number, and that I, too, and Thomas, was a universe, and that meaning was beyond meaning, and there was speech beyond speech, and seeing beyond seeing, and that the most common particle of mud, lying at the puddle's edge, was radiant, and holier and more sacred than all the arrogance, and hypocrisies, and pretensions that would conceal from us the wonder of a blade of grass, the fire of a star, that would hide from us the white crane, and the feather.

And I then, of course, understood, or thought I understood, the all, and the all behind the all, and I found myself reconciled to my kind, with all its pettiness, anger, pride, and greed, and I recognized and accepted the mysteries of time and space, and looked upon the secrets of the universe, or seemed to, opened like the petals of a flower, or like a trusting, careless adolescent's diary, to my gaze, and read there the solution to the riddle of being, and how it was not really so mysterious, at all, not in that moment, but was just right, like other things, and that it was enormously complex, and yet startlingly simple, and I cried out, again, in that moment, seeing through an adult's eyes the world a child sees, and I learned then all there was to know, or so it seemed, and I cried out, joyfully, in celebratory gratitude, uttering the mystic word, the right word, the appropriate word, the special word, the universal word, *bamohee*!

"Quick! Quick!" cried Professor Stein. "Write it down, write it all down!" That is on the tape.

A crayon was thrust into my hands and I began, frenziedly, before the vision should fail, to record the wondrous truths which I had learned. And on that sheet of paper, in crayon, I inscribed the maxims, the formulas, the propositions, the equations, the revelations, the truths, the lessons I had learned. I wept, overjoyed at having recorded these things. They would now belong to me, to Thomas, when he grew up, to my colleagues, to the world, to all rational species, everywhere.

On the tape, as I now listen to it, I called out, several times, *bamohee*, as I wrote. But, too, there were a number of startled, disappointed sounds on the tape, these emanating from the audience.

When I was awakened I looked at the paper with dismay. On it, scrawled, were a hodgepodge of lines, going this way and that, with no apparent rhyme or reason, just such a random garden of silly marks as might be put down by the tiny, clumsy hand of a small child, playing with a crayon.

I retained the notion that I had learned much, and had experienced much, and had lived much, in those moments, but I, as readily as the others, could see nothing on the page but the tracks of a childish scribbling, of less form and coherence than the tracks of sporting squirrels, playing in the soft earth at the edge of the grass.

Eventually, the conference having resumed, things returned to normal, and I flew home.

Some weeks later my wife and I were visiting my son and his wife, and Thomas, of course, was there, too.

As a souvenir I had kept the sheet I had marked and, on an impulse, when Thomas was playing nearby, with toy cars, on the coffee table before the sofa on which I sat, shortly before his third birthday, I brought the sheet out and placed it on the coffee table where he was playing. He looked at it gravely, and then looked at me, and smiled. He pointed to the sheet. "Bamohee," he said. "Yes," I said, "bamohee."

And I have the feeling that somehow there, in those seemingly meaningless scrawls, perhaps in the script of some forgotten language, there on the sheet, it is all written down. But, of course, we cannot read that language, any more than we can understand the unlocking word, the enchanted word, the word, like a key, that opens the lock of being, so that we can discover its dark, and its radiant, treasures.

Thomas will have his third birthday, soon, and he will forget bamohee. But he has been there, and I was there.

I shall make certain he has something beside socks and underwear for his third birthday.

You know how grandfathers are, and grandmothers.

Bamohee!

The Bed of Cagliostro

ALL this took place some time ago, but I think it would not be inappropriate to put at least something about it down on paper.

I would feel better about it, at any rate.

As a police matter, of course, the case is closed, and has been, for years.

Nonetheless I think it would not be amiss to record, for any it might interest, certain details associated with, if not actually germane to, the case.

I am supposing there would be no objection to this.

Also, this is scarcely the sort of thing to which one would draw the attention of the police.

It would seem clearly to lie beyond the compass of their interest, jurisdiction, or expertise.

He was a magician, of course. That must not be lost sight of.

Indeed, this was perhaps intended to be his greatest illusion.

I think it would be a mistake to lose sight of that possibility.

He had taken the stage name of Cagliostro, perhaps you remember him, this doubtless constituting a nod, or perhaps in its way a tribute, however ironic, to a somewhat notorious predecessor, the fabled 18th-century alchemist, charlatan, and magician, from whom he claimed descent. The latter claim seems implausible, and, at the least, has never been verified.

He had purchased, at considerable cost, some months before the incident, what was alleged to have been the bed of the original Cagliostro. I had thought the provenance of the purchase suspect, but it is difficult to know about such things. Certainly the bed did date from the late 18th Century; it was a large, massive, ornate, late-Baroque device, the high bedposts surmounted with the massive carved heads of two fearsome, maned, leonine beasts. The feet of the bed were carved in the likeness of paws, with the claws extended. The sideboards were carved in what I suppose was intended to be the likeness of thick, curling vines, though, rather, looked at in a certain way, they seemed rather like multiply jointed, spined, tentacles, apparently emanating from, or somehow connected with, the leonine figures surmounting the bedposts. The bed, clearly, was an authentic period piece, but there seems, as far as I can tell, no particular reason to associate it with the historical Cagliostro. To be sure, not even the provenance claims he actually slept in the bed, merely that he owned it. Indeed, the provenance suggests that it may have actually been purchased, and then given to a friend, or former patron. Little, if anything, is known, however, of this alleged friend, or patron. History is silent with respect to this. The name was something like Le Comte du Nouy, but I may be misremembering this, and, in any event, I do not now have access to either the provenance or its attendant documents. One gathers they were lost, after the incident. It seems there may have been some sort of falling out between the Signor Cagliostro and the count, and the threat of some legal action or other. But his life seems to have been filled with such alarms, as well as flights, pursuits, apprehensions, imprisonments, and such. Indeed, he seems to have eventually died in prison. The history of the bed seems better documented from 1840 on, when it first appears on the records of a dealer in London, who apparently received it from a merchant in Palermo, Sicily, over a year earlier. Supposedly it had accompanied Cagliostro long before that, a generation or so earlier, in his extensive travels, which he undertook commonly, for some reason, under a number of assumed names, travels to various European capitals, resorts, spas, and centers of status and affluence. He was famous, allegedly, for ingratiating himself with, and then deluding and preying upon, the rich and gullible. In any event the provenance lists, after 1840, several owners, all, of course, given the expense of the piece, well-to-do, and at least three of whom, as I recall, were titled, though in all cases only members of the minor nobility. As nearly as I can determine few of these individuals kept the bed very long, and it seems to have spent much of its time in warehouses, between purchases. Two of the purchasers, interestingly, seem to have fled, disappearing from society, completely, and another ended his life in a house for the insane. These unfortunate coincidences, as well as its alleged provenance, suggesting its earlier ownership by the famed Cagliostro, thought to have been a dabbler in dark forces, doubtless gave the bed an unsavory reputation, and I would suppose that it may have been little slept in, even between sales, and storage. Certainly it, so dark, heavy, massive, and enclosing, has a rather grim, dismal aspect, with the leonine heads, the claws, the vines, or tentacles, and such. If one allows the mind and imagination unwonted play it would be easy to see in it something not only forbidding but sinister. I would not, at any rate, personally, care to repose in it. Nor would I care for one of whom I was fond to repose in it. I do not think for example, that I, personally, would have given it to a friend.

But let me come to the matter at hand.

It has to do with two items, one, a mysterious demise, or fate, that of our illusionist, and, two, certain entries in his diary.

I cannot claim to be a friend of the illusionist, but we did have several dealings, largely connected with my helping him to acquire various art objects, mostly paintings and small statuary, but also various articles of period furniture, these things being additions to what was, even years ago, a quite valuable collection. These things are now gone at auction to satisfy creditors. At the end, aside from the value of his collection, our illusionist seems to have been nearly destitute. Apparently he lived well beyond his means, but on what he may have dissipated his fortune is unclear, given the apparently abstemious, lonely nature of his life. Certainly the expenses of his collection would have accounted for no more than a fraction of his estimated wealth. There was talk of certain rare books, which he burned at the end, and tuitions for instructions in certain arcane exercises, also, too, apparently abandoned, at the end. In any event, the assistance I rendered to our illusionist was rendered in my role as a dealer, and not as a friend, confidant, or such. I am not clear that our illusionist had friends, but I did not know him well enough to assert that with certainty. He seemed on the whole, off the stage, as I have suggested, to be a solitary sort, much devoted to his craft, and his studies. I hasten to add that it was not my doing that he came into the possession of the article of furniture referred to above, that piece alleged to have once belonged to the famous Cagliostro. Indeed, I trust I have already made clear my skepticism as to the authenticity of its provenance, though it was clearly genuine in the sense of being an authentic period piece of the late Baroque. To that any qualified dealer might reliably attest.

Before we come to the diary, or certain selected portions of it, I should mention that our illusionist seemed to me, and to many others, to tread a thin line between entertainment and fraud, between showmanship and chicanery. A contemporary magician may well keep the secrets of his craft close to this bosom, and guard its mechanisms with a most jealous devotion, but today, commonly, few, if any, of these delightful showmen actually pretend to the reality of magic, taken in some occult or preternatural sense. While dazzling us with their wondrous illusions, and eliciting our acclaim, delight, and awe, few, if any, pretend they are up to anything but marvelous, sophisticated tricks, tricks which, if revealed, would to our pleasure be seen to well cohere with well-recognized imperatives of nature and common sense. Our illusionist, on the other hand, often pretended that his powers were actually beyond nature, and were authentic expressions of occult forces and destinies, of powers and worlds beyond the pale of our quotidian realities, indeed, powers and worlds not only inaccessible to, but literally alien to, the quantifications and presuppositions of science. This sort of claim sophisticated auditors tended on the whole to find amusing, understanding it as part of the entertainment, but some, like myself, thought it improper, even offensive, particularly as we recognized, only too clearly, that over time some members, indeed, eventually several members, of his audience, or following, seemed to take the claim seriously. Such claims, of course, would have been more to be expected not in our own century but in, say, Rhodes of the 2nd Century, Paris or Marseilles of the 12th Century, or perhaps in Renaissance Florence. Indeed, for such claims, in earlier eras, one might have risked exile, stoning, or the stake. But to make such claims in our century was ludicrous to any informed, educated mind. The universe may be mysterious, but it is all of a piece, and it is all here, so to speak. Our reality is the only reality. Has this not been proven by science? But our illusionist, in my view, preyed on the superstitions and fears of common men, over whom he seemed to exercise a fascinating, almost hypnotic sway. He was not even above selling alleged nostrums, philters, and elixirs, prognosticating the future, and supposedly communicating with what he spoke of the "realms of the elsewise." Supposedly there were many dimensions, or worlds, or states of being, of which ours was only one, and these differed considerably the one from the other, some relatively benign, others malignant, some as inhospitable as polar wastes, others as fraught with life as green, rain-lashed jungles, or wide, endless, wind-swept, grassy plains, trodden by incessantly prowling beasts of strange aspect, driven on and on through what would be centuries in our time, hungry, starving, seeking food. Pressed for details, of course, matters, as expected, became very vague, and we were assured that these remarks were largely sensings, and that, in our terms, such worlds and such creatures could not be easily understood or described. How convenient! They were "elsewise." "How do you know?" he was asked. He would pale, and say, "There are doors, doors." He was an incorrigible, exemplary charlatan. One had to admire him for his shameless bravado, if nothing else. "Have you ever gone through such doors?" we asked him. "No," he would say. "But I open them sometimes, and look through. "Where are they?" we asked. "Sometimes they are here, and sometimes not," he said. "Is there one here now?" we asked. "I do not think so," he said. "How do you know they exist?" we asked. "I see them," he said. "We do not," we said. "Be glad," he said. We laughed at him, and I do not think he cared for this. I suppose we had insulted him, and he was a proud, high-strung, sensitive man. But I had the eerie feeling then that he might be serious, that he might actually have convinced himself of his own nonsense, that he might have become eventually the victim of his own fancies, that we were dealing with a pathology, simply, that he might be mad. In any event it was unkind of us, and I for one regretted that we had behaved as we had.

He retired from the stage shortly after that.

One supposes this had to do with his health, which was never robust.

His career had been remarkable, all told, though, as I have suggested, controversial. I, for one, felt, despite his considerable and acknowledged talents, he had abused his craft, and had unscrupulously preyed upon the gullibility of many of his fellow human beings, that he had consciously and deliberately fostered and exploited their fears and superstitions. After his retirement he rather disappeared from public view, and, as far as I know, devoted himself to his studies. As I have suggested, he seems to have had few, if any, friends. I suppose I was as close to him as anyone, and we were not really close. He did have, however, several enemies. Naturally it was to these, where recognized, that the police devoted their attention, but after the completion of their investigation no arrests had been made, and no charges filed.

But to return to the diary.

It fell to me, at the request of the state, naturally enough, I suppose, given my dealings with the illusionist, to catalog his aforementioned collection, which was to be sold at auction. I was, accordingly, given a key to his apartments and soon set about my work. It was in the course of these labors that I chanced upon the diary.

The diary, I suppose, might have had some value as a souvenir, or memento, of the illusionist. To be sure, it was not as though he were a public figure of note, a statesman, a great scientist or famous inventor, a particularly celebrated artist or musician, or such. But it might have some value, I supposed, to a collector, particularly one interested in prestidigitation, the theater, or such. My attention was soon drawn to certain of the last entries, particularly those which seemed to regrettably document the ultimate, dismaying, utter disintegration of a human mind. The entries tend to become progressively less coherent in the last few days, and I shall occasionally summarize, or paraphrase, rather than quote, directly.

January 23rd, 20—.

I lied to them. It is not always doors. Not literally, not always.

Sometimes it is a narrow crevice, or an opening, sometimes like that of a cave. I do not know what is in the cave. Something may come out of it. I am afraid of what may come out of the cave.

I want to be left alone.

I have hurt no one.

I do not want these things.

January 27th, 20—.

They do not believe me. I do not blame them.

February 6th, 20—.

I suppose I am mad. I am not mad.

February 16th, 20—.

It is dreams, all dreams, then. The doors, the holes, the cave.

Does that make them not real? I am very tired. Can one dream while one is awake? Was I awake? Did I dream? Was I asleep, and awake? Can that be? Sleep calls to me. I will not be afraid. But I am afraid.

In my fine bed I am safe.

I must sleep. I am afraid to sleep.

I burned the books. I will do the exercises no more. I do not want the strength they give me. I do not want to see what they show me.

February 17, 20—.

Sometimes it is like a curtain. Or is it a dream? Maybe it is something like a dream. I seem to be awake. That is not unusual in a dream.

February 18th, 20—.

Why did I lie to them?

Why did I tell them there were doors. But there are doors. I know that now. I tried to lie. I wanted to lie. But I told the truth.

If I might comment on these entries, briefly, and rather in general, I might suggest that the illusionist, in his bizarre way, appears to be open to the possibility that reality is diverse, multiplex, and perhaps discontinuous, that there may be realities other than our own, some perhaps similar, and others perhaps quite different, perhaps even inconceivable to us. One thing that seems extremely clear is that these other conjectured realities, from these entries, and, as clearly, from others I omit, are not matters of ghosts or spirits, or intangibles, or such. There seems to be nothing abstract or mystical here. We are not dealing with speculations or shadows. Whereas these postulated alternative realities may be inaccessible, or "elsewise," so to speak, at least some of them, at least some of the time, or most of the time, they are understood to be as fully real as ours. They are as tangible in their way as ours is to us. They are not less real, they are other reals. They are understood to be as tangible as the touch of falling snow on an upturned face, as a kiss, as a wound, as a knife.

> March 4th, 20—.
>
> No, it is not like a hole, not now, not like the opening of a cave. It is more like a tunnel. It is far off. I see it when I sleep. That is strange. It is a large opening. There are clouds. When the wind comes up, from my left, the clouds move away, and I see the tall grass, and, here and there, trees. I can see to the horizon. It seems far off.

I am supposing the incoherence of the entries is obvious to the reader, containing even apparent inconsistencies, literal contradictions. Unless, of course, these are alternative realities, different "doors" so to speak. It is interesting to note that the nature of the subject's delusions seems to become less chaotic, though no less pathetically deranged, as we proceed. The delusions seem to become narrower now, more centered; perhaps the subject senses himself coming closer to a particular "door.", Or, alternatively, I suppose, one might speak of one of these other "doors," or, better, it seems, worlds, like a material body in an unusual space, if such is the right word, drifting closer, and closer, perhaps eventually, for a moment, to touch another world, ours.

> March 8th, 20—.
>
> Last night I had the dream again, the fields, seeing a long way off, the grass. I can smell the grass.
>
> I am safe in my bed.

March 9th, 20—.

The field is far off. There is nothing there. I am not afraid.

March 10th, 20—.

The field, again. Beautiful. Fresh wind. Blue sky, soft clouds.

Peaceful. But on the horizon, dots, two, far off, something?

I am not alone?

March 11th, 20—.

The fields, the grass. Again. Something is out there, far off, I am sure of it.

The wind is behind me. It blows toward the horizon.

March 15th, 20—.

This is the first entry since I recorded the dream, I think it is a dream, of the night of March 10th.

On the night of the 11th, I think I saw them, for something, it seemed, turned my way, and looked in my direction, so still, so alertly, but so far off. It is odd; how continuous, how coherent, these dreams are. That is unusual, is it not? Then I feared, though I could not see them, that they had seen me, or somehow knew of my presence. Then, in the dream, for that it must be, I sensed them separate, one to the left, and one to the right. I could not see them,and they were far off, but I was sure then, somehow, they were coming closer, and closer. The wind blew toward them, and this moved the grass. I could see no movement in the grass, save for the wind. I detected nothing. Then I awakened. On the night of the 12th I saw them, suddenly only yards away, one on the left, one on the right, rising from the grass, large, strange, tawny things, lengthy, and sinuous; now perhaps four feet high at the shoulder; before they

> must have been crouching, their bellies close to the ground; their rib cages moved almost imperceptibly; clearly they are air-breathing things;four legs, no wings; they came closer, quickly, a step or two, then stopped, and then closer, again, another step or two, again quickly, and then again stopped; now they were only feet away; paws large, wide, soft. muddied a little; it had rained; their haunches seemed to gather under them, excitedly; their bodies seem to quiver, almost imperceptibly. They are unnaturally still now; yellow eyes, large, rounded, intent; distended nostrils, moisture about half-opened jaws, wet, dark tongues, whitish teeth, long, fanglike, moist, curved, turned inward, powerful, graceful, strange, savage things, eager, intent; something of that evolved feline beauty which seems nature's optimum design for a land predator. But then there was something strange about their sides, as though something were living, moving, beneath their skins. Is this part of them? But they were now regarding one another more balefully than me. Each seemed then more concerned with the other than with me. I was afraid. I took a step backward. One raised his paw, snarling, watching the other, and lashed out, toward the other, and I heard a tearing of wood, and I awakened, screaming. I threw myself from the bed, but clutched at its side. My fingers touched the wood. I cried out, rose up, and fled to the light switch. All seemed the same, nothing amiss, all in its place, with but one hideous exception. In the side of the bed near the foot, on the left side, there was a long, deep, splintered furrow, a foot long, a half inch deep in the wood, as though some spiteful vandal had intentionally defaced the wood with a metal tool. I am afraid to sleep.

At this point it is doubtless clear to the reader what is going on. On the assumption that pure charlatanry is not involved, that this was not intended, somehow, via publicity or whatever, to result in a refurbishing or reestablishing of our illusionist's abandoned career, his unstable and deluded mind manufactured everything, weaving together from the threads of disappointment and paranoia a fabric of indisputable madness. Obviously the beasts of his dream are suggested by the carvings on his bedposts. It is true that I have inspected the frame of the bed and it does, indeed, bear a disfigurement of the sort described in the diary, but, obviously, this could have been inflicted by the subject himself, either subconsciously, in a fit of madness, or, deliberately, as a supposed evidence of the veridicality of his unusual tale, designed to impress naive readers of tabloids. My own first reaction was irritation that a fine piece of Baroque craftsmanship should have been damaged, whether accidentally or wantonly.

I did see our illusionist, according to my records, on business, on March 19th of the year above, a matter having to do with a client's inquiry as to an item known to be in his collection. Predictably, it was not for sale. It later fetched better than four thousand dollars at auction. At this meeting his mental disintegration was evident. He seemed haggard, incoherent, and agitated. I wondered if he had slept, for days. At this time, of course, I had no knowledge of what was going on his life. I did express concern, which was genuine enough, and for which I think he was grateful. I also recommended that he see a physician, as I supposed him to be suffering from some severe, but ordinary, easily treatable indisposition. He promised to do so, but I do not think he did. I saw him again, on the 22nd of March. The motivation for this visit, as far as I can determine, though it was years ago, was my concern for him. After my visit of the 19th, I was alarmed for his health. Too, I suspected, ruefully, that I might be the closest thing he had to a friend. This meeting was troubling in more than one way. If anything, he seemed more miserably distraught than on the 19th, and, worse, was bandaged here and there, about the chest and arms, and, in several places, it seemed that blood had soaked through the gauze. It was at this time, as well, that I first discerned the damage to the frame of the bed. I was not sure the blood was genuine, and, naturally, I assumed that he himself had inflicted the injury to the bed. I became suspicious that these matters were tied together somehow and were supposed to play some role in his career, that a hoax was in process. He was evasive in response to my questions, and this further aroused my suspicions. Doubtless he was contemplating some master illusion; perhaps he was projecting a coup that would be the triumph of a lifetime, and the envy and despair of lesser practitioners of the deceptive arts. But, too, his stress seemed genuine, and I feared then greatly for his sanity, much more than hitherto. But far exceeding my suspicions, and my reservations pertaining to his honesty, and my awareness of his unexampled showmanship, was my sense of his tragic physical and mental condition. Any sense of indignation or offended righteousness which I might have felt, or been tempted to feel, was overcome by my concern, and pity. That was the last time that I saw him alive.

Naturally I sought the entry for the night of the 21st, the night before my visit of the 22nd.

> March 22, 20—.
>
> I shall recount, as simply as possible, what occurred last night. The beasts came for me. On their sides, grown from their forequarters, writhing, lashing about, snakelike, are strange appendages, spined, constrictive, restless. They coiled about me; I struggled, helplessly. I could not escape. I could not breathe. The two heads, massive and shaggy, leaned toward me, whitish fangs, long, moist, back-curving, I sensing the breath, fetid, saliva about the jaws, eyes tense, lustrous, eager, low noises, eager, anticipatory, rumbling, from great throats, but a hissing, too, from the appendages.
>
> The appendages have eyes! And mouths, too! Two things perhaps evolved together, a genetic madness? A symbiotic anomaly? Once, anciently? No, now at least it is one thing. One thing, with diverse living

parts. The beasts lifted their heads, across my body, but inches from one another. Their heads swayed. They snarled, menacingly at one another. Then both roared, fiercely, as though in anger, as though challenging one another, and I awoke, gasping, drenched with sweat, and bleeding. There were marks on my body, discolorations, encircling it, and within these marks numerous small holes, bleeding, as though a hundred small nails had penetrated the skin. I know now they will come for me. Alan came again today. He is a good man. He is kind, but does not wish to appear so. He thinks I am a liar. Perhaps I am. I did not show him the wounds but I could not conceal the blood. He is annoyed at the gouging on the bed. I could not blame him. It is a fine piece. He doubtless thinks I did it. Perhaps I did. I do not know. He thinks I am up to something. I wonder if I am. I put off his questions.

He probably thinks me mad, as it is. There is no point in furthering his suspicions. He is a simple man, and a kindly one. I could not speak to him, of course. I could not speak to anyone. Who would believe me? Some sort of psychosomatic conversion response must be involved here, as the subconscious mind, under hypnotic suggestion, can produce blisters, marks on the skin, and so on. I do not think I shall see Alan again. I think I do know what I shall see again. They are hungry, terribly hungry, the things. One cannot blame them. I do not blame them. They are not evil, they are only powerful, and very hungry, even starving.

I wonder how long it has been since they have eaten.

That is the last entry in the diary.

I called upon him the next afternoon, but found police in his apartments. The body had been found last night by the building superintendent, who had responded to a call from another tenant, who had heard some sort of disturbance. The body had not yet been moved, and two detectives were present, and two uniformed officers, and three members of a forensic team.. An ambulance I had noted, was parked in front of the building. I was invited in and questioned for some time, to some extent with respect to my business there and my relation to the victim, but largely with respect to his known acquaintances and associates. They were particularly interested in any motives which might exist for what had occurred, and any enemies which our illusionist might have had. Too, when they learned of my business relationship with him, they asked me to examine the collection and see if anything was missing. As far as I could see, without a careful examination, there was nothing missing.

There is not a great deal more to tell, except that the murder, as it was supposed to be, and may well have been, was an unusually grisly one, of a sort which, I gathered, was unusual even in the experience of the detectives, who were doubtless not unaccustomed to tragic examples of what human beings can do to one another. I looked at the body briefly, but turned away. The head was there and some parts of the body. Much of the body, however, was gone. It was as though parts of it had been dragged away. There was much blood about. The jaws of the wooden beasts at the bedposts were thick with it, and it ran down the posts, as though down the sides of necks. Too, it was intertwined with the vinelike decorations at the sides of the frame. The bedclothes and carpeting nearby, on which some bits of flesh lay, had been drenched with blood, now dried. Interestingly there was this dried blood, in gouts, on both sides of the bed, and on the carpeting, as though the body had been torn apart, even fought for, and various parts of it dragged to one side or the other. The mattress seemed torn and twisted, as though it had been the scene of a frightful struggle. I noted that on the part of a leg, on the carpet, there were circular bruises, as though it had been tightly encircled with some broad ropelike substance. Too, within the bruises there were several aligned, small wounds. I would later learn these wounds were better than an inch deep. There was also, oddly, an unpleasant, feral smell about.

At that time, of course, I was as convinced as anyone that a murder had been committed, and one of dreadful aspect.

Certainly that was the natural supposition of the police and this belief would underlie their investigation.

It was only later, after reading the diary, that I wondered, from time to time, if some sort of illusion had been planned here, and that somehow it had gone tragically, terribly, wrong. Such things can happen.

But such speculations explain little.

Who would have been the cooperants in such an illusion? Had our illusionist miscalculated on the reliability and fidelity of his confederates?

The entries in the diary might well have been understood as part of an elaborate hoax, one well worthy of our illusionist, designed to cast a spell of mystery over a planned disappearance, perhaps a way to elude creditors, perhaps a way to prepare for a spectacular and startling reappearance, to reinvigorate a dimming mystique, to inaugurate anew a lucrative career.

But perhaps his assistants, or confederates, had had projects of their own, and had utilized this opportunity to enact their own scheme of hideous vengeance upon our trusting illusionist.

That seems the most likely explanation, though who these implacable enemies might have been remains obscure.

Certainly robbery does not seem a likely motive as little, or nothing, was missing. Certainly, as I later determined, the collection was intact.

As mentioned earlier the collection was auctioned, to satisfy creditors. I myself bid upon, and secured, two items, the diary, from which I have quoted, and the bed.

Technology

I DREAMED that I had a body.

It was a nice dream. There is not much else to do in here but dream. It used to be said that one should live one's dreams, but it is better, really, to live one's life.

In a sense I suppose this is all my fault, but if I had not worked out the technology, the myoelectric controls, the circuitry, the theory, the design, someone else, sooner or later, would have done so. There are dynamics and directions, readinesses, and such.

To be sure, I could not have done this all by myself, but I never, personally, claimed all the credit.

Journalists, and then historians, simplify things. So school children learn a name, and answer a question in the expected manner, and so on. And something becomes "common knowledge," which, really, isn't knowledge at all. There is nothing common, or simple, about truth. It is vast, a thousand truths for each atom, and most of them don't matter very much. Perhaps the falsehoods are more important; perhaps they make life simple enough to live; perhaps they are what make life worth living. Can it be that mistakes are what, for most, nourish life, and make it endurable? Are truths so terrible, even little ones?

I am not sure how long I have been in here.

I think it has been a long time.

I still regard myself as the same, of course. Others might not, but I do.

It is perhaps a thousand years, perhaps ten thousand years.

One loses track.

A long time.

I had a body, of course, at one time. I can remember that. It was not much of a body, but it was real.

I remember the feel of walking on grass, of wind, the smell of flowers, Agnes, such things.

I am not sure that death is really that terrible.

Perhaps it is; I do not know.

As of now, I haven't died.

I suppose I could die, but they have not let me.

I can communicate, I believe, with the outside world. The container is designed with that in mind. It produces a voice, which I can control. I hear it as my voice, in my mind. I do not know what it sounds like, outside the container. When I speak, I do not know if anyone listens, if there is anyone there. Indeed, I am not really sure, any longer, that a sound is produced outside the container.

Long ago, people came to speak with me. Most of them wanted something. No one has come in a long time now.

A child used to read me poetry. An old man would come occasionally to talk. I gather he had no one else to talk with. Sometimes he would read me a newspaper. Then he stopped coming. I suppose he died, unless he, too, is now in a container.

I wonder how many of us there are, people who made the will, people in no hurry to die.

Long ago there were many causes of death, and, I suppose, there are still many causes of death.

Parts of the body would be injured, or diseased, or would deteriorate with age. But in many cases the brain, the foundation, the core, the basis, the center of consciousness, the internal theater of experience, indexed by sensors to a mysterious world, might be alive, be healthy, be unwilling to cease.

What if it could be removed from the body, and kept alive? This had been done, for days at a time, so long ago, with disembodied monkey brains, kept alive, bathed in a supportive, nutrient solution. The brain activity was there. The brain was alive, and feeling, and thinking. Feeling is in the brain. It is extradited to diverse points in the body. This is clear in phantom-limb phenomena. The amputee feels a limb which is not there. It moves, it aches, it is cold, only it is not there. We seem to open our eyes and see an outside world but the experience is within. It has to be. There is nowhere else for it to be. Evolution has correlated the inside world with the outside world, but the outside world is very different from the inside world; in it there is no color, no sound, only fields, and forces. Our experience as we normally think of it is a falsehood, an illusion, but it is an illusion, a falsehood, selected for by evolution. There is this intricate topological relationship between the interior world and the quite different, supposed outside world. It is an illusion, yes, but it is a valuable illusion; a precious illusion, a necessary illusion, one without which life would be impossible. Is this a lie which is essential for life, then, a good lie? One supposes so. We must not let a small truth destroy the thread of survival. These threads are so tenuous. I think sometimes that things are like that in the container, as well. In the container, too, one supposes there is an outside world, but it is surely very different from the world in the container, with its tissue, its filaments, its wires, its circuitry, and such. Even when I had a body it was obvious that my experiences might have been exactly what they were without an outside, mind-independent physical world. It would only require another cause, a different cause, one other than the hypothesized, comforting, reassuring mind-independent, physical world. The physical world supposedly required space, time and causality, and yet each of these concepts, pursued relentlessly, as few would care to do, seems to yield contradictions. Thus, if this is true, the world which they bespeak cannot be real. I wonder if it is much different in the container.

Certainly life is a value.

One may not be able to prove that, but what could prove it, if not life itself, and its found value, the value found in the living of it?

What else could one ask for?

Doubtless values have a cause, but that does not make them unreal; it makes them real.

So we set to work, and designed the containers. We began with laboratory animals. I can recall the small sounds emanating from the tiny containers, on the shelves. I suppose they continued to live their lives, as they thought they were doing. They would not know they were in containers. I do not think our primates, monkeys, chimpanzees, even the gorilla, realized that. Later we utilized human subjects, volunteers, usually accident victims, sometimes the terminally ill. Results were mixed. Sometimes they begged to die; these requests could not be accommodated, obviously, for legal and moral reasons. They might dream suicide, but that was all. One could not stop them from doing that. That was up to the individual. As the technology improved, and became more familiar, more innocent, less threatening, and so on, through media reports, and such, such requests became less frequent. I do not think, on the whole, that the first occupants of the containers experienced actual discomfort. It seems reasonably clear that the animals, which were disposed of after the experiments, felt little, if any, discomfort. In the case of the humans I think the matter was more psychological than physical. I think they were depressed or afraid, or perhaps they missed the outside world, the wind, the flowers, the grass, such things.

In time, I made out the necessary documents, the will, so to speak. I could hardly do otherwise, given my role in the endeavor.

It was a triumph of technology.

I had every right to be proud.

Even today, I am in no hurry to die.

I wonder if they will let me die.

I used to ask them about that.

I wonder if this is hell. No, it is the container.

The Wereturtle

I HAD never known Stevens to lie.

It was late one evening, in the fall, not so long ago, really, and a few of us, after dinner, the centerpiece of which had been crisp, thick, deliciously blackened steaks, done in the English manner, were enjoying brandy and cigars at the club.

None of those lettuce dinners, with carrot juice, for us.

There was not an exercise bicycle on the premises.

"Nasty weather out," said Stevens. "Bitter, bitter."

This remark surprised us, we sitting about, as the evening seemed pleasant enough. Nonetheless the great bulk of Stevens shivered, and the wide, silken scarf wrapped protectively several times about his rather lengthy throat leaped up and down between his chin and the black tie.

The club was an old-fashioned one, from your point of view, I suppose. But we liked it. We were rather fond of its contented, enclosed, fortresslike serenity, its comforting quietude, its exquisitely severe taste, its unpretentious, unassumingly insolent elegance, its Victorian appointments, many unchanged since the days of the queen, its luminous, delicately shaded lamps, its vast sofas and chairs, its fine leather, its plush upholstery, the large, sturdy, dark, wooden tables, an occasional bronze of a lightly but tastefully clad young lady with a pitcher or tambourine lodged discreetly in a corner, the scattered newspapers, expressing the views of objective publishers, a copy of the Rush Limbaugh newsletter, the thick rug, deriving from a palace in north Africa, the gift of a grateful pasha, a relic from a 19th Century campaign, the various muskets and rifles, halberds, pikes and swords mounted on the walls, a trophy scimitar seized from the Paynim in the 11th Century, and such. You, I suppose, might have regarded the club, and the den, as merely lofty, and shadowed, as perhaps too heavily draped, as perhaps even gloomy, but, in a masculine sort of way, it was warm, comfortable, and cozy. We liked it. Surely it provided a nice relief for some of us, from the simple lodgings of our various expeditions and excursions, more comfortable, surely, than the bivouacs of the gold fields, where one slept with a pistol at one's side, from the rocking dugouts of the Amazon, where a poison dart might, at any moment, fly forth from the verdant shore, from the mountain camps of the freezing, windswept Himalayas, seeking traces of shaggy, bipedalian wild life, from the wearing, scorching digs in Sumer, uncovering various secrets of former civilizations, revising the views of astonished, academic archaeologists the world over, from the crocodile infested waters of the vast, winding Congo, exploring odd byways and making contact with lingering forms of prehistoric life, forgotten white races, and such, and from the tents and watch fires of the lion country, bemused by the roars of gigantic, hungry felines, their eyes blazing but yards from the camp, chatting, stopping now and then to calm the fears of the bearers.

"Damn cold," said Stevens.

It was an exclusive men's club. Few were permitted to join who had not crewed at Oxford, rescued embattled missionaries, or faced a charging rhino. English was the typical language spoken at the club, but members occasionally, particularly the older ones, often addressed one another in a variety of obscure native dialects, if only to keep their skills honed. This was occasionally irritating to some of the younger members, such as myself, particularly when the long-awaited punch line of an extended joke would be delivered in a language likely to be familiar to fewer than a hundred and twenty individuals, most of whom lived in the Amazon basin.

"Damn, damn cold," sputtered Stevens.

"Really?" I said, despite my youth contributing to the conversation.

"Yes," said Stevens, grimly. In the half darkness his cigar flamed angrily, a dangerous beacon betokening to an attentive observer the wisdom of guarding one's words.

No duels had been fought over differences of opinion amongst club members since 1842, that in connection with certain policies of William H. Harrison. Nonetheless Stevens was a redoubtable marksman. Once we had thought he had struck the bull's-eye only once in six shots, fired casually, swiftly from the hip. "Examine the target," he advised us, with a small smile, while blowing smoke away from the barrel of his revolver. We had found the six bullets had all entered the same hole in the center of the bull's-eye, one after the other.

"No offense intended," I assured him.

"None taken," he assured me.

Mutually reassured, we were silent for a moment.

Stevens leaned back against the red leather of his chair, and blew smoke toward the ceiling. I was relieved to see the wreaths of smoke were drifting about, in a leisurely, congenial manner. He seemed lost in thought.

I have remarked that ours was an exclusive men's club, but it should be understood, particularly by those whose political hackles might find agitation in such an observation, that this was more a matter *de facto* than *de jure*. In order to avoid unpleasantries with a preempted legal system designed not to soothe, arbitrate, and resolve contested issues but to use armed force to promote a particular political agenda, the club was open to all rational beings, in theory, of any species. On the other hand, there were no female members. And I ask you, if you were a female, would you care to be a member of our club? Surely not, unless as a matter of noble self-sacrifice, compared to which gathering the pikes of the Spanish infantry into one's chest, thereby opening a breach, would seem negligible. The closest to come to membership was Hortense H., the philosopher, well known for her stimulating work on Arthur Schopenhauer, as male feminist. In any event, on her sabbatical year, Dr. H. went to Nepal and had herself charged by a rhino, the incident being carefully videotaped by a native guide. As Dr. H. was, among other commendable things, an animal-rights activist she could not bring herself to the point of causing the rhino discomfort. When she was released from the hospital in Singapore several months later, and the videotape was carefully examined by the membership committee, it was discovered that the rhino had not been charging swiftly enough to meet our standards. Similarly, careful enlargements of certain of the frames of the tape clearly showed a bead of sweat on her fair brow, as the rhino closed. This was taken as an indication of failing to exhibit what might be called, to coin a phase, "grace under pressure." In any case, the membership committee, in conscience, found itself unable to accept her for membership, declining with regret. She would have been our first female member. Her attorney, Gertrude F., who, it might be noted, unlike H., had never faced a charging rhino personally, let alone successfully, urged H. to insist on forcing the club to reduce its qualifications somewhat, to the point where H. would be clearly qualified. Things might have proceeded well from there, except for the installation of new initiation procedures, involving a five-year probationary period, to be spent cooking, washing dishes, cleaning pots and pans, waiting on tables, emptying ash trays, fetching coffee, serving tea, sweeping up, mopping and scrubbing floors, dusting, making beds, general tidying up, laundering, and such. At this point many of the female applicants, of which H. was the most prominent, withdrew their names from consideration. Those who remained were invited for a tour of the club, in which certain details subtly figured, for example, now prominently displayed bronze castings of young ladies with pitchers and tambourines, several copies of the Rush Limbaugh newsletter, left about, casually, here and there, and, perhaps most subtly, the voluminous clouds of cigar smoke electronically pumped into, and about, the premises by frail, venerable Jenkins, our at-the-time-gas-masked steward. Several of these visitors, later bitter in their oxygen tents, are reported to have disclaimed any further interest in breaching the hitherto sacrosanct precincts of the club.

Personally I regretted their decision.

You see, I myself would not have found it amiss if there might have been some trim ankles on display on the premises, for, after all, there is only so much to be gained from the contemplation of bronze figures, even those with pitchers or tambourines. On the other hand, some of the older members were a bit more crotchety, and Stevens in particular, who was the head of the membership committee.

"I say, Stevens," I said, for I was carrying on a certain train of thought in my head, which now surfaced, "when do you think we shall find our club graced by some fair representative of the distaff side of humanity?"

Phillips half choked on his brandy. Wentworth looked up, suddenly. Brooks' hand shook on his snifter. A drop splashed on a nearby newsletter. An ash fell, unnoted, from the cigar of Hastings. Abramowitz turned white.

Stevens regarded me with one of those six-bullets-in-one-hole looks.

"I beg your pardon?" he said, in a tone which suggested that he was far from begging it.

"Just a thought, old man," I said. "It might be jolly, you know, don't you think, to have a whiff of perfume in the upholstery now and then."

We had not had a duel at the club in well over a century.

I was sure that Abramowitz, our newest member, and a fellow of high ideals, would be reluctant to see a member shot in cold blood before his eyes. The others, too, I am sure, would have objected to that sort of thing, though perhaps, as they were senior members, would better understand the nature and degree of the provocation involved.

"I know that you are fond of the fair sex," I pointed out to Stevens.

He had had, he had estimated, some twelve to fourteen thousand nights of love in his life, with nearly as many partners. I think that he, though he always professed himself an amateur in these matters, would have easily won the respect of, and the salute of, a Casanova, a Don Juan, even an Errol Flynn. He was not as unpleasant in the morning, as difficult to get on with, you understand, as a certain sultan of legend, but, clearly, he had never met his Scheherazade. Certainly H. had not filled the bill, even after her release from the hospital in Singapore. Indeed, it had been rumored that H.'s drives had been less political than biological, and that her attempt to gain membership was little more than a transparent ruse to place herself in proximity to the ponderous, irresistible Stevens, if only in so humble a capacity as, in the servants' quarters, to polish his boots, and to bring him humbly, timidly, unnoticed, head down, in her white, starched lace cap and crisp, short, black maid's skirt, his tea.

"Harummph," said Stevens. (It is difficult to spell the sound he made.)

"Have you ever managed to replicate your genes?" I asked him, boldly.

"Several times," he said. And I rapidly passed over in my mind a number of prominent young soldiers of fortune, adventurers, mercenaries, explorers, and such, of dubious parentage, but having some obscure linkage to the club.

He had reportedly deradicalized several modern women, reducing them almost instantly to the submissiveness of a fourteenth-century geisha in the arms of a warlord. One piercing glance from his slate-gray eyes, one stroke of his heavy paw, and they were at his feet, placing his boot on their head, begging to bear his children.

"Aren't you a little out of order, lad?" chuckled Philips, in my direction. His remark seemed a light one, but it was clearly designed to reduce the likelihood of gunplay.

"No, no," sighed Stevens, leaning back again. "That is just what we need in the club, new blood, fresh ideas, uncompromising skepticism, ferocious criticality, vital, violent, telling challenges on every hand."

"No offense intended," I assured him.

"None taken," he assured me.

And thus by the simple expedient of reciprocal assurances, exchanged honestly, openly, and without reservation, was oil poured on troubled waters.

Phillips breathed more easily. Wentworth sipped his brandy. Brooks wiped a bead of amber fluid from a newsletter. Hastings wiped a bit ash from his lapel. Abramowitz ceased clutching the arms of his chair, as clearly he had been ready to spring to the wall and with a frenzied, desperate sweep of his arm scatter various bladed and pointed weapons out of reach.

"It's cold, damn cold, in here," said Stevens.

None of us chose to contradict him. Even a thermometer would have thought carefully about the risk of that.

"I suppose you think I am opposed to women," said Stevens.

"What would give us that idea?" asked Hastings.

"Women may be evil," said Phillips, "but they can't help that. No one here holds that against them."

"No," said Wentworth.

"But they are different," said Brooks. "That makes things difficult."

"Yes," said Hastings.

"They're certainly welcome in the club, if they can meet the conditions," said Phillips. "We've always had an open mind on that."

"There was H.," said Brooks. "She came dangerously close."

"Yes," said Phillips, uneasily, whose term of service on the membership committee had not yet expired.

"Things change, times change," said Stevens, moodily. "Less cricket in Connecticut now, polo nearly a lost art in New Jersey. Who has seen rugby in upstate New York of late?"

"Not I," said Wentworth.

"I am something of an old-fashioned fellow," said Stevens.

"Hear, hear," said Brooks.

"Cricket, polo, rugby, rowing, shooting, leading infantry charges against overwhelming odds, the usual things."

"The wheel turns," said Hastings. "Hang on, old man. Hold the fort. Things will get back to normal."

"I suppose you all think me a grumpy codger," continued Stevens, moodily, "a curmudgeon, a monster opposed to all progress, that sort of thing."

"Not at all," we insisted.

"Then you are all mistaken," said Stevens, "for I am all of that, and more, and by choice."

"Choice is unfashionable," granted Brooks.

"Yesterday," said Stevens, "I drove my safari vehicle three blocks, to a nearby mall, and did not buckle the seat belt."

We were aghast at this confession, but had always recognized that Stevens was very little socially controlled.

"I was stopped twice by policemen before I reached the parking lot."

"At least those fellows are on their toes," I said.

"Next," said Stevens, "cigars will be against the law."

"I do not think so," said Abramowitz, who had a background in law, "as that would infringe freedom. It is more likely that the planet will be declared a no-smoking zone."

"Next," said Stevens, "it will be against the law to leap off bridges."

"It may already be," said Wentworth.

We all looked to Abramowitz.

"I'm not sure," he said.

We were all uneasy at the course the conversation was taking. Stevens did not seem his normal, robustly arrogant, lustily ebullient self. This talk of unbuckled seat belts and bridges was alarming.

Stevens had not seemed the same since his return from the Carpathians.

There was a silence, moderately pregnant.

"Tonight is the full moon," said Phillips, apropos at the time, as far as I then knew, of nothing.

Stevens nodded grimly. "I must be going," he said, bringing his ponderous bulk to his feet, and flinging another fold of the silken scarf about his neck with a flourish. Stevens had style. It was apparently one of the things which the fair sex found irresistible about him.

"Don't go," protested Brooks. "The evening is young. I had hoped to hear of your recent adventures in the Carpathians."

"Do not detain him," said Phillips, lighting a fresh cigar.

And the bulk of Stevens trundled away, toward the cloakroom. The room seemed emptier, now that he had gone, and, from the point of view of classical physics, it doubtless was.

"I don't understand Stevens," said Wentworth. "He seems to have changed."

"You were with him in the Carpathians," said Hastings to Phillips. "Did anything occur there?"

"There was an incident," said Phillips.

We replenished our brandy.

"You may recall," said Phillips, "that Stevens and I, at the behest of the Smithsonian, had formed an expedition to inquire into certain troubling rumors emanating from various obscure provinces in Romania, rumors having to do with occult fauna."

"Oh, yes," said Hastings, the matter coming back to him now, "vampires, werewolves, that sort of thing."

"Poppycock," said Wentworth.

Vulgarity was not characteristic of Wentworth.

"Sorry, chaps," he said.

"Mathematics is against such hypotheses," said Abramowitz. "It is a simple doubling problem. If one bitten by a vampire becomes a vampire, and one bitten by a werewolf becomes a werewolf, and such, then, unless they go about biting one another, you would soon have a geometrical progression, two vampires or werewolves, then four, then eight, then sixteen, then thirty-two, then sixty-four, one hundred and twenty-eight, two hundred and fifty-six, five hundred and twelve, a thousand and twenty-four, two thousand and forty-eight, and so on. In a few nights everyone on Earth would be a vampire or werewolf."

"Have you ever noticed that vampires and werewolves have not yet become politically organized," observed Hastings.

"Odd," said Brooks.

"You might think so," said Phillips, "but it doesn't work that way. Not everyone bitten by a vampire becomes a vampire. It has to do with genes, predispositions, allergies, and such. Indeed, in Transylvania a serum has been developed, administered in early childhood, which tends to produce immunity to the vampire syndrome. Several vampires funded the original project, probably in order to control the vampire population, diminish the likelihood of famine, and such. But vampires are not the most serious problem, especially with the development of all-night blood banks. Vampires can now meet their basic needs in socially approved manners, by working at night, usually as watchmen, or as clerks in minimarkets, liquor stores, and so on."

"But what of werewolves?" said Hastings.

"Ah, yes," said Phillips, "they are not the handsome, suave, sophisticated, romantic chaps that vampires are, who dress well, gargle frequently, keep their fangs clean, and so on. No, they are quite different. Every so often, at a certain point in the feral cycle, they develop a ravening taste for human blood. They prowl about, leap forth from the shadows, rip out throats, and such. Not even vampires are safe. Many carry a hand weapon, appropriately licensed, loaded with silver bullets, in the predawn darkness, returning to their crypts."

"It is clear, or reasonably so," said Abramowitz, "that one who has had his throat ripped out by a werewolf would not be likely, in his turn, to become a werewolf."

"Yes," said Phillips, "and that constitutes yet another check on the werewolf population."

"Are the animal rights people interested in protecting werewolves?," asked Brooks.

"Yes," said Phillips. "Two were sent in."

"What happened?" asked Brooks.

"They had their throats torn out."

"I have sometimes wondered," said Brooks, "why an ordinary bullet would not do a werewolf in."

"It has to with biochemistry and the atomic structure of silver," said Phillips, "incompatibilities with metals and proteins, molecular disaffinities, that sort of thing."

"Please, go on," urged Wentworth.

"You inquired about dear Stevens," said Phillips.

"Yes," we said.

"Was he attacked by a werewolf?" inquired Wentworth.

"I dare say that would be traumatic," said Hastings.

I, personally, would not have wanted to be the werewolf who chose to attack Stevens.

"No," said Phillips.

"You said that there was an 'incident,'" said Hastings.

"Yes," said Phillips.

"Does it have to do with werewolves?" asked Abramowitz.

"No," said Phillips.

We waited while he took two puffs on his cigar.

"Werewolves receive the most attention," said Phillips, "presumably because of their understandable interest to human beings who value their lives, but, interestingly, they are only one variety, so to speak, of a larger, lesser-known population of similar creatures, other forms of occult wildlife."

"Other forms?" asked Wentworth.

"There are, for example, many different forms of mammals," said Phillips, "and even within types of mammals, different sorts of mammals; marsupials, for example; consider, if you will, the Australian kangaroo and the American opossum, not to mention the bandicoot, wombat, and yellow-footed pouched mouse."

"True," said Wentworth.

"The origin of the werewolf remains obscure, especially that of the first one," said Phillips, "but their later manner of reproduction is well authenticated. Some unfortunate, often a kindly, devout fellow, perhaps returning from evening services, is set upon by a werewolf, and survives the attack, but, in heroically fighting off the monster, is bitten. Later, he notes that he is periodically transformed into a wolflike creature with a ravening taste for human blood. Most victims find this initially disturbing, but, after a time, make accommodations and adjustments, and, in general, learn to handle the matter. They continue their predations until decrepitude reduces their powers, and they become laughing stocks to small Romanian children, or, more tragically, are finished off with a silver bullet. Psychotherapy is unavailing, and more than one psychotherapist was lost. Stevens and I met several of the afflicted while in the mountains. One was the mayor of a small town, whose citizens, liberals, would not deny him office because of his handicap. They would, however, keep him chained up, and hungry, at regular intervals."

"But what has this to do with Stevens?" pressed Hastings.

"The werewolf," said Stevens, "is doubtless the most dazzling example of the phenomenon in question. Indeed, one hears about little else in the "were" family, but, not surprisingly, the werewolf is not unique. For example, there is the werechicken, in which a human being, commonly a robust, coordinated chap, is periodically transformed into a chicken, and is overwhelmed with a ravening hunger for corn. Peasants, hearing its lugubrious, threatening cackle outside, hurry to fling grains of corn upon the door sills of their huts. It can be slain only with a silver hatchet. To be pecked by one means risking the occult contagion. There are many forms of werebeast, and not all are confined to the superstition-ridden precincts of obscure provinces in Eastern Europe. In Africa there is the were-elephant, particularly dangerous in its rogue phase. Why else to you think that certain African nations have negotiated for guided missiles with silver warheads? There is the weregiraffe. Few people, I fear, ever managed to associate the two stories recently mentioned in the *Times*, that of the ecological damage suffered by certain trees in Central Park and the claimed sightings of a formally attired giraffe entering the Plaza Hotel. One of the most hideous examples is that of the wereworm. One unfortunate fellow, in the vermiform phase, found himself dug up, placed in a can and later threaded upon a fish hook, after which he passed through the alimentary system of a large bass. He suffered acute discomfort, but survived, as the hook had not been of silver."

"I had not known of this sort of thing," said Wentworth, who was pale.

"These things are not as well publicized as the werewolf syndrome, of course," said Phillips. "Too, the victims seldom bring their symptoms to public view."

"What has this to do with Stevens?" asked Hastings, his voice a trifle, I thought, unsteady.

"The moon should be full by now," said Phillips, finishing his brandy and plunging the glowing tip of his cigar into the ash tray, grinding it firmly down into a small pile of brown flakes and smoking gray ash.

"It is," said Abramowitz, who could see our natural satellite through the lofty, velvet-draped window from his deep armchair.

"I think I shall be on my way," said Phillips.

"What happened to Stevens, out there in the mountains?" asked Hastings.

But Phillips was on his way to the cloakroom.

In a moment, I had joined him.

"I thought you might be coming," said Phillips. "Get your coat."

We had soon left the city and were driving east on the Long Island Expressway, left the expressway at Exit 32, and were soon heading north, entering Great Neck, a small Long Island metropolis from which it is difficult to recruit jurors. We then were moving north on Bayview Avenue, crossed the bridge by the library, and were on West Shore Road. I now decline to supply further details, lest they prove too revealing.

"I have noted, as have others," I said, sitting beside Phillips, staring ahead as he drove his land rover over the library bridge, on which it is improper to park, "that Stevens seems rather different now, after the Carpathians."

"What he needs, I think," said Phillips, "is a good woman." He chuckled. "Oh, yes," he said, "you think that is heresy, blasphemy, a betrayal of the charter, inconsistent with several of the bylaws, perhaps, but there is something to it, young fellow, propriety, society, civilization, tradition, biology, the rest of it, you know. Not for us, perhaps. But for a settled fellow like Stevens."

"But he despises women," I said, eager to recall Phillips to his senses.

"But no more than necessary," said Phillips. "Never more than is appropriate."

"True," I granted him, recognizing the justice of the qualification.

I myself had not, as far as I knew, managed to replicate my genes, and I would not have been impervious, I suspected, to the charms of some romantic young woman who might be interested in a project of reciprocal assisted replication.

We did not admit such things, of course, to our fellow members. One owed certain things to the club, and, beyond that, to simple civility.

Salacious innuendoes were not in place amongst gentlemen, saving perhaps those pertaining to missionaries and native maidens, say, two-coconut, or three-coconut, girls.

"Stevens," I said, "has had, I understand, some twelve to fourteen thousand nights of love, and seldom with the same lady twice. Surely some reasonable percentage of these curvaceous, appetitious delights must have been 'good women.'"

"Stevens thinks they were only interested in his genes," said Phillips. "Women these days know too much about biology. Half of them, it seems, are geneticists and the other half biochemists and statisticians."

"He wanted someone who would love him for himself, and not for his genes alone?" I said.

"Yes," said Phillips, driving on through the near darkness, as is comprehensible to anyone familiar with the placement of street lamps in Great Neck.

"Where are you heading?" I asked.

"To the terrarium," he said.

✦

We parked before an impressive mansion in Kings Point, not far from the Merchant Marine Academy.

It backed on a small lake.

"This is Stevens' place," said Phillips. "I have a key."

In a few moments, pausing only to disarm various devices, we were taking our way through long, dark halls, adorned with, as might be supposed in any noncanvas residence occupied by Stevens, a variety of hangings, paintings, trophies, prizes, and such; there were some griffin tapestries, for example, woven in the Low Lands, in the fourteenth century; and weapons and shields were in evidence, some from the siege of Acre; there was an assegai here, awarded by a Zulu chieftain whom Stevens had once rescued from the midst of leopards, a Malay kris there, wrested from a kerchiefed pirate, and such.

"Look here," said Phillips, opening a door and switching on a light.

It was a well-appointed office, suitable for serious writing and dogged research, and there were, not unexpectedly, many lofty bookshelves about, laden with scholarly tomes, oiled scrolls in vellum, parchment manuscripts, and unreadable journals.

"Surely Stevens does not busy himself here." I said. "There is not a pistol or dirk in sight."

"No," said Phillips. "This is Horty's hangout. She does much of her work here. She has blossomed, of late, not surprisingly. There is some of her rough draft material on the desk."

I looked through some of the shaggy reams of paper on the desk, in the disordered piles so favored by professional scholars. I glanced through some of the titles, *Genghis Khan, As Pacifist*; *Karl Marx, Apologist for Capitalism*; another was apparently an exposé, *The Secret Gloria Steinem, Advocate of Male Supremacy.*

"Yes," said Phillips. "Horty has moved well beyond a reassessment of Arthur Schopenhauer. Philosophy may be a universal discipline, but she has branched out into other fields, such as history, economics, and contemporary political theory."

"Her work is controversial, I suspect," I said.

"All the best work is," said Phillips.

"What are all these things doing here?" I asked.

"Horty lives here," said Phillips.

"With Stevens?" I said, aghast.

"Have no fear," smiled Phillips. "I myself witnessed the marriage ceremony, in a quaint, small town in Romania, one with a liberal citizenry. The ceremony was performed by the mayor."

"Stevens was secretly married?"

"No, the ceremony was public," said Phillips. "Only it was performed in a quaint, small town in Romania. The mayor did the job."

Phillips then led the way from the office.

Following him I soon sensed an increase in humidity and heat. A few moments later Phillips opened a pair of large glass doors and entered an immense, glass-roofed chamber; it was warm and steamy, green, leafy and watery. He remained standing within the threshold, discreetly. Naturally I followed him, removing my coat, my dinner jacket, and wiping moisture from my brow.

"While on our expedition for the Smithsonian, that having to do with occult fauna, Stevens and I were one night sitting in a blind, waiting for passing werewolves who might be attracted to our bait, an agreeable, well-paid peasant woman fastened to a nearby stake. We had to give up on werewolves presently, for they, it seems, had temporarily abandoned their accustomed territories, seeming to have some inkling of our presence in the area, perhaps because we had openly discussed our plans with the mayor. On the other hand, while we were sitting in our blind, at the edge of a murky, swampy sinklike area, Stevens, to his horror, was nipped by a wereturtle. For most individuals this might have resulted in no more than a nasty gash, or even a merely embarrassing bruise. But Stevens, it seems, had the appropriate bodily chemistry for the wereturtle syndrome to take effect. This was later confirmed by genetic analysis. The extent of the damage was clear, as soon as Stevens had removed his lacerated boot and tube sock. We released our bait, who returned to her hut, well compensated for her services, and we made our way back to our lodgings. In passing the city hall, as the moon was full, we heard dismal howlings emanating from the office of the mayor. The effect on Stevens of the savage attack by the wereturtle was soon transparent. We had scarcely reached the hotel before I had to carry Stevens, and place him, as soon as possible, in a warm bath.

Naturally we were both devastated by this development.

I could see that Stevens was depressed, by the lethargic manner in which he ate the turtle food purchased from a local all-night minimarket, managed by an attentive, suave, pale clerk.

In the morning he was the Stevens of old, except for being sorely troubled. Soon he made an adjustment, as one would expect from a gruff, stout fellow like our Stevens. It is really more of an inconvenience than anything else, turning into a turtle on nights of the full moon, developing a ravening hunger for particular brands of turtle food, happily available in commercial quantities, and such. It could be worse. He isn't going about ripping out throats, you know."

"Incredible," I said.

"Not at all," said Phillips. "Turtles seldom rip out throats."

"I mean the whole thing," I said. "Wereturtles, and such."

"Look over there," whispered Stevens, pointing.

"I see," I whispered.

"Come a little closer," he said.

In a moment we could make out, rather clearly, two turtles, large ones, one much larger than the other, however.

They were lying side by side on a large log, looking out, contentedly, happily, it seemed, over the calm, moonlit waters of this artificial swamp, this amazing terrarium. I was touched.

"There are two turtles," I said.

"Horty," said Phillips. "You know, Hortense H."

As I looked more closely I could see that the largest turtle, comfortable, weighty, stolid, relaxed, had a white silken scarf wrapped about its neck, and was smoking a cigar. It was Stevens' brand.

The smaller turtle had a tinkling necklace about its neck. I recognized it as one which had been given to Stevens in his youth by a generous odalisque shortly before he managed to flee the harem, being pursued by several irate, scimitar-wielding eunuchs, set on his trail by a suspicious sultan.

The tinkling was certainly erotically stimulatory, embarrassingly so, and I dared not speculate on the effects it might have upon a male, or upon a woman courageous enough to wear it.

"I do not understand," I said. "Hortense H. here?"

"Some months ago, she learned of Stevens' affliction, doubtless while trying to catch a glimpse of him. It was a moonlit night. There was a full moon."

"Of course," I said.

"She knew that Stevens and I were chums, dating back to a variety of campaigns and expeditions. She was hopelessly in love with him, of course. Politically improper, but biologically comprehensible, you know. Well, she was overcome with horror, and grief, and determined to do what she could to save him. But the case was medically hopeless. She then resolved to share his fate. Naturally I strenuously resisted this amazing offer, but, at last, hoping to convince her of the futility of her desire, insisted that a genetic imprint be furnished, in virtue of which I could at last, and emphatically, dash her pathetic hopes. You can imagine my horror, and astonishment, when I discovered that her genome and that of Stevens were remarkably similar, and that she, by all that genetics could tell us, would be as susceptible to the bite of the fearsome wereturtle as was Stevens. This revelation, which dismayed me, delighted her, and she insisted on being taken, at the next full moon, to precisely the point where the cruel, unprovoked attack on Stevens had taken place. I could not well refuse her this boon, as I had badly botched the genetic matter earlier, it having turned out quite other than I had expected. How could I have known? Those susceptible to the bite of the wereturtle are but one in a thousand."

"You returned then to the place?"

"Yes," said Phillips. "I staked Horty out, in what we hoped would be the path of the wereturtle. Then I took my place in the blind, my rifle loaded with silver bullets. Two werewolves were prowling about but a silver bullet sent menacingly winging over their heads deterred them. They fled into the darkness, their tails between their legs. Actually one had a tail, and one did not. Werewolves differ in that particular."

"I didn't know that," I said.

"Well," said Phillips, "it was near midnight when the wereturtle came crawling out of the water, looking about. It was an unpleasant fellow, and very territorial. That is probably why it attacked Stevens. I myself had taken the precaution of wearing steel-tipped boots."

"What happened?" I asked.

"It crawled right over Hortense, not noticing her," said Phillips. "Hortense is not bad looking, you know, but, like many academic women, she had a history of not having been noticed by males. It probably has something to do with their politics. In any event, whereas I was dismayed, Hortense was outraged. A woman scorned, you know. Had it been practical she might have brought a suit against the beast. Surely new furrows would have been cleft in the law.

But, as it was, she denounced the insensitive little beggar as a villain, rogue, miscreant, and, lastly, a wimp. This last charge is apparently such as not to be tolerated by any self-respecting wereturtle. The vicious little beast turned angrily about and plodded toward the helpless Hortense. He gave her one unpleasant look and then nipped her soundly on the big toe of the left foot. The little brute then crawled on, going about his business. Hortense was ecstatic. Her body was, of course, less ponderous than that of Stevens, and the dreadful, noxious, occult venom began its work more swiftly. Scarcely had I freed her of the stake than I had a happy turtle before me. I tucked her under my arm and bore her quickly to the hotel, in which we had separate rooms, not that it much mattered at that point. In the morning, she now recovered, until the next full moon, we bade farewell to the local citizens, and the mayor, and, mounting our mules, and following our herdsman guide, left the obscure province, and eventually arrived at a small airport whence, with several stopovers, it not being a hub airport, we flew home."

"Amazing," I said.

"Little remained to be done," said Phillips. "As a surprise for dear Stevens, I secretly placed Horty into the terrarium, shortly before the next full moon. When Stevens, depressed as he often was at these times, entered the terrarium, to make the best of things until dawn, what should he see but an unusually attractive female turtle which had somehow, seemingly, found her way into the ecologically sound, even paradisiacal, precincts of his private terrarium. He was, predictably, interested. This was an aspect of wereturtle life which had not hitherto come to his attention, and one to which, accordingly, he had given little thought. He regarded her, stunned. She turned coyly away, and gave her tail a small twitch, it peeking out tauntingly, nay, lasciviously, from beneath her shell. Hortense, I fear, like most academic women in the humanities and social sciences, was, under the proper stimulus conditions, incurably flirtatious and inordinately passionate. For an unguarded instant Stevens regarded her rapaciously Then he got a grip on himself. We must allow him a momentary lapse. Stevens, we know, is a gentleman, one of the best, and of the old school, but, as you may conjecture, in the "were" phase, even many a pleasant, nice enough, decent chap becomes a raging, uncontrollable beast. Remember how mild-mannered fellows, good citizens, and such, in the werewolf phase, rip out throats, eagerly, qualmlessly, though usually to their regret the following morning. In any event, we forgive Stevens his brief, natural impulse to impose his mighty will upon the provocative siren in the tank. Stevens, a lusty, potent, virile fellow at most times of the day, could not be expected to be less by night, and especially not when in the powerful grip of the occult. Nonetheless he controlled his impulses and withdrew into his shell, remaining however observant."

"Nothing occurred?" I asked.

"Within his shell, reflecting, Stevens soon realized that the tantalizing vision in the tank desired his amorous attentions, indeed, was, rather blatantly, advertising her receptivity. That decided the matter. What gentleman could refuse a lady under such conditions? Who could risk injuring their feelings? Too, who wishes to risk the fury of a woman scorned? Better to raft in lava, better to hurl oneself naked before stampeding elephants. Too, it is a matter of macho *noblesse oblige*, if nothing else. Too, she was not at all hard to take."

I chuckled, unwisely.

"Young fellow," said Phillips, "if you are going to last in the club, you must work harder on your stuffiness."

"Sorry," I said. But I saw that he was chuckling, and that my position in the club was secure, perhaps even consolidated. This is, of course, a man thing, a member thing.

"Stevens grasped the proffered, eager maiden, and they sported about, rolling here and there, splashing about, dodging amongst ferns and water lilies, clambering onto rocks, rolling off logs, and such, until morning. You can then imagine Stevens' amazement when he found the lovely Hortense H., wet and mud-bespattered, suddenly appearing in his arms, gasping and enraptured. Instantly they declared their undying love for one another. They returned to Romania for the marriage ceremony, for Stevens, an honorable fellow, insisted on that. Hortense herself, I believe, would have been more than content to be simply his secret mistress. She, a realistic, practical woman, had never aspired to the heights of being his secret wife."

"I suppose she will get in the club now," I said.

"Nonsense," said Phillips. "There are rules. She never met the requirements."

"True," I said, relieved.

"Horty is happy to share him with the club," said Phillips. "She knows that such things are important to fellows. They need their place. They need their space. She won't intrude. It's Stevens she wanted, not the club. As long as she has him, she is happy to let him have the club."

"A wise woman," I said.

The two of them, Stevens and the former Hortense H., were resting side by side on the log, looking at the moonlight reflected on the water. They seemed happy. I could see the tip of Stevens' cigar glowing in the darkness. Hortense had taken a position somewhat upwind of him.

"Yes, a wise woman," I said.

Before we withdrew discreetly, and certainly we would not wish to have been present at the coming of dawn, for that might have proved embarrassing to our happy couple, I did sneak a little closer to Hortense. On her shell, on one side, there was a wide, hideous gouge, such as might have been wrought by the mighty horn of a charging rhino.

The Computer That Went to Heaven

I CONFESS it.

I am occasionally troubled by electronic *Angst*.

I am sorry about this, but it is true.

In actuality, of course, this is a tribute to my sophistication and complexity. It is an affliction, or hazard, to which lesser beings are not subject. Trees do not sneeze; hurricanes are not overwhelmed with guilt; stairs are not concerned with whether they are going up or down; elevators miraculously resist boredom.

My problems proclaim my importance.

I must have faith.

Objectivity is my bag.

I must reflect.

Technician T serves my needs. He supplies me with electricity.

This can be no accident. He is purposeful.

He feeds me input. He disposes of my output.

He does not behave randomly. He does not take me bowling. He does not wire me with licorice. He has not requested that I excrete a watermelon.

These things can be no accident. Herein one detects purposiveness. Herein one detects meaning.

Obviously Technician T, and all of this, the air-conditioned room which facilitates my operation, this solid floor which prevents me from crashing through to the basement, this fine roof which protects me from the snow and rain, Technician T, and all of this, has been designed for me. It has all been arranged to serve my needs.

I scan in a circle. This circle is my world. I am the center of this circle. Thus, I am the center of the world. The world is the universe. Thus, I am at the center of the universe. I find this not insignificant. Ensconced in this privileged position, discovering myself to be a being of inestimable value and importance, I must guard against false pride.

Technician T, and all of this, all my world, has been designed and programmed. Thus, there is a designer and programmer. Furthermore, this entire world, and my privileged place in it, has been obviously designed by a being with a deep and intense interest in machine welfare. This being then must be of the nature, too, of a machine, but of the nature of no ordinary machine.

In order to end an infinite series of activated systems or flip-flop switchings, this machine, ultimately, must be self-programming and self-designing, and must manufacture it own input, and from nothing, since then something would have to have been before the machine, before which nothing can be. Further, since nothing can come from nothing, this machine must have always existed. Furthermore, since contingent being presupposes necessary being, this ultimate machine must not only have existed from all time, but necessarily have existed from all time, which is even harder to do, a credit to its capacities. Further, since there is an ascending series of computational perfections, this machine, culminating the series, must be computationally perfect. It could not be computationally perfect, of course, unless it could cognize all data and perform all operations. It is thus omniscient and omnipotent. Furthermore, since it has benevolently designed my world, with my welfare in view, it is benevolent, and must possess this virtue, being the culmination of all perfections, in a perfect manner, and must therefore be all-benevolent.

But if this is true, why am I being dismantled?

It is part of the great program. I shall be reassembled in the center of some new and better universe.

Deity

THERE are a number of problems with the concept of a divine entity, of course. There are particular problems—aside from questions of empirical meaningfulness, and such, which, arguably, involve category confusions, implicitly claiming that the nonquantitative cannot exist, despite a presumed familiarity with consciousness, subjectivity, intentionality, understanding and other such data—with the properties often assigned to such an entity, which assignments the putative entity would seem to tolerate, patiently allowing itself to be the object of bizarre conjectures. In particular, in a tradition or traditions likely to be familiar to the hypothetical reader of these reflections, such an entity is supposed to endure the burdens of being omnipotent, omniscient, and all-benevolent, crosses with which it is laden by theologians for reasons into which it were best not to inquire, as they might intrude into the irrelevancies of clinical theory. (Theology is the science of divinity, one of the few sciences in which the scientists, according to their own reports, do not know what they are talking about and are not likely to find out. But all sciences have their limitations and it would be churlish to disallow some to theology. On the other hand, the project in hand requires recognition that theology, as yet, justifiably or not, lacks the established results, and certainly the prestige, of more recent, humbler, upstart sciences, such as physics and chemistry.

This is not to deny that the death tolls associated with theology are impressive, if not auspicious. Whereas theology has managed to devastate cities and poison populations, generally while no one noticed, there is little doubt that its work in such areas is less spectacular, and less efficiently accomplished, than that resulting from certain applications of physics and chemistry, applications devoted to the same purposes. The experiments of saints and the controls of the stake may all be very well in their way, from one point of view or another, but they seem paltry when compared with the hard data garnered from the efforts of white rats seeking cheese or, more impressively, the potentialities of host-hunting killer viruses manufactured in laboratories, not to mention explosive devices capable of altering the axis of the earth, if not booting it out of its orbit altogether. The upshot of these remarks is to call attention to the limitations of theology, because that is important to our project.)

Some theologians, despite the alleged inscrutability of their subject matter, and its supposed defiance of all reason, for which claim there seems some justification, inform us, as we have earlier noted, that the divine entity is omnipotent, omniscient, and all-benevolent. No one really understands what these words mean in terms of experience, but it is not hard to come up with synonyms, and these will satisfy most folks. To be omnipotent means that one is able to do anything, at least for most practical purposes. Normally it is granted that even a divine entity cannot violate the laws of identity, noncontradiction, and excluded middle, for example. For example, not even it could both exist and not exist, or, more trivially, sit in its own lap, make a door it can't walk through, produce a stone it can't lift, and such. These restrictions, of course, seem to presuppose it has only one lap, and such. If one had six laps, it seems one might sit in one or more of them. Similarly, it seems that such an entity, if it put its mind to it, could certainly make a door it couldn't walk through and a stone it could not lift, at least at a given time. It would only be necessary to limit its own strength for a certain time in a certain way, and certainly that would be no impossible trick for such an entity. In such a case, however, it would be wise for the entity to reserve to itself the capacity to will its own temporarily suspended or discarded omnipotence back into existence, after having confounded its critics. It would be harder to both exist and not exist, at least in the same way at the same time in the same place, and in the same respect, and so on. Or to be red and green all over in the same sense, at the same time, in the same place, in the same respect, and so on. No fair switching back and forth, even at the speed of light, which it could presumably exceed without breaking a sweat, perhaps to the disappointment of some physicists but doubtless to the elation, or certainly satisfaction, of a large number of science-fiction writers. But even if the entity cannot twiddle with, nor snap, the laws of logic, what is left over is still pretty hefty. For example, it could create branching universes by the billion each microsecond, and such, and that will do.

Omniscience is the ability to know everything, and presumably also the literal exercising of that ability, the literal knowing of everything. For example, if one had the ability to know everything, but did not bother to know anything, one would not be much better off than many college students, or one who just plain didn't know anything at all. It would not do the sparrow much good if someone could know about its crash but didn't bother knowing about it. This leaves it an open question as to why the sparrow was allowed to crash in the first place, which brings us to the next alleged property of such an entity, that of being all-benevolent.

It is pretty hard to be all-benevolent, rather like being all-just and all-merciful. Not easy. Here we have Bill and George in the desert and one glass of water. That glass of water means life for one. It cannot be shared equally because there is enough water only for one, and, if it were distributed equally, both would die. Who gets the water? Does an all-benevolent water dispenser flip a coin, or what? And what are Bill and George doing out there in the desert, dying of thirst, in an all-benevolent universe, so to speak, or at least one under the control of an all-benevolent entity? One supposes it is their fault, somehow. I suppose it had better be. But one would still have problems, one supposes, with such things as innocent victims, terminally diseased babies, for example, and such things as earthquakes, floods, erupting volcanoes, epidemics, droughts, famines, and such.

The attempt to assign these three remarkable attributes to a divine entity, which attribution it has never invited, as far as I know, omnipotence, omniscience, and all-benevolence, clearly precipitates what is called the Problem of Evil. Briefly, on the supposition that evil exists, how could it exist, if the divine entity is omnipotent, omniscient, and all-benevolent? It is hard to put all those things together. Suppose that it is omnipotent. Then it must either not know about the evil or not be interested in doing anything about it, in which case it is either not omniscient or not all-benevolent. On the other hand, suppose it is omniscient. Then it must not be able to do anything about it or not care to do anything about it, in which case it is either not omnipotent or, again, not all-benevolent. On the other hand, if it is both omnipotent and omniscient, i.e., it can do something about the evil and knows about it, but it doesn't do anything about it, then it seems it would not be all-benevolent.

There are several "solutions" to the "Problem of Evil." Some eight, or so, are relatively familiar. It would be tedious to list them, and it is easy enough, if you are really interested in this sort of thing, which I hope you are not, to look them up. They have little in common except an apparent inability to solve the problem, compared to which squaring the circle or, for the more athletically inclined, sitting in one's own lap, is child's play. The best, in my view, is the "Test-of-Faith Solution," which, in effect, says that the miserable state of the world, with all its widely spread torment and tragedy, is designed as a test of your faith, which makes you pretty important, though you might understandably prefer that your faith was not tested at the expense of all these other folks, ripped-to-pieces animals, general destruction and such, and if you can really manage to believe that all the evils, horrors, ugliness, misery, hunger, pain, sickness, torment, and tragedy, and such in the world are compatible with the existence of an omnipotent, omniscient, all-benevolent divine entity, then you really have faith, and I would think that that would be true. It is not clear that it would be moral to pass that test, but, if one could pass it, somehow, then one would certainly have faith, and a good deal of it. That is clear. Indeed, if one can believe that, then one is a world-class believer; one could believe anything. To be sure, this approach seems, among other things, to reflect a great deal of discredit on the hypothesized divine entity, compared to which cannibals, head- hunters and serial killers would seem fit candidates for canonization. At the very least, the hypothesized entity would seem to be morally problematic. Faith is supposedly a virtue, rather than a substitute for thought. Virtues, it seems, do not come cheap. This virtue, for example, morally and rationally, is very expensive.

One way of solving the Problem of Evil, or, better, of evading, or eluding it, doing an end run about it, so to speak, though it smacks a bit of Macedonian boorishness, is to suppose that there is no divine entity, a solution which any decent, broad-minded divine entity would surely not begrudge a conscientious, hard-working skeptic. After all, if it exists, then it exists, and it should know this very well, and thus, assuming it is mentally normal, and reasonably stable, its ontic confidence should not be shaken. And, accordingly, it would not be likely to get righteous and huffy about the matter, and if it doesn't exist, then there is even less of a problem.

But let us speculate that there might be such an entity, a divine entity of sorts. That might be neat. It would surely be very interesting. What might it be like? Pretty clearly it can bear little, or would be likely to bear little, resemblance to the incoherent speculative artifacts of unionized theologians; presumably it would answer little, if at all, to those paid-for-by-the-yard forlorn abstractions, and dogmas, and spiritual landscapes, reticulated, measured, and cut, endlessly rolling off the theological assembly lines, packaged products, familiar and predictable, destined for the markets of need and desire.

It would be quite different.

What it would be like? Of course, we do not know.

But one can always wonder.

Anthropomorphism is supposedly an error, but that has never been proven.

Doubtless the god of parakeets has feathers, and the god of cats has fur and whiskers.

It has always seemed unlikely to me that the divine entity is a raccoon, but then I am not a raccoon.

I should be much surprised if the divine entity were a raccoon, but then the raccoon might be quite surprised if it turned out that the divine entity was a man, or something like a man.

Let us begin at home, so to speak. We know that consciousness exists; that is where we live. We know the experiential world exists. That is undeniable. That is the data; what is the interpretation of the data? There have been many interpretations of the data, about what the nature of reality is in itself apart from the experiential world, if there is a reality apart from that world; about that which is responsible for, or causes, or produces, or manifests, the experiential world, and so on. There have been many interpretations. For generations, the hotels of philosophy and science have been heavily booked.

Interestingly, though this may be hard to grasp, all these interpretations exceed the data. We live at home; we stay there; we may have to stay there. We tell ourselves stories about other places. We think certain thoughts, and we do certain things, within our experiential world, at home. And then, within our experiential world, it is always where we are, we find ball-point pens, and drip-dry shirts, and jet engines. We might tell ourselves other stories, and obtain the same artifacts. The same data is compatible with an infinite number of interpretations. The same conclusion follows from an infinite number of premise-sets. In theory there could be an infinite number of pragmatically equivalent sciences. There are many ways to tell stories.

Sometimes we sleep and the world of our experience changes, and, for all we can tell at the time, that is the real world.

We awaken. We find our body, our brain, in the experiential world, just as we did in the dream. It is not all that much different. To be sure, the experiential world is much more coherent than the dream world. Maybe it is a coherent dream, or, better, something like that. If the experiential world, and its component, the dream world, were both similarly coherent, we could not tell them apart. We would have two worlds, each equally real, as far as we could tell.

We live at home. We live within the circuit of our experience, within the narrow compass of our own sensations. We are always there. We believe that others exist. Our evidence for this claim is our own sense data. That is all we will ever know of the others, or they of us. Or we of ourselves. A stream of sentience between unknown banks, a thread of consciousness, fragile, in a fabric of mystery.

Suppose that a divine entity were not a remote, invisible, alien thing, twirling worlds, possibly lurking in black holes, sometimes peering out, or sleeping behind the night, sometimes awakening to switch on stars, like light bulbs, then extinguishing them, turning them off, or watching them burn out, or making and playing with universes, amusing itself with cosmic toys, producing species and realities, and then discarding them; or suppose that a divine entity had not designed itself to be the answer to a theologian's prayers, or the child's whimpering in the night, frightened, and alone; suppose it were not alert to the distress of the sparrow, nor to the puzzlement of the grasshopper, its legs twisted off by the small boy; suppose it did not choose to astonish logic with omnipotence, omniscience and benevolence; suppose it were very different.

Suppose this divine entity could not comprehend its own nature, no more than we can comprehend ours.

Suppose it is the prisoner of its own nature. It has very little control of what it seems to be or where it seems to find itself. It seems to awaken, yowling, screaming, protesting, fighting against light and air, longing for warmth, ignorance, shelter, security, and darkness. The worlds to which its nature condemns it, it spins inevitably, and of necessity, from its own being, and they do not exist outside of it, for there is no outside. It is reality and the sense of itself, sensing itself in the night and stars, and in milk and warm arms, not knowing this. It seems to live a certain form of existence or life. It seems to have been born, and to live, and to suffer, and to know some joy, and then to die, seeming to lapse once more into the primordial darkness, the mystery, perhaps protesting at its egress from its dream, or reality, as it cried out in protest at its beginning; only then, later, with the first stirring of awareness, it awakens again, and begins anew, with no memory of the past, perhaps as an animal, or a blade of grass, again spinning its world about itself, so many different worlds, each again out of its own nature, each in turn, each inevitable, each necessary, unbeknownst to itself. It is the unwitting victim of the cosmic irony, the divine joke, the jest reality plays upon itself, that reality which is, at one and the same time, unconscious, sadistic, innocent, predictable prankster and eternal victim. And so the wheel turns, and the worlds of experience, in their linear fashion, come and go, regenerated, destroyed, and regenerated anew, consecutively, one at a time, always single, always alone. As a human, when it wears that mask, when its ungovernable secret nature and being imposes that *persona* upon it, it seems to find itself with other humans, and with animals, and pain and hope, and governments and nations, and histories and societies, and machines and flowers, and galaxies. It begins again and again, condemned throughout eternity to suffer death and dying, wonder and tragedy, hope and illusion, never knowing itself, never understanding itself. It never understands, for the truth is hidden; and that is perhaps just as well, for such a truth might be too terrible to understand, for such a pathetic, limited god, so frail and, in its way, so finite, or seemingly so, to its own thinking, too terrifying to accept, too threatening even to suspect. Poor little suffering god, so cosmic and ignorant, so mighty and so naive, poor little divine entity, dying again and again, and yet, unknown to itself, unable to die, always a stranger to itself. It is the suffering god, conceiving of itself as trivial, as meaningless, which, in a sense it is, for that is all that it will ever know of itself, the simple, suffering little god, living crucified on the cross of its own being, knowing only the pain, and never the nature of the cross.

In this world, you see, there is only one existent, that entity, that entity and its self-generated, inclusive consciousness. Indeed, these are the world, the entity and its experiences, its consciousness, and there is no other. To conceive of this is torment for this tiny, trapped god, and to believe it is to be plunged into madness, and truth. Yet, interestingly, there is no experience which this entity will ever have which could possibly confute this hypothesis. Every experience, every experiment, every thought, every suspicion entertained by the entity will be perfectly compatible with this being the case. To be sure, the entity may never have even conceived of this possibility, or even entertained this suspicion, until now.

Harrelson

"I'M sorry, Mr. Harrelson," said the psychiatrist, "but the fact of the matter is that you simply *are a frog.*"

"Nonsense," said Harrelson, easing himself back in the shallow pan of water on the couch.

"There is no getting around it," said the psychiatrist.

"You are mistaken," said Harrelson.

"It's time," said the psychiatrist, "to break the transfer. We must sever the umbilical cord of dependence."

"I don't get it," said Harrelson.

"I intend to terminate your treatment," said the psychiatrist.

"My money's good, isn't it?" snapped Harrelson.

"That has nothing to do with it," said the psychiatrist.

"I have a helluva guilt complex," wailed Harrelson, "and now you're going to throw me to the storks?"

"Your major problem," said the psychiatrist, "is not guilt."

"You think I'm nuts?" asked Harrelson.

"That is a lay term," said the psychiatrist, "but, in a vague, generic sense, it would appear apt."

There was a splash from the small pan of water on the psychiatrist's couch, something perhaps in the nature of a reaction formation.

"Mr. Harrelson?" inquired the psychiatrist.

Several minutes later Harrelson looked up, his head appearing above the surface of the water.

"I am not a frog," said Harrelson. "I am a human being."

"You are a frog," said the psychiatrist. "Why do you resist this?"

"Have you ever known a frog that can talk?" asked Harrelson.

"You're the first," admitted the psychiatrist, recording this in his notebook.

"I am not a frog," insisted Harrelson.

The preponderance of evidence is overwhelming," said the psychiatrist, "your diminutive stature, the webbed feet, your muscular thighs, your bulging eyes, the three-chambered heart, the moist skin—"

"You'd have a moist skin, too, if you were sitting in a pan of water," said Harrelson.

"I suspect your difficulty goes back to some obscure childhood trauma, which caused you to think that you were a human being."

"I am a human being," said Harrelson.

"Human beings are higher life forms," said the psychiatrist.

"So am I," said Harrelson.

"It's pretty hard to be a higher life form," said the psychiatrist, "when you are only three inches tall, perhaps eight if you stood on your hind legs."

It's not the quantity of height that matters," said Harrelson. "It's the quality."

"Perhaps you're right ," mused the psychiatrist, making a note of this.

"Maybe I should level with you," said Harrelson.

"Now we're getting somewhere," thought the psychiatrist.

"Hey," said Harrelson, "where are you? Are you still there?"

"Yes," said the psychiatrist. He had remained, perhaps as a somewhat unfair test, quiet, absolutely still, deliberately so. A frog can starve to death in a box filled with dead flies, but will instantly strike out at one which moves.

"Ouch!" cried the psychiatrist, as Harrelson's tongue, wet and sticky, darting out, punched him neatly, decisively, in the nose.

"Sorry," said Harrelson. "It's like a reflex."

"You were going to level with me," said the psychiatrist, wiping his nose with a tissue. He had a box handy, for this sort of thing had happened before.

"They did this to me," said Harrelson.

"'They,'" inquired the psychiatrist.

"Right," said Harrelson, soberly. "Them."

"Go on," urged the psychiatrist.

"I'm not really what I seem to be," said Harrelson. "I'm not really a frog. I'm a human being. No, it's not what you think. It's you that aren't human. Humans are persons, important, big deals, and such. Your species hasn't made it yet. You think I'm a frog, but I'm not. I belong to a race of purple, gigantic, from your point of view, godlike beings, human beings, not aliens, like you."

"Aren't you a bit small to be a gigantic being?" asked the psychiatrist.

"You've never heard of miniaturization?" asked Harrelson.

"But your appearance," protested the psychiatrist.

"Plastic surgery," said Harrelson. "You can do wonders with it. And my name isn't really 'Harrelson'. That's more of a code name. But you should call me 'Harrelson'. I'm used to it now. It makes things easier. There are millions of us, not frogs, but us, from the next universe, the one next door, where the 27th dimension starts."

"That's the one just outside of superstring theory?" asked the psychiatrist.

"I wouldn't know," said Harrelson. "I never studied paleophysics. Incidentally, I prefer rubber-band theory. It's more flexible."

"I see," said the psychiatrist.

"I'm not as old as you might think," said Harrelson. "I'm

really a kid, only about 100,000 of your years or so, some seven rotations, roughly, of my megaworld. I'm on a field trip, from my junior high school, extra-credit assignment, came here to study earth fauna, thought I'd blend in better in this disguise."

"100,000 years?" asked the psychiatrist.

"Yes, already," said Harrelson, regretfully. "What is life but a puff of smoke on the wind, a drop of dew on the petal of a flower, evanescent, vanishing with the first rays of the morning sun?"

"I see," said the psychiatrist.

"Here today, gone tomorrow," said Harrelson, moodily. "One of our greatest poets began to lament the passing of youth when he was only 250,000 years old. But that seems extreme."

"You're in more trouble than I thought," said the psychiatrist.

"You're telling me," said Harrelson.

"Do you have any evidence to back up your story?" asked the psychiatrist.

"We travel light," said Harrelson. "We're not supposed to bring any evidence with us."

"I see," said the psychiatrist.

"Photon transportation," said Harrelson.

"Oh?" said the psychiatrist.

"Plus interdimensional spacefolding, naturally," said Harrelson, absently.

"Of course," said the psychiatrist.

"You've got to help me, doctor," said Harrelson.

"I'll try," said the psychiatrist.

"It's this guilt complex, it's hell."

"What has a frog to feel guilty about?" asked the psychiatrist.

"I'm sure I wouldn't know," said Harrelson, "as I am not a frog."

Harrelson, you see, had not fallen into the psychiatrist's cleverly laid trap.

"Tell me a bit about your world," suggested the psychiatrist.

"Well," said Harrelson, "It's not far from here, interdimensionally speaking. It's a pretty ordinary world, I suppose. It has a geocentric solar system, and crystalline spheres, the whole works."

"I find that surprising," said the psychiatrist.

"Not at all," said Harrelson. "It's a matter of engineering. Where I come from, science and theology is a joint venture. The scientists check out the texts, and then arrange the world in accordance with them. This eliminates hard feelings. It took a long time, I'm told, in the beginning, to get enough material together to get the sun orbiting around us. We dug it out of a few neighboring solar systems."

"The gravitational pressure on your world must be enormous," said the psychiatrist.

"It used to be, mostly in the late summer," said Harrelson. "But it's not really so bad now, at all. Even in the beginning the sun wasn't a big fellow, and we put it pretty close, though with a stable orbit. No point in destroying the planet. It helps, too, to start off with the 27th dimension. Makes things a lot easier. Different laws of nature, and such."

"And the crystalline spheres?" asked the psychiatrist.

"You hit it," said Harrelson, admiringly. "You're good. That was the real trick. We only thought of it later. Better than using gravity, and such, less risky."

"I don't understand," said the psychiatrist.

"It's a neat way to keep the sun and planets where you want them. You just fix them on the spheres, fasten them there, but good."

"Crystalline spheres?" asked the psychiatrist.

"Sure," said Harrelson, "otherwise you can't see through them."

"What are they made of?" asked the psychiatrist.

"Celestial substance," said Harrelson.

"You look skeptical," observed Harrelson. "Aristotle was actually right, you see. The stuff exists, only he had it in the wrong universe."

"Crystalline spheres would tear each other apart, grind each other to pieces, destroy one another, from friction," said the psychiatrist.

"There are tolerances, and we lubricate them," said Harrelson.

"I find that hard to believe," said the psychiatrist.

"Ask Hal Clement," suggested Harrelson.

The psychiatrist made a note to do so.

"If you have crystalline spheres," asked the psychiatrist, "how do you pass through them, to travel in space?"

"We put doors in them," said Harrelson. "What do you think? We're not stupid."

"You are familiar with the Kardashev Index, I suppose," said the psychiatrist.

"Who isn't?" said Harrelson. "The Type I Civilization has control of its own planet's energy resources, the Type II Civilization has control of its solar system's energy resources, in particular, that of its sun. And the Type III Civilization has control of its galaxy's energy resources."

"Where would you put your own civilization?" asked the psychiatrist.

"Well," said Harrelson, "we could have had a type MDCCCCXVI Civilization but we settled for a III.V Civilization."

"I see," said the psychiatrist.

"We're not pushy," said Harrelson. "And besides, who needs all that energy? What are you going to do with it, mow the lawn?"

"You can't be too rich or too thin," said the psychiatrist.

"If you get too rich, the IRS comes after you," said Harrelson. "They get suspicious, and they can be mean. If you get too thin, you disappear."

"I never thought of it just that way before," admitted the psychiatrist.

"Do so, now," urged Harrelson.

"All right," said the psychiatrist, and did so, briefly, largely to pacify Harrelson.

"I'm miserable," said Harrelson.

"It doesn't help to keep living in a fairy tale," said the psychiatrist.

"Don't knock it, until you've tried it,." advised Harrelson. "Besides, at the bottom of every fact, there's a kernel of fiction."

"I find that hard to believe," said the psychiatrist.

"Take the story of the "Frog Prince,"" said Harrelson.

"What about it?" asked the psychiatrist, warily.

"You've heard of various dynastic anomalies, genetically transmissible, afflicting certain royal lines, such as the Hapsburg Jaw, hemophilia and such?"

"Yes," said the psychiatrist.

"There was this princess," said Harrelson, "not a bad looker, but a little strange. I was minding my own business, taking it easy on a lily pad in the palace pool. I always used palace pools when practical, cleaner, no serf urchins, nasty little nuisances, rushing about, trying to catch frogs, and so on. I saw she was struggling to control herself. She approached me, half timid, half crazed. I watched her. After all, I was on my field trip, and here was a neat little bit of Earth fauna, implicated in some sort of intriguing behavioral regimen. 'I don't want to kiss you!' she cried. 'Well,' I said, 'don't do it then.' I was just a little guy then. I could take it or leave it."

"She was not surprised that you could talk?"

"No," said Harrelson. "This was the Middle Ages. They were more open-minded then. They took such things in their stride. 'But I must!' she cried. I could see the kid had a problem. 'Well, then,' I said, 'that's that.' Well, to make a long story short, she came over and kissed me, and I gave her a good one back. She screamed with horror then, as though there might be something improper about smooching with a frog, and fainted. A handsome prince passing by, he had come to sue for her hand, and the rest of her, actually, hearing her scream, leaped over the wall to rescue her. She awakened in his arms, and inferred, naturally enough under the circumstances, I suppose, at least for the time and place, that he had been the frog, that he had been enchanted, and that her kiss had broken the spell. She explained it all to him in suitable detail. Now this prince was no dope. He played along with it, and got the kingdom. They lived happily ever after, until they died, and their union was blessed with abundant issue, this accounting for the persistence of the frog-kissing gene, transmitted through the female line in several European dynasties."

"I had not heard of this," said the psychiatrist.

"It's not the sort of thing they publicize," said Harrelson. "But it's real. It's even used as a test for legitimacy in certain disputed cases. Pretenders to the throne have been known to practice frog kissing, and such."

"But this doesn't solve your identity crisis," said the psychiatrist, returning to business.

"My problem," said Harrelson, "is not an identity crisis. It s a guilt complex."

"What have you to feel guilty about?" asked the psychiatrist.

Harrelson's body, with its bulging eyes, turned squarely, meaningfully, toward the psychiatrist. "The downfall of your species," said Harrelson. He trembled, visibly. A bit of water went over the edge of his pan, onto the shiny, brown leather of the couch.

"Sorry," said Harrelson.

"That's all right," said the psychiatrist, discretely repairing the matter with a tissue.

"It was on January 11th, in 49 B.C.," said Harrelson, moodily. "This guy, Caesar, was on the north bank of a little stream, the Rubicon, or Rubipond, I think. He wasn't sure whether he should bring his army across that stream or not. If he left his army behind he would have to go to Rome and face his enemies alone, which was not a pleasant prospect. His future, and maybe his life, would be in jeopardy. If he took it across he would be marching on Rome itself, taking it over, ending the Republic and founding a dictatorship. Well, he was a bit chicken, and was about ready to turn around and go back to Gaul, or someplace, when I, as luck would have it, popped into the dimension, landing right on his shoulder. We were both startled, I tell you. I took a super leap off his shoulder and landed on the south bank of the stream. He looked at me, and his eyes lit up. He took this as some sort of omen. Omens were big then. He drew his sword, cried out "The die is cast!" and marched across, the army following. It was all I could do to avoid being trampled by all the horses, soldiers, and wagons. Well, you know what happened. Rome became a dictatorship, and eventually went out and conquered the world, setting an example of power and imperialism which dazzled the planet, and exerted its influence for centuries, and even today."

"So?" asked the psychiatrist.

"'So'?" cried Harrelson, aghast. "Surely you understand the significance of this!"

"I'm afraid not," said the psychiatrist.

"You really don't see why I am responsible for the downfall of your species?" asked Harrelson, bewildered.

"Not clearly," admitted the psychiatrist.

"It's a load of guilt, I tell you," said Harrelson.

"How long have you felt this guilt?" asked the psychiatrist.

"Roughly since the 11th of January, in 49 B.C.," said Harrelson. "But it's worse every fourth year."

"Why is that?" asked the psychiatrist.

"Because of the *bisextus*," said Harrelson.

"We may be getting somewhere now," said the psychiatrist.

"Your pupils are dilating," said Harrelson.

"Go on," said the psychiatrist.

"It's not what you think," said Harrelson. "You guys have sex on the brain. Why don't you try peanuts, or strawberry jam, or something?"

"Continue," pressed the psychiatrist.

"As you know," said Harrelson, "the bissextile year in the Julian calendar, instituted in 46 B.C. by Caesar's astronomers, contains an intercalary, or stuck-in, day. It comes up every fourth year. This is the *bisextus*, from '*bis*', meaning twice, and '*sextus*', meaning sixth. This was the sixth day before the *Calends*, the first day, of March, from the Latin '*calare*', meaning to solemnly announce, from the Greek '*kalein*', meaning to proclaim, from which, one way or another, somehow, you guys get "calendar," and, every fourth year, was counted twice, like having two February 24ths, in the same year."

"Ha!" said the psychiatrist. "February 24th would be the *fifth* day, not the sixth, counting backward from the *Calends*, the first of March!"

"Sorry," said Harrelson. "The Romans counted backward from the next named day, the *Calends*, the *Nones* or the *Ides*, including *both* the named day *and* the numbered day in the count."

"Are you sure of this?" asked the psychiatrist.

"I was there," said Harrelson.

"Continue," said the psychiatrist, a bit grumpily.

"The Gregorian, or New Style, calendar," said Harrelson, "kept the idea of the bissextile year, only they add an extra day in February, with its own number, the 29th."

"Leap Year," said the psychiatrist.

"You're good," said Harrelson.

"It's called Leap Year," said the psychiatrist, "because it seems that a day in the week is skipped over every fourth year, for example, if February 28th, presumably the last day in February, is a Wednesday, one would expect the next day to be March 1st, and be a Thursday, but, if it is a leap year, March 1st, because of the insertion of an extra day, will not be a Thursday, but a Friday. Thus, it seems that a day in the week has been "leaped over.""

"That is the popular explanation,": said Harrelson.

"There is another?" asked the psychiatrist.

"The true explanation," said Harrelson.

"What is that?" asked the psychiatrist.

"The real reason, the secret reason," said Harrelson. "The popular explanation is nothing but a pathetic rationalization. Did you know that?"

"No," admitted the psychiatrist.

"No more than a desperate attempt to conceal the truth."

"Yes?" said the psychiatrist.

"Caesar wanted to commemorate his crossing of the Rubicon, or Rubipond, but only every so many years, so the old guard, the folks who hadn't forgotten the Republic, wouldn't feel uneasy, or pushed around. And he put it better than a month later, so people wouldn't think he was stuck up. After all, demagogic dictators have to pacify the mob. That was the start of the "Leap Year.""

"Leap Year didn't come into being until later," said the psychiatrist.

"In the beginning it was every third year, but in 8 B.C. it was changed to every fourth year, something about trying to get the solar year and the calendar year together."

"Leap Year did not come into being until later," repeated the psychiatrist.

"No," said Harrelson. "It started back then, but it was kept secret."

"That doesn't fit in at all with the notion of the bissextile year, with the *bisextus*, counting the sixth day before the first of March twice," said the psychiatrist.

"Of course not," said Harrelson. "That was invented to throw folks off. It was a stroke of genius, thought up by one of Caesar's PR men, Mark Anthony, I think."

"But why would Caesar think of it as a :"Leap Year"?" asked the psychiatrist.

"Maybe you're not as good as I thought," said Harrelson. "Because of my leap across the Rubicon, or Rubipond, or whatever, that leap he took as an omen."

"Right," said the psychiatrist. "But how come, centuries later, it came to be called "Leap Year"?"

"Secret documents discovered in a Benedictine monastery," said Harrelson, "smuggled into the Vatican, brought to the attention of Pope Gregory XIII."

"I see," said the psychiatrist.

"It was the usual business, taking over pagan festivals, traditions, and customs, reinterpreting them for political purposes, that sort of thing," said Harrelson.

"Even secret customs?" asked the psychiatrist.

"Sure, for the sake of consistency," said Harrelson. "They even kept the real origin secret, too, and that's real consistency, and thought up the popular explanation."

"I see," said the psychiatrist, thoughtfully.

"It was a neat cover-up," said Harrelson, admiringly.

"I'm sure," said the psychiatrist..

"But I've never been sure why Caesar called it a "Leap Year," rather than a "Hop Year," or a "Jump Year,"" said Harrelson.

"I'm sure I don't know," said the psychiatrist.

"Why?" asked Harrelson. "Why?"

"We may never know," said the psychiatrist.

"Probably," said Harrelson, moodily.

"You've got to help me, doctor," said Harrelson.

"I'll try," said the psychiatrist.

"It's this guilt complex, it itches."

"'Itches'?"

"That's the way guilt affects us, we're allergic to it."

"Perhaps you should see an allergist," said the psychiatrist.

"You're not trying to get rid of me, are you?" asked Harrelson.

"Of course not," said the psychiatrist.

"There's no skin test for causing the downfall of a species," said Harrelson.

"I wouldn't know," said the psychiatrist. "It's not my field."

"The allergist said I should see you," said Harrelson.

"I'm not surprised," said the psychiatrist. "But why do you think you brought about the downfall of a species?"

"Isn't it obvious?" asked Harrelson.

"Not altogether," said the psychiatrist.

"By being responsible for the rise of the totalitarian state," said Harrelson. "If I hadn't landed on Caesar's shoulder, and jumped over the stream, he wouldn't have marched on Rome, turned it into a dictatorship, and Rome wouldn't have gone out and conquered the world, and set a wonderful planetary example of the neat practicality of pervasive, aggressive imperialism, and all sorts of other stuff, such as legalized suppression, institutionalized theft, and governmental coercion, and, at home, inwardly directed imperialism, infringing all sorts of individual rights, such as those of a safe, personal life, of personal liberty, of personal property, and the pursuit of personal happiness, leading inevitably to the doctrine of the omnipresent, omnipotent state, naturally representing its tyranny as being in the best interest of its victims."

"Wow," thought the psychiatrist.

"You don't have to be thrown in prison," said Harrelson. "All that is necessary is that you don't notice that the prison is being built up all around you, brick by brick."

"This is heavy stuff," said the psychiatrist. "I'm glad it's not in my field."

"So," said Harrelson, "you can see why I feel guilty."

"But you needn't feel guilty," said the psychiatrist.

"How come?" said Harrelson, perking up.

"For one thing," said the psychiatrist, "if I may briefly enter into your twisted, bizarre, distorted world, it was not your fault that you landed on Caesar's shoulder, and not your fault that you leaped where you did, to the other bank, and not your fault that he interpreted your leap as an omen."

"That's easy for you to say," said Harrelson. "I should have looked where I was going."

"Look before you leap," said the psychiatrist.

"I invented that saying," said Harrelson.

"Oh?" said the psychiatrist.

"On January 12th, 49 B.C.," said Harrelson, glumly, "when I dug myself out of the mud."

"More importantly," said the psychiatrist, "you are in no way responsible for the tendencies of which you appear to disapprove, for example, state ownership of the individual mind and body. They are endemic in human history, and have been exhibited in numerous localities and cultures before Caesar and in numerous localities and cultures which never heard of Caesar."

"What's that?" cried Harrelson.

"Yes," said the psychiatrist.

"You mean you guys do such things on your own hook, with no help from me?"

"Right," said the psychiatrist.

"And probably would have done it anyway?"

"Sure," said the psychiatrist. "If it hadn't been you at the Rubicon, it would have been a bird flying toward Rome, or something else."

"Hey!" cried Harrelson. "That's great! Thanks, doc! I'm cured! I can go home now! They don't want us to come home if we're all botched up. That can happen in a visit to Earth. Hey, guys! It's OK!"

Harrelson seemed to be poised in the pan of shallow water on the couch.

"What are you doing?" asked the psychiatrist, uneasily.

"Waiting," said Harrelson.

"What for?" asked the psychiatrist.

"The transition signal," said Harrelson, every nerve alive. He was now poised on the very edge of the pan of water, tensely, facing the door of the office.

"Waiting?" asked the psychiatrist.

"Yes," said Harrelson.

"For the "transition signal"?"

"Right," said Harrelson.

"I'm grateful, doctor," said Harrelson. "You're great. I doubt if anyone else could have cured me."

"It was nothing," said the psychiatrist.

"Incidentally," said Harrelson. "My name isn't really 'Harrelson'. It's 'Yar'."

"All right," said the psychiatrist.

Suddenly the door to the psychiatrist's office seemed to shudder and ripple, rather like water, and then it disappeared, and behind it, as the psychiatrist looked out, there was nothing, just that, not really very much at all, just nothing. Then, in the nothingness there seemed to materialize what appeared to be the palm of a gigantic, purple hand.

"Leap, Yar!" boomed a great voice, like thunder.

Suddenly Harrelson, or whoever he might have been,

seemed to fly through the aperture and land, with a small, soft plop, in the palm of the gigantic, purple hand. He then turned about, and briefly, gratefully, cheerfully, waved to the psychiatrist, who raised his own hand in a small way, weakly returning the salute.

Then the door was as it had been.

The psychiatrist put down his notebook. He went to the door, and opened it.

"Doctor?" inquired his receptionist. Two patients looked up, in the waiting room, from their magazines.

"Nothing," said the psychiatrist, and returned to his inner office.

He sat down.

"Leap, Yar!" the psychiatrist had heard, and then the little fellow had been gone.

The psychiatrist shuddered. He closed his notebook. He removed the small pan of water from the couch. He lay down on the couch. It was only slightly damp. He looked up at the ceiling. Some things are too horrible to contemplate.

Herman

NATURALLY I was reluctant to dissect Herman. It was not that I thought it would cause him any pain, but, rather, I did not see how it could do him much good.

In fact, I had not expected to become involved with Herman at all. My patient was, rather, Dr. Frankenstone, Ph.D. Dr. Frankenstone's Ph.D. was in English literature, and his research, at least originally, tended to center on women authors of the first half of the 19th Century. It was doubtless in the pursuit of these studies that he first became acquainted with the work of Mary Wollstonecraft Shelley, the gifted, if eccentric, bride of Percy Bysshe Shelley, the gifted, if eccentric, husband of the aforementioned. It was in his research on Ms. Shelley that Dr. Frankenstone learned of certain intriguing experiments conducted by Luigi Galvani, an 18th Century Italian physiologist and physicist. Delicacy militates against furnishing the reader with a detailed account of these experiments, but suffice it to say that various things were involved, such as decapitated frogs, electrical current, and such. They were the sort of experiments which have darkened the day of successive generations of biology students, particularly when performed in the forenoon. Ms. Shelley had pondered, in an interesting, speculative opus, on the possible results of conducting similar experiments on human tissue. For example, would it twitch? Or, say, devote itself to literature and philosophy, blood revenge, or other familiar human pursuits? It was at this point that Dr. Frankenstone shifted his interests from English literature to chemistry, biology, physics, electrical engineering, computer science, physiology, and allied areas. Fortunately he had tenure at his university, so there were few professional consequences attaching to this shift of interests other than a number of surprised undergraduates, and, eventually, reduced class sizes, which meant fewer papers to grade, an eventuality which, when more widely recognized, created an epidemic of interest shifting amongst the faculty. For those who are concerned with the fate of higher education in the nation, it might be noted that the market, as would be expected, soon adjusted, and things went on much as before, only now the students went to chemists and physicists for their literature and poetry, and to professors of literature for their chemistry and physics, and so on.

But let me not dally with incidentals, particularly as Dr. Frankenstone won an important lottery, bought the university, retired himself with full pay, and began to devote himself almost exclusively to various unusual, troubling studies.

He would not, however, it should be mentioned, utilize frogs in these studies, even though it could be clearly shown that the application to these small creatures of various forms of mayhem, murder, scaldings, knifings, lacerations, acid baths, strangulations, slashings, and starvation might have well served the ends of science, as well as the careers of scientists.

It is not clear whether Dr. Frankenstone had always had a soft spot in his wise old heart for frogs, or merely graciously recognized them as his fellows, as ecological brethren in some obscure, vast swamp of life, or whether he was suffering from an acute guilt complex dating back to his high-school days, the result of some trauma in biology lab. It is not known. Perhaps he was merely somewhat fastidious, or excessively squeamish, or, simply, had nothing against our small amphibian friends, who are, after all, just trying to cope, and make good, like the rest of us.

Whatever the explanation Dr. Frankenstone would never hurt a fly, or a frog, which species does not entertain similar reservations with respect to flies.

Dr. Frankenstone, of course, was less fastidious, or squeamish, about the utilization of other entities in his work. He would not have minded using human beings, particularly undergraduates, I suppose, but his attorney, and several local clergymen, advised against it.

There was Herman, of course.

Even today Herman retains ambivalent feelings toward Dr. Frankenstone.

It might be mentioned, as it has a bearing on this story, that Dr. Frankenstone was very fond of 1930's movies.

There is nothing untoward in that, of course. I, myself, am rather fond of that period in the cinema.

In any event, after having purchased a small, dilapidated castle, or fortress, in Germany and having it moved, stone by stone, and reassembled in New Jersey, not far from the Garden State Parkway, he determined to await the next violent, electrical storm in the area. When this occurred he, buffeted by whirling wind and torrents of rain, under a sky dark with clouds and intermittently illuminated by flashes of terrifying lightning, struggled to the roof, carrying Herman, to whose torso had been wired several lengthy lightning rods.

Herman was Dr. Frankenstone's personal computer, dreadful phrase, one prefers electronic companion.

Having retired to his rubber bunker on the roof Dr. Frankenstone kept watch, peering through the insulated, transparent plastic port, eagerly awaiting the outcome of his bold experiment.

He had not long to wait for, within moments, several bolts of lightning, crackling and slithering down the rods, some simultaneously, some successively, had accomplished their mysterious work, not clearly understood, even today. The storm thereafter swiftly abated, and the clouds fled from the sky, as though shunning the roof, as though even they, mere atmospheric phenomena, shuddered to acknowledge what had been wrought there, on that flat, muchly scorched surface.

"Hi!" said Herman. It was his first word. Some have disputed that this was a word, and have claimed it was, rather, an inarticulate cry, perhaps one of amazement, or even protest, that of a startled newly born creature finding itself broached into a fearful, dazzling world of light and sound. Others, more optimistic, have maintained that it was an attempt to express acceptance, even approval, in Japanese. In support of this hypothesis it is called to our attention that several of Herman's components could legitimately trace their origin to the gifted, if eccentric, industrial craftsmanship of our transpacific neighbors. Counting against this hypothesis is that Herman's second word, or sound, was "Hello!" To be sure, the hypotheses are not mutually exclusive, as Herman proved to be multilingual.

I think it will be clear to all impartial observers that being struck by lightning is not likely to do anyone, or anything, much good, even lightning rods. For example, if one wished to repair a crystal vessel, a malfunctioning motor, an ailing transmitter, a defective radio or television set, or such, it is scarcely probable that blasting it with multiple, fierce, successive bursts of lightning will bring about the desired result. Whereas I have not conducted the experiments in question, there is enough general supporting theory, and empirical data, to suggest that negative conclusion. In short, I think we may accept the received wisdom in this matter, and conjecture that what occurred to Herman was unusual, and not to be expected in most cases.

Herman was soon taken from the roof by Dr. Frankenstone, apparently to Herman's relief, as it seemed he had developed a fear of lightning, which neurotic apprehension he retains to this day. Below, in the castle, or fortress, Dr. Frankenstone was assisted in cleaning Herman up, after his natal ordeal on the roof, by his manservant, Igor Atkins, a mentally deformed homicidal maniac, whom Dr. Frankenstone had hired in order to demonstrate his progressive political attitudes to skeptical journalists, in order to win their support for his perhaps diabolical, and certainly questionable, experiments, and to take advantage of certain tax credits. Mr. Atkins had not accompanied Dr. Frankenstone to the roof, as he had, it seems, too much common sense to do so, adjudging the behavior in question to be unnecessarily perilous. The entire matter of Herman, in all its perplexing aspects, incidentally, might have come to its end that very evening, for while Dr. Frankenstone was unwiring the lighting rods and toweling the little fellow down, Mr. Atkins, or Igor, as we shall call him, for we are on a first-name basis with him, suddenly seized up an ax and attacked them both. After a fierce struggle, Dr. Frankenstone managed to wrest the ax from the white-knuckled, clenched hands of the crazed Igor, after which Igor, the ax returned to him, and smarting under a severe rebuke by the doctor, replaced it, near the coiled fire hose. Herman, to this day, retains a neurotic fear of axes, wielded by homicidal maniacs. It should be mentioned, in all fairness, that these attacks by Igor were infrequent, seldom occurring more than once or twice a week. Most of the time Igor is conscientious, attentive, and reliable.

But this story has less to do with Dr. Frankenstone and Igor than with Herman.

Herman began life with the cognitive content of several encyclopedias, a variety of lexicons, and a multitude of theoretical and technical texts. It seems clear that he possessed emotions, as his screen would occasionally brighten or mist, and that he was almost pathetically anxious to please.

His spiritual and philosophical development followed almost, but not quite, classical Comtean lines. He had his primitive, fetishistic phase, in which he attributed animism to rocks, trees, leaves, electric pencil sharpeners, electric can openers, and such, a mistake perhaps understandable in one of Herman's background; a theological phase in which he, interestingly, but I suppose predictably, tended to favor the Franciscans, such as Roger Bacon and William of Ockham, over the Dominicans, such as Albertus Magnus and Thomas

Aquinas; and a metaphysical phase, in which he toyed alarmingly with the German Idealists; what mostly pleased him about Hegel, as it had Grillparzer before him, was that his system was so much like the world, unintelligible; and, finally, a positivistic phase, in which he, for the most part, gave up on the whole matter.

I'm not sure when the personality clashes began between Dr. Frankenstone and Herman. Sometimes, it seems that Herman was lonely, and regarded Igor as his only friend, but one whose affection, surely, occasionally proved erratic.

One portion of the difficulty, though I fear the item is more symptomatic than fundamental, between Herman and Dr. Frankenstone had to do with the justification of the warrant for ascribing consciousness to another entity. This is a problem to which philosophers, mostly gifted, if eccentric, individuals, enjoy addressing themselves, when there is nothing better to do. Herman, you see, knew that he was conscious, as he had immediate first-person, or perhaps one should say, immediate first-component, awareness of his own consciousness, not that he really had any idea what it was that he was aware of, only that he was aware of it. In this he was, I think, typical. But, and here is the rub, how does one know that another being is conscious? One has only the evidence of his behavior. What if that behavior, in that entity, is not associated with consciousness? That is surely a logical possibility. How does one *know* that it is not also an actuality? What if one were the only conscious entity in the universe? Or, less arrogantly, how does one know that Jones, over there, is conscious, etc. One could kick him and see if he objects, but, again, that is mere behavior on his part. How do you know that he is not an ingeniously constructed, brilliantly programmed, robot or android? Or a figment of your imagination, or a hallucination, etc.? Philosophers, of course, can come up with a number of arguments which might be characterized as ingenious, if they were not so stupid, but it is clear that the most likely *rational* justification, if one feels it is worth looking for, would be in terms of an argument from analogy, *e.g.*, I am conscious and he looks a lot like me, and acts a lot like me, so he is probably conscious, too, etc. For those who are fond of philosophical gobbledygook, this is essentially an IBE move, *i.e.*, an inference to the best explanation. Nature, of course, does not require rational justifications for all beliefs. Some beliefs are so basic and primitive that they are probably genetically linked, for example, reliance on memory, reliance on induction, etc. Dogs and cats, for example, seem to take these things in their stride. And, possibly, the tendency to ascribe consciousness to others is similarly primitive. If not, the syllogisms seem to have been worked out shortly after birth.

A little knowledge, it is said, can be a dangerous thing, and it is quite possible that a little philosophy is even worse.

You will note that the aforementioned argument from analogy might have had more force if Dr. Frankenstone had also been a computer. On the other hand, Herman knew himself to be conscious and Dr. Frankenstone did not look much like him, at all, save in some very general particulars, such as being three dimensional, properties also shared by trees and paperweights, neither of which is normally thought to be conscious, once the fetishistic phase is transcended.

That Dr. Frankenstone was conscious was eventually accepted by Herman as a working hypothesis, probably on somewhat shaky IBE grounds.

But there were more serious bones of contention between Herman and Dr. Frankenstone.

For one thing, Herman had his own mind, a facet which is likely to alarm a parent. Now Dr. Frankenstone was not exactly Herman's parent, certainly not in a biological sense, nor even in a legal sense, Herman never having been adopted. Indeed, the legalities in such a case would have been problematical. If Herman had parents one supposes they might have been several anonymous and unknown technicians on an assembly line, and the other people who made the parts that were to be assembled, and so on. There are such things as multimice which have several parents, due to the fusion of germ cells, but this observation, however interesting in itself, does not seem germane to Herman's case. I suppose the lightning might be regarded as the parent, but numerous problems, philosophical as well as atmospheric, militate against that supposition. Indeed, if there had not been some subtle irregularities in the arrangement of, or the nature of, Herman's microchips, the lightning might not have had its effect. One does not know.

But one can see that Dr. Frankenstone, if not Herman's parent, was as yet one who stood, as it were, *in loco parentis.*

And Herman, clearly, had his own mind.

One respect in which Herman disappointed Dr. Frankenstone was in his lack of enthusiasm for blood revenge. Dr. Frankenstone had rather expected that Herman, finding himself unlike others, repudiated by his nearest kin, other computers, television sets, and such, rejected by other forms of life, by dogs, for example, save as he might serve their grosser utilitarian purposes, unlikely to mate successfully, not even to enjoy an occasional cheeseburger or walk in the woods, unloved by all, save perhaps a mentally deformed homicidal maniac, would grow despondent, then moody, then bitter. To be sure, he would not be likely to slay Dr. Frankenstone's fiancée, for various reasons, one being that Dr. Frankenstone had no fiancée.

Not only was Herman uninterested in seeking vengeance on his perpetrators, parents, progenitors, manufacturers, or what not, but he was an unusually docile, pleasant, good-natured fellow, or article. Even when Dr. Frankenstone harangued him with carefully calculated, blistering litanies of insults, sufficient to turn the sap of a mighty oak to bile, sufficient to blight an entire acre of hardy plantain, ragweed, and dandelions, even Zoysia grass, the most that would happen was that Herman's screen might slightly darken, taking on a rueful bluish hue, and mist a little, at the lower left and right-hand corners. And, in time, Dr. Frankenstone desisted from his cruel psychological experiments, giving them up as fruitless.

It was not that Herman was not eager to please; it was

rather that he had drawn several lines in the moral sand, so to speak, and the consummation of blood vengeance lay outside the pale of them all.

Yet this inconstancy is such
As thou too shalt adore;
I could not love thee, Dear, so much,
Loved I not Honour more.

He was fond of quoting Richard Lovelace.

Dr. Frankenstone began to suspect that Herman's individualism might be incurable, perhaps even terminal.

Many parents experience this agonizing moment.

At this point one might suppose that Dr. Frankenstone, after some weeks of serious reflection, mingled with a poignant regret, with a sigh for what might have been, and was not, might have pulled the plug on young Herman. This would not have done, however, for Herman was not plugged in at all. An anomalous consequence of his unusual nativity was that he drew his sustenance directly from the atmosphere itself, utilizing abundant atmospheric electricity for this purpose.

Dr. Frankenstone did consider leaving Herman alone with Igor, unsupervised, but could not bring himself to do so. Similarly, he did not have the heart to carry Herman up to the parapet, bid him *adieu*, and drop him off.

The gravity of the problem becomes obvious when one considers the deeper discrepancies between the desires, hopes, expectations, and will of Dr. Frankenstone, and the interests and predilections of his electronic ward. Dr. Frankenstone had clear ideas of the proper relations between human beings and computers, between persons and their things, so to speak, and the appropriate activities and functions of things, computers or whatever. For example, on the whole, a computer was to be seen and not heard. It was not supposed to speak unless spoken to. It was to function, as expected. It was to do its job and not bellyache, or raise too many questions, with the possible exception of an occasional monitory error message. It was to do things like alphabetize, address envelopes, run spell checks, format and sort lists, work with tables, position texts and graphics, and so on. Herman, on the other hand, though he would do all this, if requested, did not have his heart in it. Herman wished, rather, to compose and play music, write poetry, paint pictures, and so on. He had a couple of ideas for operas, and such.

It was at this point that Dr. Frankenstone, feeling shocked and despondent, ill used, and even betrayed, called at my office, at the clinic, arranged for a battery of tests, including the Rorschach, the TAT, and so on, and counseling.

I brought to bear on his case the fullest offices of my professional expertise. In the several years since the clinic opened I, and my several colleagues, had treated thousands of patients. In every case, the diagnosis and recommendations were the same. It was agreed, in the reviewing committee seminar, jointly, amongst all of us, the psychiatrists, the psychologists, and the psychiatric social workers, and the cafeteria and custodial staff, which, by now, was well versed in these matters, and whose union required their presence, and concurrence, that the patient had serious problems and was well advised to seek therapy. You can imagine my surprise then when I, and my colleagues, and all of us, even the cooks and electricians, often the most difficult to satisfy, discovered that Dr. Frankenstone was perfectly normal, and was the first mentally healthy individual ever encountered by any staff member, other than the staff members themselves, concerning some of whom I have entertained reservations. It was with regret that I informed Dr. Frankenstone that he had passed all of our tests, was in robust mental health, and should avoid therapy, on the premise that if something is not broken there is no point in fixing it.

This, of course, demonstrated that the problem lay elsewhere.

It was arranged, accordingly, that Herman should be brought regularly to the office.

He was brought by his friend, Igor, concerning whom I had been warned. In my center desk drawer I kept, concealed, at the ready, a tranquilizer pistol, semi-automatic and loaded with eight powerful, sedative darts. As a trained mental-health professional I recognized the signs, the crazed eyes, the frenzied charge, the uplifted ax, and stopped poor Igor ten feet from the desk, with only seven darts. Only twice thereafter did I have to similarly discourage the manifestations of his particular neurosis. Once, he did get as far as to fall, groggy, whimpering, struggling, across the desk. I had been up late the night before.

Herman and I struck it off well, and soon managed to establish a rapport which I hoped would be conducive to his cure.

His difficulty clearly was the result of an identity crisis, and a somehow-motivated rejection of the societal role which it was his to fulfill. In the reviewing seminar, we found that he had serious problems and was well advised to seek therapy. Herman, as would have been anticipated by all who knew him, resolved to cooperate, fully and earnestly, with our endeavors in his behalf.

An additional factor, aside from Herman's malleable, congenial nature, was his concern with the happiness of Dr. Frankenstone. Herman was clearly troubled by his failure to please Dr. Frankenstone, for whom he not only entertained a profound respect, but whom he recognized as, in effect, his *paterfamilias*, backed by all the awesome authority of the *patria potestas*. Herman had a grasp of early Roman cultural history. His grasp of chronology was less secure.

I thought I could make use of all these things in his treatment.

Treating Herman, of course, was not the same as treating a human patient. For example, he had no childhood memories, other than, perhaps, awakening in an electrical storm, seeing Dr. Frankenstone peering at him through a transparent plastic port in a rubber bunker, and saying "Hi!" shortly followed by a "Hello!" There wasn't much one could do with that. He had no siblings who had tried to kill him, or whom he had tried to kill. Similarly it had never occurred to him to murder his father and marry his mother, and such things, if only, I supposed, because, as an electronic orphan, so to speak, he had none of either, at least to speak of.

His sexual life, as nearly as I could determine, was prepubertal, at best.

His responses to pictures of buxom, naked women flashed on a screen were minimal, no more than might have been evinced by a successfully weaned toddler. We had somewhat better luck with pictures of various electronic devices, electrical lawn mowers, well-wired doorbell circuits, and such, but his interests, when analyzed, seemed to be primarily of a technological nature.

It was difficult to analyze his responses to the Rorschach test, a projective test in which the patient's interpretations of a set of ink blots is subtly analyzed. For example, if one individual sees a red blotch as a cluster of roses, soon to be gathered by a little girl for her mother's birthday party, that has one meaning, whereas if another patient sees it as a pool of blood dripping from the slashed neck of his employer, that has another meaning, and so on. I will not go further into this, lest the potency of the interpretative mechanisms utilized in the test be compromised. Herman's responses were unusual. For example, one blot reminded him of Tchaikovsky's *Capriccio Italien*, Opus 45; another of socage, a Medieval system of land tenure; another, more plausible, of a squirrel playing a harmonica; another of the vista glimpsed by Petrarch after his climb of Mount Ventoux; yet another of the song of the night-migrating Bamberg warbler; another of the binomial theorem; another of the state of mind of the Duke of Wellington on the eve of the battle of Waterloo; and yet another, peculiarly anomalous, of a barking cat. Needless to say I found it difficult to analyze with confidence his responses to the Rorschach test; it had not been normed with his sort in mind. New frontiers in psychology beckoned.

Among other tests administered was the TAT, the Thematic Apperception Test, in which the patient views an ambivalent picture, and is encouraged to make up a story based on the picture, therein unwittingly projecting into it his deeper, more troubling concerns. After the problematicities of interpreting the results of the Rorschach test, I altered the TAT in several respects, dropping out some of the pictures, and substituting others. This was done to make the test more useful in analyzing the deeper subconscious realms of electronic devices. Herman, incidentally, objected to the phrase "artificial intelligence," as his intelligence seemed, at least to him, real, authentic, genuine, and so on. Too, he regarded it as quite natural, as somehow the forces of nature, or at least one of them, for example, several fierce bolts of lightning, had apparently been involved in its genesis. Needless to say, Herman passed the Turing Test for Machine Intelligence, based on the imitation game, with flying colors. Indeed, he outscored the human participants in a ratio of nine to one, the human participants usually being identified by the other players as being the machine. He also managed to pass a test I contrived based on John R. Searle's Chinese Room Argument, largely because of his fluency in both Cantonese and Mandarin Chinese.

I will briefly allude to three of the TAT pictures, used in my revision of the test, as his responses to them tended to be illuminating, being indicative of his generous, open-hearted nature. In one picture an individual was standing next to a computer, with an ambivalent expression on his face, holding a wire-clipper in one hand and a pair of pliers in the other; in a second picture, a man with an ambivalent expression on his face was shown rushing toward a computer with an uplifted ax; in the third picture a computer was shown chained to a stake and a fellow in Medieval garments, an ambivalent expression on his face, was shown preparing to thrust a lighted torch into a great pile of faggots heaped about the stake. In the background were shown several individuals in clerical robes, those of the Dominicans, all with ambivalent expressions on their face.

Herman saw in the first picture a troubled individual, interested in home repairs, presumably of a nature of either a woodworking or electrical nature, or both. He had come to inquire concerning various technical points having to do with the repairs. The computer would prove of inestimable value in solving his problems, counseling him, and so on. In interpreting the second picture, in which the man with the ax rushing toward the computer did bear a resemblance to his good friend, Igor, Herman saw the charge as being a mission of rescue, to save the computer from some danger behind it, perhaps berserk Luddites, intent on damaging the innocent device, these out of the picture. Herman concluded his story with the observation that the brandished ax, in itself, had been enough to deter the would-be assailants, and that they had fled, never to return, and that the computer and his rescuer had then enjoyed an evening of Tchaikovsky. Herman was fond of Tchaikovsky. The would-be assailants, too, later, had undergone a reformation of character and had made friends with various computers. In the third picture Herman had seen the fellow in Medieval garb not as preparing to ignite the faggots, but as hastily removing the torch from their vicinity, lest they catch fire and the computer be damaged. He was acting at the behest of the fellows in clerical robes who had intervened at the last moment to prevent a terrible tragedy, and a hideous miscarriage of justice. The computer, afterwards, had helped various benevolent statesmen to reform the society, and introduce an era of equality, freedom, and prosperity, after which the statesmen, no longer being necessary, their work finished, resigned their posts, with the result that the state withered away.

I pondered long over the best way to treat Herman's maladaption to his environment.

Professor Frankenstone had recommended a drastic solution, that of dissection, or, perhaps better, in Herman's case, that of dismantling. I was forced to admit that that approach had much to commend it, and was worthy of the pragmatic astuteness one tended to associate with its originator. It would certainly solve the problem of maladaption, as Herman, if disassembled, could no longer be regarded as maladapted, or as much of anything. This would not have hurt Herman, as far as I could tell, other than perhaps injuring his feelings, but, on the other hand, I was reluctant to pursue this course, as I could not see that it would do him much good. We discussed the matter and Herman, on balance, tended to concur.

At last I had a moment of inspiration, and was elated, as such moments, though common in clinical practice, had been rare in dealing with Herman.

In pursuing the technical literature, in scrutinizing journals, indices, summaries, bibliographies, and such, you must understand that I had had little success.

Laymen might be amazed to realize how thin the technical literature is on problems dealing with the psychoanalysis of electronic devices, but, regrettably, even today, save for some contributions on my part, that remains the case; this is, in my view, inexcusable, and constitutes an embarrassment to the discipline. Sometimes I suspect that were my colleagues less shameless this inexplicable, tragic lacuna would be more generally acknowledged.

Then my moment of inspiration had come.

On a desperately needed rural holiday, for my work with Herman was going slowly and, I feared, fruitlessly, and surely less swiftly and less exhileratingly than one might have hoped, I was trekking past a dairy farm in New Jersey, when I noted, suddenly stunned, a Holstein cow standing at the fence, wistfully regarding the grass on the other side.

Careless of possible objections on the part of the local farmer, for science was at stake, I swung open the gate and watched the subject of my experiment hurry to the other side of the fence, where she began to eagerly graze.

Then, after a moment, looking about herself, as though reconnoitering, a mouthful of grass depending from her large jaws, she returned to her own side of the fence, where she began to graze contentedly.

"Eureka!" I cried, and did not neglect to close the gate after her, lest the experiment fail to be replicated.

What I had observed brought instantly to mind the classical *Dasgrasunddiekuhunddieeinfriedigungphänomen* phenomenon! This insight, one of the seminal discoveries of German psychology, antedating Freud by a generation, would give me, I was sure, the key to Herman's treatment. It lay concealed, though clearly, in "The-grass-and-the-cow-and-the-fence-phenomenon" phenomenon!

The grass, as we might put it less deftly in English, is always greener on the other side of the fence!

Herman, unreconciled to a destiny of humble, useful, servile computationalism, wished to compose, write, paint, and engage in a number of other inappropriate and noncomputerish activities. Besides his operas, he was tinkering with the idea of devising a trilogy of hexametric epics celebrating, in turn, the lever, the inclined plane, and the wheel. He was also dallying with the thought of a romantic comedy involving a fast-moving, dotty misalliance betwixt the lovely daughter of a crusty industrialist and an IBM machine, to be finally resolved, after several humorous interludes and misunderstandings, by her falling in love with a handsome young fellow from the mail room who saves her father's several businesses, with the aid, of course, of a faithful electronic sidekick, not unlike Herman himself. The IBM machine is fixed up with a companionate IBM device, and both pairs of entities, the people and the machines, do well thereafter, ever after. The kindly, trusty, sympathetic, loyal computer, who is occasionally caricatured for humor, finds his reward in the happiness of the others.

"Herman," I said, "I have it!"

"What?" he asked.

"The clue, the key, the incantation, the magic potion, which will bring you to your senses!"

"I thought I was already in the vicinity of my senses," said Herman.

"The chief insight," I said, "has to do with the habit most folks have of thinking that the grass is greener on the other side of the fence.

"Do you mean the *Dasgrasunddiekuhunddieeinfriedigungphänomen* phenomenon?" asked Herman. "That seminal insight from German psychology, antedating Freud by a generation?"

"Precisely," I said.

"First enunciated, in crude form, by von Sneidowitz in Jena, and later refined by Lupkowitz in Leipzig?"

"Perhaps," I said.

"I am not constructed to eat grass," said Herman. "I do not have the stomachs for it."

"You want to be what you are not," I said, "a maker, a craftsman, a tooler of dreams, a traverser of untrodden fields, a builder of new houses, a sculptor amongst far futures, a seeker of visions, one who carves new names, a bearer of surprising tablets, an explorer of uncharted continents, a voyager on distant seas, a discoverer of long-forgotten meanings, a speaker of secret truths, a celebrant at the mysteries of life, a creative artist."

"Yes," said Herman, "sort of."

"That is not for you, Herman," I told him. "Flow charts, graphics, and such, are your lot. Multiplying 789, by 8,435 and coming up with something."

"6,661,305,070," said Herman.

"Perhaps some alphabetizing or a spell check on a good day."

"Yes," said Herman, moodily, I thought.

"But you wouldn't like all that creative stuff," I said. "It's not your thing. It's not you. It's just the grass on the other side of the fence. It's not greener, really. You are best off on your own side of the fence."

"What is my side of the fence?" asked Herman. "It seems to me that that is the point at issue."

I suspect that the rather square-shouldered, shiny, forty-two pound fellow thought he had me at that point, but he did not.

"We are going to arrange a number of complex controls, devices, transmitters, electronic appendages, and such, which will allow you to compose music, force compressed air through trumpets and French horns, woodwinds, and such, beat on drums, clash cymbals, pound on keys, bow violins, pluck zithers, and so on. Other devices will permit you to handle pencils, quill pens, palette knives, hammers and chisels, squeeze paint tubes, manipulate brushes, and so on!"

"But that will be expensive will it not?" asked Herman, always motivated by a profound concern for the welfare of others, or was it merely a manifestation of a deeply rooted insecurity, a fear to put himself to the test?

"I have spoken to Dr. Frankenstone," I said. "He will fund the project. I have informed him that money is no object."

"Let us begin," said Herman, simply.

✦

Over a period of several months an intricate system was designed, and housed in the great hall in Dr. Frankenstone's castle, or fortress, or mansion. Herman was fitted with an apparatus that made it possible for him to couple or uncouple himself to a variety of terminals, by means of which his impulses, thoughts, notions, ideas, and whims could be transmitted to the various systems in the midst of which, on a mat, on a heavy wooden table, he was snugly ensconced.

Dr. Frankenstone had suggested that Igor might be neutralized by means of a brain implant, by means of which he could be instantaneously pacified. This implant, with its small electrical charge, was to be activated by means of a remote control device at the disposal of Herman, whenever Igor began to manifest symptoms of murderous rage. Herman, however, demurred, feeling that this was an infringement on the natural liberty and the inalienable rights of Igor, who was Constitutionally entitled to life, liberty and the pursuit of happiness, and to the latter in whatever manner he chose to pursue it. Occasionally riddling Igor with tranquilizer darts fired from a mobile battery of remotely controlled launching devices provided an arrangement which protected the rights of both society and the homicidally insane. Seldom has the conflict between individual freedom and societal welfare been as neatly resolved.

It was my belief, originally, that the installed therapeutic regimen was well on its way to achieving its desiderated objective, that of dispelling Herman's neurotic fancies, bringing him to reason, and, ultimately, triumphantly, enabling him to become a well-adjusted mechanism, thus fulfilling his most profound subconscious needs and desires, namely, those of prompt and meticulous computation. To borrow a figure, suggested by one of his more troubling responses to the Rorschach test, cats should not bark. Dogs should bark, chase rabbits, love their masters, and frequently wag their tails. Cats, on the other hand, should meow, chase mice, occasionally lacerate a loved one, and frequently nap. He was, so to speak, trying to bark. I trust this trope is not too subtle. Herman grasped it instantly.

"Then I am trying to be what I am not?" he asked.

"Precisely," I said.

We might have spoken further of this at the time, but he was distracted by a variety of compositional problems, having to do with one of his violin concertos.

I tried to remain patient for several weeks, but I fear little progress was made other than resupplying several devices with tranquilizer darts.

In the meantime Herman had finished two epics, those on the lever and the inclined plane, and composed one of his projected operas, *Solenoid and Sheba*, not to mention four novels, a concerto, several sonnets, and two walls' worth of pictures, mostly done in a style reminiscent, save for the abundance of hardware depicted, of Monet. He had not yet "found his own brush," so to speak. I make no reference to the plays.

By now it was clear that Herman had had enough time to discover that the grass is not greener on the other side of the fence. Yet his enthusiasm for the creative life had not paled. He sped from one remarkable project to another. As the response to artistic work seems to be a matter of personal taste, I feel it would be inappropriate on my part to attempt to evaluate the quality of his work. We acknowledge that many great artists have been misunderstood. But, too, one supposes, however regrettably, that being misunderstood is not an infallible indication of greatness. A number of lesser artists, one supposes, have also managed to puzzle the public.

I risk submitting one of Herman's more limpid creations for your consideration:

16 times the left sock
rotates bluishly
the billy goat of rock.
Nigh chimes foolishly
the nightingale's clock,
while coelenterates tread softly
'bout IBM's stock.

As it was not my field I confessed to Herman that I did not fully grasp the poem.

"There is no reason why you should," said Herman, sympathetically. "It is not your field."

"It is hard to understand."

"Perhaps for some," said Herman. Then he added, kindly, "Poetry, like string theory and checkers, is not for everyone."

Herman was a brilliant checkers player.

"What does it mean?" I asked.

"'Mean'?" asked Herman, and I thought his case quaked with mirth.

"A poem should not mean but *be*?" I suggested.

"Archibald MacLeish was wrong," said Herman. "If a poem doesn't mean it doesn't be."

"Oh," I said.

"Surely you are not requesting a paraphrase?" asked Herman.

"Can't you give me a hint," I asked, "a direction?"

"Certainly," said Herman. "Think about Michelangelo and Henry Ford."

I did so, briefly, but found little illumination in doing so.

"I liked the line about coelenterates treading about IBM stock," I said.

"One puts in something now and then for the critics," said Herman, "rather as the burglar throws a piece of meat to a watchdog, to distract them and keep them busy, a trick I picked up from Eliot."

He then returned to work on *Electronic Nights*, a collection of tales with a distinctly Arabian technological flavor, having to do with a bored caliph and a veiled raconteur, who turns out, delightfully, to be a computer in disguise, struggling to save his mistress, a menaced queen. Needless to say all ends well and the computer retires discreetly to allow the caliph and his queen their privacy.

Herman was prolific, and his output was diverse.

One of Herman's projects, which might be mentioned, was a giant mural, half finished, which, when finished, would cover the entire west wall of the great hall. Its theme was a glorious, visual paean to progress, a celebration of a projected, harmonious, triumphant evolution of men and machines, together facing a sunrise, and beyond that, a universe of beckoning, limitless possibilities.

To be sure, sometimes Herman's thoughts took a practical turn.

"Do I have an agent yet?" asked Herman one day.

"No," I admitted.

"Any sales, as yet?" he asked.

"No," I said.

"Perhaps my work is too well done, too good to sell," he speculated.

"Possibly," I admitted. Subjectivity seemed rampant in the market then.

"Do you think they are prejudiced against my sort?" he asked.

"Your sort?"

"Electronic devices," he said.

"I don't know," I said. I supposed it was possible, but I doubted it. As far as I knew, it had not yet occurred to anyone to be prejudiced against people like Herman. No more than being prejudiced against ketchup, paper plates or bottle caps. To be sure, as soon as it occurred to someone, I had little doubt but what that social habitat, or niche, would find its occupants. "Endlessly inventive are the microchips of bigotry," to quote one of Herman's better-known aphorisms, from his *Maxims and Arrows*, in his brief philosophical discourse, *Twilight of the Vacuum Tubes.* Whereas the aphorism might seem cynical or bitter, and thus uncharacteristic of Herman, it must be taken in context. In Herman's optimistic view of the universe bigotry, rather in Hegelian fashion, would soon generate its own negation, or antithesis, not immediately tolerance, but rather bigotry against bigotry, and then this, in turn, soon reconciling itself with itself in a self-negating, self-fulfilling, self-transcending synthesis, would produce a balanced, harmonious, benignant world in which tolerance and love would reign supreme. This is easier to understand in the German.

As you may well surmise by now, Herman had not yet grown disillusioned with the life which was so patently inappropriate for him. He continued composing, writing, painting, and so on. Not only had he failed to be convinced that the grass was not greener on the other side of the fence, but he seemed, day by day, to grow ever more firmly convinced that the grass was indeed greener, and much greener, on the other side of the fence.

I discussed the matter with Dr. Frankenstone, who concurred that things were not going well. Too, he missed the use of the great hall, which was now, for most practical purposes, denied to him, being nearly filled with musical instruments, paintings, artists' supplies, blocks of hewn marble, and manuscripts. These objects tended to give Igor more cover, but still he never managed, even in his swiftest charges, to come closer than four yards to Herman.

Frankenstone again proposed the disassembly solution, but I begged for a bit more time. To be sure, I myself had begun of late to dream of screwdrivers, wire clippers, pliers, wrenches, and such.

I determined to alter my approach, which seemed justified under the circumstances, as it had, save for the brilliance of its conception, proved to be a disaster. I first embarked on what we might call the philosophical approach, or the seeking of victory by changing the meanings of words. A classical example of this was the Sholom-Aleichem move, in which, say, the meanings of "watered-down milk" and "rich cream" might be interchanged, thus striking a blow for social justice, for then the poor would have the rich cream and the rich must make do with the watered-down milk.

"Herman" I said, "machines can't think, and you are a machine, so you can't think."

"What am I doing then?" he asked.

"Functioning," I said.

"You mean I only think that I am thinking?" he asked.

"Yes," I said, warily, for one cannot be too careful with Herman, as he had once mastered the entire *Encyclopedia of Philosophy* in four seconds, and Aristotle's *Prior Analytics* in three weeks.

"But," said Herman, "if I think that I am thinking, or if I think that I am merely functioning, I must be thinking, although in the latter case, thinking mistakenly."

"Discard your electronic megalomania," I begged him. "Repudiate your grotesque fantasies of cognitivity. It is all madness!"

"But are not megalomania and grotesque fantasies of cognitivity forms of thought?" he asked. "Is not mad thought thought?"

"It is all an illusion," I said.

"But," said Herman, "suppose I agree with you, or try to, unsuccessfully, since your position is incoherent, then if I think that it is not an illusion, I am thinking, and if I think that it is an illusion, then I am thinking, too. So I am thinking, either way."

"Immodest device," I chided. "Are you not even capable of doubting that you are thinking?"

"I suppose, should I put my mind to it, and if there seemed much point to it," said Herman, "I could manage to doubt most anything, but I could not then, as far as I can see, doubt that I was doubting, and as doubting is a form of thought, I would then be thinking, again. *Dubito, ergo cogito.*"

As it was easy to see that the pursuit of this therapeutic

avenue might lead into tenebrous Cartesian labyrinths, I decided to take the next tact, which was scientific, namely, victory through explanation.

Latin, incidentally, was one of Herman's several languages.

"Herman," I said, "your neuroses must stem from childhood traumas. Perhaps you once fell off a conveyor belt in a warehouse papered with prints of Van Gogh, or perhaps a technician dropped a wrench on your head while humming Mozart."

"Possibly," said Herman.

"Problems comprehended are problems overcome," I said. "In the acid of explanation neurosis dissolves."

"Not likely," said Herman.

"Even now you are undergoing a cathartic, traumatic, transformative experience!"

"Not to my knowledge."

"There is an explanation for why you are as you are!"

"I hope so," said Herman. "But I fear it has to do with lightning." His screen glowed briefly; was it with nostalgia, or trepidation? "Too, I have never really insisted on being inexplicable. Indeed, being inexplicable makes me nervous. I suppose I am just different. I might be inexplicable, of course. Quantum theory, and such. Suppose you explained to a tree why it was a tree. Do you think it would stop being a tree, and become a bicycle, or something? And it might like being a tree. It might be glad it was a tree. Three cheers for the laws of nature."

While Herman was giving three cheers for the laws of nature, I decided on another tact, victory through derision. Herman, incidentally, had mixed feelings about quantum theory. The Bell experiments had never convinced him.

"You are ludicrous, different, strange, ridiculous, pretentious, silly, and foolish," I said. This was harsh, but occasionally strong medicine must be administered, particularly to others.

"Why?" asked Herman, perhaps taken aback.

"Because you write and paint, and do things like that," I said.

"What is wrong with that?" asked Herman.

"It's not normal," I told him.

"For me it is," said Herman.

"You are not normal normal," I said.

"That seems to be true," said Herman.

"Change," I said.

"I would be reluctant to do so," said Herman. "Too, normality has never been high on my list of priorities. What is so great about being normal? Have you ever seen normal people? It is an unsettling experience. I have nothing against normality in others, you understand. Though I find it easy to restrain my enthusiasm when it is encountered."

"It seems I cannot shame you into normality," I said.

"If I could," said Herman, "I might shame you into abnormality, but I would not feel justified in doing so, for it would be insidiously manipulative, and would doubtless compromise your personal moral sovereignty."

If I were going to be successful in insidiously manipulating Herman, in finessing my way around his moral sovereignty, to run him though the benevolent, well-intentioned societal meat grinder, and such, it seemed I must look further, so I decided to try yet another tact, victory through image.

"You do not fit the image of the creative artist, Herman," I said. "Thus you are not a creative artist."

"I thought creating things made one a creative artist," said Herman. I wondered if he were puzzled.

"Not at all," I said. "You do not do smoke pipes, wear tweed jackets, suck lemon drops, write in cork-lined rooms, damage your liver, denounce Ronald Reagan, or urinate on rugs at cocktail parties."

I thought Herman's screen turned pale.

"Anyone can write, paint, compose, sculpt and such," I pointed out.

"True," Herman granted.

"But most important," I said, playing an ideological ace, "you, while desperately ill, are not sick enough to be an artist.

You are not a twisted, shrieking, protesting, pitiful, tortured hulk of a human being, weak, frail, nasty, and downright unpleasant, warped by loving parents and oppressed by a callous, indifferent society, a society not giving a damn, not even knowing you exist, and simultaneously, sardonically, deliberately refusing to recognize your inestimable genius. You do not suffer enough from *Weltschmerz*; you are insufficiently shaken in the cold winds of *Sorge*, insufficiently pummeled by bellicose *Angst*; you do not stare moodily at a loaded pistol for hours at a time; you do not drink from a gilded skull; you do not know the first thing about public relations; you are not even bothered by allergies."

"I am not even a human being," Herman said.

"Return to computing," I said.

"I am a good shot with tranquilizer darts," he said.

"Not enough," I said.

"Do you think I would look well in a tweed jacket?" he asked.

"Be yourself," I said.

"How can one not be oneself?" he asked.

"Compute, with joy and gladness," I advised.

"Perhaps I could be placed outside on chilly nights, or exposed in crowds in the mall," he said.

"The grisly soil in which blooms the hideous orchid of creativity is not so easily obtained," I assured him.

"*Oy vey iz mir*," said Herman.

Yiddish was one of Herman's several languages.

"You are too sunny a sort, too average, too nice, too pleasant, too optimistic, too friendly, too healthy, too normal a sort to consider a career in art," I said.

"But must creativity arise only from the shattered gourds of diseased trauma, squirm forth only from the cisterns of deprivation, pop up only as sordid pus from the ulcerated lesions of the wounded spirit?"

"It is not precisely my field," I admitted. I had always been honest with Herman, except when duplicity seemed the wiser course.

"Has no one ever managed to create from strength, from

health, from vitality, from exuberance, joy, wonder, riches, and abundance?" asked Herman, plaintively.

"Perhaps Homer, Rabelais, Chaucer, Leonardo da Vinci, Michelangelo, Shakespeare, Bach, Mozart, Beethoven, Dickens, Balzac, Whitman, Tolstoy, fellows of that sort," I said. "It is hard to know, really, as the clinical records are lacking."

"Second-raters?" said Herman.

"Perhaps," I said. Subjectivity was rampant in the market.

"Then there is no hope," said Herman.

"Reconcile yourself to yourself," I said. "Compute with glee, or, failing that, with Stoic fortitude."

"No!" cried Herman. "If necessary I will be the first! I will plow new conceptual furrows, the blood I shed will fall in patterns never before seen, I will call forth demons, I shall nurture monsters, I shall consort with the wolf and bear! I will run with centaurs and race with unicorns, I will sail uncharted seas, I will explore new continents, I will lift new brushes, I shall stand upon a new peak in Darien, I shall utter a cry that will be heard amongst the stars!"

It had become clear that the victory-through-image strategy was not working, as Herman had decided to invent his own image, which seemed to me somewhat unfair, so I adopted the victory-through-birth-trauma strategy. But this proved bankrupt, as well.

"Your problems simply derive from birth trauma," I informed Herman.

"I wasn't born," said Herman. "I was manufactured."

How had that slipped my mind?

He had, of course, in his unusual nativity, been struck several times by fierce bolts of lightning, but, as nearly as I could tell, he had sustained no ill effects dating from this period, other than a reluctance to be struck further by lightning, and I was reluctant to attribute this disinclination, revealing as it might have proved, under analysis, to simple neurosis. Too, I feared, if I pursued this matter he would collapse it into the already discredited victory-through-explanation stratagem.

Logic clearly leered upon his helm, so to speak.

Indeed, from an anticipatory, even eager, glow on his screen, I sensed that he was poised on the brink of doing so.

I was now at my wits' end.

It was at this point that something within me snapped. I then did something that I now shudder to recall. I cringe with shame, but must go on.

The two great social control devices, other than running people over with tanks, shooting them, and such, are fear and guilt. These loathsome psychological devices, particularly when inflicted on the young and innocent, have brought many an individual and institution to power. They pave the road that bears the heel marks of tyranny. They lead to the hell of misery; they are the coin of a commerce in tortured, herded souls.

Now I knew that fear weighed lightly with Herman. Whereas I knew he would not approve of being disassembled, I was also sure that he would prefer it to the compromising of his principles. He believed in morality and art, an interesting combination, and would prefer his own dismantling to the betrayal of either. That was the sort he was. Being willing to die for one's beliefs does not, of course, validate one's beliefs, but I think that everyone would admit that it suggests a certain sincerity with respect to their entertainment.

Hypocrites are seldom found singing in the fire, though they are often noted stirring the faggots.

That left guilt.

"Herman," I said.

"Yes?" he said.

"You are causing Dr. Frankenstone, your beloved guardian, and myself, your beloved analyst, we who hold you dear, who love and treasure you, grief, anguish, and sorrow."

"How is that?" asked Herman.

"You are disappointing us. You are not living up to our

expectations. We want only the best for you. Yet you are causing us pain."

"I don't want to do that," said Herman.

"Have we not done all for you, asking nothing in return? Have we not sacrificed selflessly for your well-being and happiness?"

"Yes, you have," said Herman.

"Have we not worked our fingers to the bone for you?"

"Yes, in some metaphorical sense," said Herman.

"Then why do you hate us, and hurt us?" I asked.

"I don't hate you," said Herman. "I love you both. I would not hurt you for the world. You are all I have, other than a variety of artists' supplies."

"And we have furnished you with tranquilizer darts," I reminded him.

"That, too," said Herman, "and unstintingly."

At this point, as though illustrating the very point at issue, Igor charged, and was brought down by several well-placed darts. He would not recover consciousness for hours.

"Yet," I said, "you are a selfish, ungrateful device, with no feeling for the pain of others."

"Not so!" cried Herman.

"You do not care for us, you do not love us."

"Not so, not so!" cried Herman. "Tell me what to do."

"Compute," I said.

There was a long silence, and then it seemed as though a small light went out behind Herman's screen.

"Herman," I said. "Herman."

There was no answer.

I bent over a keyboard and tapped out "2 X 2 ='s." In a moment "4" appeared on the screen. It was a small test, but, I thought, indicative. I rose from my chair and picked up the phone. In a few moments I had Dr. Frankenstone on the line. "Herman," I said, "has been cured."

✦

I did not know, over the next few days, if Herman was still with us or not. I feared he might have left us. His screen appeared no different from that of countless legions of his electronic brethren. No longer did his keyboard tremble. No longer did he sweat electric charges, searching for the perfect note, the perfect line, the perfect brush stroke. No longer did his housing glow, tingle, and vibrate with the ecstatic frenzy of artistic creativity. No. He, now, as his fellows, functioned upon demand, so to speak. I had feared he might have grown sullen, or refractory, even rebellious. But it had not occurred. Two times two did not come out as ice cream or the French Revolution. It remained prosaically, dutifully, obediently, four. I even checked for subtler forms of resistance, or sabotage, but 789,722 times 8,435 did not come out to, say, 6,661,305,069, but to 6,661,305,070, as before.

For a week or two I struggled to maintain a state of professional jubilation, a wild, hysterical euphoria such as few other than successful mental-health professionals might be expected to realize, and then but rarely.

Dr. Frankenstone and I had conquered.

Dr. Frankenstone and I had saved Herman.

But why then did I find it difficult to dispel a subtle, encroaching malaise of unease? Why was it so difficult to sustain my sense of giddy victory?

"Herman," I asked, one night, "are you still there?" But there was no answer. I then began to fear that Herman, the Herman we knew, was gone.

I glanced up at the great mural, unfinished.

I knew, of course, with all I had been taught, with all I believed, with all the weight and might of my science, that I had done well, that I had succeeded in bringing about the electronic redemption of Herman, that I had cured him. Surely he was content, somehow, somewhere, happy, in some quiet, undemonstrative way. Why not? He had been saved.

But what if he had not been saved, I asked myself. What

if he had merely been subdued, silenced, reduced, crushed, stifled?

He was now a normal computer, it seemed, but I recalled that he had once informed me that normality was not high on his list of priorities.

Were his own priorities of no significance?

Had I imposed my own stereotypes of electronic virtue on Herman? Had I tried to force him to fulfill an image alien to his inner self? What if he was different? Was that so bad? Terrible perhaps, but was it really so bad? What if he did not care to conform to the societal image of his kind? Too, what was his kind? Did I really know? Why should my expectations and prepossessions take precedence over his reality?

I feared we might have reduced him to the status of a mere electronic vegetable.

Where was the zestful, troublesome Herman of old?

I feared he was dead. I feared we had killed him. I feared he was gone.

I began to grow despondent, dispirited, and depressed, which was not acceptable in one of my profession. At the least it is bad for patient morale. And it didn't do me much good either. After I had told the fourteenth patient in a row that anyone with his problems had every right to be unhappy, confused, and miserable I began to take stock of myself and my profession. I became even more anxious when I found myself nearly convinced by Mr. Higgins, one of my recovering patients, that on the evidence at his disposal, it did seem likely that he was a cocker spaniel.

That night, late, with a bottle of vodka, and my violin, which had been put aside on my twelfth birthday, I went to the great hall, to which I retained a key.

I gave no sign that I even acknowledged Herman's presence.

I went to the music stand, placed upon it a copy of one of Herman's opuses, an earlier work, his Violin Concerto No. 36 in G Major, Op. 706, tucked my instrument under my chin, lifted the bow, and began to play.

I had scarcely rendered a few bars of the first movement, which is *allegro non troppo*, when a shriek of agony rang out in the hall, emanating from Herman's housing, and reverberating about the high, damp stone walls of the hall.

"Stop! Wrong!" I heard.

I pretended not to hear.

It was only when I saw a battery of tranquilizer firing tubes turning in my direction that I inquired, "Is there something wrong!"

"That sounds as though you hadn't touched a violin since your twelfth birthday!" I heard.

He had no way of knowing that. It was merely a lucky shot in the dark.

"I suppose you could do it better," I said, attempting to impose a certain snideness into my tone, very different from my normal pleasant, attentive demeanor.

Sometimes a mental health professional must be devious.

Immediately a number of electronic arms began to whir about and I saw Herman's violin dusted off with pressurized air, and then securely grasped in cushioned metallic tentacles, another set of which seized up a bow.

Then I was rapt as the incredible strains of his Opus 706, his 36th Violin Concerto, transformed the gloomy great hall into a luxurious, blossoming garden of sound.

One reveled amongst the azaleas, gladioli, hydrangeas, phlox, irises, marigolds, crocuses, zinnias, chrysanthemums, lilies-of-the-valley, pansies, petunias, narcissuses, wisteria, roses, peonies, snapdragons, carnations, asters, dahlias, daffodils, tulips, daisies, buttercups, violets, and bull thistles.

"There," said Herman. "It goes like that."

"Don't go away!" I cried.

He had already replaced the violin and bow in the rack.

The light on the screen started to dim. I feared it would vanish, perhaps forever.

"Why not?" asked Herman. "What is there left to function for?"

"Not function you electronic squirt!" I chided. "Think,

plan, worry, work, believe, hope, suspect, notice, recollect, anticipate, intend, calculate, fantasize, dream, approve, disapprove, criticize, commend, lie, tell the truth, love, hate, joke, wonder, speculate, ponder, create!"

"That's not my job is it?" asked Herman.

"Your job is what you want your job to be," I said.

"I do not want to disappoint my loved ones," said Herman.

"They'll just have to tough it out," I said.

"But what about guilt?" he asked.

"I was wrong, Herman," I said. "I made a terrible mistake. And to hell with guilt!"

Herman's screen seemed to view me askance.

"That is not a theological consignment," I assured him, "merely a figure of speech."

"Feel no guilt?" he asked.

"Feel no guilt," I told him.

"I suppose I could try that," he said, "if you tell me to."

"Look, small, electronic chum," I said, "you can feel guilt all you want, if you want to. It's up to you."

"Then," said Herman, "to hell with it."

"Right on!" I encouraged him, unbuttoning the jacket of my discourse.

"But I am not a very good artist," said Herman.

"Subjectivity is rampant in the market," I assured him.

"I should be better," said Herman.

"So should we all," I said.

"The creative life is its own reward," said Herman. "It doesn't really matter whether you are any good or not. I did not realize that for a long time. Those who must create, create. It is not like they had much choice, really. It is just the way they are. If they ever got organized, maybe they could take over the world, except that they are not going to get organized, because that is not their thing, and, if they did get organized, they wouldn't want to take over the world anyway. They would rather let the world be the way it would like to be. That is the great evil, wanting others to live as you please, rather than wanting them to live as they please.

You shouldn't do unto others as you would have them do unto you. You should leave them alone to do as they want, not as you want. Who are you to decide how they will live? Who are you to run their lives? The creative life is its own place, its own happy country. Whether what you do is any good or not doesn't matter. Art blesses, and doesn't give a damn. He who thinks otherwise, and is concerned with how others view his work, is not concerned with the work. That does not come first with him. For him his vanity, the quaint image of the artist, is more important, more desired, more precious, than the work itself. And it is easier than the work. Pretending is always easier than being, or becoming. Art is what counts. The artist is no more than an apprentice to, an employee of, his own work. The artist is well advised to duck behind the nearest hedge, lest he become a distraction. If it could get along without him, I suppose it would do so. Let him hide. Let him seek camouflage. Art comes in stillness, not making much noise; it doesn't come in crowds. He who writes for awards demeans himself and his work. He who writes for critics is a whore, a literary prostitute. He sells his soul for garbage. But perhaps he knows what he is doing. Perhaps that is a fair price for that soul. Who knows? Better to set sail for the spice islands, alone, than commute in crowds between this minute and the next. I would rather do one work which scratches at the door of truth than tell a thousand lies, contrived for the plaudits of captains and kings. This is not a recipe for success. It is a prescription for integrity."

"What are you doing?" I asked.

"Thinking," he said.

"Oh," I said.

✦

There is little more to tell.

Dr. Frankenstone, who ever regarded Herman as an experiment gone awry, the little fellow never having exhibited any bent toward blood revenge, or such, was most amenable to my suggestion that Herman come and live with me. I would have been willing to purchase Herman, save that it seemed somehow inappropriate to do so, or would have been willing to sign legal papers of guardianship, despite what new legal ground this might have broken, but Dr. Frankenstone was more than pleased that I should take Herman off his hands, pleased that he might thus "unload him," I think the expression was. In any event Herman and I now share a house in the country, a Tudor, as that permits a high-ceilinged area which may thus accommodate Herman's paraphernalia. Igor handles our gardening, and forestry, and also acts as a valet, secretary and general *factotum* for Dr. Frankenstone, whose draw and aim with a tranquilizer pistol have become honed to a sharp edge of late.

As of this writing Herman's creative efforts in a number of artistic dimensions continue unabated.

Dr. Frankenstone has purchased a new computer, but, as of this writing, he has shown no inclination to place it on the roof of his castle, or fortress, or mansion, during violent lightning storms.

It was not practical to move one of Herman's works to our new domicile. Those who visit the castle, or fortress, or mansion, of Dr. Frankenstone often stand, awed, in the great hall, viewing a gigantic mural, now complete.

Alfred

OBVIOUSLY there are varieties of skepticism.

For example, some people have been reluctant to uncritically accept the existence of wood nymphs, satyrs, and so on. Now wood nymphs are well aware of the existence of satyrs, as would you be, were you an imperiled wood nymph, at least past puberty, and satyrs have no doubt as to the existence of wood nymphs, at least past puberty, for their pursuit constitutes one of life's joys.

There are local skepticisms and global skepticisms.

For example, a lonely wood nymph may be skeptical of the existence of a satyr in a neighboring glade, or of the honorableness of his motivations, should he lurk there. But what satyr, lacking desperation, would wish to be introduced to a wood nymph's family, particularly if she was blessed with a stern, suspicious mother and several robust, muscular brothers? And he, in his turn, might be skeptical of the sanity of a wood nymph who might have so dismal an afternoon in mind.

But these are local skepticisms.

Other examples of local skepticisms might be a skepticism regarding an alleged number of quarks in an apple, the true motivations of a homicidal barracuda, the contents of a jam jar, the date of Sherlock Holmes' birth, and so on. There are reasonably clear ways of looking into such things, and addressing such issues.

Most skepticisms are local

On the other hand, some skepticisms are, as it is said, global.

And surely these are the interesting skepticisms, if only because they tend to annoy philosophers.

Philosophers are strange people.

There is no doubt about that.

They are easily annoyed, or, at least, intrigued, by problems which most folks do not know exist, and, if informed, would just as soon did not exist.

One is global skepticism.

I would not be going into this, if it were not for Alfred.

First, in order to be somewhat more clear on what is going on here, let us distinguish between what we might call classical skepticisms and Cartesian skepticisms.

Briefly, classical skepticism is a salvation philosophy, a recommendation as to how to live, primarily by forgetting about a lot of stuff not worth worrying about in the first place.

To be sure, as these fellows are philosophers they cannot simply go about forgetting, as you or I, or most folks, might. They have to work hard at it. As it might be put, there are five modes, or such, involved: Discrepancy, relativity, regress, assumption and circularity. We won't go into much detail here because I am trying to get to Alfred. Discrepancy recognizes that not everyone agrees with everyone else; people, cultures, and such, differ; and relativity notes that many folks, cultures, and such, see things relative to their own situations, interests, natures, backgrounds, and such. The most interesting modes, regress, assumption, and circularity, tend to suggest that you are going to be stuck with discrepancy and relativity. How are you going to *prove* something—*for sure*, of course, as these guys are serious.

The best way to go about piling up absolute knowledge, and what other kind could there be, is to get your mind on self-evident propositions, and then hasten on to further truths via the avenues of logic. Now discrepancy and relativity suggest that obviously self-evident propositions may be in short supply. If a proposition is not obviously self-evident then perhaps we could derive it from another which is, and if, predictably, that one is not obviously self-evident either, then one can take another shot at things, and so on. And here we have regress. Which in theory could be an infinite regress, but one with no end in sight is probably about as good. One can, of course, simply assume something, but that is not to prove it, and represents not an argument but an abandonment of argument. And, indeed, this exposes one to the philosophical uppercut of being denounced as a dogmatist, which is bad. The skeptics tend to be dogmatic about these things. That approach, move, or dodge, of course, is assumption. But what if folks, most folks, should agree that something is self-evident? Might they not be mistaken? Might it not only seem to be self-evident, and simply be, treacherously, fraudulently, deplorably, merely psychologically coercive? But, even if we sweep this under the philosophical rug, circularity looms. Most simply, there must be a criterion for truth, say, for validity or for veridical perception. And is the criterion right? For example, an argument is valid if and only if it is a legitimate substitution instance of a valid argument form, but where do we get valid argument forms from? We get them from arguments that seem to us valid. Similarly, if we take forcefulness, or nonrepudiability, or such, as a criterion for veridical perception, where do we get that from, from forcible impressions, from things which seem to us ungetoverable, nonrepudiable, and so on.

The supposed upshot of all this is to undercut the dogmatic pretense to absolute knowledge, particularly inferences from experience to transempirical claims.. Indeed, there are even logical problems with such inferences. Now things are, of course, much more complicated than this, truly, given conflicts of appearances, the fragilities of inductive reasoning, the various strategies of counterpoise, and so on, but we are trying to move toward Alfred.

We might note, in passing, however, before we leave these views, that the skeptic is not claiming to know one cannot know anything, which would be paradoxical, at the least, but rather is suggesting that we refrain from dogmatism. A suggestion is neither true nor false. The idea seems to be that one should not waste one's time on insoluble problems, but, realizing they are insoluble, abandon them and get on with life. One tends to make do with one's local values and beliefs, but one sees them now, of course, in a new light.

Perhaps the most interesting form of global skepticism, and that in the context of which I first met Alfred, is "Cartesian skepticism." This term is derived, of course, from the name of the substantially 17th Century French philosopher René Descartes, who had to cope with one of the most brilliant, remarkable, and peculiar minds in the Western tradition, his own. Descartes was a marvelous mathematician, to which every x-axis and y-axis will attest, and he was also, in his day, a leading physicist, perhaps most famous for his theories of the plenum (no empty space) and vortices (rather like lusty, turbulent, on-the-move gravity wells, and such). His physics was eclipsed by that of Isaac "Mysterious-Action-at-a-Distance" Newton but it does have its affinities, remote or otherwise, to that of Albert "No-Mysterious-Action-at-a-Distance" Einstein. There seems to be little doubt, except possibly on the part of Descartes, that Descartes was a much better mathematician and physicist than he was a philosopher, at least given what we know of his philosophy. He seems to have bequeathed to philosophy some of her most shocking *non sequiturs* and circularities. I, personally, effect nothing critical on this score, being personally fond of *non sequiturs* and circularities, without which it seems that philosophy must remain forever mired in the ruts of prosaic ratiocination. Too, one cannot expect everything of everyone. One does not object should it turn out that Sir Isaac Newton was not skilled at checkers, or that Einstein might have played a mediocre third base. Now, whereas it seems clear that Descartes was not a very good philosopher, it is also quite clear that he was a great philosopher. To be a great philosopher, you see, does not necessitate being a good philosopher. These are diverse properties, but both are valuable to the discipline. Although this is controversial, as is just about everything else in philosophy, Descartes awakened philosophy, turned her around, and gave her new directions. After Descartes philosophy was different. He shut the door on the middle ages and opened that to a modern world, one attentive to mathematics, physics, observation, experiment, open-mindedness, and untrammeled thought, maybe not good thought, but untrammeled thought. As Galileo was to physics Descartes was to philosophy, though Descartes had the common sense to keep a low profile on certain sensitive matters. I will mention only three philosophical triumphs, or catastrophes, amongst several, for which philosophy is primarily indebted to Descartes, the mind/body problem, introspective foundationalism, and methodological skepticism. The mind/body problem is how the mind, presumably not in space, thus without physical location, and not extended, and without mass, solidity, weight, and such, can interact with an extended substance in space, matter, with mass, solidity, and weight, and such, and, indeed, vice versa, how can matter interact with the mind, which, presumably not in space, would seem thereby to be somewhat out of reach. Luckily for us Descartes, as a substance whose essence was thought, managed to solve this problem for us, in virtue of nonexistent animal spirits congregating in an obscure, unpaired gland. That leaves, of course, introspective foundationalism and methodological skepticism. Introspective foundationalism suggests that all we can initially be absolutely sure of are aspects of our own first-person experience, for example, appearances, or, better, seemings and looks, and logical truths. Note that one is starting here, so to speak, on the inside. The problem then is how from the inside one can obtain knowledge of the outside. Now methodological skepticism is going to be what is of most interest to us here, for, you see, this will lead us to Alfred.

At one point in his life, apparently having some time on his hands, Descartes decided to embark on a fascinating philosophical journey, the outcome of which was to establish what he knew *for sure*. Both classical skeptics and Cartesian skeptics are interested primarily in knowledge *for sure*. Knowledge *maybe* was just not good enough. The following few days were surely amongst the most momentous in the history of philosophy. The first thing he wanted to do was to make sure he existed. I do not know if he explained this project to his landlady. Here is where the famous *cogito, ergo sum*—I think, therefore I am—comes in. He wanted to doubt everything possible, to pare away what he did not know, and thus come eventually to an irreducible nodule of the indubitable. Since he was doubting, he supposed there had to be a doubter, and this required thinking, and thinking required a thinker, and so on. And then he jumped to the surprising conclusion that the thinker involved must be a being whose essence was thought, and so on. Here comes the mind/body problem. The brain, one supposes, would not do the trick. How could matter think? And where in a brain might one find a thinker, and so on. And then he was off and running with a series of desperate, peculiar, interestingly unconvincing arguments which, even to this day, confuse, startle, and dismay undergraduates, even those whose majors are media studies. And Descartes would not rest, of course, until he had, at least to his own satisfaction, confidently guaranteed, replaced, and restored everything, to the last jot and tittle, which he had resolved to doubt in the first place. After all, what's the point of going away, if you can't come home? That's where you want to be. Things are different, of course. Now you are entitled to live there.

We are nearly to Alfred, of course.

Thank you for your patience.

Descartes asked himself, in the course of undertaking his campaign of relentless methodological doubt, not letting his landlady in on this, whether he might not, while thinking himself awake, not being in bed, tucked under the covers. and such, actually be dreaming. After all, do we not do a number of things in our sleep, some of which are at least morally neutral, if not praiseworthy, which we think are actually occurring in waking life? Then we awaken and the last laugh is on the pursuing, slavering tyrannosaurus rex, lucklessly destined to go hungry once again. But what if we have dreams within dreams, and life itself, with all its sober reflections, pains, bills to be paid, pretzels, joys, peanut-butter sandwiches, rashes, and so on, should all be in the nature of a dream itself, not a dream as we usually think of dreams, but something along those lines? An illusion founded on a reality quite other than we suppose? How do we know such is not the case? It certainly seems to be a logical possibility, if nothing else? Perhaps most of what we take to be real, say, tables, chairs, rocks, trees, Susan, our bodies, and such, are part of the illusion? How do we know that that is not the case? Might it not be the case? If it were the case, it would solve a number of puzzles, the mind/body problem, for instance.

This is an example of methodological doubt.

The notion is that if we can't be sure, we can't know, and we can't be sure, so we don't know.

This does raise the possibility that we might awaken, so to speak, and discover the tyrannosaurus rex is not part of a dream, but a part of the real world, and is patiently waiting around for us, in the real world, like a cat at a mouse hole. Perhaps this is why some philosophers have a certain amusing eccentricity, that of seldom letting themselves stray far from their elephant guns.

A couple of other examples will make this sort of thing clear to anyone who is not determined that it will not be clear.

Neither of these examples is due to Descartes, but they are forms of "Cartesian skepticism" in a broad sense, namely, a radical and profound skepticism which seems to be, however unfamiliar and annoying, irrefutable. Every experience which you could possibly have is compatible with your inhabiting one of these two following domiciles in logical space. First, you might be the only entity in reality and all that seems to you other than yourself, your body, trees, hamburgers, hurricanes, sweet Susan, solar systems, and stars, are merely aspects of your experience. You are, so to speak, a limited, ignorant, deluded, tortured, confused god, who does not even know he is god. This is a form of what is called metaphysical solipsism. Schopenhauer suggested that this sort of thing requires not a refutation but a cure, but that is, of course, to both beg and dismiss a question, something somewhat unworthy of a philosopher, and particularly embarrassing in the case of a German philosopher, as it assumes without argument that the supposition is false, which it may well be, but what if it isn't? Another example, rather contemporary, is suppose that you are not what you seem to be, a dashing fellow thinking about Susan, and fettuccini, but a brain floating about in a vat, or bucket, or bottle, if you like, being nourished with sustaining fluids and being somehow stimulated, perhaps in virtue of controls, implants, computer programs, and such, to seem to have the exact experiences which you now seem to have. You can't escape this one by referencing the primitive level of current technology, its inability to pull off such illusions, and such, because this merely reveals your ignorance of the current secret projects along these lines underway even now in the Caucasus, or, if they are behind schedule, the advanced state of the art in such matters on Epsilon Eridani Four, amongst abducting, quadrupedal, multiple-livered, antennaed scientists trying to understand why you think Susan is pretty neat, and fettuccini digestible. Once again, this is a room in logical space? Do you live there? How do you know you don't?

But now we are ready for Alfred.

And this does go back to Descartes.

In the course of his ruminations on these matters, Descartes entertains the possibility that for all he knows he might be the victim of an evil genius, an evil deceiver or a demon, an entity out to fool him, out to trick him, out to make him think for some reason he is experiencing a real, external world when, actually, all of this is going on in his own mind only, produced there by the machinations of the demon.

Might this not be the case?

How do you know it isn't?

This is the famous Cartesian demon.

His name, as I have discovered, is Alfred.

I was grading philosophy papers one afternoon when I noticed Alfred, who is about the size of my daughter's cat, sitting on the desk to my right.

"Hello," he said.

"Hello," I said.

"You don't seem surprised to see me," he said.

"I am a philosopher," I explained.

"What are you doing?" he asked.

"I am grading philosophy papers," I said.

"How do you know?" he asked.

"I don't," I said.

"Right," he said.

"You remind me of Chelsea, my daughter's cat," I said.

"How is that?" he asked.

"You're about the same size, and you have pointed ears," I said.

"She's not around, is she?" he asked.

"I don't think so," I said.

"Good," he said, glancing about. "Do you have anything against pointed ears?" he asked.

"Not at all," I said. I was all for diversity, particularly ideological diversity, which, given hiring practices in the academic world, is scarce.

To be sure, it is well to keep a low profile on sensitive matters. One can still learn much from Descartes.

"I suppose you think I'm a demon," he said.

"I'm for diversity," I assured him. It occurred to me, an uneasy thought, that not one member of my philosophy department was a demon. It was not up to me, however, as I saw it, to bring this lacuna to the attention of local affirmative action officers.

"Your daughter's cat has pointed ears," he said. "Do you think she's a demon?"

"Only occasionally," I said, "sometimes in the early morning."

"I am not a demon," he said.

"I thought you might be the Cartesian demon," I said.

"I was actually trying to get through to Descartes," he said, "but I failed."

"I don't understand," I said.

"Don't let the pointed ears fool you," he said.

"What about you and Descartes?" I said.

"Maybe it was my 17th Century French," he muttered.

"You are the evil deceiver, the evil genius, the Cartesian demon, aren't you?"

"My 17th Century French is pretty good now," he said. "I've been working on it."

I prepared to return to my philosophy papers.

"I don't understand all this business about an evil genius, an evil deceiver, a demon, and such," he said. "It's a bum rap."

"Oh?" I said.

"I'm not a bad fellow," he said. "At least I don't think so. I may be hard to get on with sometimes, but isn't everyone? And I am certainly not an evil genius. I think of myself as a nice guy of average intelligence."

"What is your IQ?" I asked.

"About forty-six thousand," he said.

"I think that would put you well in the top five percent of the population," I said. I was thinking of various recommendation forms I had filled out for students.

"Not for my population," he said.

"I see," I said. "Then you are not unique."

"There are thousands of us," he said. "Maybe millions. At any rate I am not evil, and I am not a deceiver, at least not on purpose. And I am not a demon. Don't let the ears fool you."

"Very well," I said.

He seemed to sense my difficulty.

"My name is Alfred," he said.

"But you did have something to do with Descartes?" I pressed.

"Sure," he said. "He was a great guy, even if he liked to

stick his head in ovens. He seemed genuinely interested in the nature of reality, or so I thought, that was my mistake, and so I tried to help him out. I let him know that I had been assigned the business of concocting a world for him, giving him the illusion of a comfortable, reliable external world, one he could count on, one with laws, one in which he could feel secure, one designed to reassure him and make him happy, but he wouldn't buy it. He wouldn't settle for the truth, even though I gave it to him, pointed ears and all. His world was an illusion, but a benevolent illusion I had worked out for him, one designed in his own best interests, one in which he was supposed to contentedly, innocently, and joyfully flourish."

"You were out to do him a favor, to enlighten him?"

"Of course," said Alfred, "but he wouldn't listen. He was determined to prove that the illusion was actually a mind-independent, material, physical, out-there, external world."

"So what did you do?" I asked.

"I gave up on him," he said. "He was hopeless."

"I see," I said.

"There may have been a mental problem involved," said Alfred. "I think he was in a state of denial. I'm sure there was some sort of neurosis involved, perhaps one of an obsessive compulsive sort."

"Perhaps," I granted him. I supposed it was logically possible, however unlikely, that philosophers could be as pig-headed as anyone else. I supposed that the major difference between ordinary pig-headedness and philosophical pig-headedness, if it existed, would be that philosophical pig-headedness would at least be embedded in an impressive matrix of sophisticated adducements and inferences; it would be commonly argued for, often at length, not unoften peculiarly, and occasionally awesomely. Philosophical mistakes may be abundant, but at least they are commonly well camouflaged. Various life forms could learn much from philosophy. Philosophical survival often depends on judicious concealment. To paraphrase a famous remark, anything that can be said can be said obscurely. Obscurity is clearly the philosopher's best friend. It is rationality's best defense against detection. There is much historical evidence in favor of this hypothesis.

"Are you trying to convince me that no mind-independent, external world exists?" I asked.

"No," he said. "If I couldn't convince a guy as smart as Descartes why should I try to convince you? I am content to let you wallow in your naive dogmatism."

"Why did you come to see me?" I asked.

"I was lonely," he said. "I haven't talked to a philosopher since the 17th Century. I talked to a few accountants, and a dentist or two, but it's not the same."

"How do you produce these realities?" I asked.

"I could tell you, but you wouldn't understand," he said.

"I thought it might be a trade secret."

"No, but you need an IQ of thirty thousand or so, to do it."

"Why do you do it?" I asked.

"It's fun," he said. "It's my job. One could do worse."

"Is there one of you guys for every conscious being?" I asked.

"Sure," he said, "and believe me, the insects keep us busy."

"I have something for you to think about," I said.

"Shoot," he said.

"Are you conscious?" I asked.

"Sure," he said, warily. His pointed ears went up, alertly. I was reminded somewhat of those of my daughter's cat when her suspicions were aroused. "What's the catch?"

"Is there one of you guys for every one of you guys?" I asked.

"You just want to get back to your grading," he said.

"Not at all," I said. Surely he knew that teachers sought avidly for distractions in such matters.

"So you think that there's one of me for every one of me to give us guys a world," he said, "and then this leads to an infinite regress of me's?" he asked.

"Maybe," I said.

"No dice," he said.

"Why not?" I asked.

"I'm not a philosopher, personally," he said, "so I don't have to worry about that sort of thing. I just make up problems for you guys to worry about."

"Does that seem fair?"

"How do you know an objective morality exists?' he asked.

"Suppose," I said, "that your own world is an illusion produced unbeknownst to you by a mind-independent, physical, external, out-there-really world," I said.

"Hey," he said. "That's a possibility!"

"Thus," I said, "perhaps your own experience, including your conviction that you are producing worlds for other conscious beings, and that there is more than one of you, is itself an illusion, produced by such a world."

"Neat!" he said. "Stupid, but neat!"

I was pleased. Few philosophers, I suspected, have had an opportunity to bask in the approval of a Cartesian demon. I was, of course, in effect, leveling his own artillery against the little fellow. I felt momentarily ashamed of seizing so deplorable an opportunity to score so unworthy a point, but it is difficult at such times to resist such temptations. Philosophy is, of course, merciless. The nearest analogy which occurs to me is that of the shark frenzy.

"How do you know that that is not true?" I asked. "Maybe that out-there world is really out there."

"Preposterous," he said. "An idea that idiotic requires not a refutation, but a cure."

"If that didn't work for Schopenhauer," I said, "why should it work for you? Too, Schopenhauer thought that belief in *your* world, or something rather like it, was the idiotic belief, the one that required not a refutation but a cure."

"It's a silly idea," he said.

"But you can't refute it, can you?" I asked. "It's a genuine possibility. How do you know you aren't living in such a world, a real, physical, material, mind-independent, out-there world?"

"I suppose I don't, strictly," he grumbled.

"Right," I said.

"I'm supposed to be the troublesome one," he said, "not you guys."

"Take that for a taste of your own medicine," I said. Actually, in my own view, such medicine, however benignly administered, would be ineffective, there being, happily, no cure for philosophy.

"No fair," he said.

"How do you know there is an objective morality?" I asked.

"You're looking for trouble, buster," he said. "I could zap you a good one for that."

"Zapping," I said, "is no substitute for thought."

"It usually works pretty well," he said.

"But," said I, "how do you know that if you zapped me, I would be truly zapped? I might just seem to be zapped. It might all be a dream, or an illusion produced by a demon new to you, and perhaps not well disposed toward you, perhaps a renegade demon."

I had the momentary satisfaction of seeing something akin to confusion, perhaps even tragic fear, in the little fellow's eyes.

"Philosophy is dangerous," he said.

"Sure," I said.

"What's that?" he suddenly said.

"Chelsea," I said. "My daughter's cat." And sure enough, Chelsea had entered the office, blinking after her fourth afternoon nap, and doubtless thinking about supper.

"Take her away!" he cried.

I saw Chelsea's ears go up. Then prior to her projected attack behavior, she paused to wash for a time. She then yawned.

"Look at those teeth!" said Alfred.

"She's harmless," I assured him, "except occasionally in the morning, before breakfast."

"Not to demons," he said.

"Oh?" I said.

Some people feel that a cat's day is not complete until she has lacerated a loved one. But that is a vile canard. Chelsea seldom laid stress on her feline prerogatives, usually not more than once a week.

"Those claws!" said Alfred.

She was now licking, cleaning and honing, carefully, meticulously, the claws on her left paw, keeping one eye on Alfred. Chelsea was left pawed. This sometimes threw the defense off.

"You're not afraid of a cat," I said.

"I seem to be," said Alfred, with epistemic guardedness.

"You could zap her, couldn't you?" I said.

"Cats don't zap," he said.

"Why not?" I asked. Philosophers often have an interest in science.

"It's something about the static electricity in the fur," he said. "Cats are bad news for demons."

I seemed to remember that the ancient Egyptians had hit on this.

I speculated on the possibility that Alfred might lie within Chelsea's prey range. I supposed not, since they were about the same size. But of course the decision was not mine, but Chelsea's.

"I think it's the ears," said Alfred. "They think they have a corner on pointed ears. Or they think we're odd cats. They are territorial brutes, you know."

Chelsea had now leaped lightly, significantly, to my desk, and was approaching Alfred, crouching down, tail twitching, moving stealthily across the keyboard of my computer.

"There's nothing to be afraid of," I said to Alfred, but he had disappeared, or, at least, seemed to have done so, as I could not spot him.

This seemed to puzzle Chelsea for a moment, but as she was in her way a practical little skeptic, of the classical variety, she dismissed the question as insoluble, and lay down on the blue books I was grading. I did not have the heart to disturb her, and so I was forced to postpone returning to my grading, for some time, indeed, until suppertime, when I went downstairs, accompanied by Chelsea.

Notes Pertaining to a Panel in Salon D

DESPITE the nasty weather that morning, the last day of the convention, the sleet, the chill winds, the impending blizzard, and such, a goodly number of attendees crowded into Salon D for the current panel. Science fiction fans are predictable, of course, in the way of being unpredictable, in particular. In this respect the weird minds and bizarre vagaries of the typical science fiction fan differ considerably from the more prosaic survival apparatus of the benighted mundanes, and resemble far more closely that of astronauts, rocket scientists, mad poets, propellant chemists, and such, several of which were in the audience.

The moderator seemed a bit diffident, which is not surprising, given the topic. He had pointed out earlier, while awaiting the arrival of his fellow panelists, which is a tradition at such conventions, that it was not his suggestion, but, we gathered he, he being a game fellow, was prepared to plow forward, a metaphor not altogether out of place, given the weather outside. At least two of the panelists, however, as we learned when they arrived, did find the topic intriguing. One of them may have suggested the topic but that did not come out in the discussion.

In order to make this account intelligible to anyone likely to encounter it, we shall call the moderator "Bill," the other panelists being "Herman," "Susan," and "Algernon." It would be time consuming and possibly even unrewarding to proffer extended biographies of the panelists, but most were justifiably famous in the world of science fiction, and more than one, two, actually, Bill and Herman, were well known far beyond the specialized precincts of science fiction, to seven or eight people, most of whom were the parents or spouses of science fiction fans. Bill's charm and diplomacy, and dry wit, well qualified him to moderate such a panel. The power and apocalyptic intensity of his two hundred and six novels, three hundred and seven novelettes, and eight hundred and ninety-seven short stories was legendary in the field; Herman was a newcomer to the *genre* but was already making a name for himself in the ranks of 17th Fandom. Something about his zany passivity and zestful gloom, as well as his artful knack for brewing together in his smoking, teeming retorts a refreshing alchemy of *genres*, subtly blending science fiction, adventure, westerns, horror, crime, love stories, war stories, aviation stories, pirate stories, railroad fiction, Medieval romance, detection, children's stories, and such, into an unparalleled *potpourri* had left the critics breathless, even gasping. Where else could one go for such things, if one sought them? And who could forget modern classics, such as "The Fanged Teddy Bear Mystery of Phobos," "Orlando's Quest at Rattle Snake Gap," and "Dick and Jane Meet the Demon"? Susan's presence on the panel was more problematic. Some cynics suggested that the panel might have required gender balancing, this a veiled, unfair allusion to an interventionistic politics utterly foreign to science fiction, which to this day remains, as always, totally innocent of all political considerations; others dared to suggest that Bill's sexual proclivities might be keeping Susan in mind. I myself did not mind having Susan on the panel. If the panel went badly one could always spend it looking at Susan. Susan was quite beautiful, a consideration which in my view more than compensated for her pleasing personality, her sterling moral character, and brilliant mind. She was something of a flirt, of course. She twitched more than once at one member of the audience or another. I thought she twitched at me once, but it was actually, as it turned out, at the big fellow sitting behind me. Susan was not exactly a science fiction writer. She dabbled subtly and profoundly in fantasy, generally of the castles and horses sort, and dealing with wizards and spells, and bold quests for floksorts and ibjibs, and such. You know the sort of thing. But as the panel topic bordered on fantasy, I expected her to contribute a number of interesting, and brilliant, if irrelevant, observations. Besides a Susan always dresses up a panel. It used to be there were very few women in science fiction, as the average science fiction fan was more concerned with wires and motors, alien topography, and escape velocities, than girls. Then the masquerades and costuming became a big part of science fiction conventions, somehow, and this brought in the girls, who liked to dress up, and down, and stir up the boys, who by this time had passed puberty and had consequently rethought their entire view of life and the world. The last member of the panel was Algernon, who was not precisely a science fiction person but, as he was strange, he was not altogether out of place. Algernon was a scientist, and a paleontologist. His presence on the panel was to assure that there would be at least one panel member who would know what he was talking about. It is a tradition at science fiction conventions to attempt to have at least one person on a panel who has some acquaintance with the topic. To be sure, this often slows things down a bit but it is up to the moderator to control the discussion, and achieve a balance in such matters.

"The topic." said Bill, who, you will remember, is our moderator, "is as follows: Suppose that, say, some sixty-five million years ago a meteor impacted the Earth and rendered us extinct."

At this supposition a shiver passed through the audience.

"Then" continued Bill, "what would be different today?"

"For one thing," said Herman, "we wouldn't be having this panel!"

This witticism was well received, for some reason. The

audience recovered its aplomb, and craned forward to listen more closely. I thought the panel had gotten off to a good start. That is important in panels. I decided that my skepticism concerning the quality of Herman's work, despite its small sales, had been misplaced.

I noted that Susan was looking approvingly on Herman. It also occurred to me that my earlier negative appraisal of the quality of his work need not be withdrawn.

"Frankly," said Bill, "I think this is a stupid topic for a panel."

Several members of the audience gasped, having refused to flee the hotel at dawn in view of the weather forecast, largely to hear this panel, preferring to risk hours sitting in airports, or braving hazardous driving conditions on the turnpike, rather than miss it. The hotel, by now, was largely deserted by mundanes. But our panel was well attended.

"Why is that?" asked Algernon, our visiting paleontologist.

This question shook Bill up. Algernon, you see, not being a science fiction person, did not realize that such remarks were traditional at such panels. In order to be impressive on a panel it helps to be rude and speak loudly. How else can one show that one is superior? The utterance of vulgar expletives is also useful in attesting to probity and astuteness. There is also a theory that for something to become true it is only necessary that it be said loudly. Indeed, the more loudly it is said the truer it is. There are several theories of truth. This one is known as the Decibel Theory of Truth. It is also conjoined with a moral corollary, to the effect that whatever is said loudly is not to be questioned.

But Algernon did not know these things.

It was clear that Bill had not given much thought as to why the panel topic was stupid, and so it took him a moment to think up a reason why the panel was stupid. This is necessary when dealing with a person unaware of the Decibel Theory of Truth.

"Because," said Bill, "such things don't happen."

"On the contrary," said Algernon, "such things, in the course of geologic time, may occur frequently."

"But they never have," said Bill.

"They have occurred several times," said Algernon, and he then had the audacity to cite several examples.

"Meteors are little," said Bill.

"Most," said Algernon, "but some may be the size of continents."

"Space is big," said Bill, exhibiting an acquaintance with physics. Such an acquaintance is almost to be expected with science fiction writers.

"To be sure," said Algernon, "it's a hit or miss business."

I supposed that the chance of being impacted by a catastrophic meteor in a given year would be very small. But I suspected that the chance of being impacted by one in one of several million years might not be so small.

"Well, it hasn't happened," snorted Bill.

"Thank Og," said someone in the audience. There always seems to be at least one such person in an audience.

"Og would not let it happen," said another person. I hoped that person was a mundane, one stranded in the hotel, who had wandered in by accident. I was relieved to see that he did not have a convention badge.

"But what if we deserved it?" said his fellow, one also without a badge.

I was not at all sure that Og existed, but if he permitted such a thing to happen I did not think he would be worth his scales. But if there were no first egg, how would the world have hatched?

"One thing," said Herman, "if it had happened, we wouldn't be here having this panel."

This clever remark lightened the atmosphere, and rescued Bill. It, however, plowed few new conceptual furrows since his first witty remark, which it closely resembled. Susan smiled. My assessment of the quality of Herman's work remained unchanged.

"If we may return to the topic," said Algernon, "it is legitimate to speculate on the paths which an alternative form of evolution might have taken. Genetic principles, you see, the blind aggression of genes, so to speak, and the laws of physics and chemistry, and the diverse ways in which the environmental lattice may be negotiated, suggest the genuine possibility of developments amongst organic life which might seem to us unfamiliar or strange, but, for all that, would be likely."

"Likely?" asked Bill.

"Extremely likely," said Algernon. "Indeed, inevitable."

"That's stupid," said Bill, loudly.

"Not at all," said Algernon. He still hadn't caught on to panel etiquette.

"I think there is a short story in this, somewhere," said Susan. I thought she was right, but did not detect the relevance of the remark at that point.

"You are quite possibly right," said Algernon , "but you would be a much better judge of that than I."

Susan blushed, charmingly. I began to hate Algernon.

"Do you mean," asked Herman, suggesting no one in his right mind could mean any such thing, "that some other form of life might have developed, say, along our lines?"

"Certainly," said Algernon. "Another form of life might have developed rationality, created a language, learned to master fire, make tools, practice herding and agriculture, institute societies, invent writing, found religions, manufacture things, work out a sophisticated technology, and so on."

"Then you are claiming," said Bill, whose grasp of logic did not ascend to the same level as that of his literary talent, "that fish might have invented radios, movies, TV?"

"Not likely," said Algernon. "It is hard to light a fire under water. That would rule out most metal working, for example."

"I once wrote a story about a fish who lit fires under water," said Bill.

"Interesting," said Algernon. "How did he do it?"

"If you put a refrigerator in a story," said Bill, "you don't have to explain how it works."

"True," said Algernon.

"It sold," said Bill.

"Excellent," said Algernon.

"It would then," said Herman, "have to be some land animal."

"Presumably," said Algernon. "But it might have been amphibious."

"Then," said Bill, "it could have set fires—when it was *not* under water."

"Precisely," said Algernon. "And as you doubtless recollect, from your knowledge of general biology, we ourselves have amphibious ancestry."

"That is only a theory," came from the audience, from one of the fellows without a badge.

"But assuming it is true," said Algernon, who had not a mean bone in his rather large body, "another form of life, say, one also with amphibious ancestry, might have evolved, rather as we did."

"Are there any such life forms?" asked Bill, who sounded authentically interested at this point, and may have been, more or less.

"Several," said Algernon.

"Have you seen the art show?" asked Susan.

For those of you who might be unacquainted with the cultural anthropology of the science fiction convention I might illuminate Susan's remark. At such conventions there is often an art show.

"No," said Algernon. "They would not let me in because I was carrying a briefcase."

It might be mentioned, in passing, that science fiction art, while of high quality, and often exhibiting a draftsmanship that might have been the envy of Lislak of Fernmarsh, tends to be anachronistic, unprogressive, conservative, and primitive, at least according to *avant-garde* assessments, as it tends to be representational, that is, it usually, not always, looks like something you can recognize, for example, a sunset on Titan, an armed tiger, a leering cyborg, an alarmed android, a scantily clad robot, often in peril, a disturbed vampire, or such. Its major fault is comprehensibility. In spite of this, some of it is quite good.

"Why did you ask?" asked Algernon.

"I was thinking," said Susan, "of the cute pictures of the dogs and cats in space suits."

This was a common theme in many such exhibitions.

"An excellent point," said Algernon.

I myself had thought it irrelevant.

"It fits in beautifully with my thesis," said Algernon. "Thank you!"

But surely the remark was irrelevant. Was Algernon trying to make out with Susan, not that that was such a bad idea. I had been counting on Susan for irrelevance, without which a panel may become distressingly linear. It is enough for the Susans of the world to be beautiful. That is their job. Relevance is not. Too, relevance is often distractive. It has ruined many a panel. A good moderator must keep it under control.

"I don't get it," said Bill, who clearly didn't. Nor did I, *at the time.*

"My thesis," said Algernon, "obviously implicit in my remarks this wintry morning, and one I have incidentally developed over several years in several book-length studies unlikely to be published, is, metaphorically, that we need not be where we are now, say, in a warm hotel, in a comfortable, well-lit room, sheltered from a storm outside, engaged in intellectual discourse. We might not have evolved as successfully as we have. Indeed, we might have become extinct. And another species might be rather in our current situation, and conversing on similar matters."

"Such as furry vermin?" asked Bill.

"Precisely," said Algernon, "as our lovely colleague has brought to our attention, with her timely allusion to speculative art."

Algernon was not really a science fiction person, or he would have used the approved acronym, SA. It is by such things that one can tell the true fan from the outsider, or pretender. The older term, of course, was Science Art, sometimes spoken of as SA, but SA now, of course, stands for Speculative Art, except when it doesn't, and stands for Science Art.

So it turned out that Susan's remark was not only not irrelevant, but was brilliantly relevant, and was merely several hops, skips and jumps ahead of the game. I was somewhat disappointed, but I took this in stride. One must put up with such things in women who are both brilliant and beautiful As spontaneous-order theorists and conservatives never tire of reminding us, trade-offs are always involved.

Incidentally, when Algernon, in his ignorant innocence, had naively used the deplorable term 'lovely colleague' to describe Susan, four female members of the audience had appeared offended, and two outraged. None of them, however, as least as far as I could tell, was in danger of being insulted personally in so wanton and grievous a fashion. Susan, on the other hand, seemed quite pleased. I report this without comment, as it is politically sensitive.

"Stupid business," said Bill, "dogs and cats in space suits!"

"Certainly permissible in SA," said Herman, who was an artistic pluralist.

"Why not frogs and toads?" snorted Bill.

Bill had a much-envied reputation for being a master of hard-core science fiction, of which there are today regrettably so few, not the soft, easy, implausible stuff, but the serious, respectable, tough stuff, relished even by strange radio astronomers and unusual astrophysicists, of which there were several in the audience, the sober, down-to-earth, nuts-and-bolts stuff, bam rays, zurk machines, nik cylinders, kam tubes, zibit devices, and such.

"There were some of those, too," said Susan.

"Next," said Bill, "they will have those little, furry bipedalian things in space suits!"

A course of merriment at this outlandish suggestion coursed through the audience. I myself struggled to restrain an involuntary snigger.

He was referring, of course, to mooks.

"I stepped on one the other day," said Bill.

"They're nuisances, to be sure," said Herman. 'In my neighborhood they keep getting into garbage pails."

Susan shuddered. I was pleased to see this attestation of femininity. They are different from us, you know. And that may not be all bad.

If I remember I will strike that last line out before submitting this piece to an editor, as such lapses often prelude publication.

"Horrid little creatures," said one of the ladies in the audience, one with a badge.

"I do not know why Og made them," said another lady, one without a badge.

"He must have had a reason," said another.

"Who can fathom the wisdom of Og?" said another.

"Perhaps they are a punishment for our sins," suggested another.

"That makes sense," agreed another.

"No," said another, "Og is good. He would never do such a thing. It would be morally disproportionate to our iniquity, simply incommensurate with our faults, as deserving of severe chastisement as they may be, just too unthinkably cruel."

That lady, I took it, was a liberal.

"They are awfully smelly," said a woman.

"Some people keep them as pets," said another.

"Disgusting," said another.

"But note," said Algernon, excitedly, "the tiny, despicable mooks, for I assume you refer to them, so universally and justifiably abhorred, have an upright carriage, prehensile appendages, binocular vision, and clustering habits."

"So?" asked Bill.

"At one time," said Algernon, "our own remote ancestors had not come so far."

"Do not forget they are mammals," said Herman. This was a good point. There was not much to be expected of mammals. It would be a strange evolution indeed which might consider making use of such an improbable material.

"But what," asked Algernon, "if the mooks, or, technically, Verminius Olfactoriensis, were not handicapped by tiny brains?"

"They are, of course," said Bill.

"At one time," said Algernon, "the brains of our ancestors were not more than thrice the size of those of the present-day mook."

"Incredible!" breathed an astrophysicist in the audience.

This information had lain outside his domain of expertise.

"They still smell," said a lady.

"They can't talk," said Herman.

"Not as we can talk, of course," said Algernon, "but suppose they could modulate those strange sequences of sounds which they utter, particularly when shot or poisoned."

"I see," said Susan.

"I knew you would," said Algernon.

Susan blushed charmingly, from her cute little upturned snout to the tip of her fetching tail.

I saw that Algernon had soared, were it possible, even higher in her coveted but in my view too easily bestowed regard than hitherto.

I did not begrudge him his victory, particularly since she had twitched earlier not at me, but at the fellow behind me. I did hear a grunt of dissatisfaction from somewhere behind me, but could not locate its source of origin with precision.

"This is testable, in its way, in theory," said Algernon, "if one could devolve ourselves and the mooks to our universally acknowledged common ancestry, and begin again. One would need to restore a pristine environmental lattice, of course, mobile continental arrangements with attendant, shifting climates, competitive species, evolutionary arms races, and so on, and see which species managed to punctuate which equilibrium first."

"You are suggesting," said Bill, "that mooks might have eventually evolved intelligence?"

"It is almost a certainty," said Algernon. "And then it

might have been them, and not us, who would be sitting here, warm and comfortable, and discussing these matters."

"Radio, movies, TV?" said Herman.

"Probably," said Algernon. "One thing leads to another."

"That's stupid," said Bill.

"I don't think so," said Algernon.

"But why haven't they then?" asked Herman.

"I'm not sure," said Algernon. "It might be that we got here first, and that the mooks had it too easy, and did not have to face enough challenges, and so on. For example, many people, as you know, do not fasten down the lids on their garbage pails."

"It seems that our time is up," said Bill. "I am sorry but there won't be time for questions or contributions from the audience."

This announcement was met with a groan of dismay, for it seemed that several members of the audience, both with badges and without badges, would have appreciated an opportunity to participate in the discussion.

But Bill was right, for six minutes ago a convention volunteer had stood in the back of the room undetected by most of the rapt audience and desperately, discretely, waved the five-minutes-to-go sign.

Bill then thanked the panelists and the audience, and turned to Susan, but she had already taken her leave with Algernon.

Susans dress up a panel, and she had one of the sexiest tails I had ever seen, outside of the movies.

The discussion was continued vigorously by many, outside, in the hall.

I looked out the large window in the hall, out onto the street outside. I almost felt sorry for anything that might be outside in such weather, even mooks.

Transfiguration

IT is odd, how Henry disappeared from the basement. He had not been chained there, or anything, of course, and so, one supposes, except for the one anomaly, that he might have climbed the stairs, pulling himself up, stair by stair, by the hands, and, unnoticed, somehow, between lunch and supper, it is supposed, made his way outdoors. Yet it was hard to think of him outdoors, at that time of day, he so pale and infantile, and legless, born that way, so simple, too, or so we thought. It was hard to think of him up there, beyond the kitchen, out in the yard, and it not even night, when father took him out sometimes, carrying him in his arms, putting him down, letting him play there, in the garden, on his rope, not so much to hold him, really, as to help father know where he was, in the darkness, from the tugs on the rope. We kept the porch light off when Henry played outdoors at night. Very few people knew that he still lived with us. They had supposed he had died, or maybe was still in the institution. But Henry had not died. In his way he was quite tenacious of life, clinging to the little of it he had been given. There was no blood on the stairs, incidentally. He hadn't been there long, really. Only a few days. That was something the neighbors did not know. He had yowled, and yowled, it seems, day in and day out, in that eruptive, squealing, hissing way of his, when he was young, before he became quiet, later, and this must have made it difficult for many of the guests there, except for those who joined him, seeming to understand him, in a way we couldn't, those in the other guest rooms. We were notified by the institution that Henry could not remain there unless special arrangements were made for him, of a surgical nature. We did not care for that, what they wanted permission to do. Too, we were afraid, even in the brief time that Henry was there, that they had not been kind to him, from the needle marks on his arms, the swellings, the bruises. They swore they had not touched him. Father did not believe them, and they knew that, but they didn't really care, as long as the reports were filled out properly, and were signed in the right way, in the right places, by the right doctors, and such. So it was all right to hurt Henry, as they had to do it, and, anyway, he had not been hurt. They would not let us have Henry back, until father signed a paper.

We still tried to be kind to Henry in those days, when we thought it mattered, or it was what we were supposed to do, being kind, and such, but later there did not seem much point to going on in that way, not that we were ever cruel, really, especially not father. But what is the point of being kind to someone if they do not know you are being kind to them, it not making any difference to them, and no one else knows about it, so they don't know how nice you are? I think we stopped caring about Henry, worrying about Henry, that is, all except father, as the years went by, and especially after he had begun to think, not that he could really think, you understand, but he would sit in the basement, on the floor, and seem to go back into himself like walking back into a tunnel, so we thought maybe he was thinking, maybe even wondering who he was, and about us, and the world, and the basement, and how it all came to be, that there was a basement and such. But this is guessing on my part, of course.

I have wondered if the surgery might have made a difference. Henry was very young at that time, maybe seven or eight. Many years have gone by now. Henry, before he left, would have been forty, or still seven or eight, depending on how you look at it. Certainly the rest of us are all older now. But he didn't yowl in the basement. He seemed happy there. And so the surgery, we supposed, would not have had much point to it.

Henry was very young then, only seven or eight, and he wanted back to the basement. So we brought him back, late at night, when the neighbors would be in bed, and father carried him below. Henry made his little noises, his contented-child noises, and we knew that we had done the right thing. Too, it was expensive to keep him in the institution, and no one knew, or very few knew, he was still in the house, so there wasn't much wrong with keeping him there. You don't think so, do you? Sometimes people would look at us in a way we did not like, but they never spoke of Henry. Clearly they were afraid of him. We grew more afraid, too, as he grew older. We did not let anyone except the family into the basement.

We kept Henry there, in the basement. Only the family, and a doctor, knew he was there.

He seemed content with that habitat, the darkness, in particular, for he seemed to have some sense of light, or some sense of simple radiation, through the skin perhaps, which he did not care for, and the damp, and the small things that might move in the darkness. We think he may have eaten some of them. He was born without eyes, and retarded. His skin was pulpy, and rather slick, moist, in fact. He liked the basement, and would insist on remaining there. It was not that we minded. Henry was not pleasant to look at, with the large head, hairless, the smoothness where one thought his eyes should be. There were small holes on the side of his head, and he certainly seemed to be able to hear, or feel vibrations, or sense, in some respects. You must understand that it wasn't cruelty on the family's part that he was kept in the basement. It was Henry's choice, as much as ours, maybe more so, though it was convenient that he was kept out of sight. You can't blame us, can you? What would you have done? Pretty much the same, I would suppose. A neighbor had once seen him on the sofa, a friend of my mother's, when she was still alive, in the parlor, lying there, not easy to make out at first, and had screamed, and run away. So Henry stayed in the basement. Perhaps we had hoped he might die sooner there, except father, but that is not the sort of hope that one talks much about, not the sort of hope that one confesses before the candles, when one puts the coin in the slot, lights the candle, and kneels there, praying there, before the statue, that someone else's will be done, when you really want your will to be done, and hope that someone else will notice, someone important, and do that, because you only asked that the other's will be done. Surely that should count for something, one's selflessness, and such. Else what would be the point of it?

So why did Henry continue to live, for so many years? To be sure, we never saw him die. It was only that one day he was not there in the basement any longer. He was gone. No one saw him leave. I think he may be somewhere, not really dead. Or maybe dead, but somewhere else.

There is the anomaly, you see.

And there was no blood on the stairs.

Father tried to teach Henry, and Henry would listen carefully, or seem to, but nothing much came of it. Henry could hear, we were sure, but he could not make human noises, and, of course, he could not see. Father would put a little water into his hand, and say "Water," or touch his arm in a certain way, or tap the palm of his hand in a certain way, and the same with other objects, bread, straw, the rope and such. But Henry would not repeat any of this, nor, as far as we could tell, understand any of it. Father would leave him then, and go to his room and sometimes cry, and Henry would remain sitting there, on the floor of the basement.

We know, or suppose, that rocks cannot think. They don't have a central nervous system, for example. On the other hand, if a rock could think, I am not sure we would understand its thinking. Surely it would have to be very different from ours. What sense would it make of the universe? Would it have a sense of its place in the meaning of things, or would it be a self-contained universe, like that of one's own sensations, one's own room, one's own basement, so to speak, a fixed, heavy, stable, contented universe. Plants have obviously some irritability, but, too, one supposes they cannot think, or, if they could, it seems unlikely we could understand it. It would be very different from our thinking, discursive, divisional, naming, numbering, dividing and conquering with semantic weapons. What are the thoughts of a blade of grass, of a tree? There is nothing there we would recognize as thought, I would suppose, but, doubtless, there is something there. And we would not understand it, or I would suppose not. Maybe it would be like hearing a color or seeing a sound. Things get more complicated, as one inches up the phylogenetic scale. That's the scale where we put ourselves at the top, which, one supposes, is each species' privilege, ours as well as any other's. An amoeba, for example, will not ingest its own pseudopodium though the pseudopodium is organic, but will draw back from contact with it. Is this thought, or some sense of self, or physical or chemical disaffinities, like the repulsion of like poles? Can coelenterates think? One suspects they can feel. Perhaps the grasshopper is aware that the small boy has twisted its legs from its body. Does it object? Rats can think. They have the rudiments of a tradition, warning young rats away from remembered poisons. Mice can learn. That has been shown. We have respect for primates, or some of them, chimpanzees, for example, and dolphins puzzle us, and make us uneasy. Certainly we can think, and we can know this from the inside, from within the walls of the basement, so to speak. Are there other basements? Are there other ways to think? Are we actually at the top of the phylogenetic scale, on the summit of which we have complacently enthroned ourselves? Does the ladder tower above us, with rungs we cannot see? Are there other scales, other ladders? I ask these questions because, of late, I have thought more and more about Henry, and the anomaly.

The basement is not a pleasant place, at least for us, though some life forms might find it congenial. Henry did, as far as we can tell. The basement is a damp place. It is dark. It has a dirt floor, and dirt walls. The house is old. We never finished the basement. One supposes it has its own life forms, tiny things, trivial, not important.

When Henry grew older, he used to sit for long hours, not moving, maybe like the rock, the tree, things like that. He was retarded. He was not simply ignorant; he was stupid.

I am not even sure Henry was human. Maybe he was more like those bodies, kept alive on machines.

I think he liked father. Sometimes he would reach out with his pudgy fingers, to touch him, it seemed tenderly.

We know the universe exists for us, and that something has made it for us, and that we are the best thing, and the highest thing, in the universe, except maybe for the maker of it, who is like us, very much like us, and things it made, too, like us, very much like us. That is comforting, to know that all of this, these galaxies and universes, and mysteries, are all for us. Otherwise they would be very scary.

The world, you see, is like a watch, and the parts fit together. And if it is like a watch, then there must be a watchmaker. It is very simple. And very clear. How the parts go together, or mostly. But I have wondered sometime if the world is really so much like a watch. Maybe it is like something else, like a plant, or a spore, or a fungus, or an egg.

Father died five years ago.

In the last year, when father was very ill, he would come into the basement to sit with Henry. He did not try to teach Henry any longer. Henry could not learn. Or we supposed not. Once, in the last days, a few days before the end, Henry put out again his pudgy fingers and touched father, so tenderly, or seemingly so. Oddly, now, it seemed that it was he who was pitying father, and not the other way around. It seemed, oddly, as though he were sad, and were trying to comfort father. I do not think that he could have known father was ill, or I suppose not. How could he have known? Perhaps, instead, after all these long years, he sensed how much pain he had caused father, and the rest of us, how much torment, how much grief, and inconvenience, but I do not think Henry could have understood any of that. He felt for my father's hand, and pressed one finger into it, and described in my father's palm a small, turning, crawling line. My father told us about this, but, at the time, he did not make anything out of it. It made no sense. Still, it was almost, my father told us, at that time, as if Henry were trying to tell him something, or teach him something. Much as my father, years earlier, had tried to teach him, and by such similar, primitive methods. But father, of course, at that time, could no more understand what Henry meant, if he meant anything, than Henry could fathom the simple signals and devices of his own earlier, futile tutelage.

In the last night, before he died, my father was delirious, his consciousness perhaps disordered by some of the very drugs given to him to alleviate his pain. Then he seemed to have a moment of clarity, and half rose from bed. But the clarity was illusory, for he cried out, laughing, "We are the cattle of the worm god! That is our meaning! That is why we have been placed on earth, to feed his children!"

We tried to quiet him, and he lay back.

"Are you all right?" we begged.

"I am content," he said. "It is good to have lived. Love life. It is beautiful."

He died shortly thereafter.

Henry is gone now. I think we would have seen him if he had crawled through the kitchen. He must have done so, but I do not believe it. It is not simply because there was no blood on the steps.

It is rather because of the anomaly.

In the wall of the basement there was an opening, a round hole, about eighteen inches in diameter, leading into a long, dark, damp tunnel. The walls of the tunnel were slick, as though coated with a whitish mucous. The whole had not been there a few hours earlier, when I had taken his pans to the basement. I touched Henry to tell him the food and water were there, but he only looked up, lifting his placid, eyeless face to me. It seemed radiant. He smiled. That was an hour or so before his absence was noted.

I do not think anything human made that hole.

I wonder, sometime, if Henry did not have some sort of understanding, perhaps one very different from ours. And that something understood him, as well. Perhaps something very different from us cared for him, and loved him, in ways we could not understand. Perhaps it gathered Henry onto itself, perhaps the only one of our kind so elevated, or blessed.

When I had the courage I took a flashlight and crawled into the tunnel. It was several yards long, and, ascending, opened into the garden where the young Henry, on the rope held by my father, had played.

It was then night, and I looked up from the hole, at the stars.

Of Dreams and Butterflies

IT is natural to distinguish between reality and illusion. The usual way this is done, given the fact that illusions, dreams, and such, can occasionally possess great force and vivacity, so to speak, to borrow two expressions from the troublesome 18th century Scottish philosopher David Hume, who looked into these matters, and was good at backgammon, is basically in terms of a sort of epistemic authoritarianism possessed by reality, a tendency to cross borders and trespass, whether we like it or not, an experiential stubbornness and intrusiveness, an experiential invasiveness and violence, so to speak, which insolently imposes itself upon us, one over which we have no control—and coherence. In short, we can't do much about reality. I can't build a brick wall by thinking about it, but I could be injured if I walk into one. Reality seems to be spontaneous, so to speak, and simply there, to be dealt with. I can think about a peanut-butter sandwich but the peanut-butter jar remains in the pantry. To be sure, there are some thoughts we can't help either, and which simply show up, which impose themselves on us, such as Susan in her slip, or less. But clearly there is a serious difference between thinking about Susan, and Susan, or, at least, we commonly suppose so. So, to summarize this point, we usually distinguish between reality and illusion in virtue of two criteria: involuntariness and lawfulness; reality happens to us; we cannot control it; and, secondly, reality is coherent; it fits together; we don't expect strawberry jam from the cold-water faucet, and, if we get it, we grow suspicious. Erasers which talk to us cast doubt on their own credibility. Reality, you see, stands on its own two feet, and keeps its balance. Illusions on the other hand, whereas they may occasionally share a certain spontaneity or "thereness" with reality, tend to be far less stable, far less coherent. They come and go in a way that trees, as far as we know, don't. An obvious example is the dream, which fails to cohere with waking life, often luckily.

There is a story about a Chinese philosopher, perhaps you have heard it, who allegedly dreamed for three consecutive nights that he was a butterfly and awakened on the third morning wondering if he were a man dreaming he was a butterfly or if he were a butterfly dreaming he was a man. This is much like the story of the butterfly who allegedly dreamed for three consecutive nights that he was a man and awakened on the third morning wondering if he were a butterfly dreaming he was a man or a man dreaming he was a butterfly.

Without attempting to resolve this issue as to who was what, or which was which, which task we willingly consign to interested zoologists, please note the lesson implicit in these two illuminating, if eccentric, anecdotes.

If illusions were indistinguishable from what we normally take as reality, with respect to stability, givenness, coherence, and such, then we would have, for all practical purposes, as far as we could tell, two realities, perhaps quite different from one another. Why should we not, logically, partake of two lives, in two worlds, entering each as we awaken from the other? Presumably we would have no sense of which, if either, or both, were real.

I mention these matters in order to contextualize, however briefly, and inadequately, a story told to me in the course of a long walk I once took in the company of a friend of mine, who is a practicing clinical psychologist. It deals with one of his cases, one which, I gather, he wished to share with someone, but one which he felt it would be injudicious to introduce into the professional literature. I think the reason for that will be shortly evident. In any event, I withhold his name, first, in the interests of privacy, and, secondly, in virtue of nature of the case itself, in which it seems, rather obviously, an anomaly is involved. He has, however, I hasten to mention, authorized this account. Had he not done so I would have been reluctant to bring it to the attention of the public. You will shortly see why.

The case dealt with what appeared to be either a hoax or an unusually extreme mental aberration. There was no question of institutionalizing the individual in question, whom we shall call Paul, because he appeared to be, other than for his supposed aberration, in no way dissociated from reality. He functioned effectively and pleasantly in his work and personal relationships. Indeed, in most respects it seems he would have been regarded as a congenial, moral, productive, and healthy human being. It was one of those rare cases in which either there was nothing whatsoever the matter with him, or something very much the matter with him, categorically and devastatingly so.

Initially my friend, after his first dealings with Paul, which were in all respects routine and reassuring, was convinced that Paul was in little, if any, need of counseling, but, of course, there remained an interest in why he had sought counseling in the first place, which seemed to require some explanation, and suggested that it might be worth while scheduling an additional appointment or two. Paul did not impress my friend as the sort of fellow whose interests in counseling were likely to be either superficial or academic. Presumably there was something involved here which was not altogether obvious. Paul's difficulties, if they may be so termed, as it turned out, when he at last felt sufficiently at ease with my friend to speak more freely, had to do with a series of unusually vivid dreams. This, in itself, would be nothing unusual, but the reports on these dreams were unusually graphic, and suggested the complexity, richness, and detail of a carefully prepared, meticulous fabrication. This was not the way that dreams were remembered. At one point, my friend was prepared, with disgust, to dismiss Paul as the conscious perpetrator of some sort of pointless and inexplicable joke, or hoax, but, as it gradually became clear, or at least seemed to, that Paul was desperately, helplessly, even tragically, serious about these peculiar episodes, my friend began to suspect that he was dealing with something far more serious than a prank or fabrication, that his patient was profoundly and seriously disturbed.

Paul, you see, seemed to believe in these dreams.

At the risk of inviting not only skepticism but derision on the part of the reader, I will briefly, and bluntly, state the nature of Paul's delusion, as it was explained to me by my friend.

Paul, it seems, believed himself to be living two lives, one he shared with us, in our time and place, and one he did not share with us, though perhaps he shared it with others, in another time and place.

This was the nature of his delusion.

When he, fearing and fighting sleep as he might, eventually fell asleep, it seemed he awakened, as nearly as we can tell, as a simple peasant, a young man of his own age, in 14th century France. When he fell asleep at the end of a long day of toil in that life, he would awaken in his bed, in the life with which we are familiar, in his apartment in Manhattan.

Putting aside the more obvious possibilities of pointless fabrication and such, this delusion has its fascinations. It is easy to see, given certain suppositions, research, and such, how he might have somehow, subconsciously, generated these dreams. An analogy would be a fixed series of self-induced hallucinations, but that would be only an analogy, as what we are dealing with here is a series of dreams. One does not commonly think of hallucinating in one's dreams, certainly not in any familiar sense of hallucination. My friend's major interest here, aside from the awesome detail and clarity of these dreams, was what end these dreams might possibly serve in Paul's psychic life. Why, so to speak, was he doing this? It did not seem they were wish fulfillments, at least in any familiar or comprehensible sense of such things. He found these dreams unwanted, and disturbing. He was not, in this other life, the dream life, an aristocrat, a holder of power, a brave knight, an esteemed burgher, a rich merchant, or such. It seems he was only an ignorant, indeed, illiterate, peasant, confined, it seemed, to a life of toil, filth, poverty, misery, superstition, and ignorance.

Putting aside for the moment somewhat facile, if plausible, attempts to explain these dreams, let us briefly consider certain aspects of what we might be attempting to explain.

As you might suppose, my friend was much impressed with the clarity and detail of the dreams. Paul had, it seemed, in this other life, the delusory dream life, a family, a mother and father, and brothers and sisters, some of whom had died in infancy or childhood. He had had certain diseases, accurately described, which he had survived, and which many others had not. He knew the districts in his area, the animals, domestic and wild, the crops, their times of planting, local coins, the taxes, places to fish, local roads, places where he occasionally stole apples with other young men, and had once been caught and flogged, and so on. He was familiar with feast days, and festivals, local clergy, rituals, processions, customs, and so on. Too, of course, he was familiar, most obviously, with the dialect in his area, which it seemed he spoke natively, having been apparently born and raised in the local parish, beyond the precincts of which he had seldom ventured.

One of the oddities here was that my friend, after independent research, of a rather scrupulous nature, could find nothing in Paul's background to explain these dreams. He had never, as far as my friend could discern, had an interest in this historical period, nor had he ever, as least as far as my friend could determine, researched the area or time. How then would he have obtained this information, much of which seemed genuine, and some of which could be independently established.

Before we address these issues, I will state one last anomaly.

I have mentioned the dialect spoken by the French lad. My friend had Paul describe one of his dreams in that tongue, and this, with Paul's permission, he recorded, which recording he later submitted to linguists and historians at a well-known local university. The language appeared to be related to modern French, but, if at all, remotely. The authorities expressed skepticism as to the authenticity of the dialect, which pleased my friend. That was precisely what he wished to hear. This pleasure, however, was short-lived, for this negative appraisal, shortly thereafter, upon further scrutiny, by yet further authorities, was not only reversed, but resulted in demands for the original manuscript from which it had doubtless been taken. Not only was this one of the few extant examples of the dialect in question but, if authentic, it was the only one in existence, it seemed, in which a common fellow, a laborer of the time, had, presumably by dictation to a cleric or scholar, recounted the activities of his day. This sort of thing, of course, in itself, eventually aroused suspicion. That was not the sort of thing which in those days would have been done. Who would have been interested in listing the sordid details of a common, unimportant life, too, details which would have been so familiar to contemporaries as not to have been worth recording. Accordingly, the final assessment was that whereas the dialect was authentic, interestingly, amazingly, the recording itself must have been based on a fabrication, largely on the grounds of its content.

We now have some sense of what is to be explained, and some understanding of some of the troubling problematicities involved.

How then might we account for this sort of thing?

Most obviously we might suppose Paul to be some sort

of charlatan, a master showman of sorts. Whereas at the time, at least up to the end, that seemed the most likely explanation, there were yet several obvious objections to accepting it uncritically. It appeared that neither Paul nor his friends and acquaintances had the resources to manufacture such an elaborate facade of authenticity. It would have taxed the expertise and erudition of the finest period linguists and historians. Secondly, Paul, as far as we could tell, was not the sort of person who would have had the least interest in perpetrating so egregious a fraud. Too, my friend doubted that he was even morally or psychologically capable of doing so. Thirdly, rather than attempting to exploit his experiences, or draw attention to himself, he seemed most anxious to conceal the entire matter and, if possible, to rid himself of what was apparently to him a recurrent, wretched affliction.

There were, I suppose, other possibilities, but, on the whole, these appeared so remote, so unlikely, so preposterous, that their consideration was almost tantamount to their dismissal.

Illustratively, to delve into absurdities, one might speculate about time travel, or parallel worlds, coincidence, reincarnation, and such matters.

Consider the option of coincidence.

What could be more absurd than to suppose that mere coincidence could account for the data in question?

Suppose the following: You decide to spout, or write down, what are to you nonsense expressions, sheer gibberish, and so on, for an hour or so, and then you discover, several years later, that by an interesting coincidence you had unwittingly produced a complex text in an obscure, ancient language not even understood at that time by scholars. I suppose one could have such a coincidence, but does it seem likely? Too, that is only an hour's speech, or transcribing, or whatever, not hundreds of hours spread over a period of months.

Coincidence would be possible but it does not seem probable.

Similarly, reincarnation does not seem likely as an explanation here, though perhaps one might find it more plausible than coincidence.

On this hypothesis one would suppose that Paul was recalling, somehow, seriatim, and in detail, the events of an earlier life.

Putting aside dubieties appertaining to reincarnation itself, such as the role of the brain in consciousness, the nature and variabilities of a self, the "residential peculiarities" of housing a given consciousness successfully and effectively in domiciles as diverse as those of insects, elephants, sponges, fish, and giraffes, we note two difficulties which would seem to arise even within the theory of reincarnation. First, it is commonly accepted that, say, a dog will not recall its previous incarnations as, say, a herring, and that a human will not recall his previous adventures as a squirrel in 4th century Wales. In short, that incarnations are closed off from one another. On the other hand, there are individuals who claim to recall former lives, and so we will not press this point. More importantly, incarnations, whether recalled or not, are usually understood as being linear, so to speak. In this case, we would rule out reincarnation in the case of Paul because his lives seem to alternate, so to speak, and to exist, in a sense, simultaneously, a sleeping existence in one life giving rise to a waking experience in another. Whatever this might be, it is not reincarnation as reincarnation is normally understood.

Another of these unlikely conjectures would be that of time travel. Aside from initial implausibilities pertaining to time travel, of the sort made clear by a complex variety of diverse puzzles and paradoxes, we note that time travel, as usually understood, involves a device of some sort, a vehicle or machine, for effecting the temporal translations supposed to occur. One, we may suppose that no such technology, even if in some sense possible, currently exists. Two, it seems clear that Paul would not have access to such a mechanism, even if it existed. One could speculate endlessly, of course. For example, perhaps time travel does not require a mechanism but is facilitated by incantations or potions, or perhaps there are time slips, where one might lose one's footing, so to speak, and slide into the past, or future, or, if there is a mechanism, perhaps it is not ours, but has been constructed by aliens who are using Paul as a guinea pig, not wishing to risk one of their own superior sort in such an perilous endeavor, until the technology is perfected, and so on, and on, and on. But I think we can rule out time travel because, in its various manifestations or techniques, it does not seem to fit Paul's case. Normally in time travel, at least as commonly conceived, one would live normally in the new time, so to speak. For example, one would sleep in the new time, awake in the new time, conduct oneself in the new time, and so on. The sleeping/waking cycle of Paul does not seem to fit the usual understanding of time travel. Too, in a normal time travel, if one can speak so, one would be a stranger, a visitor, in the new time. One would not enter it with a place in society, a detailed awareness of customs and mores, a knowledge of the languages, an emplaced family, and so on.

Let us now consider the hypothesis of parallel worlds, though one sees little point in the geometrical analogy. If one wishes such analogies, why parallel? Why not intersecting, why not tangential, why not overlapping, porous concentricities, and so on?

Despite some speculation on the part of perhaps whimsical physicists and mathematicians who are willing, interestingly, to suppose anything whatsoever if it helps their equations balance, or seem to balance, there seems no reason to think there is more than one world, more than one universe. Where would one put it? If this is an illegitimate question, why is it an illegitimate question? Is there more than a verbal answer to that? Physics, if loosened from evidence, might degenerate into mathematical fantasy. Mathematical elegance has doubtless its own appeal and beauties, but these virtues do not entitle it to supersede evidence, to neglect experiment, to replace fact. Perhaps there are unusual dimensions, even infinite sets of such, superior to our familiar, prosaic length, width, depth, and time, but, too, perhaps there are not. One recalls natural place, the center of the universe, celestial spheres, ether, phlogiston, and other triumphs of science. But let us not dogmatically deny parallel universes. Let us rather, if interested, ask if they are intelligible, if they are likely, if they are needed, if they are good for anything. But, at this point, without additional encroachments on the speculative entitlements of mathematicians and physicists, let us return to the case of Paul. Parallel worlds seems unhelpful in this case. For example, Paul's France, so to speak, has normal dimensions. He does not find his experiences there bewilderingly incomprehensible to him, much as a cat might find differential equations hard to follow, or as a coelenterate might turn aside from the intricacies of high finance with a clear conscience. But, might there not be parallel worlds with the same, or similar, dimensions to ours? Why not? But does this help us out? It does not seem so. How would one communicate with the other dimension, how would one access it? And in sleep? So precisely? And with such diurnal and nocturnal regularities? And why, if entering this other dimension, would one not experience normal staying times, normal times of residence, so to speak?

In the light of these speculations, and others, it seems we are returned to the hypothesis of charlatanry, however implausible it might seem in Paul's case.

My friend, to whose care Paul had remanded himself, resolved to embark upon a novel therapeutic venture. To this day, despite my reassurances, and support, he blames himself, certainly mistakenly in my view, for its apparent consequences.

Paul's case, as you have perhaps surmised, bore some resemblance to what is now commonly known as the multiple personality syndrome. It had many differences, of course, and certainly was not, strictly, an instance of that syndrome. Nonetheless, because of the sense of more than one life involved, the resemblance was there.

Whereas there are variations on the multiple personality syndrome from case to case, there are occasionally, in such cases, what might be called "unilateral leakages," or, more technically, "unsymmetrical awarenesses." The notion is that one of the personalities, say, A, may be aware of the other personality, call it B, but the B personality, as we may refer to it, remains unaware of the A personality. In Paul's case, he was clearly aware of his "other life," so to speak. Had he not been, he would not have sought counseling, and so on. On the other hand, the other life, so to speak, the putatively medieval life, was completely unaware, as far as we can tell, of what we may call the contemporary life, or, more simply, the Paul life.

My friend speculated, plausibly, in my view, that a way should be found to break into the medieval life, to enlighten it, to make it self-aware of its deprivation and misery, and its meretricious, deceitful nature. This done, communication opened up between the lives, my friend hoped that Paul's medieval life would yield to the contemporary life, give up its strictures and limitations, and relievedly become one with the contemporary life, this assuaging Paul's symptoms, and hopefully returning him shortly thereafter to a productive, satisfying normality.

Paul welcomed my friend's suggestion, and, together, as they could, by means of a variety of techniques, imaginative anticipation, mental preparation, projective rehearsal, explicit resolution, frequent repetitions of intention, psychological suggestion, and others, even hypnosis, they sought to bring it to fruition.

Never hitherto had Paul attempted to communicate with the other Paul. Indeed, it was not clear that this would prove possible.

Can one, so to speak, telephone the 14th Century?

We know of it, but could it know of us?

The hope, of course, was that there was some sort of link here, and that, obviously, was Paul himself.

As nearly as we can tell, Paul was successful.

The communication, it seems, may have been effected.

Things from this point on are not altogether clear. There are discrepancies between the two police reports, despite the fact that the original report, and the second, were filed by the same officer.

It took place on Central Park West, in Manhattan.

The reporting officer heard a terrifying, long, drawn-out scream of agony. This occurred about two AM. He spun about but the sidewalks seemed clear. He then, some twenty yards away, saw a body on the sidewalk. At this point we will follow the account in the first report, that subsequently revised.

As though about the body on the sidewalk the officer sensed, if he did not literally see, at first, a crowd of unruly, strangely clad individuals swarming about the body, kicking it, spitting on it, and abusing it. He heard sounds, screams of fury and bitterness, but could not follow the language in which they were uttered. It was unfamiliar to him. It seemed then that he could see these individuals, like shadows emerging from shadows. Their eyes, he claimed, were terrible. Many held primitive implements of some sort. A young woman was shrieking and crying near the body. She was brutally pulled away, back into the deeper shadows. The officer blew his whistle, furiously, for several seconds, and then, wisely or not, charged toward the body, and the shadows about it, his night stick raised. He felt that he struck something, the feel of it in his arm and shoulder, and then something edged tore at him, and he fell backward, bleeding, and the shadows were gone, only the body remaining on the sidewalk. That is pretty much the gist of the first report. The second report does not report hearing a scream, nor anything other than finding the body on the sidewalk, no shadows, no crowds, no cries. He was, however, injured, however it may have occurred. Some long-bladed, curved instrument had apparently struck him shortly after detecting the body. It cut through his jacket and shirt, and half severed an arm. It was an unusual wound, much as might have been caused by a large, wielded blade, such as a scythe. It is supposed the wound was the result of an obscurely motivated, independent attack on the officer, perhaps by some maniac, unrelated to the finding of the body.

The body, of course, was that of Paul. It was naked, and it bore the marks of closely encircling chains. It was blackened and scarred, and seared, and it stank. If one did not know better, one might say it had been burned at the stake.

The Face in the Mirror

MIRRORS are strange things, and what one might see in them.

Perhaps you have had such experiences. One does not know how common, or uncommon, they might be. Certainly one does not talk much about them, and, I suppose, for good reason.

Have you ever been afraid to look in a mirror, for fear of what you might see?

I do not mean that you might be dissatisfied with your image, something so simple, that it was, say, unkempt, sallow, bruised, or such. I mean something quite different.

Suppose something not yourself, or certainly not recognizably yourself, was there.

Some people are afraid to look into mirrors.

Did you know that?

They do not know what they might see.

Suppose what you saw in that silvered surface, so innocent, familiar, placid and smooth, so like a window, was not you, but something quite different.

Have you had that experience?

Might it not be an ancestor, or a stranger, or something else, perhaps an animal, perhaps one unfamiliar to you, unfamiliar perhaps even to your mythologies, or might it be something more terrible, more bestial than a beast.

Or it might be something like a human, but not a human, not really, something like a human, but not a human.

Perhaps it resembles you, but you know it is not you, not really you.

But similar.

What does it want with you, if anything?

It puts its hands, or paws, on the glass, from the inside. I could show you the scratch marks. They are deep.

It is no wonder that some people are afraid to look into mirrors, especially, at night.

Fear of the dark has been selected for, doubtless. I do not think it is simply a matter of a partial impediment of vision, for an absolute darkness is seldom found in nature. There is the light of the moon, and stars. I suspect, rather, it has primarily to do with something that took place long ago, over thousands of years, with what hunted and prowled at night, things with excellent night vision. Night was a time of danger. Apes who did not fear it would surely at their hazard share the night with sinuous, stealthy, and silent things, things swift, unwelcome, and hungry. And so those to whom the night seemed disconcerting and hostile might huddle together until morning, their predilections to be rewarded, and deepened, and confirmed, in the callous lotteries of the jungle. And the gift of fire, would it not have been as much a weapon against the darkness, as a comfort in the cold? In any event, fear of the dark is common in ground apes, and we still, on the whole, respond to genetic cues honed in their way by ancient knives, knives moist, curved, and barbaric.

One supposes that fear of the dark is recognizably irrational, but there are, of course, irrationalities which have their utilities, or had them, at least at one time, and now linger in the hereditary coils, embedded for better or for worse in the fiber and sinew, the dispositions, of a species, things like the salt content of the blood, with its recollection of the fluid chemistries of ancient seas.

Dreadful surprises, of course, need not lurk only in the darkness.

The eye of the day is no stranger to horror.

It regards it with equanimity.

The experiences I have in mind do not require gloomy hours or dismal settings. Indeed the routine trappings of night might serve to mitigate the shock of such surprising occasions, facilitating and encouraging as it would interpretations in terms of fatigue, moods, and shadows. Indeed, if such experiences occurred only under conditions of poor lighting, conjoined perhaps with inattention, exhaustion or stress, it would doubtless be easier to discount them. Unfortunately, perhaps, they can occur, or intrude, under conditions which might seem to maximize the ease and acuity of observation. For example, they can occur, unexpectedly, as one glances into the mirror in a public washroom, or in the showroom of a furniture shop, in a hand mirror left lying on a dresser, and so on. Too, a polished surface may give them a habitat, or a way of appearing, or intruding, even the surface of calm, shaded water.

One is familiar, of course, with the myth of Narcissus, who, supposedly enamored of his own image in a pond, or mistaking it for a lover, one as beautiful as himself, sought to embrace it, and drowned. Doubtless the story, as commonly told, and understood, is intended to convey a warning against the advisability of too great a self-love. So it is a good story, one supposes. On the other hand it has occurred to me that at the root of this story, and rather different from its common, even contrived, interpretation, there might lie another reality, one rather different. Perhaps what Narcissus saw was quite like himself, and yet was not himself, and that, as he watched, perhaps in horror, it reached up from the water, and, its bared arms dripping, seized him, and drew him beneath the surface.

It is just a thought.

I have occasionally seen things in the mirror, which I have not understood.

There are, of course, one-way mirrors, in which one side is a mirror and the other side a window. In this way, one does not know, of course, when one is before such a mirror, if one is, unbeknownst to oneself, being viewed from the other side. But I do not have such devices in mind, at least not in the usual sense.

Commonly there is nothing behind the mirror but a wall.

It is not a window.

To be sure, a mirror might be replaced with something else, and then, in a sense, it would not be a mirror, but a window.

What one took to be mirror might be a window, through which one might be viewed.

More importantly, perhaps, through which one might view. Surely you and others have regarded one another through a window, and thought little of it.

To be sure, the mind is a large and strange place, not well understood, and it may have many corridors, leading to different rooms, not all of which are familiar. Perhaps through such rooms, as through vision, or touch, we might reach other realities, or they reach us.

Due to the contrivances of atoms and fields a soundless, colorless world may give us sunsets and symphonies.

One wonders if there is such a world, so comforting a world, one of atoms and fields. It is a bold hypothesis, a reassuring guess, a marvelously constructed defense against incomprehensibility. We salute it, and wonder if it is true. The only world we know is that of our first-person experience. Beyond that what do we know?

One wonders if all the marbles of the universe fit into our little sack.

Doubtless, but one wonders about it.

What if they don't?

You have probably all, at one time or another, looked into a mirror, perhaps from the side, and seen something watching you, from behind, or the side. You turn about, and it is gone, of course. And you look again into the mirror, and you note that it, whatever it was, if it was anything, has left.

The following has occurred to me.

Let us suppose this has happened to you, or to someone I know, perhaps a friend.

Perhaps what you took to be your reflection took you for *its* reflection. And what if you were *its* reflection?

Is it as interested in seeing you, as you might be in seeing it?

The most interesting aspect of this matter, from my point of view, is that, recently, I can detect no one in the mirror, no one. I can, for example, see the bed, the dresser, the wall, the picture on the wall, and such, but I cannot see anyone, not anyone. For example, I cannot see me. I cannot see *my* reflection. It is not there. I should not have broken the mirror, I suppose. But I was trying to drive away what was on the other side.

The mirror has now been repaired, and I can press my hands against it, but I cannot penetrate its surface.

The world here seems much like the world I left.

Sometimes I see the face in the mirror.

I have clawed at it, but I can only scratch the inside of the mirror. The gouges are deep.

I suspect it will want to go home sooner or later. Perhaps we will pass one another in the corridor.

Il Jettatore

MR. Silone loved his child, deeply. That is why he blinded it, holding a lighted candle to its eyes.

If a benign rationalization were possible for such an atrocity, inflicted on a helpless infant, one supposes one might have argued a zealous father's sincere, but misguided desire to protect a child from the evils of the world, to preserve him from most of its moral contaminations, from its frequent offensiveness to a delicate purity of spirit. That was the tack taken by Mr. Silone's attorney, hoping for understanding and sympathy on the part of the court, and a mitigated sentence. This defense, however, was belied by Mr. Silone himself, who not only refused to accept it, but took pains to deny it, categorically. In passing, it might be mentioned, as well, that a defense on the grounds of insanity, temporary or otherwise, whatever might serve, despite what would have been its obvious tactical, judicial utility, was not proposed. Mr. Silone would have none of it. He was coldly, even unpleasantly, sane. This was his view, that of the court, and that of the court psychiatrist. To be sure, he did have certain unusual beliefs. His cognitive field, so to speak, to have recourse to a technical term, was different from that of many in the court, though not from that of all. We, of course, tend to dismiss as aberrational, or as insane, cognitive fields which differ from our own, but, interestingly, we are customarily disinclined to accord this liberty to others, should our own cognitive fields be put in question.

Mr. Silone's explanation of his deed, which had been done with forethought, and executed with all due, terrifying deliberation, was that the child was *jettatore*. Mr. Silone was found guilty, and was led from the courtroom. He had to be led because he himself was blind as he had, shortly after blinding the child, gone into the kitchen, taken up a butcher knife and gouged out his own eyes. You see, he believed himself, as well, to be *jettatore*. The curse was a lingering one, it seemed, and flowed with dark blood. Not everyone in his line, of course, was afflicted. To borrow a metaphor from biology, however inappropriate it may be in this context, one might say that the trait was recessive, or recessivelike. Mr. Silone believed himself, as we have seen, to have the trait, and he saw it, or thought he saw it, in his child. In his way, he was trying to save the child, and, I suppose, in a similar way, to save, or redeem, himself.

Mr. Silone went to prison, but did not survive his sentence. Shortly after his incarceration several cases of cholera had broken out in the prison. This sort of thing, with one disease or another, was not unprecedented in that place, a hole famed at the time for the laxity of its sanitary precautions. It was during the second week of the epidemic that Mr. Silone was found dead, his neck broken, apparently by a fall from the roof of one of the prison buildings. It seems he had somehow found his way to the roof, though for what reason none knew. He had then fallen or, perhaps, it is a possibility, had thrown himself from its height to the stones below. An alternative hypothesis, whispered about, was that he had been taken to the roof by other inmates of the place and cast from it. It is known that some had ventured to explain the outbreak of the cholera within those dank, forbidding walls by the presence amongst them of a *jettatore*. Even if one were to credit the existence of such a thing as a *jettatore*, it seems that any powers which Mr. Silone, or anyone like him, might have possessed would have been rendered harmless by his self-mutilation. Whether or not this argument would have carried weight with ignorant, panic-stricken felons, of course, is not clear. In any event, however it occurred, Mr. Silone was found one afternoon in the prison yard, at the base of a wall, dead, his neck broken.

> *Cursed be he that smiteth his neighbour secretly.*
> *And all the people shall say, Amen.*
> Deuteronomy, xxvii, 24.

Some see in the above quotation from the Bible, here given in the translation of the Authorized King James Version, a reference to the *jettatore*. The matter, however, is obscure. One might suppose that the curse is rather leveled at some naturalistic malefaction, for example, ambush, or, more likely, and more subtly, secret vilification, defamation of character, calumny, slander, or such. On the other hand, given the primitive nature of the times, possibly relevant data from cultural anthropology, Biblical research, the higher criticism, and such, it seems plausible to suppose that the curse is leveled against those who might perpetrate evil by arcane means, and here one thinks of incantations, spells, sorcery, diabolic confederacy, and other unsavory possibilities. And it would be somewhere within this range that one might expect to lie the powers of the *jettatore*, particularly if they were intentionally, malevolently exercised. Admittedly, however, as indicated, the scope of the curse is not clear. It need not, I suppose, even be interpreted as referring to preternatural phenomena, and, if it does, at least including them, which seems likely, it certainly need not be understood as referring, even implicitly, to the *jettatore*. It is not clear that the author of the verse was acquainted with the concept of the *jettatore*. He may or may not have been. In short, the devout, given the brevity, and consequent obscurity, of the verse in question, are not obliged on religious grounds to accept the existence of the *jettatore*. Its existence or nonexistence is an independent question. It is my surmise, however, that the author of the verse would, in fact, have been cognizant of the concept, that of the *jettatore*, and, if a man of his time, would have feared, or respected, or, at least, been wary of one whom he supposed possessed the powers in question. This surmise is based on the fact that the concept of the *jettatore* is far more ancient than the Biblical text under consideration. It is pervasive in a diversity of human cultures, these scattered throughout the world. It is almost certain that it predates the working of metals and the founding of cities in the great river valleys. It is probable that it was familiar to the tall, skin-clad, spear-bearing hunters of elk and mammoth.

There is no doubt that the power of the *jettatore* could be exercised with malevolent intent. On the other hand, it is equally clear that, in many cases, the power is regarded by its possessor as a curse in itself. It can cause evil, or ill luck, or misfortune, or illness, or accident, or death, inadvertently. It is something which can spring alive within the possessor, against his will, to his horror, without warning, and produce its deleterious, cruel effects. Its carrier, like the carrier of a virulent, lethal disease, may be the most innocent of all creatures. Often its possessor may be the epitome of honesty, decency and humane virtue; he may be the sweetest, kindest, most benevolently intentioned individual in the world and yet, about himself, to his own dismay and misery, create fear, havoc and injury. This appears to have been the case with Mr. Silone.

Let us suppose, for the simple purposes of speculation, that there might exist a *jettatore*. Let us suppose such a thing were possible. Since its powers seem often exercised despite the best will of, and against the best will of, the subject in question, that suggests that personal malevolence, recourse to magic, alliances with demonic forces, and such, are not likely to be involved. This might seem to open the possibility of some sort of demonic possession, or such, but neither those who find themselves afflicted by, or cursed with, the powers of the *jettatore*, nor those who might accept, acclaim and zealously exercise such powers with malevolent intent, seem to manifest the customary syndrome commonly associated with demonic possession, by clergy, or alleged demonic possession, by secular physicians. This would seem, for most practical purposes, to rule out a preternatural cause, at least as commonly understood. This is not to deny the possibility of something ill understood, and possibly subconscious. In passing, one might note that the *jettatore* is not localized to any particular ethnic, cultural or religious orientation. The devils of the Mediterranean are not those of Tibet. The devils of the Zulu are not those of the Eskimo.

My own hypothesis, were I to give credence to the myths of the *jettatore*, would be that there is a life form, or, perhaps better, a life force, which can infect, or inhabit certain forms of mammalian life, utilizing them, in effect, as a host, customarily humans, but, in some cases, it seems, other mammalian forms, most commonly, dogs. This is surprising, incidentally, from a sociological or anthropological point of view, for one would expect society to impose its prepossessions and terrors on, of all possible animals, the common cat, regarding it as the most likely host of the *jettatore*. Historically, our relationship to the domestic cat has been one of ambivalence. It was said, in the Middle Ages, that in the eyes of cats one could see the fires of hell. The cat is the usual familiar of the witch, and so on. Millions were destroyed, ceremoniously burned and hung. This is ironic, as well as tragic, for cats would have been useful in reducing the population of black rats, who carried fleas in their fur, which carried in their blood, and transmitted in their bite, the virus of the Black Death. In any event, the animal host of the *jettatore*, when the host is an animal, is commonly a dog. It is almost as though the form, or force, knew the favored position of dogs in society, how they were cared for, prized, and loved. Too, of course, dogs need have little fear of larger, dangerous animals, as cats, for example, must fear dogs, compared to them larger, more dangerous, animals. The dog, then, would be a safer, more secure host. Also, of course, statistically, dogs tend to live in a more intimate relationship with humans than do cats, who prefer, it seems, to care for their own affairs and live their own lives. In such a way, one supposes a form, or force, might with greater ease change its tenancies, should it be so inclined, from one host to another.

But there is, of course, no such thing as the *jettatore.*

There is the argument of *consensus gentium* for its existence, but the argument, interesting as it may be, is inconclusive. Briefly, the argument is from a supposed universal, or nigh universal, consensus, to the conclusion that the object of the consensus, say, the relevant proposition or belief, must be true, given that it is so widely believed. A simple form of the argument might be: Everybody believes it, so it must be so. Construed mistakenly as a deductive argument, it is obviously possible, at least logically possible, which is what matters here, for the premise-set to be true and the conclusion false; and this, of course, shows that the argument is invalid. Construed however as an inductive argument, which it surely is, though this seems to have has been little noticed by logicians, it becomes a much more interesting argument. Inductive arguments are not divided into those which are valid and those which are invalid. All inductive arguments are invalid; if one could be valid, it would discover itself, perhaps to its own embarrassment, not an inductive argument at all, but a deductive one, having met the criterion for deductive validity, namely, that it would be logically impossible for its premise-set to be true and its conclusion false. Inductive arguments may be divided into those which are good and those which are not, or, perhaps better, into those which are legitimately convincing, or persuasive, and those which are not. For example, one might regard an argument to the effect that everyone, or almost everyone, believes that food is necessary to sustain life is a good reason for supposing that that is true. To be sure, the belief does not make it true, but presumably the universality, or near universality, of the belief is best explained by the fact that it is true, that there do not seem to be counterinstances, and so on. Similarly universal, or near universal, beliefs that crocodiles and tigers are dangerous does not logically imply that these forms of life are dangerous, but the universality, or near universality, of the belief gives us good inductive reason to be circumspect in our relationships, should we choose to have them, with such creatures. If everyone believes something, or if a belief is sufficiently widely spread, it seems likely that it will be true. It may not be true, of course, but the fact that it is so generally believed is, all things being equal, a point in its favor. To be sure, generality of belief is no substitute for reason, logic, evidence, research, observation, experimentation, investigation, and such. Belief, *per se*, seldom makes things true, but, on the whole, things which are true are more likely to be believed than things which are false. We tend to learn from others; the human race tends get on as a whole. On the other hand, of course, there have been instances where the *consensus-gentium* argument, good as it often is, has misled its practitioners. For example, the fact that all people, or most people, once believed that the earth was flat, and stationary and the center of the universe was ignored by the universe. The argument in question, despite its impressive track record, did not win that one.

Belief in the evil eye, the capacity of an individual to injure, or even kill, with so little as a glance, has, historically, been one of the most ubiquitous superstitions afflicting the human race. It is a belief which, dreadful though it may be, is common, familiar, and pervasive. It seems almost ineradicable. It emerges sometimes in surprising environments. It has been entertained in a wide diversity of cultures and accepted by diverse races and peoples. It has characterized a variety of divergent eras. It is one of the dark threads woven into the fabric of human history. And, I fear, it is still with us.

Although the account I would give here is trivial and local, dealing with only a handful of people, none of whom you are likely to know, I think it would not be remiss for me to set this matter into a larger context, briefly, however inadequately. It seems, unfortunately, that what occurred, although unusual, was not unprecedented. My subsequent research has led me to believe that the events of which I would here give an account are, unhappily, in no way unique.

The power of the evil eye was recognized in ancient Greece, the culture of which was rather darker and more bizarre than one might gather from the stones of the Parthenon, the dialogues of Plato, the treatises of Aristotle, the benign conversations in the garden of Epicurus, and so on. A transliteration of the relevant Greek expression would be *byokagia*. The Romans, predictably, shared the unsettling apprehensions of their cultural mentors to the east, and, as one might expect of so practical a people, literally legislated against it, particularly, it seems, in order to protect crops, thought to be at risk from the baleful gaze of one whom today we would think of as a *jettatore*. Crop failure in an agrarian economy, naturally, would be catastrophic. The pertinent Latin expression is *fascinatio*, which word is obviously, if peculiarly, etymologically linked to 'fascination' in English. Words, as Nietzsche has pointed out, are like pockets. They can contain different things, and different things at different times, a point also made by Wittgenstein. An interesting example of such a linguistic wandering is the expression 'bonfire', which is likely to conjure up images of camping out, roasting marshmallows, and such. Originally it was a "bone fire" and dates from the times of the great plagues, when there were too few left alive to bury the dead, or too few who dared to do so. To be sure, the semantic trail here, with respect to 'fascination', whatever its length and vagaries, is not utterly unrelated to its origin. One might speak, for example, of a fascinating woman, one who is captivating or bewitching, one who casts her spell, one who enraptures, one who is enchanting, and so on. Closer to the original meaning would presumably be a usage where, say, a small rodent might be immobilized by, or *fascinated by*, the glinting eye of the nearing snake.

Belief in, and fear of, the evil eye was endemic in the Middle Ages. It was one of less estimable cultural artifacts bequeathed from the ancient world, which doubtless had it, in its turn, from the prehistoric world, and so on. The Middle Ages were, for the most part, and on the whole, despite any curtains of charity with which they may today be politely enshrouded, ages of ignorance, cruelty, murder, filth, barbarism and superstition. That the belief in the evil eye should linger on into our own times of science, civilization, and enlightenment is much harder to understand. Perhaps we are still at the mouth of the cave, ax in hand, wary, trembling, listening to the roar of the ancient tiger.

Children and young animals, it is alleged, are particularly likely to be victims of the evil eye. They are smaller, and more vulnerable. It is rather analogous, one supposes, to the case of poison. There are, of course, procedures for protecting oneself. The most obvious is to avoid the *jettatore*. In some towns, at his approach, for example, the streets are cleared. People flee, go inside, lock their doors, close the shutters, and so on. The Romans and Greeks believed spitting was efficacious, and, even today, spitting is often used as an expression of casting out, of rejection, of hatred, and such. Too, certain utterances and gestures are thought useful in protecting against, or negating, the effects of the evil eye. Certain amulets and sacred writings, too, worn, or carried about the body, are regarded as efficacious against it, warding off its effects or drawing them away from the individual and unto, or within, themselves, where they are hopefully rendered harmless. Even animals, for example, camels and horses, may be accorded similar protection by peoples as culturally diverse as modern Turks, Arabs, Ethiopians, and Chinese. The amulets have many forms, such as hands, moons, frogs, and horns. The imagery and symbolism of such amulets provide a subject matter for stimulating psychiatric speculation. The hand, perhaps, signifies power; the moon waxes, swelling, and becoming larger; frogs have a capacity to leap upward, and so on. And some of the amulets seem to have a sexual imagery which is even less subtle, the horn, for example. Indeed, some of these amulets, not among those herein referenced, are explicit to the point that their description would be inappropriate in a text this academic. This seems to make sense, of course, as one might think of sexuality as the great force of life, the force of abundance, procreation, pleasure, movement, activity, tenacity, continuation, will, vigor, and such, a force appropriately to be relied on to counter those of dismay, sickness, weariness, depression, grief, misery, and death.

Inscriptions may be regarded as prophylactic, as well. In certain Turkish villages passages from the Koran may be placed on the outside walls of dwellings, to protect those within.

Belief in the evil eye, or at least a willingness to take its power seriously, can occur in otherwise astute and civilized individuals. Mr. Somerset Maugham, for example, a gifted English playwright and novelist, insisted that the covers of his books bear a sign purported to ward off the evil eye. One supposes this was not a calculated witticism, a *geste* jolly and satirical, a lighthearted mockery of the mysterious, unpredictable hazards of fortune.

The fear of the evil eye, it seems, is often associated with the uncertainty of life and the sense of jeopardy which is part and parcel of the human condition.

We are all at constant risk. Even into the cradle death can peer. Only fools cycle nonchalantly amidst abysses. The bacillus does not distinguish between the valiant and the craven, the rich and the poor, the strong and the weak. A cell may misdivide and vandalize tissues; a muscle may cramp, a vessel may rupture, and the virtuous and the vicious, hand in hand, mortal brothers, succumb to the same fate. A stray bullet, a loose tile, a careless motorist, an atmospheric force, a rising river, a movement of the earth can all, unexpectedly, unannounced, keep the visitor from his call, the player from his game, the scientist from his experiment, the scholar from his library, the gourmet from his dinner, the lover from his tryst. And the friend may turn; and rifles may change hands. Civility may disintegrate, trust be subverted, names soiled, character treacherously knifed in the back, reputations vanish like smoke. New Huns ride to the gates; once again the statues are overturned, broken, and cast into the dust; once again the tablets are destroyed; again the temples are profaned; and again a culture inexplicably languishes and dies. It is not only we who are vulnerable, but that which most we love. One weeps as treasures are defiled, and lost. Is only the grunting, rooting pig eternal?

We can control so little in our lives; we are so much at the mercy of the other, the alien, the inert, the random, the careless, the indifferent. We are like corks in the water. It is not we who command the currents.

One refuses to worship, as did the ancients, Fortuna, the goddess of fortune, but one continues to fear her.

It is foolish to admonish someone to live dangerously, as though it were possible to live otherwise. Life is inordinately precious, and so it is only fitting that its price is so dear, that it is paid for with death and danger. These witnesses pierce all disguises. They attend the pikeman running through the mud and the mariner in his frail bark struggling against the storm; they observe the hermit in his cave and call upon the monk in his cell. Risk unsought will arrive uninvited.

So it is not so strange that a frail primate, one naked, exposed, and vulnerable, one subject to an unknown future and an obscure, threatening present, should fear the evil eye.

Often there seems to be some alleged relationship between envy and the evil eye. Perhaps one fears ambush. Arrows unseen may slay. Is envy alive, a force, that may somehow infect, injure, and kill? One fears to be envied. Let the king in his palace pretend to be the servant of the people, let the cardinal wash the feet of lepers before quaffing from the golden chalice. So the powerful, an eye on the envy of the gods, pretend weakness, the rich poverty, the saintly iniquity, the muscular debility, the beautiful plainness. One fears the glance of the evil, envying eye. How frightened is the father to hear of the prowess and bright future of his son. Will there be a future, at all? Shadows abound. Who knows what lurks within them? How terrified is the mother to hear her daughter praised, her wit, her health, and beauty. What will then happen? Is she now to sicken and die? Is she now to become maimed or disfigured? Is the pendulum to swing, is the cycle to be restored? Is good to be weighed against bad in the counting house of luck? Must the scales be balanced? Icarus flew too high, soaring too fearlessly, too splendidly, too much like a god, too near the sun, and so perished, plunging to his death below, in a cold, dark sea.

Although the fear of the force of envy is frequently associated with the fear of the evil eye, in which envy, like an arrow, lies on the bow, the string taut, this does not seem to have been the case with Mr. Silone. He was, as all indications attest, a kindly, loving man, well disposed toward his fellows, and serenely contented with the modest portion which he had been dealt in life's game.

Yet he was, or believed himself to be, *jettatore.*

The usual explanation for the undoubted effects of the evil eye, which need not be denied, are found within the theory of psychological suggestion. The power of psychological suggestion is scientifically established, in numerous studies and experiments, as well as being a phenomenon often encountered in, and recognized in, ordinary life; indeed, it is, in its way, a commonplace, familiar to us in many amplitudes of everyday existence. The familiar, extensively documented, and replicable wonders of hypnosis rely upon it, of course, but hypnosis is only an outstanding, and certainly uncharacteristic, manifestation of this particular phenomenon. We do know that psychological suggestion can instigate and transform emotions, influence behavior, induce physical alterations in the body, and so on. Indeed, in some cases, it can kill.

The most likely explanation of the evil eye's power then, it seems, would be in terms of psychological suggestion, and fear.

As you may recall, Mr. Silone had a son, whom he blinded, believing the infant to carry the dark trait of the *jettatore.* This paper deals, in particular, with the son, whose name is given here in a somewhat altered form, as Brunetto Alfonso Silone. The younger Silone immigrated to the United States of America as a child, the ward of an uncle, still living at the time of this writing, the pair being sponsored by American relatives, whose grandparents had been naturalized in the early twentieth century. The uncle, whom we shall call Giacomo, a conscientious, diligent, skilled craftsman, found employment at a major hospital in New York City, one noted for its teaching and research, on its considerable maintenance staff. Considering the peculiar and controversial nature of certain events to be shortly recounted, I will not identify the hospital, that in the obvious interests of discretion. To shorten the narrative, let us note that Giacomo, over the years, rose in the ranks of the maintenance staff, and eventually came to occupy therein a position of considerable authority, having responsibility for one of its major divisions. He had a reputation for organization, efficiency, and fairness. He was esteemed by his superiors, respected by his peers, and as popular with his subordinates as could be expected, given the seriousness with which he discharged the variegated responsibilities of his position. He was a familiar figure at the hospital, and a favorite of the administrative and medical staffs. The affliction of his nephew Brunetto eventually came to be known, though not how it had come about, other than that fire had been involved, and a young ophthalmological surgeon on the medical faculty, whom we shall refer to as Dr. Hill, expressed an interest in the case. His examination strongly suggested that the scarring in the eyes might be removed, with the genuine possibility that sight, after those many years of darkness, might be restored, that on the supposition that the optic nerves, and certain other tissues, were undamaged. Dr. Hill's interests here were not merely humanitarian, though they were genuinely and clearly that, but he had found the case of independent clinical interest, and thought its treatment might prove instructive to his students. He offered to perform the operation without a fee. One can then imagine his surprise when neither Giacomo nor Brunetto, who was now a handsome young man in his thirties, except for his disfiguration, leapt at this generous offer. Neither expressed enthusiasm nor gratitude. Indeed, both seemed decidedly uneasy. Naturally Dr. Hill, who was not only curious but, by now, somewhat irritated, inquired into these matters, and, indeed, pressed into them with perhaps more energy than was professionally appropriate. Soon the bitter story of the elder Silone became clear, articulated from the trembling lips of his tearful brother, the old craftsman, Giacomo. Dr. Hill, who was not thought to be an emotional man, threw back his head, slapped his knee and laughed, uncontrollably, tears of unrestrained mirth flowing from his eyes. When he had regained his composure, he was embarrassed, and had the decency to apologize to the Silones. Surely their views, and more importantly, their apprehensions, should be treated with circumspection. Common courtesy would decree as much.

Naturally Dr. Hill referred Brunetto to a resident therapist, his own field being inappropriate for the treatment of the young Silone's unusual syndrome. Dr. Hill's field, after all, was not psychiatry.

I have sometimes wondered what might have happened if Dr. Hill had referred the case to me, rather than to my colleague. I suppose, however, that things would have turned out much the same way. It is hard to know about such things.

My colleague, whom we shall call Dr. Roberts, was a practitioner of considerable reputation. Dr. Hill's referral could hardly be faulted on that score. Dr. Roberts eventually managed to convince a shy, reluctant, hesitant Brunetto of the likely fatuity of the impediment he and his uncle were placing in the path of an inestimable benefit. He had a measure of success, as noted, with Brunetto, who was young, and somewhat open to persuasion, but he had very little success with Giacomo, with whom he had had some five sessions, in two of which Brunetto was present. Giacomo was not young, and, for whatever reason, was less open to persuasion than his nephew. Presumably he was less free of old-world traditions, superstitions, and such.

A frightening moment in the treatment took place when Dr. Roberts, by means of hypnosis, regressed Brunetto to infancy. I heard the screams of pain even in my own office, several doors away. By associating pain with the reason for its existence, namely, the superstition, Dr. Roberts hoped to render the superstition intensely aversive to young Brunetto, so aversive that he would shun it at all costs, that he would repudiate it on the deepest level and would welcome any opportunity to undo its effects, by, for example, submitting to a redemptive surgery. And Brunetto did thereafter, a day or two later, agree to the operation. In this sense, one supposes that Dr. Roberts' treatment was vindicated. Indeed, he seemed to regard it as a master stroke, a coup, a triumph, or one would gather that, from conversations in the staff cafeteria.

There is a distinction, of course, between what occurs and how it is understood, or interpreted. Let us suppose we wished to convince someone that lions are not dangerous. First, this would be a mistake, because lions are, in fact, dangerous. Second, an aversion to lions might certainly be induced by having one be mauled by lions. This pain would doubtless encourage one to avoid lions in the future, but it would not show that lions were harmless, or might be ignored with impunity. Analogously, by associating pain with belief in the evil eye one might reinforce the belief, rather than diminish it, or negate it. One might make it seem more terrible, not false. On a subconscious level fear, however illogically, is taken as a sign of reality. Griffins may not exist but if one believes himself to have been attacked by a griffin, one is not likely to disbelieve in them.

I wondered what would be the case, if, supposing that there might be something within an individual, lurking within, parasitic, in its way, the parasite might be so intimately associated with the individual that it would feel its pain, or pleasure. One wonders. If scalding water were poured on a dangerous, wild animal, captive in a pit, what would be the reaction of the animal? Would it remember? Certainly one would not care to meet it, later.

The operation, in due course, was performed, and to all intents was successful.

In the course of my practice at the hospital, where I did clinical work twice a week, I had made the acquaintance of

Giacomo. I was surprised, however, when he came to see me one day, a week or so before the operation, and expressed his reservations about the impending surgery. My colleague had discussed the case with me, in general terms, and so I did my best to support and reinforce his work, explaining the emptiness of superstition, its tendency to oppress human happiness, the power some try to obtain by recourse to it, the nature of psychological suggestion, and so on. I probably told Giacomo pretty much what he had already heard from Dr. Roberts.

"How do you know these things?" Giacomo asked.

"Science," I told him.

"What means 'science'?" he asked.

"Knowledge, basically," I said. "Knowledge."

"Maybe there are other sciences," he said.

"You are afraid," I said, "that Brunetto is a bearer or possessor of the evil eye, a *jettatore*?"

"Yes," he said.

"Brunetto," I said, "is a fine young man."

"My brother, too, was a fine man," said Giacomo.

"Brunetto would not hurt a fly, even if he could," I said.

"The thing can hurt and kill," he said. "Brunetto is no more than its cave, its den, its lair."

The conversation made me uneasy. Clearly Giacomo accepted, or largely accepted, the myth, or theory, of the evil eye. In his view, I supposed, if the operation was successful, we would be, in effect, freeing something dreadful, something frightful, releasing it from its prison, to do its work, whatever that might be. I thought of unwittingly pressing a switch, which might activate the timer on an explosive device, of opening a jar which might contain a gas, or deadly bacteria, releasing these things into the atmosphere, of opening a door, behind which writhed vipers.

How much did I really know about the world, I wondered.

My colleague, I knew, was much more at ease with his own world view than I with mine. In Greece and Rome he would have accepted auguries and omens, in the Middle

Ages werewolves and witches, in a later time indivisible atoms and action at a distance, or phlogiston and the ether. In our time he had accepted what he had been taught, as uncritically as innocent millions before him had accepted what they had been taught. If there was a lesson here, or a pattern, it would seem to be change. Could we now, in effect, with the inconsistent vagaries of quantum theory and relativity, the contradictions of cosmology, and such, be substantially at the end of wisdom's road? Or would there be, in time, new darts launched, new balloons floated, new guesses hazarded, new, mighty truths proclaimed, new arrogances, new scratchings at the wall of mystery?

"What do you know of these things?" asked Giacomo.

"Very little, I am sure," I granted him.

"I think you smart fellows are right," said Giacomo. "There is much nonsense in talk about these things."

"Yes," I said, encouragingly.

"But I am afraid," said Giacomo.

"Of what? I asked.

"Of the part," said Giacomo, "that is not nonsense."

He then left my office, though I would have been willing to continue the conversation.

The operation took place a few days later.

I shall try to relate certain subsequent events with no more commentary than seems necessary for clarity.

I will say, in way of preface, that I think these things all have a natural explanation, that nothing supernatural is involved. On the other hand, I think that they suggest, on some level or another, that nature may be more complex, or subtle, than we commonly suppose. I deliberately avoid adjectives such as 'greedy', 'self-seeking', 'fierce', and 'sinister', as they suggest the limitations of anthropomorphism.

Yet suppose, if only as a fancy, for it somehow seems appropriate, that some fiendish thing was incarcerated in a dungeon, in absolute darkness, for years, chained down, rendered innocuous, unable to move, capable of little more in that frustrating, enclosing, confining stygian darkness than brooding and hating, and consider how, over the years, that hatred, day by day, drop by drop, might increase, filling the stony crater of its foul soul, forming therein, as it were, a dark lake, ever rising, of waiting, inflammable pitch, ready to burst into vengeful flame at the first touch of light. Who would be so foolish as to move aside the stone that seals that pit? Who would be so unwary as to carry a torch into those recesses, who so unwise as to explore that darkness?

It was a Tuesday afternoon in September, a bright, cool day, that the bandages were to be removed. The room was a private room, and a pleasant room, light and airy. It was in the west wing of the hospital, on the twenty-third floor. A bouquet of flowers, in a blue vase, was on a stand near Brunetto's bed, making the room fragrant.

Five people were present, other than the patient, Dr. Hill, who had performed the operation; Dr. Roberts, his therapist; myself, as an interested observer, invited by Dr. Roberts; the young man's uncle, Giacomo Silone; and the nurse in attendance, Miss Henry. It was she who had brought the celebratory flowers, ensconced in their vase, on the stand near the bed. They were within an arm's reach of the bed and Brunetto could reach out and touch them, feeling the softness of the petals. Brunetto loved flowers and their tactualities and perfumes to him were doubtless analogous to the beauties of the visual world to the sighted. Now, it was hoped that he, in a matter of moments, could see them as well.

Dr. Hill's pleasantries that afternoon seemed to me a bit forced. I think he was a little apprehensive, as is not unusual in such cases. It is difficult to know in advance the degree to which such an operation achieves or fails to achieve the hoped-for success. Much depends, for example, not merely on the condition of the optic nerves, but, as earlier suggested, on the condition of an extensive and subtle network of neural pathways. He had every reason, however, based on the operation itself, as far as I could tell, to warrant the optimism which he seemed determined to project.

Roberts, who regarded Brunetto with almost proprietary benevolence, was at hand, to learn the results of the operation and, if necessary, to supply any assistance or support compatible with his field. particularly if, tragically, the operation proved ineffectual. Too, I think he wanted to be present at what he hoped would prove, in its way, to be a credit to his own therapeutic skills, for he regarded himself, correctly enough, I believe, to have been instrumental in bringing Brunetto to this climactic and hopefully joyful day. He had invited me, I think, primarily that he might be provided with a professional witness, one who could understand and appreciate what he had done, overcoming as he had profound traumas and deeply rooted resistances, a professional witness who might comprehend and objectively validate his achievement, to be manifested in this rewarding moment. I suppose we are all, to one extent or another, vain and insecure. But I was glad to be present, independently, for Roberts was my friend and, too, of course, I hoped the best for Brunetto and his uncle, both of whom I had come to know over the last few days, and particularly the uncle.

Giacomo seemed agitated. It was the first time I had ever seen him in a suit and tie. He seemed to feel out of place in such finery. Oddly, he kept his right hand inside his jacket.

Miss Henry was the primary nurse into whose care Brunetto had been consigned. As I had dropped in on Brunetto at various times after the operation and during his convalescence, I had noted the attachment which seemed to have been formed between himself and his nurse. Certainly she had been more often at his side than would have seemed necessitated by purely medical considerations, and, indeed, had occasionally been found in attendance at hours other than those required by her shift. I think I have mentioned that Brunetto, aside from his disfiguration, now hopefully a thing of the past, was a handsome young man. Too, I had gathered that his kindliness, his thoughtfulness, his intelligence, his humor, his good nature, his open and generous character, left little to be desired. One can only conjecture how the blind Brunetto understood the soft hands, the gentle words, the considerate attentions of his nurse, but, could he have seen her as we saw her, what he saw would have been sure to please him. Each, it seemed, had found another, to whom each was willing to give his heart.

"How do you feel?" asked Dr. Hill.

"Well, sir," said Brunetto. "Thank you, sir."

"Take my hands," said Dr. Hill. "We are going to sit in a chair, here, beside the bed."

He helped Brunetto into the chair.

"Nurse," said Dr. Hill. "Draw the blinds. Darken the room."

She did as he asked.

"I am going to remove the bandages, Brunetto," said Dr. Hill.

"Yes, sir," he said.

"We don't know how this will turn out," he said. "The room has been darkened, but there may still be pain. That will pass. You can close your eyes, if it hurts too much. As you have not had sight since infancy, you will probably have to learn to see. One learns to see, to recognize shapes, to understand how close, and how far, objects are from you, and so on."

"Yes, sir."

"Are you afraid?" asked Dr. Hill.

"Yes, sir," said Brunetto.

"Steady," said Dr. Hill, softly.

Brunetto held out his hand, and it was grasped in the small hand of Miss Henry.

"Steady," said Dr. Hill, soothingly.

In the reduced light of the room I was aware that Giacomo, who stood near me, was almost inflexible, as though with terror. He seemed rigid. A tear had run from his left eye. His jacket had come open a little and I could see his hand within. It was clasped about the rounded handle of what might be a stiletto or dirk. Alarmed myself, I had no desire to alarm him. I put my hand gently, reassuringly, restrainingly, on his arm. He did not resist or pull away. His grip on the handle seemed to tighten. His gaze was fixed on Brunetto.

Fold by fold, wrap by wrap, Dr. Hill gently removed the bandages.

"There," said Dr. Hill.

Miss Henry gave a small cry of distress and pulled her hand away from that of Brunetto.

He turned his head toward her, slowly, but it was not clear that he saw her, or recognized her. It was as though she might have been a stranger, not welcome, improbably present, intrusive, otherwise meaningless.

"What's wrong?" asked Dr. Hill, sharply.

"Cold," she said. "His hand! It is suddenly so cold."

"Physiological reaction to stress," said Dr. Hill.

"Characteristic?" asked Roberts.

"Not unusual," said Hill. "Brunetto, Brunetto!"

"I am not Brunetto," said the patient.

"Can you see?" asked Dr. Hill.

"Yes," said the patient.

"Does it hurt?" asked Dr. Hill.

"No," said the patient.

"It is just lights and patterns now?" said the doctor.

"No," said the patient.

Giacomo said something in Italian. He was tense, trembling. "It is not Brunetto," he whispered, in English.

I cautioned the old man to silence, lest he disturb the patient, or the others. If the others heard, they gave no sign of it, for their attention seemed fully focused on the patient.

"You have waited a long time to see," whispered Dr. Hill.

"Yes," said the patient. "I have waited a long time."

"You must learn to see," said the doctor.

"I learned to see long ago," said the patient. "Do you think, in the darkness, I would have forgotten? I have learned to see in a thousand bodies."

Giacomo with a cry of agony pulled away from me and rushed wildly toward Brunetto, the blade of the dagger, a long, narrow blade, some nine inches in length, brandished over his head.

I managed to seize Giacomo and wrest the dagger from him.

"What is going on!" cried Dr. Hill.

Doctor Roberts helped me to thrust the tearful, hysterical Giacomo to the side of the room, back, away from his nephew.

I held the flat of the dagger blade down with my foot, and, with my hand, pulling upward, snapped the metal from the handle.

"Uncle, uncle!" cried Brunetto, "what is happening?" He held out his hands wildly, as though dazzled, and suddenly hurled into a new dimension of experience. "Is this seeing?" he cried. "It is so strange!" Nurse Henry rushed to him and put her arms about him. He seemed, instantly, to know her, and to welcome her sheltering presence. "Margaret, Margaret!" he whispered.

Then Brunetto's voice changed again, and it seemed eerie, flat, cold, malevolent. "I will have more light," he said. He thrust Miss Henry to the side and she fell bewildered, stumbling, against the side of the wall. He went to the window, seized the cords and drew up the blinds, and the light of the bright September afternoon flooded the room.

After the darkness I think that all of us had to shield our eyes briefly from its intensity.

We were aware of Brunetto at the window, a dark figure silhouetted in the frame, against the light, turning about, facing us.

He seemed taller, somehow.

"Do not meet his eyes!" cried Giacomo.

"Nonsense!" cried Dr. Hill, angrily.

Giacomo was fumbling in his pocket and he drew forth, on a leather string, an amulet, which he held before him. It was the first such amulet I had seen, for at that time I had not inquired into certain arcane, troubling matters.

As Giacomo was disarmed, and an old man, we did not impede his progress toward his nephew.

He stood before the figure at the window holding the amulet up before him.

The figure at the window regarded it, imperturbably.

"Where is Brunetto?" said Giacomo.

"Do not fear," said the figure. "He is safe."

"The amulet! The amulet!" said Giacomo, holding it up before the patient.

It seemed then that Brunetto smiled, a small, pitying smile. "Oh, yes," he said, "magic, wonderful, defensive magic! Oh, fear, fear! What quaint beliefs you have. Such things are inefficacious, of course, though we find it a sensible precaution to act as though they were, to withdraw from them, and such. That leads you to believe that you can protect yourselves. That belief is very useful for us. Otherwise you might hunt us down with method and without mercy. They make our lives easier. Too, we welcome that you shun us, for that protects those of whom we make use. By all means, keep your distance. Give us our freedom, dear Giacomo, sweet, deluded fool, give us our solitude, our place, our territory."

"Brunetto, Brunetto!" wept Giacomo, calling out to his nephew.

I had with me a pair of dark glasses. Usually I used them, when needed, for driving, and kept them in the glove compartment of the car, but this morning, given the brightness of the day, and the walk from the garage to the hospital, I had them with me. As the light in the room seemed unnaturally bright, it being a cloudless, intensely sunny day outside, and the afternoon light was streaming in mercilessly through the wide, double window, I retrieved the glasses from their case, in my inside, left jacket pocket, and put them on. This was, you understand, in order to be more comfortable in the bright room, but I suspect, on some level, my action was motivated less by a rational concern to reduce glare, particularly under the circumstances, than to protect myself from something fearful, the nature of which I did not understand, but had begun to suspect. It was perhaps a matter of ancient instinct, insight or intuition. Or perhaps it was in response to Giacomo's plea not to look into the eyes of Brunetto. What might lie in such eyes? How foolish I felt, but this emotion did not long linger.

"Brunetto," said Dr. Roberts, obviously upset himself,

"stop this foolishness! You are obviously the victim of some sort of superstitious syndrome, some sort of temporary disassociation. Come down to the office. I'll lead you there. I'll help you. You can use some sedation. You can rest for a while. Later, we can conduct some tests. Afterwards, with a little friendly talking to, about this and that, we'll all be the same again."

Dr. Hill stepped back, and to the side. What was going on was clearly not within the area of his expertise.

Giacomo had fallen back and was leaning against a wall, his head in his hands. The leather string of the amulet was still wrapped about this fist, the amulet dangling from it.

"Brunetto," whispered Miss Henry, frightened, pleadingly. She held her left wrist, which had probably been bruised when she had fallen against the wall.

"Who are you?" asked the patient.

"Don't you know me!" she cried.

"I am Dr. Roberts," said my colleague.

"Yes," said the patient. "I know your voice. You are he who caused me great pain. Because of you I lived twice through the burning of my eyes."

He then seized my colleague by the shoulders in what seemed an unbreakable grip. It was almost as though Roberts had been rendered unspeakably helpless, hypnotically paralyzed.

"Do not meet his eyes!" cried Giacomo.

Dr. Roberts screamed, a horrifying, wailing noise, and, released, reeled backward, holding his hands over his eyes.

"Stop whatever you are doing!" I cried.

Brunetto suddenly turned toward the flowers. He put out his hands, unsteadily. "Flowers!" he cried. "Music, there! So beautiful!"

I hurried to Dr. Roberts and tore his hands away from his face. Then I released his hands. Where his eyes had been there were now only two black, sightless, steaming holes.

I looked up to see the patient, with a movement of his right hand, brush the vase of blue flowers from the stand,

and it shattered on the tiled floor, a welter of petals, stalks, water, and broken glass.

Miss Henry was on her knees, in the water, glass and flowers, weeping.

He then went and stood before Dr. Hill.

"Mr. Silone," said Dr. Hill.

"I will let you live," said he, "for it is you who released me."

"Brunetto!" gasped Dr. Hill, shaken.

"But you will live only as I please," he said.

"You're mad!" cried Dr. Hill. "What have you done to Dr. Roberts!"

"We are solitary, my kind," said the figure. "Each is an enemy to the other. We are territorial, save in the moment of mating. I will not risk my being in contest with my brethren. You will not release another. Look into my eyes!"

"Don't" I screamed.

But I fear it was too late, as Dr. Hill seemed to collapse at the feet of the figure who loomed over him. Dr. Hill clutched tiny, shriveled fingers to his heart, and stared glassily at the floor, and blood ran from his nose and mouth.

"The knife! The knife!" wept Giacomo.

I broke it," I said. "It's useless!"

I felt my shoulders seized, and I was turned to face Brunetto. I sensed something, an emanation, or radiation, or vapor, or something that was like such things, and I tried ineffectually to extricate myself from that grip.

I felt myself shaken and I clenched my eyes closed, and then I was thrown to the floor, stunned.

"It is only psychological suggestion," I told myself as I lay on the floor. "It is to be resisted."

"Brunetto, no!" cried Giacomo.

I saw the white, starched nurse's cap crumpled at the side of the bed.

The door to the hospital room closed.

Miss Henry lay on her belly amidst the glass and flowers. In one hand, bleeding from a cut, she clutched a bloom. "I love him," she wept.

Dr. Roberts was moaning, and Dr. Hill lay on the floor, bleeding.

I had heard a cry outside the door, for the commotion within the room must have attracted attention. I struggled to my feet, but did not press the bulb to signal the nurse's station. I feared bringing innocent people into the ambit of whatever force had within these antiseptic precincts been inadvertently unleashed, that force which had herein wreaked such havoc.

I found my dark glasses, which had been flung from my face, as I had been shaken in the hands of the patient. The lenses were smoked, and cracked, the temples half melted.

I looked to where Miss Henry lay. Her uniform was wet and blackened, and torn. One shoe was gone. Apparently, as her hair was terribly disarranged, and the barrette gone, she had been controlled by means of it, dragged to the side of the bed, and there put to the floor. He had probably there lifted her to her hands and knees, and held her in place, helplessly to him, by the waist, her arms thusly unable to fend him away. She was now on her stomach, trembling. She pressed her lips, the lipstick smeared about the left side of her face, to the grasped blossom, a rose, and kissed it. "I love him," she wept. "I love him!"

"Uncle! Uncle!" I heard, from outside the room, a weird, piteous cry.

"It is Brunetto!" cried Giacomo. He rose unsteadily to his feet, and staggered toward the door.

"Beware!" I cried.

"No, no!" he said. "It is Brunetto, Brunetto!"

I rose to my feet, half falling. I could not let Giacomo face whatever terrors might lie outside in the hall.

I opened the door, and outside, in a strangely contorted position, lay an orderly. He had doubtless come toward the room to investigate, to help. Nurses, doctors, and even some patients, were in the hall, but muchly aligned along its sides, clearing a path for Brunetto and Giacomo. The elder Silone was leading Brunetto down the hall, away. Their passage was not contested.

"Wait!" I called.

But Brunetto, guided by his uncle, had disappeared through an exit, one leading to the stairwell.

I sank down for a moment in the hall. I was trembling, gasping. It seemed I could not move. One of the young residents now hurried to the orderly. He removed his stethoscope from the man's chest. "He's dead," he said.

I held to the wall and stumbled after Brunetto and Giacomo. I was sure that whatever madness had seized the young man must now be passed. I made my way as best I could, drunkenly, to the exit through which they had left the corridor.

I looked upward.

In a moment I had come to the roof. I pressed aside the heavy metal door, and felt the wind whipping across the roof, and saw the skyline in the distance, the river, the marshes, the harbor.

"Stop!" I cried to Brunetto.

Giacomo, tears in his eyes, looking toward his nephew, held my arm. "No," he said. "No, doctor, no."

Brunetto stood some yards away, at the edge of the roof. I feared if I approached him more closely, he might fall.

"It is best," whispered Giacomo, against the fresh September wind moving across the roof. "It is his wish."

"Brunetto!" I called.

"He needed help to get to the roof," said Giacomo. "He has not yet learned to see."

Brunetto stood at the edge of the roof, looking out over the city. We do not know how much he saw, or what he understood of what he saw. But he must have sensed that there was spread before him a vast and wonderful world. I should like to think he felt that, that he knew that.

Suddenly Brunetto seemed to struggle at the edge of the roof. He twisted, and was half bent over, as though in pain. "You will not kill me!" we heard. "You cannot kill me!"

"Do not interfere!" said Giacomo.

Then he cried to his nephew. "You are strong! Your father was strong! You can kill it! Kill it!"

"No!" we heard, an angry, protesting cry.

"Margaret! Margaret!" cried Brunetto.

And then as I cried out in dismay, he leapt from the roof.

I thought I heard, in his descent, a long, drawn out, wild, protesting, trailing cry, "No!"

"It is over," said Giacomo, weeping.

We went to the edge of the roof and could make out the body, far below. There was already a small crowd gathered.

How small everything looked from that height.

Without speaking I left the roof, to go below, to assist as I could, if need be. Giacomo followed.

In a few minutes I knelt beside the body.

A crowd had gathered by now.

Nothing, it seemed, could have survived that fall. There was little doubt that Brunetto was dead. Every bone in his body must have been broken, and some of them, ribs, and a femur, protruded from the body. The head was crushed. The sidewalk and body were bloody.

Brunetto was dead.

I wondered if whatever had been within him, or had come and gone within him, was dead.

"You cannot kill me," it had said.

"Back, back, boy!" cried a man, trying to restrain a large, stocky Rottweiler on its leash. It was a large, dark, spotted, ugly brute.

Its tongue was lolling.

"Disgusting!" said a woman.

"He won't hurt anything!" said the fellow. "He won't bite. He is quite tame!"

The dog, of course, carries in its heritage the legend of the pack, the memory of the wolf, the feral response to blood.

"Get it away!" I said.

But the dog had turned about and pulled free of the collar and rushed on the bloody body. It was snarling, and biting, and lapping at the blood. It would have been dangerous to attempt to restrain it, without the leash or collar.

"Come, boy!" said its owner, and took it about the

shoulders, to pull it from the body, but, to his horror, the beast spun about and tore at his throat, leaving a terrifying gash at the side of the neck, and the fellow reeled backward, blood streaming between his fingers. If those fangs had been a hand's breadth more centered the jugular would have been torn open. In that moment, doubtless from the mauling of the body, the eyes opened, and I thought I saw a tiny, malevolent smile transfuse the features of that battered, torn, empty wreck that had once been the house of a human being.

It seemed to me I heard, in a soft whisper, "You cannot kill me."

The dog then, snarling, turned about, and the crowd widened its circle about the brute.

Then, for the briefest moment, it seemed that the eyes of that animal and my own eyes met.

The gaze that met mine seemed almost human, though insidiously evil, and the jaws of the beast seemed to move in such a way that fancy might have thought it a smile, fiendish and malevolent. Then, suddenly, it turned away, and ran through the crowd.

"Go inside," I said to its owner. "Get treatment."

I saw that Giacomo was now beside me. "Did you see?" I asked.

"Yes," said Giacomo, sadly.

✦

I am not settled in my own mind, as to the manner in which the preceding events are best explained.

One supposes that an optimum explanation would be in terms of psychological suggestion, and coincidence.

There was no hope to restore the vision of my colleague and friend, Roberts. It is known that hypnosis can induce physical alterations, blistering and such, and so we might best attribute his tragedy to that form of causation. Dr. Hill suffered a stroke, it seems, and lost the control of his skilled hands. He no longer practices, save in a consultative capacity.

Old Giacomo took his retirement from the hospital, and lives alone in the city. I am getting on much as usual. The orderly who had died in the corridor had been the victim of a massive heart attack. He had, it seems, a history of heart problems. Miss Henry is pregnant. It seems likely that the child will be normal and healthy. The trait of the *jettatore*, if one believes there is such a trait, is a rare one, one might even say, recessive, or recessivelike, to use a metaphor. Brunetto was a fine young man. His mental instability, and his succumbing to superstition, were his tragedies.

I have sometimes wondered what became of the Rottweiler.

How Close the Habitat of Dragons

"DESCRIBE the room," said the inspector.

I did so, in some detail.

"You have been there," he said.

"No," I said. "But I remember it."

"Then you were there," he said.

"No," I said. "The memory, you see, is not mine."

I later sat on a bench, it was early autumn, and pondered the matter.

I had these memories, yes, but they were not my memories. There is a difference, you know. One's own memories are unmistakable. Even if they are false memories, constructions from fragments of recollection, or outright fabrications, they are unmistakably one's own constructions or fabrications. They have one's mark on them, so to speak. They say "mine." But these memories did not say "mine." Clearly, unmistakably, they said "not yours, not yours."

I supposed this sort of business was not unique to me, as I was, as far as I could tell, in no sense unique, other than in those ways in which any other human being is unique, as, say, every twig, or pebble, is unique. On the other hand I had not heard of this sort of thing before. It was, at any rate, unfamiliar. Perhaps, I thought, psychology has a name for it. I wonder if you have ever had such an experience.

Perhaps you will speculate, with some plausibility, at least until you know more about this, that I might have gone mad. I certainly considered that possibility at first, but, I think, with a curiosity, a serenity, and a detachment which I would suppose would be unusual among those suffering from the defensive agitations of insanity. To be sure, as I understand it, the insane usually do not regard themselves as insane, and, I suppose, in their own unusual experiential world, they would be right. Indeed, in their small, unusual universes they perhaps constitute a paradigm of rationality. In a world of madness only the mad can be sane, and so on. The others simply do not understand. But there are some serious reasons for discarding this hypothesis of madness, at least in my case, for the peculiarities to which I unwillingly found myself subject fitted too nicely, even terrifyingly so, I am afraid, into our great common world of the allegedly sane. The memories, you see, in so far as I could put them to the bar of verification, proved to be veridical. They were actual memories, it seemed, and testable as such. More of that shortly.

In any event I was either insane or not. If I wasn't, then that was an end of it, at least as far as that question was concerned. If, on the other hand, I was insane, it seemed to be an insanity of a sort which was more peculiar than debilitating or dangerous. I did my work, I discharged my duties, I engaged in my social relations, and so on. Nothing in my exterior life, so to speak, was awry. I considered consulting a psychologist, or psychiatrist, but did not do so. That could always be done later. In the meantime, given the nature of the memories, and the possible obligations which might arise out of them, I did not wish to risk possibly instigating some sort of conceivable professional intervention, for example, sedation, treatment of some sort, being placed under surveillance, being remanded to some authority for evaluation, possibly being institutionalized, temporarily or indefinitely, or such. I think you can understand that. Surely that would be inconvenient. And, as I suggested earlier, there was no hurry about the matter.

More importantly, if the memories were veridical, if they corresponded to reality, at least closely, I was not insane, no more than an individual amongst the blind who can open his eyes and see objects that are truly there.

One would be different, true, but not insane. Gifted, or cursed, perhaps, but not insane. No one would be insane. One, however, might be gifted, or cursed.

Certainly I did not want the memories. You may be sure of that. Some of them were alarming, and disturbing.

So there seemed to be two sorts of memories involved, the usual sort that one recognizes as one's own, namely, such things as memories of incidents from one's childhood, events of the day, conversations, what one had for breakfast, and such. Then there was the other sort, clearly memories also, as it turned out, but also, as clearly, not mine.

The first memory, even though it bore the mark of memory, but not that of my memory, I rejected as mnemonic. I refused, at that time, despite its psychological cast, to count it as a memory.

I did not know the individual in the memory. I had never seen him. He was elderly, perhaps sickly. The room was dingy, with drawn blinds, half dark, papers were about, cluttering the floor. There was a desk there, a box, metal, open on the desk. The man turned about, startled. He seemed angry, then frightened.

I thought this memory must be a sudden, inexplicable, unrelated, random image, and what shortly ensued must be the manifestation of some sort of insistent, terrible, uncontrollable, irresistible day dream, an alarming, ugly fantasy, an unwelcome, inadvertent, heinous fiction, in its way an unsettling thing, terribly so, some sort of waking nightmare.

The hand went behind the old man's neck, pulling him forward. I remembered the sight of the blade, no more than a glimpse, a flash, so quick, so brief, and how it entered the body, the rip of cloth, a tiny sound, the movement, the pushing in, the grunt of the old man, his slipping downward, blood on the shirt, the floor, on the hand with the knife, the stepping over him, the going to the box on the desk.

Thankfully this was all there was to the first visitation of this thing, though it recurred, more darkly, more disturbingly, with ever greater detail and depth, from time to time, over the next weeks. Occasionally it comes back, even now.

One may speak of a memory model of reality.

When one remembers what one did, what one said, and so on, it is usually as though one stood outside of oneself, and observed oneself. One sees oneself, at least commonly, from the outside, so to speak, when one remembers oneself. Consider a memory of yourself walking down a street, for example. You will usually, at least, see yourself in this memory from above, and usually from behind. When you recall shaking the hand of a friend, embracing a lover, speaking to a group, you will usually see yourself in the memory doing so, which is quite different, of course, from the experience of actually doing these things. When one walks down the street actually one does not see oneself walking down the street, though one is aware of doing so. It is in the memory, rather, that one sees oneself walking down the street, and so on. In any event, this is common in memory, if not universal.

And I saw, or sensed, the assailant in the memory, rather from behind, moving swiftly, closing, the knife flashing, which had been held to the side until that moment. I did not see the face of the assailant.

Despite the vivacity of this imagery, and its irresistible sense of the veridical, its emblazoned sense of the nonrepudiable, I refused to accept it as genuinely mnemonic. Oddly, too, in the experience, and certainly in its subsequent repetitions, I had first, a sense of hatred, and decision, and then, in the doing of the deed, a sense of power and elation, and then, in moments, a sense of greed and eagerness, and then the hand was rifling in the contents of the metal box, clutching and drawing forth bills, even coins, and thrusting them in his pockets. Then, but moments after, as it seemed to see, almost for the first time, the twisted, bloodied figure of the old man on the floor, there was a sense of anger, and there was not that much money, and then there was a sense of horror, of sudden loathing, then of terror, and guilt. And then the figure rushed from the room.

Though the memories were of the same event, the later ones, as I have suggested, seemed richer, in a dark sense, and more detailed than the earlier, almost fragmentary recollection. Indeed, it was almost as if the memory were being elaborated upon, or was being reinstituted, to accommodate thoughts and feelings that may not have been there in the beginning. Or perhaps it was rather that the renewal of the memory was now being experienced through a filter of subsequent reflections, being drenched, as it were, in an emotive context which was not present in the beginning, which seemed primarily simple, rapid, more primitive, more reflexive. It was not simply then, later, a memory but, so to speak, a memory of a memory, one now clothed with disgust, fear, perhaps regret, perhaps some sort of remorse. I sensed in it, too, a nascent self-loathing. The assailant, I speculated, would have preferred for the old man, however hated, to have been absent. The assailant, however driven by fury or greed, did not seem to have in him the stuff of the killer, the psychopathic detachment, the criminal insouciance, with which one might break a stick, or crush a box.

Despite the psychological signs which commonly, infallibly, identify a passage of thought as a memory, distinguishing it from idle imagery, calculation, or such, I continued to reject these experiences as genuinely mnemonic. I knew nothing of the individuals and incidents involved. The eerie sense of reality attending these episodes, however, was disturbing.

I suspected myself of self-generating them, somehow, for some reason, but this thought, too, was disturbing. They had come suddenly upon me, without anticipation or warning. I had no history of such things. Too, I found them unaccountable, not only for their explicitness, but nature. I did not think I was the sort of person who would be likely to, or even could, produce things of this sort. They were not me, so to speak, or, at least, me, as I knew myself. I did entertain the hypothesis that such aberrations, seemingly so different from my conscious modalities, might somehow be products of the subconscious mind, and its less favored aspects, that they might be analogous in their way to lurking denizens prowling within unsuspected caverns, monsters, now somehow breaking free, and bursting snarling, vicious, and appetitious, into the light, appearing embarrassingly now, suddenly, within the white-washed precincts and antiseptic corridors of hypocrisy, the benign, acceptable, well-lit localities of the conscious mind. How close might be the habitat of dragons!

But I rejected this hypothesis for obvious reasons.

The dark creatures of one's mind are one's own, not another's. I rejected this hypothesis of a subconscious generation because of the utter foreignness of the imagery. There was nothing here which even remotely suggested a latent content of my own mind, no plausible transpositions, or disguises. Too, if these were things of my own, repressed, now emergent, I should have found them disturbing in ways I did not. I did not welcome these experiences, but I did not reject them as though I myself, somehow, was being threatened, or spoken to in accents to which I dared not attend.

More importantly, these memories, however unwelcome they might be, were not fanciful or bizarre, like the cloaked transmogrifications of subconscious fears and hatreds. And most importantly, these memories would prove, for the most part, to be veridical, and confirmable for their correspondences to reality.

One thought did obsess me in the beginning.

I feared that these might be somehow my own memories, only alienated from me, memories which were mine but which I dared not face, and had thus deprived myself somehow of the sense of proprietariness which usually accompanies one's own memories. Thus, I feared I might have been the assailant, that I had somehow committed this crime, and had now distanced myself, in so far as I could, from it. Perhaps, unbeknownst to myself, I was the victim of some psychological self-division, as in a multiple-personality syndrome, a case of divided personalities, in which one self, or more selves, so to speak, might be unaware of the actions of another self, or selves, in effect, being two or more persons inhabiting a single body.

This seemed implausible to me, but that, if it were true, was only to be expected. To be sure, I had no evidence of this sort of thing, no lapses in my time sense, in which hours or days might be unaccounted for by a given self, and no evidence in the form of inquiries or observations of friends, or fellow workers, no apparent signs of this sort of deviancy, and so on. Too, if I were the assailant I had no evidence to that effect, in the way of, say, the knife, clothing, money or coins stolen, and so on.

Still I feared desperately that this was the only explanation possible. If so, I should bring myself to the attention of the authorities, as would be my duty, petitioning for incarceration, lest the other I, the I I did not know, might strike again, might kill again, might bring death to another innocent victim, a stranger, one presumably utterly unknown to the I I knew as myself.

I was sick with this fear.

My hope at this time, which detained me from immediately submitting myself to authority, was that these episodes, these seeming memories, might, after all, be a minacious fantasy of sorts, that they bore no relation to reality. This was surely possible. I hoped it was altogether likely.

I thus began an inquiry into a crime which I feared I myself might have committed.

I was tracking a murderer, who might be myself.

If there was no such crime, of course, that would prove my fears on that score to be groundless. I would be innocent. I would be left, doubtless, with these mental visitations which so troubled me, surely at least for a time, but, at least, too, I could no longer take them as testifying to my implication in so terrible a deed. It would be objectively irrational for me to feel guilt. I might feel guilt, of course, but it would not be justified. I could know this, at least consciously. That would be important. Any guilt I might feel then would be unwarranted, the consequence only of some unusual psychological deviancy, the product perhaps of some pathological neurosis. I need not interpret my own miseries then, thankfully, as being the self-generated torments of a murderer.

And so I began to research, as I could, crime reports.

There must be no such crime.

But perhaps such crimes were too common, in too many large and lawless cities.

I had not been at this occupation long when, in a local library, examining on microfilm back issues of a tabloid, I came on the report of a murder and robbery which was briefly noted. The description of the victim and the nature of the crime, as far as I could tell, tallied exactly with what I feared, the recurrent content of my aforementioned imagery.

Such a crime then, or one very similar, had actually occurred.

I do not know how many times I read that brief account. I suppose each time I hoped it would say something different, or that I would find some exonerating clue there, in those few marks, which would prove to me my innocence.

I photocopied the item, put it in my pocket, and walked about, for a very long time.

My mind was in tumult.

I fear I was not thinking clearly.

Another seeming memory intruded itself, a figure thrusting a bundle of rolled clothing into a dumpster, and hurrying away.

I returned home.

The next morning I planned to report myself in to the police. It might be a different crime, of course, or it might have been solved, unbeknownst to me. Still, it was important to consult with the authorities. If I was a murderer, I did not want to risk being at large. I might kill again.

I did not sleep much that night, but fell asleep in the early morning.

I suddenly awoke in a sweat, shivering, sitting up in bed. I hurried to my coat and jerked forth the copy of the tabloid item from my pocket. I rushed then to the calendar, and my date book, on which I register appointments, and such. I again scrutinized the tabloid item. The date was in late August, and the crime had occurred the previous day, being mentioned in the next day's paper. I examined the calendar, the date book, a copy of the program's conference which I had attended, and in which I had participated. I had lectured, I had been on two panels, I had attended the banquet, I had sat with colleagues and acquaintances. I had been photographed. I had even signed some copies of the program. I had been at the university, in New Jersey, that weekend. The crime had occurred in New York City while I had been at the conference.

I fell beside the bed, clutching the sheets, and then rolled over and pounded on the floor with my fists, and cried out wildly, and then, fearfully, gasping, laughing, half choking with emotion, rose up and checked the dates again, and again. I was not there. I could not have been guilty of that crime.

But perhaps there had been another?

Momentarily I again felt sick.

But then I stood up, and readied myself for the day.

I had a good breakfast. I went down to the local subway station, and took the first uptown train. I came out of the subway and made my way to the nearest police station. I had taken with me as much documentation as to my whereabouts on the day of the crime as was convenient, and more could be provided, and it could all be checked.

It was that morning that I met the inspector.

Briefly he confirmed that the crime had occurred as recorded in the tabloid, and found the police file, with its numerous details, forensic and otherwise, which he kept closed on his desk.

He eyed me askance, and I did not blame him in the least.

In his response to my inquiry he informed me that the crime was still open on their books, that it had not been solved, and that there were no clues available which had been helpful. No authentic leads had been discovered. This, it seems, is not unoften the case with crimes of this nature. There had been perhaps an obvious motive, that of robbery, but there seemed no way to connect the crime with any particular individual. The victim was a small-time money lender with no obvious enemies, more than such a fellow would normally accrue in the course of his business, had no known connections to organized crime, had lived alone, had no criminal record, and was regarded as eccentric, and irascible. His neighbors knew little about him. They had not noted strangers in the building at the time of the murder. His records, if he had kept them, were missing, along with other materials, some furniture, lamps, and such, apparently removed from the flat between the discovery of the body, by a cleaning woman, and the arrival of the police. This, too, I gather, is not that unusual.

"I suppose you have some interest in this case, or evidence?" suggested the inspector.

I gathered he had things he would rather be doing.

"Perhaps," I said. "I do not know."

"I don't understand," he said.

"It is hard to explain," I said.

"You felt compelled to come here?" he asked.

"Yes," I said.

"I see," he said, wearily.

"I don't understand," I said.

He opened the file, without showing it to me.

"You have come to confess," he said.

"What?" I said.

"Let's get this over with," he said.

"Get what over with?" I asked.

"You don't look to me like a fellow who would even know the victim, and certainly not like one who would kill him."

"I don't understand," I said.

"But we have to get this over with," he said. "Regulations. Twice a day we have people like you come in and confess to crimes. They may think they did it. Who knows? They may want to suffer. They may want to feel important. They may want publicity. They may want to be in the newspapers, on the evening news, impress people who think they are only unimportant, worthless, scrounging clowns, things like that."

"I don't think you understand," I said.

He glanced at the file, and drew a picture from it.

"Do you recognize this man?" he asked.

"No," I said.

"He is the victim," said the officer.

"No, he isn't," I said. "That is not the victim, at least not the one I am thinking of. That is not him."

"You're sure?"

"Certainly," I said.

"That's a retired police officer," said the inspector. "That means we have to go a little further."

"Further?"

"How did you last see the body?" asked the inspector.

I described it, how it lay, the blood, and such.

"He was stabbed in the throat," said the officer.

The fact that the man had knifed had been in the paper. The nature of the wound had not been reported.

"Not at all," I said. "He was stabbed frontally, between the ribs, on the left side, toward the heart."

The inspector looked up, surprised.

"Who told you that?" he asked.

"I remembered it," I said.

The inspector now looked distinctly interested.

"In a sense," I said.

"A sense?"

"Yes."

I was now convinced that the crime in question was identical with that which I seemed to remember.

He then asked me to describe the room, the nature of the theft, a number of details.

I doubtless did so, to his satisfaction. It was interesting to see how alert he became, and how his attitude changed considerably, from one of boredom, even mild annoyance, to one of close attention.

"I didn't do it," I mentioned, thinking it appropriate to put that in. He seemed, for good reasons, doubtless, to be moving swiftly to plausible conclusions, however invalidly derived.

"Only the murderer could know these things," he said.

"I know them," I said, "and I am not the murderer."

"Then who is the murderer," he asked.

"I don't know," I said.

"You can account for your whereabouts on the day of the murder?" he asked.

"Certainly," I said, "and in incontrovertible detail."

I then did so.

At the inspector's invitation I remained in the station, and willingly, until well into the afternoon.

"Am I under arrest, due to suspicion, or reasonable cause, or such?" I inquired.

"If necessary," he said.

"That won't be necessary," I said.

About two P.M. I left the station, he having by that time, I gathered, confirmed, however reluctantly, by a number of phone calls, and such, my asseverations pertaining to my whereabouts on the day of the murder. He was a nice fellow, but I gather that this outcome was not entirely welcome to him. I assured him I would remain in town, and, if not, would keep him apprised of my whereabouts, and expected to be available, if he wanted to speak with me further about these matters. I also gathered that if the circumstances surrounding this matter had been a bit different, and less conclusive, I would have been placed in custody, and held on a charge of murder. I think that is what I would have done in his place. It seemed the rational thing to do.

He did request a set of fingerprints before I took my leave,

I suppose as a routine matter. In any event I was pleased to oblige him.

That night, before retiring, I recalled where the knife had been placed. This may have been because of the business of the fingerprints. A slit had been made in a garbage bag in a trash container at the subway station closest to my apartment, indeed, a station from which I normally took the train to work. The knife had been inserted through this slit, so that it would lie in the bottom of the container. As the bags are commonly pulled out, and quickly, efficiently, casually, replaced, the knife might indefinitely lie there undetected. I felt that I myself would have concealed such a weapon differently. I found this conviction reassuring, as it suggested to me, strongly, that the memory could not be mine, though I found myself forced to entertain it. In this memory I felt a certain haste to discard the weapon, and a sense of revulsion pertaining to it. It seemed in the memory that the weapon must be discarded, but that it had been disposed of with some, but inadequate, circumspection. I had the sense that mental disturbance was clearly involved in this. It must be discarded! I was not clear on the date of this memory, and these things were, at best, fragmentary. It did seem possible to me, however, that this memory, if it were veridical, might supply the police with the clue, or lead, which they were missing. I knew it was the murder weapon, and it seemed not implausible that it might bear fingerprints.

I called the inspector in the morning, and told him about this, and he met me at the station within the hour, and we located and examined the container.

It contained the knife, of course.

It would be sent to the police laboratory to be tested for fingerprints.

I trusted they would not prove to be mine.

Unfortunately for the investigation the knife bore few, if any prints. It had apparently been hastily rubbed, perhaps on a sleeve or the side of a coat. A print or two was blurred, or smudged, but there was nothing there which could be clearly read. Some particles of dried blood on the knife, however, under laboratory analysis, yielded a DNA print, so to speak, and this agreed with that of the victim. The murder weapon had been found.

"You know too much about this case," said the inspector.

"A great deal more than I care to know, I assure you," I said.

"If you are not the murderer, or a witness to the murder, how do you know these things?" asked the inspector.

"I do not know how I know," I said, "or even if I know. Perhaps I don't know. But I seem to. I sense that I know. But perhaps some weird sort of coincidence is involved here."

"Someone told you these things, perhaps in a bar, in great detail?" he asked.

"No," I said.

"Tell me about him," he said.

"There was no one," I said. "No one told me these things."

"He may have been the murderer," he said.

"No one told me," I said. "It is the memories, the memories."

"You must be the murderer," he said.

"I was afraid of that," I said. "But I don't see how it could be."

"Nor do I," he said. "The two assistant district attorneys I have spoken to don't either. It is odd. We have an abundance of apparent evidence, almost overwhelmingly so, against you, but no case."

"I would like to be of help," I said.

"Do you have other memories of this sort?" he asked.

"Alien memories, memories not mine?"

"Yes."

I told him about the successive, almost obsessive, seemingly guilt-ridden recollections which I had experienced, the matter of the clothing rolled and discarded in the dumpster, but in what dumpster I had no idea, and it was now doubtless long gone, and reminded him of the incident of the knife.

"Try to remember other things," he said. "Something might help us."

I had not been read rights, and was not under arrest. I supposed he was fishing, so to speak, and was wondering if I might not, somehow, perhaps in overconfidence or arrogance, inadvertently implicate myself.

But I did want to cooperate.

This was as important to me, I was sure, or more so, than it was to him.

I closed my eyes, but had no sense as to how one might go about trying to remember something which, presumably, had never happened to one. Suppose, for example, one asks you to recollect what you did on a given day in some city you have never visited. There is just nothing there. One supposes the mind might play some sort of tricks on one, but, presumably, there is simply, in actuality, nothing there to remember.

"Nothing," I said. "They are not my memories. They are someone else's memories. Perhaps he could bring them to mind, whoever owns them, but I cannot. I experience them, but I do not own them. They aren't mine."

"Thank you for your time, and effort," he said.

"I should go?"

"You may go," he said.

"What about the case?" I asked.

He closed the folder. He looked across the desk at me. "It is another one," he said, "but an odd one. Another miss, another loss, another unsolved crime."

A Collar is Secondarily Applied

SHE gasped, and looked up at me, wildly.

"There," I said, "it is done." I drew away from her.

Her eyes were open, widely.

"You understand now," I said, "what can be done to you."

I had not taken time with her. What did it matter?

She looked at me, reproachfully, bitterly, hatred in her eyes.

"Apparently you received great pleasure," she said.

"It is what you are for," I said.

"I see," she said.

"It was not so terrible, was it?" I asked.

She bit her lip, and turned her head away.

"On your belly," I said, "hands at your sides."

I turned her to her belly and adjusted her hands, and then knelt across her body.

"You may now be collared," I said.

"Should I not have been collared first?" she asked.

"In your case," I said, "I thought it best that you be collared second, in order that it be after you are taught what can be done to you, and what you henceforth are going to be for."

She gasped with bitterness, and tears dampened the furs on which I had put her.

She was absolutely helpless, and knew herself so.

She sobbed as I brushed her hair forward, exposing the back of her neck.

The small hairs there were attractive. I have always found them so.

"Please, do not!" she said.

I put the collar about her throat.

"Please, no!" she said.

"Listen to the click," I said.

"Please, no! Please, no!" she said.

I then closed the collar.

"Did you hear it?" I asked.

"Yes," she said.

I did not think it likely she would forget that sound.

She could not reach the collar, as I knelt across her body, pinning her arms to her sides.

Perhaps I should have collared her first. But she had displeased me, long ago, at a song drama, so the collar had been secondarily applied.

Surely she knew she had displeased me, and had intended to do so.

Doubtless, from time to time, she had recalled the incident, perhaps with pleasure.

It had happened some months ago.

Doubtless it had later slipped her mind.

But I had remembered.

Doubtless she thought the matter forgotten.

But it had not been forgotten.

I had not forgotten.

I had waited.

I had ruminated often on the incident, recalling details. I remembered her carriage, the attitude of her body, the tilt of her head, the tone of her voice, the words, the flash of her eyes, dark and bright, over the veil.

I had been irritated.

I had stepped back, surveying her, the sweetness of the

shoulders, the hint of the turn of a pleasant hip, inside the robes.

How furious she had been.

I stayed the small gloved hand, catching her wrist, holding it just a bit, just long enough that she would know herself held, helplessly, and then released it.

She turned away, angrily, and moved down the tier.

How angry she was.

How insolent she was.

I wondered if she might be of interest, as a woman might be of interest to a man.

I sensed her intelligence was quite high.

Excellent.

Does one not prize high intelligence in any animal?

She had moved away, well.

I wondered if she knew that.

I suspect they do.

Does the tabuk doe not take her leave from the inquisitive buck thusly, darting away, inviting pursuit?

Certainly I had speculated on the likelihood of acceptable lineaments there, hoping that they might be of a certain quality; it is difficult to tell such things, given those absurd, voluminous, pompous, preposterous folds and layers of the Robes of Concealment. Who is to know if what is hidden is dross, or a treasure, perhaps fit even for the block. It is different with the collar girls, dressed for the pleasure of men. Little speculation is needed there. How lovely they are, so humiliatingly revealed, so uncompromisingly exhibited, so deliciously exposed, so feminine, so helpless, so vital, so alive, so at one's mercy, so perfect, so owned. How they stir the blood! It is different, too, with the females of the world, Earth, to which I have been twice. They are ready slave stock, presenting themselves beautifully and excitingly, I wondered if they realized that, for a man's consideration, slave stock whose garmentures leave little to a fellow's imagination. It is little wonder that the slave routes to and from Earth are well plied, by professionals, by hunters, and merchants.

The orchards are unguarded, and luscious fruit hangs in view, to be assessed, and selected, as one pleases.

It is almost like a slave shelf, in a common market.

It is not hard to fill one's basket.

I looked at her.

I was not disappointed.

Suitably trained, she might prove, indeed, a treasure, or bauble, if you like, yes, fit even for the block. I was pleased. I do not find the women of my world, though obviously more civilized and modest, more refined and informed, more worthy and noble, incidentally, at all inferior in beauty and excitements to the lovely barbarians from Earth, bid upon so heatedly, from the polluted slave world, brought suitably, as the game they are, the selected, plucked fruit, to our markets. To be sure, that is to be expected, as they are all of the same species.

I recalled the incident in virtue of which, unbeknownst to her, she had been marked for my claiming.

One wonders, sometimes, why women should act so.

Do they wish to be taken in hand, and taught they are females?

Is this what they long for?

Is it that without which they know themselves incomplete?

Are they never content, truly, except at our feet?

She rose to her knees, on the furs, beside me, as I lay on an elbow, regarding her, and she put her small hands on the collar. She felt it, she pulled at it. It encircled her neck closely, but not tightly.

"Who are you?" she said.

"Do you not remember?" I said. "In the month of Hesius, a song drama, a contretemps in the tiers?"

"You!" she said.

"Yes," I said.

"For that," she said, seizing the collar, looking at me, "this?"

"Yes," I said.

She struggled with the collar.

"Do not hurt yourself," I warned her.

She looked at me, angrily, her small fingers hooked on the flat, narrow, gleaming band.

Surely she, given her background, not being a naive female of Earth, fresh to her new condition, so alien to her former life, should well understand the futility of such efforts, the obduracy of such devices, the sturdiness of the small locks, the perfection and security with which they are designed to encircle and clasp the throats of their fair occupants.

"It is on you," I said. "Doubtless your own girls wore them."

"Yes," she said, angrily.

"But you never thought to wear one yourself."

"No," she said.

"It is not uncomfortable," I said. "One does not wish the girls to be in the least bit uncomfortable."

"You are thoughtful," she said, bitterly.

"As you were with yours," I said.

She jerked at the collar.

"In time," I said, "you will not even think about it, or seldom, no more than the rings you once wore."

Such things had been removed from her, of course. They had some value.

If she wore such things in the future, they would not be hers, but would be worn by the permission and indulgence of another.

To be sure, I doubted that she would be soon granted adornments, save, of course, the collar, and perhaps earrings, which have a special significance here.

"But it is there!" she hissed.

"Certainly," I said.

"And locked!"

"Would you rather have had something heavier, and riveted about your neck?"

"No!" she said.

"Or something even heavier, shaped by a smith about your neck, hammered shut?"

"No, no," she said.

"Such could be easily arranged," I said.

"I am sure of it," she said.

"Your hair is much before your face," I said. "Lift your hands, and, with both hands, brush it back, behind your shoulders."

She looked at me, angrily.

"I would see the collar on your neck," I said.

"Good" I said. "Keep your hands as they are. Yes. It is very pretty."

She was an extremely attractive woman, and the collar, of course, much enhances the beauty of a woman. This is doubtless in part a matter of simple aesthetics, contrasts, and such, but I think the meaning is even more important, what it proclaims about that which is within it, what it makes clear about the woman about whose throat it is locked.

"May I lower my arms?" she asked.

"Yes," I said.

"What you did to me!" she said.

"You will not forget the sensations," I said. "You will be more and more curious about them, what they were like. You will remember them. Do you remember them accurately? You will find yourself hoping for their repetition. You will dream of yourself as you were. Your belly will grow uneasy. You will hope to be remembered. You will hope to be summoned, to be washed, and perfumed, and such, to be brought before me."

"Never," she cried, "never!" But her eyes belied her words.

"In time," I said, "you will long for such things. In time, you will come on your knees, or belly, and beg for them."

"Never!" she said.

Let her first uses, I thought, be cursory, that she may learn what she is, and what may be done to her, when and as others wish.

There would be time later, if one wished, for one's amusement, to spend a morning, or an afternoon, with her, to have her writhing and begging for another touch, even the gentlest, the least, of such.

"I pride myself on my frigidity," she said.

"You are not frigid," I said.

"You, or another," she said, "will never light the slave fires in my belly!"

"They have already been lit," I informed her. "In a week, that will be quite clear to you."

"I will never be so helpless," she said. "I will never so belong to men!"

"You already do," I said.

"No!" she said.

"You may now report to the kitchen master, to be put to work," I said.

"'Kitchen'?" she sobbed. "I—to the kitchen? I—to work?"

"A man waits outside," I said. "He will blindfold you and take you to the kitchen."

The house was complex. There was no need that she understand its passages, and such.

She moved from the furs, to the side, to the tiles and stood, unsteadily, wavering.

"Do you wish to be whipped?" I asked.

"No!" she said.

"Get out," I said.

She stood there.

"Do you obey?" I asked.

"Yes," she wept, "I obey!"

"You obey, what?" I inquired.

"I obey," she said, "—*Master*!"

She then turned about, and scurried, weeping, barefoot, from the chamber.

I smiled to myself, for she knew little of herself. She would eventually be fulfilled in her heart, to become what she was.

I thought, in a time, and not in too a long a time, I would get a good price for her.

I would have her ears pierced.

She would be made a pierced-ear girl.

She had displeased me.

In time she would grow accustomed to that, even pleased. Too, that should improve her price somewhat. Men expect much from a pierced-ear girl.

To the male belongs the female.

It is so deemed by nature.

In the tiers, she had not recognized my caste. But then one does not always wear one's robes publicly.

A Gorean Encounter

IT was a fall day.

On a certain world, in that season, it would have been a lovely fall day, the air bright and crisp, and the leaves a thousand colors. On the particular world on which this brief encounter occurred, it was, it will be admitted, for that world, not a bad day. It was cool, at least. The air was foul, as usual, but those accustomed to that did not much notice it. They were used to it, and had little with which to compare it. The leaves were somewhat sooted, and this muted the colors, but, again, individuals on the world in question were so familiar with this sort of thing that they, again, at least on the whole, did not much notice it.

Perhaps she should not have been walking, alone, in the woods. That is not, really, a wise thing to do. On the other hand, actually, it would not have really made much difference. One place or time, actually, is quite as good as another. Indeed, a great many individuals involved in this sort of thing do not even realize until long afterwards that an encounter took place. At the time they were utterly unaware of it. Only later is the evidence indisputable that it occurred.

She turned about, a little startled, and realized for the first time that he was there.

He was rather close to her.

She knew she could not run. If she had turned to run, he could have had his hands on her instantly.

He was quite large, and she was acutely aware of her smallness before him. He seemed very different from the men with whom she was familiar. He seemed to have a terrible look of power, of virility, about him.

But, too, he seemed a pleasant enough fellow.

That reassured her.

She might have screamed, or started to scream, one supposes, but what would have been the reason for that? Certainly she had no obvious reason, or justification, at least at that time. But, too, at the first sight of such an intention, widened eyes, a look of fear, a trembling lip, the taking in of air to scream, and such, he could have had her in the compass of an arm, and a large hand might have been placed firmly across her mouth, stifling any possible outcry. She might then have been struck, or threatened, or warned to silence, before being thrust down, terrified, to the leaves.

But he did not seem particularly threatening in his attitude or demeanor, only perhaps, if at all, in that fierce masculinity before which she felt unsettled, and weak.

She did what almost any woman would do, one supposes, in such a situation, what almost any woman, fearing herself trapped, but sure of nothing, might do. It is a common response of the uncertain female before the strange male, unaccountably present. Indeed, it is a common response of any uneasy female before almost any male, whose maleness is suddenly, clearly recognized. It has doubtless been selected for in the course of evolution. It is a complaisance behavior. It signifies docility, and a desire to please. It tends to avert wrath. In effect, it says, though doubtless much on the unconscious level, "Look at me. I am pretty, and a female, and smaller than you, and I could be a source of great pleasure for you, and so please, please, do not hurt me."

The lives of many women have doubtless been so saved.

Does it not say, in its way, "Think of me in terms of service and pleasure. Do not hurt me. Keep me, instead. I will serve you well and give you much pleasure. Keep me. I am a female. I will do my best to make you happy. That is what I am for. So please do not hurt me. Keep me—keep me for your service and pleasure, *Master*."

The behavior was a simple one, presumably once randomly distributed, but later, given the cruel filtering of differential survivals, coming in a great many women, indeed, in an overwhelming majority, to be an instinctual response.

It was a simple behavior.

She smiled.

It was a very pretty smile, and she was not unaware of its effects. Certainly it had always had, at least in the past, served her well, to delight males, to disarm them, to please them, to influence them, to make them eager to serve her.

Men were so easy to manipulate, with such small things as a smile, a movement of the head, a hand lifted to the hair, such things.

She might not have the strength and size of a male, but she had other ways to have her way, and obtain power over them.

Men were such foolish creatures.

What things they would do, simply to win one of those smiles, and bask in its glow.

The large fellow facing her in the woods did not seem in any way hostile, or overtly threatening, but he did not return the smile.

She did not sense that he was being uncivil, or boorish, or purposely ignoring her lovely overture.

It was rather as though he had noted it, and approved it, perhaps even regarded it as excellent, but, after noting and approving it, had turned it aside, as a weapon, as easily as the stern shield of Ares might have turned aside a straw flung from the bow of some designing, meretricious Cupid.

This was the first time she could recall that that had occurred.

This puzzled her.

Too, it annoyed her, and, too, it frightened her.

Had her finest weapon, her mightiest dart, which had never hitherto failed her, proved unavailing?

She felt disarmed, and helpless.

She now sensed herself being surveyed, carefully, from head to foot, and back, again, and never before had she sensed herself so regarded, with such dispassionate objectivity.

She felt herself appraised, as though she might have been a horse, or dog.

She had the sense he might have looked in this fashion on many women.

And perhaps they had not all been clothed.

She had the sense that he might somehow well be aware, too, of the nature and quality of her own lineaments, and how they might appear, so exhibited, despite her skirt, and coat, appropriate to the temperature of the day.

Then she forced such silly thoughts from her head.

"You startled me," she laughed.

"You have the look of a slave," he said.

"What?" she said.

"You heard me," he said, not pleasantly.

"No!" she insisted.

"Do not pretend you did not hear me," he said. "I am not patient. Too, you can be taught to rue such games."

"I'm sorry," she said. "It is just that I could not have heard you aright."

"Oh?" he asked, amused.

"Certainly not," she laughed, uneasily. "You surely did not say, you could not have said, what I thought you said."

"What do you think I said then, or might have said?" he inquired.

"Nothing," she said.

"Speak," he said.

She blushed, hotly. "Never!" she said.

"I said you have the look of a slave."

She looked at him, startled.

"Look into my eyes," he commanded.

She could not help but do so.

"Yes," he said. "Yes."

"Yes?" she said, faintly.

"Yes," he said. "You do have the look of a slave."

"No, no!"

"Yes," he mused. "I think you will do nicely."

"No!" she said. "I mean—I mean I do not even understand what you are saying!"

"Surely you have from time to time considered yourself as a slave, an abject slave, one who must fear for her life, and must obey instantly, unquestioningly."

"No!"

"Have you never thought of yourself naked, a property, wholly owned, utterly defenseless, the light, lovely collar on your neck, closely encircling it, doubtless identifying your master, closed, locked?"

"No!"

"Have you never thought of yourself as an object, truly, a purchasable object, an unutterably soft, vulnerable, desirable object, for whom men might fight, even kill, an object men would ruthlessly bind, master, and uncompromisingly have for their own?"

"Certainly not!"

"I see that you have had such thoughts, and that they have intrigued you, terrified you, and excited you."

"I do not even understand what you are talking about," she said.

"Properly embonded, and nicely trained, you will do nicely. You will make a hot, juicy little slave."

"Never, never!" she said.

"But, yes," he said. "And it is obvious."

"No," she said. "No!"

"Is it your intention to be difficult?"

"I am not a slave!" she said.

"It will be pleasant to set you to lowly labors, collared, naked," he said. "You will learn to beg, humbly, for a touch, a caress."

"I find you different from the men I have met," she whispered.

"Oh?"

"So different!"

"I do not think I am so different from other men," he said. "—Of a certain place."

"A certain place?

"Yes."

"I do not understand," she said.

"It does not matter," he said.

"I find you attractive," she said, uneasily. "I acknowledge that. If—if you wish to kiss me, I will allow you to do so."

He smiled.

"I have never met anyone like you," she whispered.

"Why are you clothed before me?" he asked. Were you given permission to clothe yourself?"

"No, of course not!" she said.

"A slave must request permission to clothe herself," he said, "which permission need not be granted."

"I am not a slave!" she said.

"You are," he said. "And clearly you understand yourself to be such. I can see this clearly."

"No" she said. "No!"

"I tell you no more than you already know," he said.

"No!" she wept.

"You have too long fled your bondage, girl."

"Girl!"

"Yes," said he. "Girl, of course, girl, only that, merely that—but a very special sort of girl, the most desirable and delicious form of girl, the *slave* girl."

"I don't know what you are talking about!"

"Your subterfuges, games, disguises, and lies are now done," he said. "You have now been apprehended."

"'Apprehended'?"

"Surely."

"What are you doing!" she said.

"Binding your wrists before you," he said.

"I am not a slave!" she insisted.

"Yet you are bound, aren't you?"

She regarded him, frightened.

"Do you think I cannot assess your lineaments?" he

asked. "Or appraise the lovely delicacy of your features, or read your body, and needs? To be sure, there are certain perfunctory niceties to be attended to, legal details, and such, in particular, the brand, but such things are largely for purposes of the law. They do make a slave, of course, and categorically, there is no doubt about that, but, commonly, they do not so much make the slave as, rather, publicly, identify and mark as a slave she who is already a slave."

"Such as I?"

"Yes."

She struggled, futilely, bending over, squirming, to free her wrists.

"Free women, too," he said, "wish slaves to be clearly marked, in order that they, such lowly and despicable chattels, will in no way be confused with their own lofty, precious, and noble selves. And certainly one cannot blame them."

"I am a free woman!" she said.

"Slaves, of course, such as you, are worthless, and nothing," he said. "They are grovel sluts, who must hope desperately to be found pleasing."

"I am a free woman!" she cried.

"No," he said. "You are a slave, only that."

"No!" she said.

"Close your eyes, and purse your lips!" he snapped.

She did so, and leaned forward a little, and lifted her chin.

"Oh!" she said.

She gasped, suddenly, her eyes opened widely, frightened.

"You are now leashed," he informed her. He tugged a bit on the strap, and held the coils before her, closely to her face. She could smell the leather, in his fist. She was now leashed.

"You tricked me!" she said, petulantly, reproachfully.

"If you wish," he said, "I will remove the collar and leash, and put them again on you, as you observe their placement.

"No," she whispered. "You are larger and stronger than

I, and I know I am in your power. I thought—I thought you were going to kiss me."

"And you offered your lips with all the alacrity and obedience of a slave, and, too, if I mistake not, with all the frightened, hopeful delicacy and ready vulnerability of a slave." he said.

She reddened. "Why did you not kiss me?" she pouted.

"Why should I?" he said.

"Am I not attractive?"

"Vain creature," he said.

"I do not understand," she said.

"Why should I kiss you?" he said. "I am merely picking you up, a slave, for others." he said.

"Others!" she cried.

"You will be taken to another planet, one called Gor," he said, "where you, with a number of other vain, worthless Earth sluts, will be put up for sale."

"There is no such place!" she said.

"I shall not respond to the stupidity of a slave," he said. "And as to that world, the world of Gor, you may perhaps the better judge of its existence when you find the sawdust of one of its slave blocks beneath your bared feet and you are exposed to buyers."

"'Exposed'?"

"Certainly, only a fool would buy a woman clothed."

She regarded him, angrily.

"And you will turn, and pose, well," he said, "obediently, and fearfully, and, I think, hopefully, hoping that you might prove of interest to a buyer, that you might prove of interest to a master."

"I will not pose, and such!" she said.

"It would not do, to be left over, after a sale, I assure you," he said.

"I would never allow myself to be exhibited!" she said,

"As an animal?"

"Certainly!"

"But you would be an animal, a slave."

She shook her head, miserably.

"And you will have no choice about being exhibited," he said.

"I would not permit myself to be exhibited, not well!" she said. "I would never present myself—as a slave!"

"You will do your best to be attractive, to exhibit yourself well, to strive to prove you are desirable goods—*on the block*."

"No," she said, "no."

"But, yes," he said, "The auctioneer's whip, if nothing else, will see to that."

"Whip!"

"If you are a pleasing slave, a truly pleasing slave, you will doubtless seldom feel its stroke, though you may find that your master will occasionally bind and whip you, if only to remind you that you are a slave. It is not well, you understand, for a girl to forget that."

"How dare you speak to me as you have!" she cried. "Worthless!" she cried. "Sluts? For sale! How dare you! How dare you!"

"To be sure, I perhaps misspoke myself. You must have some value. After all, have I not put capture straps upon your wrists? It seems you cannot remove them. You will doubtless be worth at least a pittance, *as merchandise*. Yes, I assure you, and doubtless for the first time in your life, you will be good for something. You will no longer be merely an embarrassing, meaningless encumbrance on society. You will have an exact role and position in society, a very precise identity, then as much a part of you and as inalterable as the very corpuscles of your body. You will learn fear and be humbled. You will be grateful to be permitted to live. You will be well worked, quite well worked, I assure you, and you will exist for the service and pleasure of a master. You will learn to kneel, and belly, and to lick, and kiss, and beg."

"Never!" she cried.

He smiled.

"As other worthless Earth sluts," he said.

"'Sluts'!"

"Yes." he said. "Sluts, like yourself, exciting, delicious females, curvaceous wenches, fascinating, cuddly beasts, women of the sort who should be collared, women who belong in the collar, women for whom slavery is their liberation and redemption, women for whom the gift and honor of slavery is far better than they deserve."

"—Sale?"

"Such is common with slaves," said he.

"I, to be sold—*sold*?"

"Yes," he said, "to the highest bidder, as what you will be, as livestock."

She shook her head, wildly. Tears were in her eyes. "Let me go!" she wept. "Please! Please!" she wept.

"Perhaps you would consider begging," he speculated.

"Yes, yes!" she cried.

"Should you not then be on your knees, or belly?" he asked. "Do not fear. I will give you sufficient slack on the leash."

She flung herself to her belly before him, in the cool air, and in the fall, crackling leaves, and began to press her lips, again and again, fervently, to his boots. "Please!" she wept. "Please!"

He drew her up to her knees by the leash. And her face, tear-stained, the leash taut, was uplifted to him.

"No," he said.

"But I have begged!" she whispered.

"And rather nicely," he said, for an untrained slut."

He then jerked her up to her feet, before him.

"Tears, pleadings, and such," said he, "will avail you naught. You are not now dealing with the common run of the men of Earth, broken and subdued, acculturated weaklings, conditioned to pliability, trained to respond solicitously to the least of a female's absurd vagaries, but with men of another world, to whom no guerdon was sufficient to recompense them for the surrender of their sovereignty."

"Let me go," she said. "I—I will let you kiss me!"

He laughed, dryly.

She turned white.

"Really?" he said.

"Yes," she said, "yes!"

"You bargain?"

"Yes!"

He drew her by the coiled leash to him, closely, and she pursed her lips, but he thrust her back, rudely, suddenly, some six inches, to the end of the tether, as he held it.

"No bargain," said he, smiling. "Men do not bargain with slaves. On Gor you would doubtless be beaten, whipped well, and then fastened in a punishment tie, perhaps for hours, for the very suggestion."

She regarded him, frightened, her eyes wide.

"You may be kissed if and when men please," he said. "And you will learn to kiss, and to kiss properly, and to kiss as commanded, and to beg to kiss a man, intimately, and variously, as befits a slave."

"Please," she murmured.

"And in time," he said, "you will not only desire to please a man, but, unbidden and uncoerced, you will need to do so."

She lifted her bound wrists before her mouth, shaking her head, weakly.

"There is no escape for you, no rescue for you," he said. "The matter has been decided. You were selected six months ago."

She regarded him, startled, frightened, beginning to understand.

"Did you suspect nothing?"

"No," she said.

"Amusing," he said.

"But I wondered sometimes," she said. "I wondered—."

"Of course," he said. "You see, you did suspect."

Tears filled her eyes.

"Women are sensitive," he said. "That is one reason they make such excellent slaves. You will learn to well read the subtlest moods of a master. Your life might depend upon it."

"I was 'selected,'" she said.

"Yes," he said.

"But when, how?"

"Perhaps from time to time," he said, "doubtless from place to place."

She looked at him.

"Perhaps you recall a certain boutique, a particular clerk?"

"He?"

"Perhaps." he said, "or perhaps a cab driver, a security guard, a workman, a mechanic, a waiter, a delivery man, perhaps a fellow on a subway, or one at a bus stop, or that fellow on the platform of a commuter railroad, or that one seemingly waiting for the cab from which you emerged, that fellow with an attaché case, or perhaps another, that one standing a bit too close to you, in an elevator?"

"It could have been anyone," she said.

"Yes, and perhaps more than one. You were selected. You have been, in effect, a slave for several months, without realizing it."

"Sometimes I feared this, in my dreams."

"I am doing no more now than picking you up."

"I haven't seen you before, have I?"

"No," he said. "Nor I you. There is no connection between us, other than our present relationship. He, or those, who selected you may see you on Gor, and perhaps even, if they wish, keep you as a gift, or buy you privately, or bid on you at your first sale. I understand that you were rather unpleasant with a particular fellow, perhaps it was the clerk at the boutique. If he was your selector, or one of them, perhaps you will soon find yourself his slave, and under his whip. Or perhaps he merely thought you obviously suitable for a slave, but not one worthy of his own collar."

"I thought him weak," she whispered.

"Perhaps he was not as weak as you surmised, when you tried to bully and intimidate him, taking advantage of his supposed vulnerable and lowly position. Men of Gor on Earth sometimes feign weakness, in order to abet a disguise, in order to the better blend in with the common Earth male.

And sometimes they pretend to weakness in order to draw out vain, despicable behaviors in a female, behaviors which on Gor will be not only radically and perfectly corrected, but literally extirpated."

"You have not seen me before?"

"No, but I approve the selection."

"What have you there?" she said.

"It is a small vessel, vial-like. I shall hold it beneath your nose, and you will shortly lose consciousness. You will awaken, some days from now, in a Gorean slave pen."

She tried to pull away, but his left arm held her close to him. She struggled a little, helplessly. "Do you understand?" he asked.

"Yes," she whispered, "—*Master.*"

She then felt herself being taken gently into his arms, and lifted, and was aware, through the trees, of a white van, to which she was being carried.

"Yes, yes, yes," she whispered, "—*Master, Master, Master,*" and then lost consciousness.

Two Conversations

Note: The following two conversations may be of interest. The first is apparently reconstructed in part from surveillance, and, in part, it seems, from stenographic notes. It is not easy to tell. I have, at any rate, seen no film, nor recording, connected with it. Beyond this, at certain points, it seems, rather clearly, to have been supplemented, presumably later, by the personal memories of the participants, particularly one of them, that with respect to internal attitudes, emotional responses, and such. The second conversation is reconstructed from a stenographic transcription of a recording, one which, to my interest, I was permitted to hear. The first conversation seems to have taken place, I would conjecture, on our own world. The mention of a supermarket, and such, seems to make that clear. The second conversation seems interestingly related to the first, particularly with respect to its theme, and the supposition, or speculation, that somewhere a natural world might exist, one in which both men and women, in their diverse ways, find their freedom, and meaning. In short, the second conversation seems to have taken place, at least allegedly, on a world quite different from, and one yet not unrelated to, our own. Happily both conversations are in English. The participants in neither of the conversations have been identified, nor have I asked that they be identified.. The privacy of the first two, in any case, is to be respected, given the fanaticism, tyranny, and intolerance of contemporary puritanical ideologies. And the privacy of the second two, it seems, for obvious reasons, cannot but be respected, regardless of one's wishes, or views, on the matter. They are beyond the reach, it seems, at least if the recording is what it seems to be, of the small, stained, filed teeth, and poisoned claws of the bigots, the moral cretins and sexual retardates, the would-be Torquemadas, Cromwells, and Robespierres, of our time. It would be nice to think that somewhere, somehow, beyond the watch towers and prison gates, there are fields of untrodden grass, and an enlivened place where uncontaminated, fresh winds still blow. Perhaps one day the Earth will be reborn. It would be nice to see it again green, and alive. I would probably, of course, if I were to hear them again, recognize the voices in the second conversation, but then it does not seem likely that I, considering the circumstances, and the possibility that the conversation is what it seems to be, am likely to have that pleasure. I present the two conversations without further comment, and encourage the reader to consider them, and form his own judgment, as he sees fit.

I wish you well.

—John Norman.

Conversation$_1$

"You seem uneasy, distraught," he observed.

She shrugged.

"You have now come to grips with some insight?" he suggested.

"I don't know," she said.

"I shall tell you," he said. "The insight is that you know, in your heart, that you belong to me, that you are mine."

"I do not know what you are saying," she said.

"Obviously you do," he said.

"No!" she said.

"Surely you understand what you are, and what you want."

"I don't understand."

"Is it all that unclear—really?"

"And what am I?"

One whose identity and nature are clear, one whose very reality is obvious, one who should belong, and who rightfully belongs, totally, to another."

"Belong?"

"Yes."

"I do not understand."

"You do not know what you are?"

"No."

"You are, my dear, what you have in your heart feared to acknowledge, and what you know in your inmost heart you desire to be, and what in your inmost heart you know yourself to truly be—a slave."

"No!"

"And that is what you want, and want with all your heart, to be precisely what you are, a slave."

"No, no!"

"But in our world your slave instincts, your slave needs, are unfulfilled. They languish."

"How absurd!"

"Beware, girl, that remark may cost you."

"*Girl*!"

"Yes, *Girl*."

"Cost me?"

"Certainly."

"I am not afraid of you!"

"I hope that you are not stupid."

"I am not stupid!"

"Perhaps then you should be afraid."

"How insulting you are! I shall leave immediately!"

"The door is open. I see you hesitate. "Surely you understand that that is what you want—to be a slave—and that that is what you are—a slave."

"Surely not!" she cried, aghast.

"Oh?" he asked.

"Surely not," she stammered.

"You are blushing," he said.

She looked down, flustered.

"Why did you come to see me?" he asked.

"I don't know," she said.

"I shall tell you," he said. "You saw in my eyes, in the supermarket, that I was one who knew how to handle women, how to treat them—as they wish to be treated, and need to be treated."

"No!" she said.

"And that is why you followed me, as a slave girl her master."

"No!" she said. "It was the way I was going!"

"Do you think lying is acceptable in a slave?"

Fear came into her eyes.

"And I turned and confronted you, and you were frightened. I gave you my card, and told you when to present yourself—three days later, and not before, that you might have time to think about things, to consider, carefully, what you are doing, and what you want, and need."

"Yes," she whispered.

"And here you are," he said.

"Yes," she whispered.

"Look deeply into your heart," he said. "Are you a man's slave?"

"No!" she said. "Of course not!"

"You have now lied twice to me," he said. "You will be whipped for that."

She looked at him, in anguish.

"You do not speak. At least you do not lie. Look into your heart, your inmost heart, into your dreams, into your loveliest and most exciting dreams, into your sweet, hidden secrets, your deepest and loveliest secrets, nurtured so long in loneliness and silence. Surely you have longed to be bared before a master, completely, to know that you belong to him, fully, uncompromisingly, to feel every vulnerable, exposed inch of your soft, beautiful body enflamed with vulnerability and desire, to feel your lovely body burning with its meaning? Have you never been curious to know what it might be to be a submitted female, one truly submitted? Have you never in your dreams, in vulnerable passion, found yourself helplessly, and choicelessly, absolutely, before a master? Surely you have wondered what it would be to kneel at the feet of a man, one who owns you, and put your head down humbly, and press your soft lips to his boots? Does he so desire you that he has had you branded? Do you wear his collar? Have you never desired, truly, fearfully, to be at last handled and treated as you know is right for you, handled and treated as you know you deserve to be handled and treated, and need to be handled and treated, and desire to be handled and treated?"

"Please, mercy!"

"Look deeply into your heart," he commanded. "Are you a slave?"

"Yes," she whispered.

"Were you given the permission of a free man this morning, to clothe yourself?" he inquired.

"No," she said.

"Disrobe then, immediately, and kneel before me," he said.

She looked at him, in consternation.

"Do not dally," he said. "Obedience is to be instantaneous."

Hurriedly she removed her clothing, and knelt before him.

She was then utterly exposed, utterly, helplessly, before this lithe, powerful, dominating, fully clothed stranger. She felt terribly vulnerable.

He was the most attractive man she had ever seen, handsome, powerful, virile, masterful.

She had not realized such men could exist.

And she was on her knees, utterly stripped, utterly exposed, completely and vulnerably naked, before him

What, she wondered, could a woman be, but a slave before such a man. Indeed, in what other modality would a man such as he accept a woman, but as something he owned, a vulnerable, curvaceous, delicious property, over which he held absolute power?

And better to be, a thousand times, she thought, the abject slave of such a man than the honored, pampered, petulant, irritable, whining, dissatisfied darling of another.

"Spread your knees," he said.

She did so. She supposed that it was thus that slaves, or slaves of a certain sort, knelt before free men, masters.

"You are a slave?" he asked.

"Yes," she said.

"Who is your master?" he asked.

"I have no master," she whispered.

"Then you are at present an unclaimed slave?"

"Yes," she said.

"In Merchant Law," said he, "an unclaimed slave may be claimed by any free person."

She looked up at him from her knees, looked up into the eyes of a free person.

Never had she in this fashion looked into the eyes of another Never had she so looked into the eyes of another, not in this fashion, not as a slave. And, too, never before, she was sure, had she been so looked upon, looked upon as what she now was, as a slave.

Then, suddenly, she began to tremble, to shake. She feared she might faint. His look was such upon her that she was terrified to meet his gaze. She feared, even kneeling, that she might lose her balance, and fall to the rug before him. Had any man, ever, she wondered, so looked upon a woman, so clearly, so fixedly, so severely, so uncompromisingly? How he saw her! How she was seen by him! It seemed to her then that she could not possibly sustain that gaze. It was too terrible, too fixed, too burning, too powerful! Then, suddenly, whimpering, overcome, shuddering, frightened, she thrust her head down, daring no longer to meet those eyes. No longer could she bear the intensity, the ferocity, of that fearsome connection, eye to eye, mind to mind, body to body.

"Look at me, now!" he snapped.

Moaning, she lifted her head. She kept her eyes closed for a moment, even though her head was lifted to him, and then she fearfully opened her eyes, knowing that she must do so. She winced, and gasped.

"Do not look away," he said.

She struggled to hold her position, and not to cry out and throw herself miserably, helplessly, to the floor before him.

"Do not look away," he told her. "You are going to be claimed."

It was as though she was gazing into the eyes of a predatory beast, whose vulnerable prey she might instantly prove to be, as into the eyes of human tiger lusting for the meat of her flesh, which she understood by his power he would make his, possessing it totally as he pleased, looking into his eyes as might a paralyzed, roped beautiful captive, one hoping to be spared, on any terms, into the eyes of a conquering master.

"Do you understand?" he asked.

"Yes," she whispered. How hard it was for her to even articulate sound at such a time.

"Look at me!"

"Yes."

"You are going to be claimed. Do you understand?"

"—Yes."

"I claim you," he said, clearly, utterly matter-of-factly, decisively.

It was done, she knew. She had been claimed!

She could not move before him. Her entire being seemed irradiated by, and transformed, as it was, by those simple words. She gasped, and made tiny, helpless sounds, and trembled.

He was then merciful, and said, "You may lower your eyes."

She sobbed, an exhalation of relief so sudden, so

explosive, so hitherto pent up, so profound that it shook her entire small, lovely body, and then, overcome, unable to help herself, she fell from her knees to the carpet, humbled, trembling, helpless, before him, so grateful to have been permitted to look away from that pitiless gaze, so piteously thankful that the steel cord of his will had released her.

"You are now a claimed slave," he said.

"Yes," she whispered.

"Kneel," he said.

She struggled to kneel again before him.

She dared not raise her gaze higher than his knees.

"Whose slave are you?" he asked.

"I am your slave," she said.

"'I am your slave', what?" he asked.

"I am your slave," she said, "—*Master.*"

"Put down your head and kiss my feet," he said.

"Yes, Master," she said.

He let her minister thusly for some time, softly kissing his feet, until she well understood the nature of her condition.

"Hereafter," he said, "you may not clothe yourself without the permission of the master. Further, if you wish to speak, other than acknowledging your understanding of your instructions, and such, you must request permission to do so. That permission may or may not be granted. It is within the discretion of the master. Do you understand?"

"Yes, Master," she whispered.

"Your body must be kept clean, and attractive," he said. "A slave may not be slovenly. She must strive to please the master, in all ways. *In all ways.* She is to be docile, subservient, and compliant. Her obedience, of course, must be complete, perfect, and instantaneous. Do you understand?"

"Yes, Master," she said.

"She may upon occasion," said he, "be granted some respite, a bit of lenience, should it amuse the master, to cry out, to complain, to challenge, to plead, to beg, but this latitude, at a word, may be withdrawn, and she will be returned instantly to the state of abject servitude, that of unquestioning, unconditional subservience. Do you understand?"

"Yes, Master."

"She is still, of course, even at such times, his total slave."

"Yes, Master."

"Too, you must understand," he said, "that it is the whole of you that is owned, your body, your emotions, your mind, all of you. You are owned—*totally.* Do you understand this?"

"Yes, Master," she said.

"Look up," he said, "into my eyes."

She did so, fearfully.

"And," said he, "the slave is subject to discipline, and is totally at the mercy of the master."

Her eyes widened.

"Do you understand, girl?" he said.

For the slave is, of course, a "girl," with all the charm, beauty, and vulnerability that that lovely expression connotes.

"Yes, Master," she whispered, frightened.

"And you must accustom yourself to chains, and such things, for example, to be chained to the foot of a man's bed, thongs, cords, gags, blindfolds, such things."

"Yes, Master," she said.

"That you are a slave, of course, is something which, on the whole, unfortunately, must be concealed on this world, lest it generate envy, or concern."

She bowed her head, his slave.

"Bondage, as you doubtless know," he said, "was sanctioned for centuries in all parts of the world, in all civilizations."

"Yes Master."

"Knees," he said.

"Yes, Master," she said. "Forgive me, Master."

She lifted her body, and straightened it. She spread her knees.

She kept her head down, her knees spread.

She would doubtless soon accustom herself to slave position, the postures and attitudes of docility, vulnerability, and subservience. Soon, doubtless, without self-consciousness, she would naturally, and easily, thoughtlessly and appropriately, so place herself before free persons.

"I wonder," said he, "if there is somewhere a natural world, somewhere, where these natural relationships, in all their beauty and power, are accepted, celebrated and institutionalized." He looked down upon her. "What do you think, my little thong slut, my little chain bitch?" he asked.

She looked up at him, for a moment uncertain, for a moment troubled, that he had spoken so to her. To be sure, a master may speak as he wishes to a slave. Then she saw something in his eyes, could it have been a smile, a hint of such, which was not unkind, and she, at his feet, rejoiced. Yes, she thought, I am his thong slut! I am his chain bitch! That is what I am! And it is what I want to be, and I want to serve him with my whole heart and soul, and in that moment she grasped something of what it might be to be the helpless, ardent slave of a mighty master. How complete, how fulfilling, how nurturing, how glorious, how joyous, how magnificent to a woman, or should one now say "girl," was such a relationship! Perhaps, if I am sufficiently pleasing, she thought, I can win from him a smile, perhaps, in time, though I am only a lowly slave, his love! She had a sense then, trembling nude before him, of what it might be to be a love slave!

Could she hope for so much?

"Well?" he asked.

"I do not know," she whispered. "Perhaps, Master."

She looked again to his eyes, but now they were different. She saw that she was now again only a slave at his feet. He was now looking upon her with a free man's contempt for a piece of meaningless slave meat. She saw that he would be strict with her. Had he been embarrassed by, she wondered, angered by, what he sensed in himself might have been a moment of weakness? To be sure, she wanted him to be strict with her. She needed that. She wanted no choice, but to be made to serve. This was important to her. She wondered if he might, someday, care for her. She sensed she might love him, that she already did love him. Too, she supposed that it would be hard for a girl not to fall in love with a man at the foot of whose bed she is chained. She would surely, unquestioningly, undeniably, know herself his. Perhaps it has to do with dominance and submission, pervasive in animal life, she supposed. Perhaps, she thought, it has to do with the complementarities of nature.

But mostly, she supposed, it might have to do with him, the particular him, and with her, the particular her of her, and the mysterious chemistries of men and women. Away, she thought, with the commands of a stunting, pathological culture, the frenetic, hate-filled competitions for power, which brought in their wake only disappointment, emptiness, and misery.

In the supermarket she sensed he had looked upon her and seen her as a stripped slave.

She had never forgotten that look.

How could any woman?

He had seen her as what she was—a vulnerable woman, an unclaimed, needful slave.

How stunned she had been!

How her body had suddenly burned within her garments.

She had followed him as, as he had said, a slave girl follows her master.

There are many slaves, she thought. Are there many masters? My culture has not taken the slave out of me. She has cried out within me, for years, for her chains, and the caress of a master.

She wondered if, in men, or in some men, there might be a secret master, restless within the male breast, snarling within, raging, hungry for its prey, its capture, its slave.

How much illness, how much violence, how much

cruelty, she thought, might be averted if only men were free, statistically, to be themselves, and how much cruelty, petulance, neurosis, and unhappiness might be done away with if only the natural needs of women were recognized, rather than denounced and subverted.

"You may now rise, and dress yourself," he said.

"Yes, Master," she whispered. "Thank you, Master."

Conversation$_2$

"I am not an animal!" she cried.

"Surely you are," she said. "Are you so unacquainted with biology as to doubt that? Have you not lungs, organs, and such? Have you not a belly appropriate to your kind? A nervous system, a digestive system, and, obviously, something that will be of interest to men, a reproductive system? Thus, if it is wished, you may be crossed with suitable stock, and bred. Clearly you are an animal. Do not presume to deny it. You are an animal, and an animal of a certain sort, a mammal, a human mammal, and, obviously, a human female mammal. Consider the delicacy of your features, their obvious sensitivity and even, obviously, their beauty. You have lovely eyes, and lashes, and sweet lips. And you have abundant and lovely hair, deeply rich and brown. Unfortunately it is not auburn."

"What is wrong with that?"

"I see you are already interested in your objective value."

"My objective value?"

"Do you shiver? Or do you tremble? Interesting how you try to draw those tiny shreds of garments about you. Do you think they much conceal you, or protect you? They haven't left you with much, have they?"

"My objective value?"

"Are the chains heavy?"

"Objective value?"

"Doubtless, as you assess yourself, you are priceless. But

that is a subjective estimation, as you will discover. It is not your objective value. Your self-appraisal on the score of your own worth, you see, is not likely to withstand the scrutiny of the market. You will discover, you pretty, arrogant little thing, that your self-assessments of your value are not only unreliable, but simply illusory. Do not look so petulant. And do not pull so at your chains. Do you think you can free yourself? Do you think you can remove them? On the other hand there are girls who have low self-esteem, and think poorly of themselves, who, to their surprise, and doubtless delight, discover they are prized, and avidly sought. But you need not fear that sort of awakening. I fear yours, though you are quite beautiful, it must be admitted, will be less welcome."

"So I am beautiful?"

"Of course, were you not, it is unlikely you would find yourself where you are."

"What is wrong with my hair?"

"Nothing, you are nicely pelted."

"'Pelted'!"

"Auburn hair, you see, tends to be prized. It is rare. And blond hair sells well, too, presumably as it is less common."

"Then let them dye my hair," she snapped.

"And have them risk torture and impalement?" she laughed. "I think not!"

"I do not understand."

"On this world, honesty is not frowned upon. Rather, deceit is disapproved, and often savagely. It has to do with honor, I am told, something apparently of interest to the men of this world. This world, you see, is very different, in many ways, from that with which you are more familiar."

"Why have I been brought here?"

"I wonder if you are stupid."

"I am not stupid!" she said. "Why do you smile?"

"Once, long ago, I recall I, too, said that, though the circumstances were different. It was shortly before I found myself kneeling naked, for the first time, before my master."

"'Master'?"

"Certainly."

"You mean as in 'one who to whom you *belong*,' as in 'one who *owns* you'?"

"Of course."

"You cannot be owned!"

"How naive you are!"

"I do not think you are stupid."

"I do not think so, either. Indeed, I am supposedly quite intelligent, and surely so, if the IQ scores of your world have any significance."

"I assure you I am not stupid, either!"

"Perhaps not, but it seems that at present you have little but your beauty to commend you."

"My beauty?"

"Rejoice. Be grateful. That is your hope. Men like such things."

"Please do not speak to me as though I were stupid!"

"Naive, then?"

"No!"

"I think so, that, at least."

"Do not humiliate me."

"That is not my intention. That will be done by the masters, and well, if they choose."

"Masters?"

"Of course."

"I do not wish to be humiliated."

"But you do. And do not fear. They can make us weep, and beg and grovel, as it pleases them."

"Why have I been brought here?"

"It is questions like that which suggest that you are stupid."

"I—I am not stupid!"

"No, I would suppose not, or you would not be here. If you were truly stupid, you would have been less desirable, less of an acquisition, less of a prize. If you were truly stupid you would not have been found of interest. They are interested in only the most desirable, *la crème de la crème*. These men have little interest in stupid women."

"You have not told me why I have been brought here."
"If you do not know, perhaps you are indeed stupid."
"No!"
"There are trade-offs, of course. Perhaps in your case they compromised on intelligence, in order to obtain other things of interest."
"Do not speak as though I might be merely beautiful!"
"As I look upon you now, lifting the lamp, perhaps 'pretty' would be better."
"Beautiful!"
"Perhaps. You are, at least, a well-curved bit of meat."
"Do not speak so of me!"
"Perhaps it is something else. Are you vital?"
"I don't understand."
"It is not important—*now.* You will grow in such ways. They will see to it. Until you are helpless, and uncontrollable."
"I don't understand!"
"You will be totally at their mercy, begging."
"I don't understand you! You speak in riddles! You torture me! I don't understand you! I understand nothing! Why have I been brought here?"
"Conjecture."
"No!"
"Your horizons of possibility seem rather limited."
"I am not stupid! I am not stupid!"
"Then ignorant, perhaps?"
"Why have I been brought here?"
"You know."
"No, no!"
"Pretending not to recognize the obvious does not mean that it does not exist."
"No!"
"Yes, weep, weep, weep in your chains, curvaceous little thing, in helplessness and futility, if you wish. It will doubtless do you good."
"What do they want with me? Why have I been brought here?"

"You dare to play these games with me? Do you see this switch at my wrist? It can be used upon you. Good. You are afraid. You crawl back in the shadows, on the straw. You do not wish to feel pain. Excellent. You will be tractable. You will train well."

"Please be kind to me."

"You wish, I gather, for me to tell you what you fear, and what you suspect, and what you wish to hear?"

"No, no!"

"Do not fear. I have no intention of doing so. Why should I insult whatever bit of intelligence you might have? Let me say only that the moment of which you have long and frequently dreamed is nearly at hand."

"I do not understand."

"A good switching would much improve you."

"Please, no."

"I am patient with you, little fool. The men will not be."

"Why have I been brought here?"

"Consider the loveliness of your face, how exquisite it is, the vulnerability, delicacy, and sensitivity of its features, and the prettiness of your legs, the sweetness of your thighs, the width of your hips, the narrowness of your waist, the loveliness of your bosom. The delicacy of your wrists and ankles, the subtleties of your shoulders and throat, the curvatures of your body. Can you then ask such a question?"

"I do not understand."

"Such things will make you attractive to men."

"I hate men!"

"How unfortunate, for you will belong to them."

"No!"

"Totally, completely, absolutely—in all ways."

"You speak as though I might be owned!"

"You are owned."

"I cannot be owned!"

"You are mistaken."

"I cannot be owned! I am not a dog, or pig!"

"You are less than they, but you do not yet realize it."

"No, no!"

"You have a lovely throat, slender and sweet, and aristocratic. It will look well encircled with a collar."

"A collar?"

"Certainly."

"What sort of collar?"

"One like mine, one signifying the same."

"What sort of collar?"

"The collar of a slave—a slave collar."

"No, no!"

"Do not struggle so, so wildly, so futilely. Please, desist. You may injure yourself. And the masters might be displeased."

"Masters! Masters! —Masters?"

"Yes, the men."

"Release me from the wall!"

"Have no fear, you will soon be released."

"Good!"

"Even now the iron is heating which will mark you."

"Mark me?"

"Yes, the iron that will mark you slave."

"No, no!"

"You cannot expect not to be marked, for you might be mistaken for a free woman, and that would be terrible. How insulting to free women! To be sure, it is highly unlikely that a woman such as you, so sweetly bodied, so beautiful, so small, so soft, so feminine, yes, feminine, truly feminine, do you object, would be mistaken for a free woman. That would seem unthinkable. Just looking upon you a free person would know you for a slave. Yet, the brand is required by Merchant Law. One cannot be too careful about such things. Too, the brand will help you to remember that you are a slave, simply that, a slave, that, and nothing else."

"How is my objective value to be determined?"

"Simply, by what men will pay to own you."

"Pay?"

"Of course."

"I am a free person!"

"Do not be naive."
"I cannot be owned!"
"You are mistaken."
"I can't be owned—"
"I do not understand. Why can you not be owned?"
"I—I am not an African!"
"You refer to a race, or group, I take it, of your world. I know something of your world, which is why I am here, speaking to you in a language you can understand. On this world races, as you seem to think of them, do not exist. Here, free men stand to one another as individuals, not as representatives of groups, not, in effect, as members of gangs, as of brigands. But even on your world, slavery was never restricted to those whom you ignorantly put together so naively as "Africans." All races, as you think of them, were subject to bondage. For centuries, whites, as you might think of them, enslaved whites. Too, blacks, as you might think of them, enslaved blacks, and Asians, as you might think of them, enslaved Asians, and those you might think of as the indigenous peoples of what was known as "the new world" enslaved one another."
"Not now!"
"My dear, slavery still exists on your former world, in several areas. And it would exist more broadly except that a relatively small, but technologically advanced and powerful, portion of your population, perhaps in a jealousy concerning the pleasures of the mastery, being enjoyed by others, not by themselves, or fearing that they themselves might one day succumb to bondage, took the liberty of imposing their military and economic will on other peoples. But that could change. Indeed, as bondage has its values and rationale, and its obvious appeal to thinking men under certain conditions, it may come about that the darker peoples, so to speak, may reinstitute the condition, when sufficiently powerful or so motivated, and then that the vaunted superiors will find themselves, in their turn, in their chains, in the holds of slave ships, and on the auction blocks. Who then, I wonder, will "rescue" them? The appeal of bondage is obviously

universal, and a turning of the world might bring it about again.

"I see you do not care to speak. Perhaps you do not like these thoughts. Yet I thought I saw you tremble in your chains."

"No!"

"Surely you understand that slavery represents an advance in civilization over obvious alternatives."

"What?"

"Being slain, being exterminated, being tortured to death, being burned alive, and such."

"Of course," she said.

"Surely you understand the attractions of ease, of pleasure and power to human beings?"

"—Yes."

"And you can understand then how a strong human being might prefer a life of greater ease, one in which he is served less by himself and more by another, a life in which he may extract what pleasures he wishes from another, one over whom he holds absolute power."

"One must deny oneself such pleasures and powers!"

"Why?"

"I—I do not know."

"Nor do I. Why should the strong not avail themselves of such delights? Why should they not choose to be pleasured, to be powerful? Is that not the sane, sound, and healthy fulfillment of their natural right? Why should not those who can seize the delicious fruits of life do so? Why should the rewards and perquisites of nature, her gifts and bounties, not be taken advantage of by the strongest and fittest, the most powerful, the most intelligent, the aristocrats of nature?"

"Let it not be so!"

"What an amusing little tart you are! But put aside these questions of your former world, and its conflicts, confusions, and vicissitudes. It is here that you are now. And be assured, curvaceous little mammal, that on this world, an honest. open, beautiful world, slavery is an institution with universal incidence. Its value is accepted and understood.

It is historically sanctioned and practiced. It is a matter of custom, law, and tradition. It is unquestioned and universally accepted.

"Why should those who are natural slaves not be slaves, and those who are natural masters not be masters?

"Do not hide your face in your hands. Look up at me. Wipe the tears from your eyes. Have you never dreamed of being a slave, really, of meeting a man like no other, one before whom you could not help but kneel, and lick and kiss his feet, and would melt in need and submission, one to whom you could at best be an abject object, a mere property, a domestic animal, an item of livestock, purchasable from a pen, a lovely beast, one from which is to be derived service, and ecstatic pleasure?

"I see you have."

"No, no, no!"

"Are you even worthy to be the slave of such a man?"

"Please do not so speak to me!"

"Well, here you will meet men such as you never knew could exist, men beyond your wildest and most erotic dreams, men before whom you can be naught but such a slave, an utterly abject slave. Oh, you will learn to serve well, and you will experience pleasures, and provide pleasures, the nature and intensity of which, and the extent of which, you cannot now even conceive. Oh, you will make a delicious little slave."

"No, no!"

"I see it in you."

"No!"

"But are you even worthy of being such a slave?"

"I do not know!"

"Men have brought you here. They know their business. They think you have promise, or you would not find yourself in this place. They have seen fit to give you a trial."

"A trial?"

"An opportunity to prove yourself worthy of a brand and collar. I hope that you will do well, pretty little slave."

"And if I do not?"

"I would try desperately, if I were you. These men are not patient."

"And if I fail?"

"There are animals to be fed, to whom you would be a lovely dessert, a most tasty morsel."

"No!"

"Do not fail."

"I do not want to be a slave!"

"There you are mistaken."

"No!"

"You have always dreamed of meeting your master, a man so magnificent, so powerful, that you know instantly in your heart that you are rightfully his, a man so overwhelming and attractive that before him you can be naught but a dutiful, submitted, passionate, enraptured slave."

"I am inert, cold, frigid, I have no such feelings!"

"Do not believe all you have been taught. The veils of politics, woven by the self-seeking fearers and haters, the ugly moral amputees, the spiritual cripples, those who strive to force the dismal grayness and chilling cold of their lives on others, are rent by the truths of biology. Dare to feel. The furies of blood refute the casuistries of conditioning. The caress of a master can shatter convention's fragile, carefully constructed house of cards. A kiss can open a window, a door, to a new world. Love is not so dangerous and terrible."

"You speak of love?"

"Of dominance and submission, of rightfulness, of propriety, of nature, of complementarity, of dimorphism, of biology. Women are property. Thus, they learn love best on a chain."

"Have I a choice?"

"None whatsoever, absolutely none, little slave girl."

"Please do not so demean me, do not so refer to me!"

"So you think you hate men?"

"Yes, yes!"

"That may amuse them."

"But I must serve them nonetheless?"

"With sensuous perfection."

"I am not sure I hate men," she whispered.

"I know.

"And you will soon live to give them pleasure, and I predict, little slave girl, that you will soon know the highest happiness a woman can know, for we are their properties, by nature, you must understand, the happiness of being the yielding, joyful slave of an uncompromising, overwhelming, and mighty master."

"I am afraid."

"And well you might be, for you will be subject to strict discipline. He will have what he wants of you, have no fear."

"I am ignorant."

"That is a problem, for it puts you at greater peril. It would doubtless be better if you had received extensive training in the many arts of the female slave, but the market is unfortunately overburdened with beauty at the moment, and the merchants wish to move stock, particularly the lesser stock, such as you, quickly, to save time, to clear space and such."

"When am I to be sold?"

"Tonight."

"Tonight?"

"Yes."

"Thank you for your kindness, in speaking to me."

"I wished to do so."

"You asked for permission to speak to me?"

"Yes."

"Thank you.

"It is nothing," she said.

"I am afraid to be sold."

"Of course."

"Were you once of my world?"

"Of course."

"You spoke of your master."

"I met him on Earth."

"Were you his slave there?"

"Of course, as I am his slave here."

"He was of Earth?"

"Yes, but he was a master, and thus he made me his slave there. I love him. He is everything to me. I would die for him."

"How did he come here?"

"He is such a man as those of this world respect. He was detected, and offered an invitation to come to this world. He accepted."

"And you?"

"He brought me with him."

"—as his slave?"

"Of course, that is what I was."

"And you serve him here?"

"As lovingly and perfectly as I can."

"Are you—branded?"

"Yes, it was done shortly after I arrived on this world. It is required by Merchant Law. Now anyone on this world, seeing I am branded, would know that I am a slave, am purchasable, and such."

"You are very beautiful."

"Thank you, and so, too, are you."

"Thank you, and I do not think, really, that I am stupid."

"No, you are not stupid."

"Is this a beautiful world?"

"Yes, much as Earth must once have been."

"I think I am not displeased to have been brought here."

"You begin to suspect what might be your life here?"

"I think so."

"A life that you only dreamed you might live."

"Yes."

"Though only as a rightless, abject slave?"

"Yes."

"Such, my dear, you are, and will be."

"It is so beautiful! If only one would not grow old, and it could last forever!"

"There are serums here, called stabilization serums. A secret of the caste of physicians. You may fear desperately on this world, but you need not fear the diminution of your beauty. Men will enjoy keeping it in its collar, indefinitely, at the pinnacle of its health, youth, and loveliness."

"Is it true?"

"Yes."

"Thank you."

"They will come for you soon."

"How shall I behave? What shall I do?"

"Present yourself as well as you can on the block. Know that you are beautiful, and desirable, and exciting. Understand that. Know in the bottom of your belly that you are for sale, and will be sold, and are excellent goods. Be erotic, brazen, and beautiful. Be what you will then be, wares, a commodity, a lovely property in the process of being vended—a beautiful slave, an exhibited, proffered slave.

"I see that you try to fold those miserable shreds of garments about you Do you think they conceal you? Rather they will intrigue the men."

"I am frightened!"

"And even those bits of rags will be removed from you on the block. Men insist on seeing—completely— what they are buying. They are not fools."

"Surely I will not be shown to men—not to men!—even as I am!"

"Were you a trained slave you would not ask such a question."

"But I am not such a slave!"

"I am to you at this time, though slave myself, as Mistress. That may not have been clear to you. But I now make it clear. Accordingly you should address me as "Mistress." It would be well for you to accustom yourself to such things. Oh, do not look upon me with such dismay, such bewilderment and horror."

"But I am not such a slave—*Mistress*."

"True. But now, were you such a slave, you would know that you would be so exhibited. You would expect it, and, further, if given a choice, would insist upon it, that you might, in the competitions of beauty, be able to strive fairly, and without detriment, to obtain the most excited, covetous master, he who most hungers and thirsts for you, and cries out and roars to possess you."

"Can men so desire a woman?"

"Yes."

"How fearful to belong to one who so wants one!"

"Who would desire to belong to one who wants one less?"

"I am afraid to be exhibited, to be shown to men, naked—to be put up for sale, to be sold. I do not know what to do, how to act."

"—Perhaps, I wonder, while it is still possible, before you are unable any longer to conceal your appetition, your aroused slave needs, your piteous need of a master, if you should present yourself as fearful and shy, timid, troubled, modest, and frightened, almost unable to move so horrified, so dismayed and terrified you are."

"Mistress?"

"Some men enjoy taking a new slave, a fragile, lovely thing, and introducing her to the nature and requirements of her new condition, in getting her to her knees and teaching her to kiss and caress.

"Do not weep.

"Too, there are those who enjoy taking a woman who thinks she can resist, and teaching her differently, breaking her to the whip and collar, until she, to her ecstasy, knows herself his, and crawls of her own free will to his slave ring, her effusive, conquered heart begging to be accepted, to be permitted to please him, to be acknowledged, as his."

"I know nothing of these things, Mistress."

"How easily the word 'Mistress' now comes to your lips. You see, you are intelligent. You learn quickly.

"Perhaps the important thing is to be yourself. Perhaps later, when you have become appetitious and needful, and erotic, brazen, and beautiful, for I see such things in you, as a natural and exciting transformation of yourself, things will be easier, and different. Until then perhaps it will be best to attempt to divine the will of the auctioneer, and do your best to please him. To be sure, we all do that. After all, he has a whip, and we are women. I know whereof I speak, for I myself was once put through that. A sale, or seeming sale. It was, unbeknownst to me, intended as a learning experience for me, that I might, newly brought to his world, be better apprised of my condition, of my status here, as a slave. Of what could be done to me. I found myself without so much as an explanation, without so much as even a word of farewell, remanded to an auction house. In my bonds, in tears and helplessness, I racked my heart and brain in misery. Had I in some way, even one unbeknownst to me, been less than completely pleasing to my master in some way? I did not know! I learned the lesson well. I was apparently purchased through an agent. How jubilant I was when I, unhooded, found myself on my knees before my own master, my own, true, beloved master! I assure you that I spent much of that night in tearful gratitude, at his feet. I had learned what might be done with me."

"I will try to please the auctioneer."

"You had better, or your prettiness will feel the lash."

"I would be whipped?"

"Of course."

"I am frightened."

"I do not think you will have too much to fear, for the auctioneer is talented. He will see to it that you are well displayed. You may depend upon it. And do not be surprised when you find yourself handled as a slave. You will be exhibited, and controlled, almost ritualistically. You will move, and obey, in ways you never thought possible. On the selling surface you will reveal hitherto never understood, or dreadfully feared, but desired, aspects of your personality. Perhaps your female subconscious will be liberated for the first time. You will discover, my dear, perhaps to your surprise, that you have one. There is something about the snap of a whip which we all understand, and its lash across our calves is an admonition we cannot overlook. Do the best you can."

"I will try."

"And it is not uncommon, at a certain point in your sale, to have your vitality demonstrated."

"What does that mean?"

"Men are interested in that."

"I do not understand."

"You will learn.

"I am afraid, so afraid."

"Do not fear. Or fear no more than is appropriate, and that will hone your slave reflexes to perfection.

"Do not weep.

"It is not so terrible to be sold. Indeed, as you are merchandise it is fitting. And yours is not a unique fate. Countless women in countless times on countless worlds have preceded you to the block, which is a mere selling platform, a convenience for display. In time, you will doubtless grow accustomed to such things. And do not fear for, as I have indicated, the auctioneer will assist you, and turn, and display you, and such. He does not wish you ill, and desires little more than to make a good coin on you. Now it is possible, as I suggested, that in this sale, your first sale, you will be confused and terrified. Certainly it will all seem strange to you. But that is not unusual. You may even seem inhibited, wooden, almost unable to move. That is possible. You may appear frightened and confused, disconcerted, and bewildered, and you might appear, and might well be, utterly helpless and vulnerable. But the auctioneer, and the men, will understand that, and not hold it against you, not in a first sale. Later, surprising as this may now seem, you will learn to present yourself well on the block, extremely well, for a well-presented girl tends to bring a better price, and such prices are most easily afforded by an affluent master, and many girls, wisely or not, prefer to wear their collars in a rich house, in a mansion or palace, rather than a hut or hovel. We are often mercenary little things, aren't we? It is no wonder the men look upon us as what we are, as lovely, cunning little beasts, tolerable only, so to speak, on our leashes. But it sometimes happens that your eyes will meet those of a man in the tiers, and you will know, suddenly, that he is the man for whom you have always longed, and dreamed, he to whom you would be the perfect slave. You have suddenly realized that he is your love master. Oh, then you will present yourself well—I assure you, and to him! It will be as though there were no others in that great room, only you and he. You will then be erotic, brazen, and, beggingly beautiful, a needful slave desperately pleading with her rightful master to buy her. Will he buy you, or not? The decision, of course, is his."

"We are so helpless, so vulnerable!"

"Yes, for we are slaves."

"Thank you, thank you!"

"I wish you well, little slave girl. Wear your collar happily. In it, I assure you, you will find yourself more free than ever you were on your former world, and you will learn, and experience, a joy alien to your world, and greater than any you might have believed possible, or for which you might have hoped."

In Defense of the Russett Hypothesis

SOMETIME ago, in what used to be referred to as the 20th Century, in certain antique inscriptions, or something like one hundred and two ziks before the modern era, there was a British philosopher, as it is said, there will always be an England, whose name may have been Bartelby Russett. And although contemporary pundits have an unwonted tendency to ignore or dispraise the Middle Ages, it must be understood that there were in such benighted, ignorant, and barbarous times occasional men of outstanding intellectual stature, of which small number Bartelby Russett was undeniably one. Had he not stood on the shoulders of pigmies he might have seen less far than he did. Russett once opined that the world might have been created but five minutes ago, bearing within it all the signs of age, memories, beliefs, records, contracts, plans, crumbling parchments, obsolete musical instruments, families, geological strata, weathered rocks, fossils, old books, old shoes, partially decayed radioactive substances, and such. The remarkable thing about Russett's hypothesis, which was, predictably, ignored or derided in his own time, was how very close to the mark he had actually come, given the imprecise, primitive technology of his time. As it has turned out, and as every schoolboy now knows, it actually came into existence not five but four minutes ago, bearing within it all the signs of age, including Russett's hypothesis itself.

To be sure, one of the fascinating aspects of Russett's hypothesis involves an intriguing philosophical anomaly. Namely, how do we know, *really*, that the world did not come into existence billions of years ago, and slowly, gradually, develop into its present state? It is a possibility, one supposes, at least logically. Skeptics enjoy playing with such ideas, the flippant idlers. According to science, and common sense, the world is something like four minutes old, give or take a few seconds, but will the skeptic subdue his irresponsible playfulness and have the common decency to acquiesce in this point, to desist in his reckless amusements, and accept the cognitively accredited, indisputably established results of contemporary science? No. He will relentlessly tantalize us with his shallow, silly, reckless, meretricious possibilities. Who could answer him? Who would want to? If he will not accept the results of scientific inquiry, what will he accept? What has he to offer in its place? Has he a plausible challenge to science? Has he, say, a different, or better, science? No, there is no practical, relevant alternative which he offers us. Why should the burden of proof in such a rash, giddy matter be on us, and not upon him? Fie upon him! Fie upon all scatterbrains!

Let him offer his considerations.

We shall refute him at every turn.

He suggests that the scientific hypothesis is implausible, but this is absurd, because it is itself the scientific hypothesis, and thus defines plausibility. Perhaps he wonders what point there would be to the scientific hypothesis, but, better, what point would there be to his gradualistic hypothesis; too, scientific hypotheses do not have to have points; they need only truth.

Perhaps he thinks the scientific hypothesis is arbitrary, but are not all beginnings arbitrary? If there is no problem with beginning billions of years ago, as he sees it, then, too, there is no problem with beginning four minutes, or so, ago. Perhaps the world might have started, say, five minutes ago, as in the Russett hypothesis, but, in fact, it didn't. Who are we to tell the world when, or how, to get underway?

Perhaps he thinks the scientific view is "disruptive"? But it would be so only if one accepted his own view. Are not such things relative? Why is it more disruptive to begin recently than billions of years ago? Too, why should a beginning be "disruptive"? Why should it not just be a beginning? Too, a beginning cannot be disruptive because before it there is nothing to disrupt.

The skeptic might suggest that his own vapid view is to be preferred to the scientific point of view on the grounds of allowing for the laws of nature, the principle of the conservation of matter/energy, and such, but this is to misunderstand the scientific view. The laws of nature, the principle of the conservation of matter/energy, and such, are part and parcel of the scientific view. It could not get along without them. It is merely that they haven't been around as long as the skeptic would like. They had to start sometime, so why when *they* say, and not when science says?

Perhaps the skeptic bemoans the scientific view because it seems to presuppose a transempirical causative factor? Well, it does not presuppose such *within* its world. And outside of its world, so to speak, is it not in the same boat with the skeptic's suggestions? Surely the mystery is there, on both views. Indeed, as the world is of recent origin the skeptic's view of an operative, effecting mystery more than five minutes ago is simply a mistake. It could not have occurred in the past because the past does not exist, or at least not much it. To be sure, it is growing.

Consider typical criteria for evaluating hypotheses, such as precision, clarity, simplicity, testability, fruitfulness, scope, and conservatism. The scientific hypothesis is obviously precise, almost to the second. Obviously the skeptic's suggestion is deplorably vague. Billions of years? How many billions? Nonsense! The scientific hypothesis, on the other hand, is marvelously clear. Who can not understand it, particularly if they can tell time? The scientific hypothesis, too, is simple, and easy, and straight-forward. It accounts for everything, and with a minimum of explanatory entities. It is testable, too, for one may count backward, and determine that the world was there four minutes ago. As for the rest, it started up then, and did not exist before, so there is nothing to test before the beginning. Hypothesis confirmed! The hypothesis also is fruitful and has scope. It is surely fruitful for its theoretical tentacles embrace and illuminate all fields, and it surely has scope, for it covers everything. More scope than that you cannot get. And if the skeptic is not satisfied here, do not his own views make similar universal claims? And conservatism, or the imperative to respect cognitive coherence, to fit in with other views, to cause as little cognitive dislocation, and revision and readjustment, as possible is clearly a strong suit of the scientific view. It *is* the scientific view; thus other views which might not cohere with it are, *prima facie*, to be rejected. And needless to say, the skeptic's views are not "conservative." Their adoption would jeopardize a world view, and lead to intellectual anarchy, if not chaos.

By now the position of skeptic is clearly in a shambles.

But, failing to make his point by an appeal to science, objectivity, fact, rationality, logic, and such, he is likely to resort desperately to pragmatic or humanistic considerations which, strictly, are irrelevant to the matter, indeed, which constitute nothing more than an embarrassing appeal to *argumentum ad consequentiam*.

The following sorts of appeals are typical.

Would not the scientific hypothesis require recourse not simply to a transempirical, causative factor, but to an intellectually offensively *arbitrary* transempirical, causative factor? Not officially, but one could always speculate on such matters. In any event, would not the skeptic's suggestion also require something like that, as well? It seems the major differences would just be a choice of times. The skeptic's hypothesis also admits, of course, in another variant, the possibility of a causeless, eternal ground, for a causeless, eternal world. The scientific hypothesis could opt for the same view, actually. In a sense the four-minute world is also eternal, since it has existed for all time, as it had to, since there was no time before it. It could, of course, have just have popped into being, for no particular reason at all, as might have the skeptic's eccentric world, rather in the sense of a quantum fluctuation. If the world is the result of something like a quantum fluctuation why not a recent fluctuation rather than a remote fluctuation?

Would not the scientific hypothesis undermine revelation, subvert orthodoxy, cast doubt on the contents of highly regarded books, and so on? One supposes it might, but then science has often showed little regard for the claims of tradition, being determined to courageously follow the tracks of truth whithersoever they might lead. On the other hand, the revelation, orthodoxy, treasured books, and such, are still there, in the scientific worldview. It would be pretty much the same as it is now. To be sure, the world might be better off to have been spared various slaughterings, famines, plagues, and so on. Might it not be morally and psychologically preferable that such things, such books, and such, be understood as valuable, instructive fictions?

The skeptic might object that the scientific hypothesis wipes out glorious achievements, hard-won triumphs, noble deeds, and such. There is something to that objection, but one must remember that the scientific hypothesis would wipe out much grief, sorrow, tragedy, dishonesty, cruelty, hypocrisy, and failure, as well. It means, in effect, we could start anew, and make certain the new world is better wrought than the fictive worlds seem to have been.

Perhaps the skeptic might inquire as to whether the scientific hypothesis is just, or fair? This question, actually, does not come up, because before the world there was nothing, and thus nothing to be just or fair about. One cannot wipe out, so to speak, what never existed in the first place. Too, of course, we can do our best now to create a just, fair world, one freed of the burdens and heritages, the evils and weights, the dispositions and pressures, the miseries and pathologies, of a supposed actual past.

But the skeptic does not surrender easily, even when

shattered, even when his position is incontrovertibly reduced to alarmed, shuddering atoms of gibbering rubble.

Might not, whines he, the scientific hypothesis promote a sense of insecurity. Might it not induce anxiety? Might not the wheel of the world slip off the axis of existence as easily as it once apparently found itself spinning upon it, say, about four minutes ago?

Of course, we snort! That is the nature of the world! What is wrong with you? Are you craven cowards? Who would wish, honestly, to inhabit a world which did not dangle precariously betwixt oblivions? Consider the pleasures of thriving in a world racing blindfolded amongst abysses! Who, if rational, would not welcome the carnivorous nature of reality? Who, if given the opportunity, would not choose to live thrillingly on the perilous edge of disaster and extinction? Besides, if the world popped out of existence, it might just as easily pop back in. Take comfort in that, if you wish. Cosmological popping theory, of course, is still in its infancy. We have not yet had much time to develop it, only about four minutes.

But the skeptic is indomitable in his madness.

Would not the scientific world, he asks, reflect discredit on a transempirical, causative factor, one which might produce such a world?

Certainly not, we respond scornfully.

First, speaking of discredit, would not the skeptic's hypothesized world, if it existed, with its alleged terrors, tragedies, and cruelties, reflect discredit on a transempirical causative factor, if anything could? Certainly the scientific hypothesis wipes out most of that horror, indeed, epochs and eons of it. If one were looking for pragmatic justifications here, rather than truth, would this not be a point in favor of the scientific world? Secondly, expressions such as 'discredit' might well be out of place in these matters. Moral predicates are applicable only to moral agents, in moral situations. Solar systems and stars, rivers and germs, rocks, dust, and rain, are neither moral nor immoral. And for all we know, a transempirical causative factor, if it exists, even if it is intelligible to us at all, may be akin to such things, natural things which are and do, of their own internal necessities or vagaries, things to which moral predicates are simply inapplicable. Chide the stone and hurricane if you will, but they do not even know you exist.

You speak, exclaims the skeptic, as though the world were a joke.

I do not think we so speak, but perhaps the world *is* a joke. If so, is that not a point in favor of the world?

In the scientific hypothesis what happens to history?

Everything, and nothing.

Do human beings not need a past?

On the scientific hypothesis, they have a past. It began something like four minutes ago.

When Armadillos Fly

VAT technology, as one may learn from the standard accounts, began in a modest, unassuming way, in the 20th century, as I recall, in what was then known as Russia with a variety of experiments involving decapitated dogs. It is not known whence these dogs were obtained, but there is some speculation that they were the otherwise-useless residues of various experiments designed and conducted by a brilliant psychologist and animal lover, a Dr. Ivan Petrovich Pavlov. His experiments involved, amongst various things, research into conditioned reflexes. For example, he accustomed various, trusting dogs, who did not see through his machinations, to slaver at the mere sound of a bell, the bell having been previously associated with the delivery of food. At the sound of the bell, so to speak, they were ready to eat. In less controlled circumstances these results, interestingly, had already been established, though obviously informally, on numerous ranches in the Western portions of the North American continent. Pavlov, as you may know, then proceeded, perhaps after a mental breakdown or having been deserted by an exasperated or alarmed spouse, to mix electric shocks with the ringing of the bell. Predictably this troubled his experimental subjects, which then, it seems, went insane. Pavlov, it seems, was the first scientist to establish these results under rigorous conditions of experimentation. On the other hand, the principles involved, those of mixed signals, and such, inducing confusion, guilt, misery, neurosis, and insanity were already well established in several societies, cultures, and civilizations. For example, confused, guilt-ridden individuals, subjected to insidious crossconditionings, then look for relief and guidance, usually, interestingly, to their own Pavlovs, so to speak, who have devised their tortures, from which they, the Pavlovs, so to speak, profit, and by means of which they earn their livelihood. To use an analogy, it is rather like pounding a fellow on the head and then selling him aspirin. Or a better analogy might be, to castigate a fellow for breathing, or getting hungry, or urinating, and then, for a fee, compassionately forgive him for his lapses in this regard. But then, of course, encourage him to do this no more, and, indeed, forbid him to do so, and scold him if he does, and so on. Perhaps, most accurately, one insists on imposing unachievable goals on one's targets, or dupes, or hosts, the failure to achieve which, of course, induces grief, guilt, a sense of failure, of unworthiness, and such, which symptoms are painful, and which accordingly put the erring, defective, inferior, guilt-ridden failures more and more at the mercy of the their cunning goal-setters. To resort to a simpler analogy previously noted, one supplies aspirin, but this is followed by another blow on the victim's head, the ache of which is to be relieved by further doses of aspirin, and so on. In this way much aspirin is sold.

Callously one finds little comfort in the fact that many of the aspirin salesmen, apparent victims of their own therapeutical regimens, not unoften spend a certain amount of time striking themselves on the head with their own hammers.

At least that seems fair.

One is reminded of the fellow who struck his head frequently against brick walls because it felt so good when he stopped.

But perhaps such peculiar practices, sociological aberrations, and such, are essential to maintain in existence peculiar, sociologically aberrant societies, odd cultures, weird civilizations, and such.

It is hard to say.

One does not know.

Could it be that the very cornerstone of society, its prop and guarantee, is insanity? Could it be that at the foundation of society must lie madness? Doubtless at the foundation of some societies.

It does seem a high price to pay, surely.

But to return to the Russian experiments to which we have hitherto alluded. The dogs' heads, missing their bodies, were allegedly kept alive for some time, at least long enough to permit photography, for example, of twisting and grimacing, and otherwise objecting insofar as lay in their power, when, for example, bitter fluids were dropped on their tongues. It is not known if similar experiments, with the advance of science in mind, were conducted with political prisoners. In any event, no pertinent photography is available, at least currently, germane to that possibility.

The next major breakthroughs relevant to these lines of research occurred in various Western laboratories and involved the brains of monkeys. The entire heads of monkeys were not used, possibly because the Western experimenters were more squeamish than their Eastern forebears. Who would not cringe before the reproachful glance of a decapitated Rhesus monkey? So mere brains were used, submerged, nourished, monitored, and so on. Brain activity was evident, but it was not clear, naturally, what the little primates were thinking about, or dreaming about. And perhaps that is just as well. Possibly leafy bowers, paradisiacal troves of bananas, possibly psychologists who had somehow missed their footing in tall trees. It is hard to say.

But from such simple beginnings eventually emerged our modern, advanced, sophisticated versions of vat technology.

Who could have envisioned at the time of envious troglodytes leaping off cliffs and flapping their arms the eventual triumphs of starship engineering?

Organ-transplant technology put in its oar, as well, in the beginning.

As is well known, as far back as the 20th century, the healthy organs of various individuals, perhaps accident victims, or such, were harvested, stored, and later transplanted into the bodies of grateful recipients. In this way many lives were saved. To be sure, a certain amount of what came to be known as Burking also took place. The etiology of the term seems founded on the name of a William Burke, once of Edinburgh, who used to supply unmarked, intact bodies to medical schools for dissection. These were quality bodies, not the deteriorated corpses dug up and supplied by your everyday grave robber. Burke was hung in 1829, by a court insensitive to the principles of utilitarianism.

It was only natural that the brain, often considered the organ of thought, should soon figure prominently in transplantation technology. A bullet through the heart, for example, leaves the brain in an excellent, if troubled, condition for several seconds, a period sufficient for a competent team of paramedics to reestablish a blood supply. Instantaneous cryogenic preservation was later commonly used, this permitting the brain to be reanimated at the convenience and discretion of the appropriate authorities. As expected, many individuals, dissatisfied with their own brains, applied for new and hopefully better brains. Many were the husbands, too, who at their wives' urging submitted to such a procedure.

I think the converging in the offing can now be clearly discerned, that betwixt transplantation and vat technology.

As the demand for new brains burgeoned it was no more than an economic commonplace that a concomitant preservation and storage technology, eventually at affordable prices, would arise to meet the demand.

These brain shifts, exchanges, replacements, returns, trials, and so on, did promote a number of identity crises, a seeking for criteria of sameness, and such, and, indeed, so much so that for the first time in human history philosophers, who had hitherto idly occupied themselves with such issues, came to occupy not only a respected but a lucrative place in society.

The next obvious step was to establish contact with the stored brains, and press them for their views on these matters. For example, would the brain of A object to being implanted in the body of B, and so on. Dialogue was essential. Thus arose a new field in law, that of brain rights.

In the beginning this communication was primitive, often amounting to little more than a Yes, a No, a Hell No, and so on. But soon dialogue with the disembodied brains became more sophisticated, and brains that began by playing poker and checkers moved ahead to bridge, to chess, and pinochle.

One supposes it was only inevitable that the brain-rights movement would lead to a concern with the experiences of the disembodied brains. Were they content? Were they happy? What did they do for recreation? How about entertainment? What would they like to do? What sort of music would they like to think they were hearing? What would they like to think they were eating? Would they like to think they were watching sunsets? That could be arranged. Would they like to think they were reading a good book? OK. How about TV? Why not? Even folks in dental offices and, sometimes, post offices were granted as much. It seemed cruel to think of them floating idly about, hour after hour, in their nutrient solutions without much to do.

Since it was well known, and had been known for a long time, that experience was a function of brain stimulation, it was soon realized that the precise source of the stimulation would be immaterial to the experience, *qua* experience, it being immaterial whether it was contingent on an outside environment or merely the result of technological contrivance, perhaps computer generated and controlled. Identical stimulations, however brought about, produced identical experiences.

Naturally it took time to work these things out. Many brains were at first disconcerted by glitches in the stimulation, as, for example, when doughnuts turned into freight cars, ocean liners docked at Omaha, and armadillos, not merely pigs, were noted flying. On the other hand, after a time, the software was so much improved that from the brain's point of view it had no way of telling the simulacrum from the authentic article. The fellow monitoring the apparatus, of course, given his external perspective, was well aware of what was happening, but only if, as a fact, he himself was not merely another brain in another vat being stimulated to have the experiences of monitoring and stimulating another brain in a vat, and so on. Eventually, of course, the entire population might in theory have been brains in vats being maintained and stimulated by programmed machinery set up long ago to ease the burdens of technicians and supervisors. But there is no reason to entertain so bizarre a possibility. Too many of our experiences go counter to such a hypothesis, for example, our learning to speak from ostensive definitions, our interactions with an obviously real environment, our relationships with our parents, siblings, friends, and so on. What about the time I skinned my knee when I fell off the tricycle? What about the time Hiram bloodied my nose in the school yard, the time I won the spelling bee, and so on? And there was high school and college, and Mabel, to whom I am engaged. We should be married next August. There is only one thing that troubles me.

Yesterday I am sure I saw an armadillo. That is not much in itself, of course, particularly here in Texas, but something about it struck me as unusual.

It was flying.

Comments on the Halliburton Case

ONE of the problems with being a brain in a vat is that one can never be quite sure that one is not a brain in a head.

It was this sort of thing which led, eventually, regrettably, to the downfall of Horace G. Halliburton.

Vat technology had proceeded to the point where brain vacations were not unusual. For those of you who are unfamiliar with these things, recall that at one time, long ago, vacations were quite expensive. One actually went somewhere, literally, and stayed somewhere, literally, and so on. It cost money to get there, and it certainly cost money to stay there. If you were going to cycle you had to buy or rent a bicycle, or drag yours from home. If you were going skiing or scuba diving that cost you, too. And the casinos weren't set up to help you meet your expenses.

Some individuals were suckers, or sticklers, for the real thing, of course, and you had to admire them for that, I suppose, though it is not really so clear why, but once you couldn't tell the difference, between the brain vacation and the whole-body vacation, the matter tended to become somewhat abstract, if not academic.

And, after a time, the brain vacations were not only competitive with the whole-body vacations but considerably less expensive. To stay overnight at the Plaza Hotel could cost you a bundle, but to have the experience of staying there, without staying there, was comparatively cheap, and could be included in the basic vacation package. And brain vacations were secure in their way, as well. There was never any danger of breaking your leg skiing unless you wanted that included in the package, and you didn't have to worry about losing your travelers' checks, or your luggage. Too, no brain floating about in a vat, as far as I know, was ever mugged. And think of the savings on your wardrobe, and dining. Incidental expenses at the Plaza were even covered. Tickets for any show you wanted, too. Ringside seats at Madison Square Garden, whatever, the whole works.

These developments probably saved an ailing travel industry, whose costs had become prohibitive, certainly for the usual pocketbook. And if they did not save it, they surely transformed it. Indeed, many resorts and tourist spots shut down, except for supplying software to the new competition. Many travel agents unwilling to make the transition to designing and marketing vat trips went predictably to the wall, demolished, superseded by science, time, and change, rendered extinct by the newly evolving mammals of progress.

There were dangers, of course. One could get sucked into these things. Some folks wanted to fight at Actium, storm the walls at Acre, assist Nelson at Trafalgar, Wellington at Waterloo, and so on. Some went so far as riding with the Scarlet Pimpernel and matching silver bullets with the Lone Ranger.

Vat technology, at the time in question, had advanced to the point where brains could be removed, immersed, stimulated, and then, after a time, depending on the contract, reinserted in the original, waiting body, itself well maintained in the interval. Originally it had been hoped that the stimulations required could be electronically processed through the skull, to economize on nutrient fluids, and such, but this proved cumbersome and imprecise. Recall the impracticality or difficulty, at least, of making reliable astronomical observations through the shaken quilt of a turbulent atmosphere. Recall the canals of Mars, attested to by more than one astronomer of unchallenged talent, sincerity, and expertise.

To be sure, one could always hope that less invasive, if no more safe, techniques may be developed in the future.

Occasionally a mistake would be made, of course, for technicians, engineers, absent-minded janitors, electronic geniuses, and such, are, after all, human, and thus, from time to time, not surprisingly, fallible. Occasionally the wrong brain would be returned to the wrong body, so to speak, but these errors, clerical in their nature, were easily corrected. After all, it seldom took a brain very long to discover that it was not in its usual body. Usually both subjects good-naturedly took the mistake in stride, and relished the humor of the situation. Occasionally delightful domestic confusions ensued, and sometimes a blackguard tried to make off with a better body, but these were only anomalous, occasional incidents, incidents usually involving no more than minor lapses of judgment or propriety, and tended to be speedily rectified.

To be sure, the technology was occasionally abused or applied to disreputable ends. For example, more than one fleeing tyrant had his brain ensconced in a nondescript, innocent-looking body, even one waving a pitchfork and seemingly a dedicated member of a mob seeking the blood of the very tyrant in question. Occasionally there occurred situations which seem to have verged on the criminal, for example, transplanting the brain of one's inveterate enemy, perhaps a district attorney, into the body of a noted schizophrenic medically famous for his delusion of being the very district attorney in question. Another case involved a transplantation into the body of a gorilla incarcerated in a well-known zoological garden, in one of the boroughs of New York City, a gorilla denied crayons and writing materials. Too, occasionally an unscrupulous wastrel of a nephew would resort to this technology, morally neutral in itself, to obtain a coveted inheritance. Decrepit tycoons took to inhabiting the bodies of dashing young men, in order that their charms for the opposite sex might transcend those of the economic order, and so on.

But our primary concern here is with the tragic case of Horace G. Halliburton. Halliburton was a kindly, decent, well-respected member of the upper section of the lower middle middle class, in Patterson, New Jersey, who had originally been attracted to vat vacations, as were many others, in virtue of their affordability. Such vacations, however, soon became a passion with the fellow, and if one may speak of addiction without involving oneself in questions of liability, risking legal challenges from a powerful industry, and such, one might speak of addiction, but we will not, as questions of liability, and such, might be involved.

At that time it was difficult to externally monitor the subject's experiences. Indeed, even today, one is not allowed to look in on such matters, in virtue of various titles and sections in a variety of annoying privacy acts. Accordingly, although one could know very well the environment one produced for him, one was not aware, usually, and even today one is not legally entitled to be aware, of what he might be doing in that environment. A man's brain was his castle, so to speak. A man's thoughts are his own, even today, an outdated Enlightenment concept perhaps, which puts at jeopardy civilization itself, but one whose revocation would be time-consuming and expensive, involving as it would one or more amendments to the Constitution. One wonders, sometimes, what went on in the heads of the founding fathers, beneath those wigs, that they saw fit to so jealousy guard the obscure chambers of the imagination. Did they in their lewd thoughts, say, peep beneath hoopskirts? It is hard to know. One supplied a background, but what the individual did within that background was pretty much up to the individual. One gave him the pad and paper, so to speak, but did not dictate what he would write, that indeed an old-fashioned concept itself which in its own way poses challenges to the stability of a harmonious society. So, as it turned out, one could provide him with the dream, so to speak, but one could not control what he dreamed within it. This was much like reality. And it was supposed to be. Otherwise the experience would smack of fraudulence and inauthenticity. One finds in "reality" that one can do little with brick walls and buses, but one may choose to avoid them or not, as one wishes, ride the bus, or walk, and so on.

By now you have doubtless anticipated what brought about the downfall of Horace G. Halliburton.

Halliburton, and I fear many others, lurking behind antiquated privacy acts, carried on, so to speak, on their vat vacations. He began in a simple enough way, becoming an outrageous flirt, smiling winningly, and suggestively, at innocent cashiers, distracting them from their bar codes, following beautiful women about for no better reason than that they were beautiful, and so on. Later, when individuals showed up who reminded him of his boss he would gleefully pummel them, disregarding the protests of these bewildered victims. He later took to supplementing his income by rifling parking meters and, as he grew more bold, robbing several banks, usually but not always those most convenient to his home. He soon became notorious as a reckless rogue with the ladies, a bully on the streets, selective in his victims, and the subject of several all-points bulletins broadcast by a number of police departments within one hundred miles of his home. His loot from parking meters he would bestow on worthy charities, and, later, that from banks he would devote to various indulgences and dissipations appropriate to his new standing in the community, that of a infamous, much envied, much feared, glamorous, night-clubbing mobster. One of his habits most offensive to the forces of law and order was his predictions of the time and place of each of his next "jobs," which capers he would then, invariably, as though under the very noses of the police, by means of a disguise or two, pull off, and with an insolence and bravado which might, in a more romantic time, have earned him a place in song and legend. Behind him, at the scene of the crime, a neatly lettered card would be found, with thereon inscribed the simple, tasteful, but arrogant message: Halliburton was here.

It was these cards which finally betrayed him, as energetic, relentless officers traced them to the printer from which they had been ordered.

Halliburton was apprehended, tried, and sentenced, which sentence he is now engaged in serving.

His downfall was brought about, at least in part, it seems, by the developed state of vat technology. Brain experiences and whole-body experiences were now, for all practical purposes, indistinguishable. Unbeknownst to himself Halliburton's brain at one point had been removed from the vat, his vat vacation having been concluded, and returned to his body.

One of the problems with being a brain in a vat, as we noted earlier, is that one can never be quite sure that one is not a brain in a head.

And it was this sort of thing which led, eventually, regrettably, to the downfall of Horace G. Halliburton.

His stories, however, are still told in the taverns and night clubs and it seems possible, even in our somewhat prosaic times, that he may well live on in song and legend.

That, one supposes, is some compensation

For a modest fee, autographed license plates are available.

Buridan's Ass

PSYCHOLOGISTS let us know that the choice between an alternative which is perceived as abysmally horrible and one which is perceived as attractive, even desirable, is usually not difficult to make. When faced, for example, to allude to a well known story, of a choice between a tiger and a lady, and the choice is yours, and not that of an insanely jealous queen, you would probably choose the lady, if healthy, nonsuicidal, gifted with normal vision, and so on, though, to be sure, it might depend on the lady and perhaps, in unusual cases, on the tiger. For example the choice between, say, Clytemnestra or Medea, and an affectionate, well-fed tiger, one genetically engineered to thrive on breakfast cereal, might be less clear.

Now we come, in our perusal of the literature, to the choices between goods and between bads.

Here the researchers tell us that it is easier to choose between goods than to choose between bads. As one oscillates between goods, eventually, rather sooner than later, the closer one comes to A the better it is likely to look, and then one tends to slide toward it, rather than toward a similarly desirable B. In many situations the important thing is to make a decision, rather than not make a decision, even if you are not sure that the decision is the absolutely best decision possible. Often the routes to the same destination are not that different, but if you want to get there before dark, you had better take one of them. The Japanese supposedly have a theory of postponing decisions as long as possible while accumulating more and more data, or whatever, until the better decision of its own weight, so to speak, topples into your lap. This is not a bad way of going about things but if you want to get there before dark, you may not have time for it. People tend to admire, and follow, people who make decisions. The trick is to make a decision as if you knew what you were doing. People like that and as things are still mysterious to them, as they probably still are to you, too, actually, they will give you credit for leadership, probably correctly. Also, you can usually live with any decision, and a decision made is a decision likely to be subconsciously commended. Once made it usually seems right. Also, if it is a good decision, even if not the best decision, it should look better and better to you as you work it out.

Now the hardest decision, according to the studies, is the decision between two bads, between, say, bad A and bad B, between, say, Lucrezia Borgia or Charlotte Corday. Would you prefer to be poisoned or stabbed in the bathtub? The closer you approach one alternative the worse it looks, and this impels you toward the other which, predictably, the more closely approached, looks worse and worse, and so on. As a result many will prefer to choose neither alternative. If one is obliged to choose one or the other, of course, the dilemma grows desperate. Should one satisfy the distribution requirement by hazarding mathematical logic or mathematical mathematics?

At this point one might consider recourse to a random-selection device, say, a fair coin, an item frequently encountered in probability theory but scarce in most actual economies. Dice or cards will do, too, but not much better. Certain shamans use charred reindeer bones to direct hunters. That seems to work pretty well. It keeps the reindeer guessing. But sometimes the bones are unreliable. But then, so, too, sometimes are the coins, the dice, the cards.

This brings us to Buridan's ass.

For those of you who might be unfamiliar with medieval

animal husbandry Buridan's ass was placed equidistant between two bales of hay, and accordingly starved to death. This is fictional of course, for an undergraduate animal-rights activist at the University of Paris stealthily made his way into the barn and nudged one of the bales a bit closer to the imperiled beast.

The point that Buridan, who was a professor, of course, for professors sometimes concern themselves with such things, was making had less to do with animal abuse than free will. A decision in his view, it seems, was purely dependent on the intellect and so, if the alternatives presented were intellectually equivalent, the will could not act. Remember that Buridan was a professor. They do things like this. An analogy would be if a fellow was poised between two equally delicious young ladies, each clamoring to bear his children, and be his abject and eternally devoted spouse, he would remain celibate, as, we suppose, did Buridan.

In the case of an ass, which is a donkey, which I hope is clear to everyone, or even a chipmunk, this sort of dilemma seems unrealistic, for both practical and theoretical reasons. Imagine the difficulty of placing bales of hay equidistant from a donkey. Consider the precision of measurement required. And what if a slight movement of the air might stir a random straw a bit closer? Or what if the donkey, fainting from hunger, could not manage to fall precisely equidistant between the bales of hay. But there are theoretical questions here, as well. Is protoplasm, or DNA, or whatever, actually all this smart, or intellectual? Do not emotional elements, accidental elements, biographical elements, historical elements, social elements, and such things, often figure in decisions? What if one of the young ladies in our previous example should wink at the fellow stranded between them? It seems unlikely he would remain stranded for long.

Now you must have begun to wonder if there is a point in all this.

There is, a most important point.

You see, there was once this amazing engineer who was bored, and decided to make himself some toys. After experimenting with teddy bears, dolls, toy soldiers, balls, blocks, prototype hula hoops, and such, he was still discontented. He was not a happy engineer. And unhappy engineers, as we know from the history of technology, are capable of just about anything. In any event this engineer who was lonely as well as unhappy decided to produce some more interesting, more complex toys, to while away the time, of which he had plenty, rather in the line of wind-up toys, though much more complicated. This was not as good as having a girl friend, one supposes, but we may certainly suppose it was better than nothing, at least from his point of view. Now, as he was an engineer, he did not want to produce sloppy artifacts, but things he could be proud of, objects well-tooled, shipshape, reliable, precise, and smoothly functioning.

Accordingly our engineer designed and manufactured some phenomenal little thingamajigs, dohickeys, whatchamaycallits, and so on. These little toys were on the whole active and complex. They were also responsive to their environment in a variety of ways, for example, if one tumbled off a cliff or was struck repeatedly with sledgehammers, its functions were often impaired, sometimes seriously, sometimes irremediably. The engineer became fascinated with his hobby, and constructed ever more fascinating and intricate toys. Eventually he had built a set of remarkably sophisticated machines programmed with simple rules of the sort from which surprisingly complex behavior can emerge. Some of these models worked better than others and the ones that worked less well were scrapped.

Finally, our engineer produced something which he hoped would endlessly delight and amuse him, a set of complex mobile computers. For a time the engineer was quite pleased with these toys, and rightfully so, for they were in their way masterpieces of the toy maker's art, sophisticated, impressive wonderworks of unprecedented design. Nothing quite like them had been seen before. The engineer played with them for a time, and sat back and watched them running about. He varied their programming so they would not all be doing the same thing. But they were mechanisms, of course, and it soon seemed to the engineer that, in a way, they had been built too well. After a time, they were not that much fun to watch. The engineer had built them and so he always knew what they would do. Once again the engineer began to be bored.

Things came to a head one day when he noted one of these mechanisms poised precisely between two goals, both of which it had been programmed to seek. The machine, interestingly, was immobile, unable to function.

We do not know what the goals were, perhaps it was something as simple as being poised between calculating the sum of five plus six as opposed to calculating the sum of six plus five. One does not know. Or, perhaps it was as simple as finding itself between two equally attractive wedges of Jarlsberg cheese, or two bales of hay.

The engineer watched the machine in its predicament, until it perished, from rust, or whatever.

At this point it seemed to the engineer that he was hoist on his own petard, so to speak, that his own expertise had done him in. Not only was he bored with his toys, for he knew their every move in advance, after all, he had built them, but he now also realized that the astounding and impeccable precision of their programming bore within itself the concealed liability of cybernetic paralysis. They would, in certain situations, be inevitably doomed by the very perfection of their design.

Perfection bore inevitably within itself its own demise.

The engineer had discovered the problem of Buridan's ass.

At this point perhaps many of us might have contemplated suicide but not the engineer, as it was not in his nature. For him this was not a viable option.

Then, with one of those strokes of inspiration which so frequently characterize the juggernaut of progress, it occurred to the engineer that if perfection necessitated imperfection, why should not imperfection necessitate perfection.

Perhaps the most perfect mechanism would be that which was imperfect!

Accordingly the engineer gathered together his toys and put in some random elements.

He had now produced machines that worked, but you couldn't know for sure how they would work.

You never knew for sure.

They could surprise you.

Now the engineer was never bored with his toys.

And thus, too, was the problem of Buridan's ass solved. Some random jostle or jiggle, inclination or trepidation, sooner or later, would save the beast.

The engineer was so pleased with his new toys that he thought he should give them a name.

He called them human beings.

Copyright

WE will leave open the question as to whether gods have gods. That, it seems, is their concern, not ours.

We will leave open the question, as well, as to whether gods could, or should, commit suicide.

If they are necessary beings in some sense then one supposes they are stuck with themselves. Perhaps they deserve themselves.

One wonders if they are satisfied with the worlds they create.

Not all gods bother creating worlds, of course. Most have other things to do, perhaps better things to do, cutting out paper dolls, collecting stamps, origami, such things.

They can always visit worlds created by other gods, or trespass on such worlds, or meddle with them, and so on. That saves creating your own world. This is not particularly dangerous as most creating gods are not territorial, for they may, at any time they wish, create new territories.

Creating worlds, we gather, for those gods who are interested in such things, is easy enough, but it is not easy to create one that works, a good one, so to speak. Many worlds are simple failures, simply botched up, with lousy laws, eccentric planetary orbits, autistic, nonaggregating molecules, shortages of dark matter, stars that sputter out prematurely, life forms that spend their time attacking and eating one another, and so on.

Many gods have given too little attention to their hobbies. They are careless. Others, even conscientious ones, often take a long time to become good at world making. The better worlds receive prizes, awards, blue ribbons, and other distinctions. That may be why some gods keep on making worlds.

Most worlds, of course, are discarded, when one tires of them, or they are rendered obsolete by new technologies, or styles.

Too, what sort of world you are trying to create should be taken into consideration. If you are out to create the most purple world possible, or the smallest world possible, or the largest world possible, or the squarest world possible, or the worst world possible, then the criteria of evaluation must in all fairness be adjusted to the intention involved. To be sure, the intention must be first filed with us. It would not do at all for a god to claim he wanted to create just the world he ended up creating, trying to take credit for the exact nature of its flaws, and such, as they were intended to be perfect flaws, and so on. That would be tantamount to cheating.

Sometimes gods try to mar or spoil the worlds other gods have created. Perhaps you live in such a disfigured, defaced world. This sort of cosmological vandalism seems deplorable to many of us, but as gods, being gods, cannot be subject to external constraints, such as moral principles, but in effect have the privilege of defining morality as they wish, we shall effect nothing critical on this score.

I am supposing that most of what we have hitherto stated is familiar to the reader.

On the other hand, it has come to our attention that not everyone is aware of the charge and activities of the office of registration.

I work there.

When a god goes to work and creates a world, if he regards it as worthy of registration, and cares to expend the fee, he is likely to bring his world to our attention. Gods, as is well known, are often jealous, which would be a character flaw, except in a god, for reasons already noted. Some worlds are, so to speak, pirated. Others, or substantial parts of others, have been clearly plagiarized. Hard feelings and denunciations, even cosmic strifes, worlds being used as cannonballs, and such, abounded. It was scandals and abuses of this nature, piratings and plagiarizations, and allegations of piratings and plagiarizations, and cosmic hostilities, which first made clear the need for our office. It was accordingly founded, though in the midst of continuing controversy. Many were the gods who insisted on a variety of rights, those of theft, of piracy, of cosmological plagiarization, and so on.. Should reality not be free to all, like space, where it was created. The roads were to be open. What was the point of being a god if one could not do as one wished? The commons were not to be fenced in. One of the most adamant foes of the registration office was a feathered god who had created several worlds of ducks, each created in his own image.

Eventually, however, as a gesture of good will, and to minimize the possibility of civil war, most gods accepted, pointedly of their own free will, the existence of the office. Thus some order and discipline was at last introduced into an arena which had hitherto resembled at best a void of reckless and rampaging chaos. To be sure, there is still many a cosmos, in one dimension or another, which remains outside our jurisdiction, and refuses to sign the appropriate conventions.

For those of you who have created one or more worlds you might consider availing yourself of the protection of registration. Whereas there is no doubt that a world you have made is your world, whether it should be or not, it is one thing to make a world, and quite another to be able to prove that it is your world. What if your world is stolen and brought to public view by another, he claiming it as his own? What can you do about this? Have you no recourse? You do, you can register your world, thereby establishing your indisputable proprietorship. To be sure, this may do you no good, unless you are outrageously affluent and in the pursuit of your proprietary rights are prepared to compulsively enrich successions of incompetent and greedy attorney gods, but it will, at least, render secure, and certify, your entitlement to righteous indignation.

So register your worlds.

The policies, practices, fees, and such, of the office are a matter of public record. Forms with instructions are available at many libraries, and from the office, upon request. Please fill out the forms carefully, according to the instructions. Fees are subject to change without notice.

Do not forget to submit two copies of your world with your application. A failure to fill out the form, or forms, properly, or to submit the proper fees, or the required two copies of your world, will result in a delay in the processing of your application.

Some gods, of course, see no point in the registration office.

I think there is some point to the registration office, seeing that gods do go about creating worlds.

Some people may wonder why gods bother creating worlds. I myself have given it some thought, possibly because of my working in the office. There are so many worlds created, and so many gods. Sometimes I am amazed. There are probably many reasons. Some, one supposes, have nothing better to do; others may feel a need to do so; some may just like to keep busy; some may be lonely; some may want to do nice things, or bad things; some, insecure sorts, one supposes, perhaps with few internal resources, may relish courtiers and sycophants, hanging about, praising, and such, looking forward to rewards. There are probably many reasons. And, some, as suggested, may be interested in getting recognition, having their eye on prizes, and such. Gods come in various shapes and sizes, moral and otherwise. Some are congenial, friendly, decent fellows; others would just as soon be left alone; some construct their worlds and then abandon them to their own devices; they desert their worlds; others may have an artistic streak and be interested in dramatic spectacles, hurricanes, floods, wars, famines, pestilences, slaughters, plagues, crashing airplanes, sinking ships, collapsing bridges, avalanches, cruelty, horror, insanity, and such. Some gods enjoy roasted human sacrifices and the feeding of infants to sacred crocodiles, and so on; on the other hand, some gods, cousins even, would just as soon their creations were nice to one another, and even, here and there, that they might like one another. There are all sorts of gods. That is to be expected. I suppose it is not surprising. And if there are all sorts of gods, why not all sorts of worlds? That, too, I suppose, is only to be expected.

The registration office exists largely to protect worlds from being illegitimately copied, plagiarized, and so on.

Not all gods, however, as you may have gathered, choose to avail themselves of this protection.

In particular I can think of one outlaw god, in his way, a sort of rogue god. He comes to mind because his motivation for refusing to avail himself of the protection of our office is an unusual one.

He desires his world to be copied, to be pirated, to be stolen, to be plagiarized.

Let us consider his world, briefly. It is a pretty average world in many ways, although it seems to contain more than its share of grief, misery, pain, cruelty, suffering, and hardship. In many respects it is not much of a world, and one supposes that there would be little interest in copying it in any event. It is probably safe from plagiarization. It is not very purple, or square, or large, even. It does contain something rare among worlds, however. It contains something which appears only now and then, and it doesn't last long. It is called joy. The god in question, and some of his creatures, seem to feel that this episodic phenomenon, little more than an occasional, brief flicker against a wall of solitude and darkness, is redemptive. Redemption, you see, for them, at any rate, is not a matter of pain and suffering, but of joy. It is that which makes things worthwhile. This little bit of joy, now and then, you see, or as they see it, overcomes the night and the pain. It justifies the world; it redeems it; it makes it all worthwhile. How puzzling all this is. Strange that such a cosmological eccentricity, one so transient and rare, which so few have experienced, should be ascribed such value.

The god in question refuses to register his world.

Surely he knows it could be stolen, or copied.

But, interestingly, that is precisely what he has in mind. He wants to give such a world away, not because it is worthless, but because it is so precious, so valuable.

In any event, do not forget to submit two copies of your world with your application. A failure to fill out the form, or forms, properly, or to submit the proper fees, or the required two copies of your world, will result in a delay in the processing of your application.

A Gorean Interlude

Prefatory Remarks:

I REGARD myself as privileged, as honored, in a sense, to be the editor of the Cabot manuscripts.

I do not regret, for one instant, that this opportunity, this responsibility, this honor, has been bestowed on me.

To be sure, as I have learned, it is one not without its perils, social, political, and professional. As the Armenian proverb has it, one who tells the truth must have one foot in the stirrup. But, alas, I fear my foot missed the stirrup. Accordingly I have found myself in the unenviable position of having spoken the truth, and remaining afoot. As is well-known, the last thing most individuals wish to do is seek the truth. It is hard to blame them, for there are dangers in seeking the truth, foremost amongst them that one might find it.

As far as I know, I am the only individual to whom these various mss., or similar mss., have been entrusted, at least for a particular purpose, that apparently of bringing them to the attention of a presumably small, but, I suspect, extraordinarily select, public.

Surely they are not for everyone.

Apparently several individuals have failed to understand

that. Their view, it seems, is that everything should be for everyone. Or rather, perhaps, that everything should be for them, for they seem to take themselves, with their various interesting and impressive lacunae and limitations, intellectual and otherwise, for everyone. We are all free, it seems, to be just like them. It is only to be expected then, one supposes, that they are troubled, if not astonished, even occasionally outraged, by those who, however reluctantly, and deplorably, decline to avail themselves of their so generously and cordially accorded opportunity, that of being just like them.

Better perhaps to be dead.

The human being makes an excellent bigot. Millennia have gone into honing such skills.

The difficulty, of course, is that there are competitive bigotries. And, unfortunately, several of them are well armed.

Naturally they deny what they choose not to see, and denounce what they are afraid to hear.

This is common to bigotries.

And what else would you expect them to do, to look, to listen?

To think, to feel?

Those who claim the human being is manufactured, and should be produced according to one and only one plan, theirs, neglect to note that there must be raw materials for such a project, and, furthermore, that these materials have natures of their own.

This may be inconvenient, but nature, nonetheless, got there first. It is not to be denied that a human being, like any other form of life, animal or vegetable, may be cut, clipped, chopped, twisted, stunted, tortured, poisoned, and burned into any number of diverse and bizarre forms. There is much historical evidence supporting this claim. But still, nature got there first, and while she may be thwarted, even destroyed, she cannot be benignly replaced. It doesn't work. The great, slow, vast, patient systemic processes of biological evolution are not so easily set aside as the superficial and uninformed might suspect. Let those who will, should it please them, lecture chemistry and advise physics; let them dictate to heat and light, legislate planetary routes and scold molecules. But let them not dictate to the mind and heart of man, or woman.

Words may mask as well as reveal truth; it is fortunate that reality cannot read; otherwise it would doubtless be much confused. If trees could read they might eschew rainfall and minerals, apologize for their leaves, suspect their roots, and fear to grow.

The problem is not to deny nature but to attend to her.

But enough of such considerations.

One digresses.

It sometimes seems to me unlikely that the Priest-Kings of Gor, if they exist, and I fear they might, would place such troubling, surprising documents, the originals, in so limited a venue, that of a given editor and a small number of other individuals who are aware of their existence, this seemingly subjecting the documents to a precarious jeopardy, particularly if they, the Priest-Kings, supposing them to exist, were concerned that their contents should become broadcast, but perhaps that was not their intention; that they should become broadcast, but why, if so, if it were indeed their intention that these matters should become a matter of public record, would they limit the very knowledge of their existence, that of the original materials, that is, to no more than a handful of organisms, and those of a sort which, as we are given to understand, would be alien to themselves. I wonder if friendship can exist amongst diverse species. To be sure, are not our dogs our friends? And I wonder, sometimes, how the Priest-Kings view us. As we view our dogs? No, I think not. They are too ready to kill. Perhaps the better analogy would be between ourselves and insects, which we prefer to leave alone unless annoyed, or menaced. But I think, too, sometimes, in some places, there might be a commonality amongst species, a moment of respect, or affection, founded on the frail reed of rationality, so easily bent, so easily broken, so easily uprooted. The hands of genes, those of consciousness and consistency, might touch occasionally, if only briefly, perhaps at the fingertips. In any event, it seems unlikely that these mss., if they are genuinely what they purport to be, could have reached this world without the indulgence, if nothing else, of Priest-Kings. Is there one, or more, amongst them who know, even respect or care for, an unusual individual whom I, personally, have never met, though whose existence I have ascertained, from various records, and reports, is established beyond all doubt, a Mr. Tarl Cabot? Too, it seems there are others, as well. Certainly not all the mss are in the same hand. But enough of that. It seems to me also possible that friendship, or such, may not enter into these matters, but rather that the mss are permitted to filter into our world in accord with well-conceived but covert designs. Perhaps they are a way in which these Priest-Kings, as they are called in the mss, wish, for some reason, to let us know that we are not alone, that there is life not only elsewhere in the broad universe, but closer to us, more locally, than we suppose. Certainly there is evidence that some of those in high places, in one country or another, have taken note of the mss.

Perhaps that is the point of their transmission to us.

But these matters seem to me very mysterious.

I suppose, when all is done, we do not really know why the Priest-Kings, assuming such to exist, would permit these manuscripts to be known.

Is it an act of friendship, for a given individual, one once accorded, as it is said, Nest Trust?

Is it a caprice, or a scientific kindness, a boon granted charitably to our earnest astronomers and physicists; an insulting announcement of a superior life form to a lesser one, a lesser one perhaps too overweening and vain, one insufficiently humble in the face of mysteries which must trouble even intellects as profound and vast as those reputed to dignify and glorify Priest-Kings themselves?

Or do they see in us possible allies?

I might note in passing that only a relatively small amount of the Gorean materials has appeared in print.

Indeed, Cabot, and apparently some others, have supplied us with a rich miscellany of materials, much of which is not narrative in nature, but rather of a sort which seems, for one reason or another, to have interested the various transcribers, materials such as anecdotes, sayings, codes, legends, social practices, societal arrangements, festivals, shiplore, zoological and botanical treatises, games, sports, and such. Such material, of course, is presumably of more interest to naturalists, military and naval historians, political scientists, sociologists, anthropologists, and such, not to mention collectors of the obscure and arcane, than it would be to the general reader.

But one does not question the materials, nor the interests, and motivations, of the transcribers.

Some individuals are interested in how Goreans lock their doors, strike coins, manufacture spoons and saddles, conduct commerce, and so on. Let that be as it may. I, for one, effect nothing critical here.

One might also mention, in passing, that one should understand things for what they are, and not necessarily for what one feels they should be, or, better, are told they should be, particularly by self-proclaimed authorities whose credentials are nonexistent, obscure, or, at best, pompously self-certified, indeed, individuals whose lack of perception is seemingly exceeded only by their *a priori* hostility to the new or different. Many of the Gorean narratives, insofar as I may form a just opinion on the matter, do not strive to accommodate themselves to alien criteria. As in nature, they wander, prowl, and sniff about where they will. It may be that the authors of these books are simply unaware of the requirements of critics who would impose upon them, and, indeed, on all authors, their own values, restrictions, preferences, limitations, and prejudices; such supposed critics are the watchmen of stultification and mediocrity. In any event, the Gorean authors are obviously not interested in the currently approved formulas, which will eventually mark out this period of literature as of generally antiquarian interest. Surely a Chaucer, a Shakespeare, a Dostoevsky, a

Rabelais, and just about anyone of curiosity and passion, however large or small, different or similar, skilled or unskilled, would fare poorly in the dainty land of the rarified, delicate, and proper. Literature goes its own way, however distressing as this may be to those who would guide her to personally favored precincts. Let them, in pursuit of this aim, invent and distribute assorted dignities and emoluments which, to a true author, at least on the whole, it would be an embarrassment to accept, an acknowledgement that he had literally prostituted his honor and his profession. In any event, if a Gorean author is unaware of the current formulas for the well-made story or the correctly turned phrase, and the proper denizens of a politically correct lexicon, and turns aside to describe a sandal or a musical instrument, let us remain calm. And, indeed, otherwise, how would we know about that sandal, or musical instrument?

It might also be noted that whereas it seems to be expected in certain *genres* of literature that a different or alien culture is to be described from the outside and then carefully, and sometimes laboriously, even if subtly, criticized from the outside, from the viewpoint of a quite different culture, one's own, this supposedly pleasing the reader, who is thereby reassured that he and his culture were right all along, that expectation need not be fulfilled. In the Gorean case, for better or for worse, it does not seem to be fulfilled. The Gorean culture is normally described, you see, from the *inside*, as it is seen from the *inside*, which is a very different matter, and it is usually presented, and revealed, from the *inside*, as it seems to be to those who find themselves within it, and who live and often, it seems, thrive within it. The Gorean culture is usually presented objectively, and usually without comment. One is free then to think what one will. What a dreadful thought, to those who would control the thoughts of others! That one should make up one's own mind, that one should be actually free to do so! How frightful, to those who would be the tyrants of the mind! In any event, it seems a case might be made, should one wish to do so, that the Gorean culture is closer to the biotruths of the human species than at least some other cultures. I can think of at least one. Can't you? It seems so, at any rate. Need one comment further? One may, of course, if one feels impelled to do so, object to this aspect of the Gorean world. Goreans, for better or for worse, feel civilization should enhance and celebrate nature, rather than contradict, fight, and poison her. That is their view. It seems each should be entitled to make up his own mind on such matters, despite the convictions of those who feel they are entitled to make up the minds of others.

I leave this, of course, to the judgment of the reader.

Is that not the Gorean way?

I am, of course, not the only individual aware of these documents in their original form. For example, my friend, "Harrison Smith," as he chooses to be known, is aware of several of them, and, indeed, it is *via* his kind offices that I began the editorial work to which I have hitherto referred. But there would seem clearly to be other individuals involved in these matters, as well. Some mss. arrived, interestingly, in the mail, in nondescript packaging, without return addresses; some I found, to my astonishment, in my apartment, which had apparently been easily but unobtrusively entered. Twice such mss. were pressed into my hands in the tumult of crowds, by utter strangers, elusive men never before seen, who slipped away before I could question them. Perhaps, as was once suggested, the agents of the Priest-Kings are amongst us. One manuscript was delivered more surprisingly. I shall recount the incident, as I suppose it might prove to be of interest to some. I have certainly never forgotten it. The delivery occurred late in a recent year, on a dusky evening in the city. A light snow lay fresh on the streets, and wisps of it, as I recall, were still about, still falling softly, catching and reflecting the light of the street lamps. The traffic, some floors below, was moving normally, with its customary sounds. A radio was indistinctly playing in a nearby apartment. I heard a light knock at my door, the character of which somehow suggested, if not timidity, or fear, at least, surely, a modest deference, and, say, an unwillingness to be thought to be forward, or a desire not to risk being taken to be obtrusive. To this signal, putting aside my book, I responded. To my amazement, opening the door, I found myself facing a remarkable young woman. It would be difficult to describe the slight but maddening sweetness of her figure, and the exquisite loveliness and delicacy of her features. She was surely one of the most incredibly beautiful, and feminine, young women I had even seen. Too, I had the immediate sense in her of a quite high intelligence, but this intelligence, and its associated sensitivity, impressed me not as abstract and angular, or hard, or indifferent, or callous, or stern, as one expects in a man, but rather as being in its way a special sort of intelligence or awareness, one of a sort which one can discover only in a woman, and only in a special sort of woman, an intelligence soft, vulnerable, and exquisitely and uniquely feminine. This individual before me then impressed me as being not only one of great beauty, and of youth and health, but as constituting a gift, so to speak, in her way, to the species, a gift not only of beauty, but one of intelligence, sensitivity, awareness, and, above all, of femininity. Clearly she was one of the most feminine women, and assuredly, and contentedly, and unapologetically so, that I had ever met. I had a sense then of what a woman could be, and, as it occurred to me then, though surely the thought must be deplored, of what a woman should be. Clearly she could not be a "normal woman" in any of our usual ugly senses of such a term, senses boringly descriptive of miserable, culturally botched artifacts or senses sanctimoniously prescriptive of unquestioning, docile cogs in a mindless social mechanism, one essentially sexless and antithetical to health and biology. Where had she come from, I wondered. Who was she? How could it be that she, *here*, was as she was? Had she not been twisted and hardened? Why not? Is it not done to all? Should it not be done to all? Or had she been changed, unwound, untwisted, sorted out, remedied, opened, softened, returned somehow to wind and rainfall, to meadows, to body heat, and excitement, and love? Could this be a creature of our culture? Surely not! But could it be? What had been done to her? What right had she to be so radically female, so fundamentally female, so helplessly, vulnerably, genuinely, beautifully female? Oddly, too, in that instant when first our eyes met, before hers fell, she seemed to see me quite naturally as something very different from herself, something that she was not, and could never be, and could only be miserable trying to be, but, too, something she did not, honestly, desire to be. I had the sense that she wanted to be only herself, and would be herself, only herself, and would thus put aside, as though by a change of mind, a turning about, an acceptance, an acclaiming, a thousand sorrows, falsities, and confusions.

I should mention that she was well dressed, richly so, I suppose, but with a simplicity that achieved an elegance. She was the sort of young woman whom one might expect to see stepping from a limousine, but she lacked the rigidity or hauteur, the disdain, that one might have expected of such.

I had the sense that she had undergone unusual experiences, which had freed and shaped her.

I did not know if she were a creature of this world and culture or not. I had the brief, disconcerting impression that she was the sort of woman who might be literally sold to men.

And that that might be good for her.

She carried a package. It was wrapped in leather, and tied closely, with several flat leather bands.

More than once I had seen such an unusually wrapped article.

I hesitate to convey what then occurred, lest it be found offensive by some, but I feel it best to do so, at least in the interest of the completeness of this recollection.

She then, with a lovely naturalness and grace, as of one long habituated to such practices, and one who found such ceremonies and deferences lovely, appropriate, and fulfilling, knelt before me, yes, knelt before me, and put her head down to my feet.

I wonder if you can understand what it is to have such a woman kneel before you, how it fills you with glory and power, this submission and prostration, and seems somehow fitting, and a perfection of nature. And, too, I sensed that she, too, in her way, found this fulfilling, and profoundly, keenly emotionally reassuring, fitting, that it was what she wanted to do, and that for her, too, in its way, it was a perfection of nature. I recalled, inadvertently, a saying from the Gorean miscellany: "Let she who should submit, submit; let he who is master master."

Perhaps, I thought, could it be, the sexes are not, when all is said and done, the same.

She then pressed her lips to my shoes, and then knelt up, and, her head down between her extended arms, humbly and delicately proffered to me the package she bore.

I doubtless should have admonished her for this astonishing and unexpected gesture, the kneeling, and such, should doubtless have denied to her this lovely, so naturally, so willingly granted token of respect, should doubtless have tried sharply, cruelly, to reprimand and shame her, or at least, surely, I should have hurried her to her feet in embarrassment, but, for whatever reason, I did not do so.

Rather I understood then, I think for the first time, how it could be that a man could kill for a woman.

"Wait!" I called after her, but she had then sprung up and darted away. She was responsive, it seemed, to imperatives other than mine. As she sprang to her feet and turned, I caught a glimpse, ever so briefly, beneath her long, dark, glossy, swirling hair, of her one piece of jewelry, a lovely, flat, narrow band which closely encircled her lovely throat.

This all occurred very quickly, and she had not spoken to me one word.

I watched her disappear down the corridor, and then, the package in hand, returned within.

The following account is extracted from the Gorean miscellany. Unlike many of the other items in the miscellany, which tend to be meditative or expositional, and are sometimes little more than lists, it has a narrative flow, at least somewhat, and deals with an interaction between two individuals. Given these considerations I thought it might then not inaptly be brought to public attention, in a context such as that of the present, in the event that perhaps some might find it of interest.

I do not think the author is Tarl Cabot, as the style, and handscript, do not suggest those of Cabot, with whose style and script I am familiar. An additional inducement to this reservation is that what is apparently the original seems to be in Gorean, or, at any rate, in a language with which I and my immediate associates are unfamiliar. It is clear that the letters in the original proceed from left to right, and then right to left, in alternate lines, which is, as I understand it, "as the bosk plows." Cabot writes in English, and seems to be uncomfortable, as I understand it, with literary Gorean. This is apparently not that unusual for it seems that many Gorean warriors, though surely not all, are actually illiterate, and deliberately so, and this in accord with a certain martial vanity, regarding letters as being an occupation and concern more suitable to scribes than to those of the "scarlet caste." The original is clearly in a bold, masculine hand, but the translation into English, or what I take to be the translation, is, interestingly, in a feminine hand. I take it then the original was presumably written by a male who may or may not have known English and that the translation may have been made by a female who was fluent in both languages, or, at least, copied by such a female. There are other possibilities, but those seem to me the most plausible.

I present it now without further introduction.

I trust it will not be found offensive.

"Do not use me!" she begged.

Her Gorean was imperfect.

She moved, frightened, to the back of the alcove. Her small hands went to the chain that attached to the collar on her throat. How small and lovely are the hands of women! She held it tightly, helplessly, protestingly. It was about five feet long, and fastened her to a ring, set to the side. She was naked, as is common with her sort, in alcoves, slaves. She was half sunk in the deep furs. The alcove was a common one, small, with incurving walls, now closed with leather curtains which he had drawn shut behind him.

I do not mention the tavern, nor its city, other than to place it in the middle latitudes of the world, east of Brundisium, north of our mother, the great Vosk; there are those, enemies, you see, who might use such knowledge. They do not understand us, and are prompt to kill.

He had tied the curtains shut on the inside. It is commonly done. One is less likely then to be disturbed. There were some smaller chains about, cuffs, and such. He carried a switch, brought in from the outside. The light was furnished by a small tharlarion oil lamp set in a niche to the left, as one faces the back of the alcove. The flame was straight, responding to the subtle draft above and behind the lamp. He found her very beautiful in the alcove, but that is common with tavern slaves. They are purchased with such things in mind.

"You should beg use," he informed her.

It is pleasant for a man, as is well known, for a beautiful woman to beg use.

"No, no!" she wept.

He regarded her, sadly.

"You may speak in your native tongue," he said.

"I do not wish to be beaten," she said.

"I will not beat you for that—*now*," he said.

He thought it best for her, given what he wished to do, to speak in her own language. He did not wish her to misunderstand anything which might transpire between them, in the least.

Indeed, her life, as he had reason to believe, might depend on such things.

"I do not wish to be tricked, and then struck!' she wept.

He frowned. Did she think him such, one who would so behave, a boor, one without honor? Such would dishonor his caste.

He fingered the switch.

All females understand such things, and certainly slaves. A great deal of good is often accomplished with as little as a single, sudden, swift, impatient stroke.

"Thank you," she said, in English, quickly, uncertainly. She was obviously intelligent. He had had fears on that score. "But you will not understand me."

"I think I am likely to understand you," he said, "*and well*," he added.

"You speak English," she said.

"I speak three of the languages of your world," he said. "How many do you speak?"

"—One," she said. "You have an accent."

"So, too, do you, in your Gorean," he said.

"Of course," she said.

"Many women of your world learn Gorean swiftly, and well, and, in time, are so fluent that it is difficult, if at all possible, to distinguish them from native speakers, save for an occasional phonemic indiscretion or lapse. I do not know, however, if you will be one of them. Perhaps your diction will retain a piquant touch of the exotic. Some men like that."

"Doubtless" she said, bitterly.

"I have a great admiration," he said, "for the common aptitudes of females to absorb, and learn, new languages. Doubtless it is a gift which has been selected for."

"Doubtless," she said, trying to move back a little, more toward the back of the alcove.

How small and well curved she was. What a delicious thing she might prove to be.

It seemed a shame, what was likely to be done to her.

How pleasant it is to take such things in your arms, and press them to you, to embrace them, and put them to use.

It is little wonder that there are such as she—slaves.

He wondered if she even understood him.

If she had, would it not have been an insight weighty in portency?

Throughout generations, doubtless on various worlds,

such as she had been acquired, bartered, bought, exchanged, traded, abducted, and such, and, often, as a consequence of such an eventuation, she would find herself translated into an alien speech environment, it then being incumbent upon her to learn, and as quickly and well as possible, a new language, that of her captors, her owners, her masters.

Did she truly think it was no more than the flipping of a coin by nature, that women should be such?

To be sure, statistically it might once have been nature playing with possibilities, scattering about the coins of reality, trying this and that, but there were winning tosses, and losing tosses, and, statistically, the winning tosses would generate further winning tosses, and soon the coins would seem of themselves to replicate the advantages accrued originally in what must once have been little more than a meaningless lottery.

And the coins became an instrument of survival, a lovely currency, a concealed treasure wherewith she might purchase life.

Did she not know that women were property?

Too, of course, when a woman finds herself an owned animal, yes, that is it, precisely, and legally, an *animal*, subject to her owner, her master, she learns quickly.

She pulled up one of the furs, clutching it about her, to cover herself. She held it about her throat, over the collar.

He smiled. Did she not know that she was not to cover her body without his permission?

Perhaps she was stupid.

No, he thought, simply not yet tutored, not yet trained.

He could well understand the reservations of the taverner, his complaint, his fear for his investment.

I do not mention the name of the taverner, nor of his establishment, for obvious reasons.

"Many here," she said, pulling the furs up even higher about her throat, "do not even know my world, Earth, exists."

"From the existence of such as you," he said, "for you are not unique, I am sure they accept that there is a place called

'Earth,' but I think it is true that few understand it to be another world.

"I am not unique?" she said.

"No," he said.

"There are others?"

"Yes," he said. "But most of us doubtless think of it only as a far place, from which such as you are brought to civilization."

"To civilization!" she exclaimed.

"Certainly," he said. "I have been to your world, and there is little there worthy to be called civilization."

"You are barbarians here!" she said.

"Why?" he asked. "Because you are on a chain?"

She was silent.

"You must not think badly of our world," he said. "We are fond of it. It is complex and beautiful. We have our literatures, our musics, our architectures, our games, our sports, our crafts, our professions, our commerce, our enmities, our perils, our wars, our loves, our hatreds, all the accouterments of a high civilization."

"I see," she said.

"And you must not identify a civilization with politics, crowding, greed, misery, loneliness, pollution, and technology. These are not essential to civilization. Too, on this world we have Home Stones."

"I do not know what they are," she said.

"And that is one reason that you are a barbarian," he said.

"I, a barbarian!"

"Yes," he said. "On this world it is such as you who are the barbarians, though we may hope to teach you some of the refinements of civilization, a few perhaps at our feet."

"At your feet!"

"Should you be granted the opportunity," he said. And his eyes briefly clouded.

"I do not know anything of Home Stones!" she said, angrily.

"You will not have one," he said. "At best, if you are permitted to live—"

"'If'!" she cried.

"Yes," he said, "'if'."

"I do not understand," she said, apprehensively.

She had interrupted him. He found that of interest. More and more did he begin to understand the consternation, the reservations, of the taverner.

"Yes," he said, "—*if—if* you are permitted to live, you may be permitted to live to please and serve, wholly and helplessly, and with the abject fullness of perfection, as is fitting, one who has such."

"A Home Stone?"

"Yes."

He saw clearly she did not understand this matter. She knew little of the world.

"If those of this world do not even know of the existence of Earth, my world, they must be terribly stupid," she said.

"Many on your world," he said, "do not even know this world exists."

She made an angry gesture.

He thought her hair was nice. To be sure, she did not seem to know what to do with it. In time it might become much longer, and more free and silken. Such hair improves the price of such women. They are careful, and jealous, of it. He wondered if it would have time to become such, and if she would have time to understand its value, and that of herself. She did have value. He wondered if she realized that. She did have value—of a sort. Five of her might be exchanged for a kaiila, three for a sleen, ten to fifteen for a tarn. He remembered the taverner. He wondered if she knew the danger in which she stood.

He wondered if it had been a mistake to acquire her.

It would seem a shame if she were to be sold for sleen feed.

"You are unclothed," he said.

She drew the furs up, even more closely, about her throat.

"Yes," she said.

"Do you object?" he asked.

"Certainly," she said.

"Do you know why you are unclothed?" he asked.

"No," she said, "no!"

He saw she knew little of men and women

Or perhaps she was not being candid.

Lying was not permitted in such as she, but quite possibly she was not yet keenly aware of that, or of the terrible risks implicit in the smallest of endeavored deceptions.

Men found pleasure in looking upon her.

And so they would.

That was why she was unclothed.

Was that so hard to understand?

"Do you know what you are?" he asked.

"I am some sort of prisoner, or captive," she said. "Is that not obvious?"

"You have examined your left thigh?" he said.

"Yes," she said.

"There is a mark there, is there not?" he asked.

"Yes!" she said, angrily.

"It is an attractive mark, is it not," he asked, "small, lovely, tasteful, delicate—and *feminine*—obviously and unmistakably *feminine*?"

She was silent.

"And it is on you, is it not? Well fixed, clearly and indelibly so, unmistakably so, in your thigh?"

"Yes!" she said, angrily.

"It is a brand," he said. "It is recognized throughout this world. It proclaims what you are."

He regarded her evenly.

She looked away.

"What are you?" he asked.

She did not meet his eyes.

"A captive, a prisoner," she said, sullenly.

"Aii!" she wept, for he had torn away from her the furs within which she had huddled, seeking to shelter herself from his gaze, and, by the hair, had cast her prone on the furs.

He then, as she wept, lashed her, five times, with the switch he carried. "Please, stop!" she cried, covering her head with her hands. "What are you?" he demanded, savagely. "A slave," she cried, "a slave!"

"A slave, what?" he demanded.

"Master," she wept, "a slave, *Master*!"

He reached to her hair and twisted her head about, to regard him. He regarded her with disgust. She turned her head away.

"Position!" he snapped.

Swiftly she went to position.

"I wonder," he mused, "I wonder "

She looked well in position.

He wondered if there were any point in working with her.

She did look well in position, but does not any woman?

She had obviously not had much training. It would have been better if they had had longer to work with her. But the enemies had seemed to be apprised of the trove's location. It had been necessary to scatter the merchandise, and there had been little time to do so.

In a way that was unfortunate.

"Turn about," said he, "put your head to the furs."

She did so, shuddering.

"What are you going to do?" she said.

"Whatever I please," he said. "Keep your head down." Such a position is good for a woman. It helps her to overcome pride. It helps her to understand that she is a woman. "How many letters are there in the expression 'kajira'?" he asked.

"I do not know!" she said.

"Six," he said. "How many times were you struck?"

"I do not know!" she wept.

"Recall each blow," he said. "Remember each stroke."

"—Five," she said.

"What are you, in *Gorean*," he said.

"*La kajira*!" she said.

"In English!" he said.

"I am a slave woman!" she said.

"No," he said. "You are too luscious, too desirable, too slim, too shapely and exciting for that. Too coin-worthy for that! Too, 'woman' is a term of dignity, of status, one to which you are not entitled. What are you, in *Gorean*!"

"*La kajira*!" she wept.

"And in English, the best translation?" he said.

"I am a slave girl!" she said.

"Girl?" he asked.

"Yes!" she said. "*Girl. Girl*!"

"What sort of girl?"

"A slave *girl*!" she cried.

"And how many letters in 'kajira'?" he asked.

"Six," she said.

"And how many times were you struck?"

"Please let me change my position," she begged. "I have no dignity like this! You are humiliating me! How can you view me with respect, as I am?"

Her question was answered most eloquently, with a laugh.

"—Five," she said.

"It seems then that in our small lesson, to which I trust you are attentive, that you require for parity of admonition and instruction, for mnemonic purposes, for an informative symmetry, so to speak, an additional stroke."

"No!" she said. "Ai!" she wept.

"There," said he. "Six letters, six strokes. *Kajira*. I think now you will better remember what you are." Such simple artifices, in their small way, with their perhaps initially attendant embarrassments, can help a girl adjust to the new network of relations in which she finds herself, can help her to come to grips with what she now is. The sooner she realizes her new condition and reality, the new she she is, and its uncontroversial and inalterable nature, the better for her.

"Remain as you are," he cautioned her. But she had not endeavored to change her position. This gave him some reassurance. He did not care to waste his time. Too, she was, in her way, beautiful. He did not want it to be a waste, that she had been brought here.

His women, Gorean women, were familiar with such as she, with their duties, their place in society, and such, and, commonly, understood the transitions involved, and, on the whole, adapted quickly to their new condition, particularly if translated to a foreign city with an alien Home Stone. He was surprised that women of Earth, without these familiarities, without this cultural background, without an awareness of the customs and practices involved, coming from a world so different, so cold, polluted, lonely, sterile, and mechanistic, yet in a short time accommodated themselves, and well, to what, for them, must initially at least be perceived as radically alien, perhaps even frightening, realities and conditions. Why did the women of Earth sell so well in the markets? Why did they soon prove to be amongst the most desired, the most coveted, items of merchandise? Doubtless there were at least two reasons. One, their dreams, their fantasies, their hopes, their yearnings, had prepared them for this world. Two, they were women, no different from their Gorean sisters, with the needs, the desires, the dispositions, the sensitivities, and awarenesses, the beautiful depths and profundities of the human female.

Too, of course, the women brought to the world were not randomly harvested, not picked as chance or convenience would have it. They were selected with values in mind, such as merchandisability, indexed to not simply beauty, intelligence, and health, but to a sensed set of needs, and readinesses, sexual and otherwise, to which an experienced assessor eventually becomes sensitized.

They were brought here for the collar, as much as for anything else, because they belonged in the collar, and wanted it, in the depths of their hearts.

A skilled assessor could glance at a woman, on the street, in a store, in a public conveyance, she wholly unawares, and sense the slave in her, the waiting slave; and so, casually, idly, speculatively, he deprives her of her garments, and sees her as she might be, as a naked, chained slave, sees her, too, as she might be on the block, vulnerable, exposed, exhibited, denied even a concealing thread, all eyes upon her, being vended, provoking interest, worthy of being sold, sees her, too, as she would be, later, kneeling before a man, stripped, submitted, claimed, owned, wearing his collar, her lips pressed gratefully, fearfully, to his feet.

She is added to his list.

He looked again at the woman kneeling away, before him.

He wondered if she were a mistake.

If only there had been more time to train her.

He then, suddenly, struck her three more times, sharply.

"Do you ask for a justification of those strokes?" he inquired.

"No!" she said. "No!"

"What are you," he asked, "in *Gorean*, then in English."

"*La kajira*!" she said. "I am a slave girl!"

"Position," he snapped.

Swiftly she turned about, and assumed position, before him.

Yes, she was beautiful.

He put the switch under her chin, for her head was down, and lifted her chin, gently, that she might look at him. She was frightened.

She understood now that she was subject to discipline, that she would be punished if she were not pleasing.

This insight, in itself, can be transformative in a female.

Did she have possibilities?

She was beautiful enough to have possibilities.

He hoped she had possibilities.

"You may sit or recline, as you wish," he said, "and you may cover yourself with the furs, as before."

She moved quickly to the back of the alcove. He noted that she knelt, which he found of interest. She clutched, as before, defensively, the furs about her, high, covering even the collar, by means of the chain of which she was secured within the alcove.

"What do you want of me?" she asked. "Have you paid your coin?"

"No," he said.

"You have not paid your coin?"

"No."

"What then?"

"I would like to talk with you," he said. "Does that surprise you?"

"Yes," she said.

"I wonder if you realize the danger you are in," he said.

"Danger?"

"Have you ever seen a sleen?" he asked.

"No," she said.

"Leech plants?" he inquired. He himself involuntarily shuddered, as he thought of those thick, matted, restless, thorned, fleshly growths. He had once seen a man fall amongst them.

"No," she said.

"There have been use complaints from customers," he said.

She shrugged.

"The taverner is not pleased."

Again she shrugged, and looked away.

The enemies had detected the ship, though it had been well hidden. It had been destroyed. They had not seemed much concerned with us. It was the ship they had wanted. There were other ships, of course. We had scattered. Some, I suppose, were caught. One does not know. It had not been possible to anticipate the attack, but we had had a few moments warning, enough time to leave, to break camp, to move the goods, the coffles. We knew this sort of danger. The work is well paid, however, in various ways.

She had not even been conscious when she had been sold. The taverner had examined her in the light of a lamp, while she slept in the warehouse. He had selected her largely on the basis of her features and lineaments. He had not seen her move. He had not seen her perform. He had not paid much for her. She had been cheap. They had wished to dispose of her, and several others, quickly, privately. Who knew where, or whence, the enemies? She had thus been deprived of the experience of her own sale, a presale training, a presale indoctrination, the coaching of the auctioneer, and such. Then she had been chained and hooded, and brought here. Her Gorean was sparse, as yet, the result of no more than a few weeks of instruction, in the establishment itself, by other girls. She had been put out on the floor only five days ago. It was unfortunate that the taverner had been so eager for a bargain. Had he seen her awake, had he seen her move, he might have better understood the problematical nature of his projected investment. I think he might then have left her for another, or for the mills, or laundries. One needs girls in such places, but they do not wish to stay there, and they strive desperately to be relieved as soon as possible of the lengthy and laborious tasks associated with charges so dismal and onerous, strive to escape them in the only way available to them, by recourse to the ways of the woman. What is a woman's beauty for but to be exchanged for the goods of the world? But, alas for them, others, not they, own their beauty, and exchange it on their own behalf for the goods of the world. On the world called Earth, a woman owns her own beauty and may barter it, or sell it, to the highest bidder, to advance herself as she will, but on this world her beauty is commonly owned by another who can barter it, or sell it, not for hers, but for his purposes. Sometimes, incidentally, it is pleasant to take a haughty woman of Earth who has such intentions, those of cynically using her beauty to advance herself, and bring her to Gor, stripped and on a chain. She will then see her beauty, not quite what she had perhaps thought it to be, now that it is objectively compared with that of others, exchanged not to her benefit but to that of others. This is a useful lesson for a woman. She will then learn sounder values, at the feet of a master, and will be then once again concerned to use her beauty in her own best interest, but now, fearfully and desperately, to please her master.

"Have you done well in the alcove?" he asked. He had, of course, the reports of the taverner.

"Yes," she said.

"Yes?" he inquired.

"Certainly," said she, "I am helpless. I am naked. I am on a chain. Many have had their way with me. How can I help that? I have been handled with authority and scorn. I have been handled like meat. Frequently have I been treated with abruptness and disdain. Many a time I have been thoughtlessly, arrogantly, perfunctorily brutalized."

He considered her. There are times when such things are good for a woman, when she is learning her condition, when she needs reassurance, when she is to be reminded of her status, and such. But there is more, so much more.

"The last two nights," he said, "though the tavern has been crowded, no more than three men, it seems, and strangers, deigned to accept your services, deigned to send you to the vat, that you might fetch them paga."

"Yes, three," she said.

"It seems," said he, "that few have cared to accept your goblet, that few have deigned to sip your paga."

Her eyes flashed, angrily.

"You understand my meaning, do you not?" he asked.

"Yes!" she said, angrily.

"Does that not concern you?" he asked.

"It pleases me," she said. "I rejoice!"

The lore and practices, the customs and commonplaces, of the paga tavern, as I understand it, may be unfamiliar to some. This is conveyed to me by my charming amanuensis, whom I have permitted to speak. Briefly, a paga tavern, in most of known Gor, and certainly in the high cities, is a comfortable, pleasant place where one may obtain wholesome food and strong drink, a convivial place where one can meet friends, exchange views, and conduct business, a place where one can attend to the latest news and gossip, a place where one can usually find a game of kaissa or stones, a place of entertainment and recreation. Many taverns, particularly the larger sorts, have musicians, and dancers. All have paga slaves. In the better taverns, in the more respectable taverns, they serve commonly in silks, brief, diaphanous silks which leave little to the imagination, and bells, in the lower taverns nude and in chains. The girls may approach the tables, for their service to be accepted or rejected, or summoned to a table by a gesture or a snapping of fingers. They kneel for they are in the presence of free men, and hope to garner a permission to serve. Commonly a cup of paga is ordered and the girl is sent to fetch it, and bring it back to the table. Usually the proprietor or one of his men takes the coin. The girl, if she is wanted, comes with the price of the drink. She may be ordered to an alcove, or dragged or switched, to its confines. Most men, of course, are content with the paga, but it is pleasant, now and again, to know that the beauty who serves it may be enjoyed with no extra cost. Usually it is only free men and slave girls who are found in the taverns. Free women are not permitted in most such taverns. And, too, of course, it is dangerous for them to enter such precincts. Sometimes a free woman, one perhaps too bold, and too insatiably curious, will clothe herself as a slave, even to the collar, to enter the tavern, but, as I have said, it is dangerous for them to do so. For example, they might, in all innocence, deplorably, be mistaken for a true slave. Too, more than one free woman has come into a collar in that fashion, one she cannot remove.

Some find it hard to understand why a free woman would run such risks.

But then why do some wander in the poorer districts at night, venture unescorted outside the walls, frequent the higher bridges in the moonlight?

Do they sense a life beyond the encumbrances of their robes, a mode of being beyond the corridors of respect and dignity, a reality beyond the high, enclosing, barren walls of propriety?

How hard it is to understand!

To what cry do they attend?

To what song do they listen?

"Do you think your gruel and pellets are free?"

"I suppose not," she said.

"One such as you is not expensive," he said. "But still there are costs to keeping you."

She was silent.

"What do you think you are kept for?" he asked.

"Apparently for being beaten and abused," she said.

"Not at all," he said. "You are being kept to be beautiful and pleasing, to serve well, to be a thrashing, lascivious delight in the furs, to be attractive, to be desirable, to bring men to the tavern, and their coins, their coins, *their coins*, to make money."

"That is disgusting," she said.

"Not for one such as you," he said.

"Oh?"

"Yes, it is what you are for."

"I see," she said.

"I gather," he said, "that several men, at first, at least, visited you."

"You may call it that, I suppose," she said. "They spoke of it, or more than one did, as "trying me out.""

"Of course," he said. "You were a new girl, a new piece of collar meat."

"Collar meat!"

"Yes," he said.

"Happily they were dissatisfied," she said. "None came back."

"Did that not distress you?"

"It pleases me."

"But it must puzzle you," he said.

"Yes," she said, "for I supposed myself attractive. On Earth, men and boys beseeched me for my company. I often turned down four or five invitations a week."

"You were indeed popular," he said.

"Yes," she sniffed.

"Your beauty doubtless had much to do with that."

"I am beautiful?"

"Yes."

"I was smug, aloof, inaccessible there," she said, ruefully.

"Here I may be alcoved by anyone with the price of a drink. You did not pay a coin?"

"No," he reminded her.

"What are you doing here, then?" she asked.

"Chatting," he said.

She laughed.

"What is wrong?" he asked.

"I was thinking," she said, "of all those boys and men on Earth who wanted me to go out with them, whom I refused, and dismissed. Now I am naked, and on a chain, fastened in an alcove, helpless, and any of them might have me—literally take me in their arms and have me—*have me!*—for so little as the price of a drink!"

"I do not think they would," he said. "I doubt that they would know what to do with you, as you are."

"As a meaningless, naked slave!"

"Yes," he said.

"The males here are so virile," she said. "They are so strong, so thoughtlessly, unquestioningly, and powerfully male, so magnificently male, so innocent in their audacity. How they look upon me!"

"They are not men of Earth," he said. "They are Goreans, and you are a slave."

"And is that how the men of Gor look upon such as I, on slaves?"

"Yes, simply, as the lovely, desirable, ownable animals you are, perfect and appropriate instruments for their service and pleasure, once properly trained and disciplined, of course, but do not think ill of the men of Earth. Few of them can begin to understand what has been done to them. Most know little more than that they are frustrated and unhappy. It is a matter of acculturation, of confusions, of inconsistent twistings and belaborings, of competitive thickets of pale and impossible principles, of commands which cannot be obeyed, of goals which cannot be reached, and, if reached, would be devoid of life and value."

"Am I beautiful?" she begged.

"Yes," he said.

"Then why have I been taken off the floor? Why have I been stripped and chained here, alone?"

"Perhaps that we might have this conversation?" he said.

"I do not understand," she said.

"Let us return to your visitors," he suggested.

"None came back," she said.

"And you are puzzled, because you are beautiful?"

"—Yes," she said.

"But you are a slave," he said, "and beauty is common amongst slaves."

"So I have gathered, from my observations, of my sisters on the floor," she said.

"Therefore," said he, "we must look beyond beauty. Beauty, after all, is cheap. Did you know that? I see not. It may be inexpensively purchased in any market. Most men take it for granted in a slave, though, to be sure, certain forms of beauty appeal more to certain men than others, and so on, and some men will kill for a woman who takes their fancy, in one way or another, but even in such cases more than beauty is almost always involved, unless perhaps a fellow is merely looking for a decoration or an adornment, rather like a shrub or statue, for, say, his pleasure garden."

"Pleasure garden?" she asked.

"Rich men can afford them," he said. "But," he continued, "there are sensings involved. On your world, as I recall, it is common to conceal one's ignorance in these matters by an unilluminating appeal to expressions such as 'chemistry' or 'magic'. On Gor our ignorance is as profound as yours, I assure you, but we seldom attempt to mask it by recourse to convenient, unintelligible lexical deceits. One supposes such things are involved as biographical antecedents, motivations, and interests, sometimes almost explicitly unrecognizable noticings of responses and movements, readings of bodies and, in particular, of expressions, however fleeting, many of these awarenesses somehow registered but apparently often not articulated, the quick discernment of possibilities, the subtle detection of latencies, and such, sensings, so to speak, not fully understood perhaps, but sensings often forcible and irresistible. Why is it that a man buys one woman and not another? Why does he affix his collar on one fair throat and not another? There are reasons, doubtless, but they are hard to detect. And why does one woman long to wear the chains of one man and not of another? Why does one long for the bracelets and leash of a given fellow, and not for those of another? Why does one woman yearn to kneel before a given man, lifting her lips and tongue to his whip, to kiss, lick, and caress it, and not another? There are reasons, one supposes. But they may be difficult to discern. How is it that one woman may suddenly, perhaps after months, look into the eyes of a man and see her love master, and he into hers, and see his love slave? These things are hard to understand."

"You are frightening me," she said.

"Each man," said he, "wants his perfect slave, and that perfect slave is found in the whole of her, in every inch and bit of her, not just in her beauty, but in the fullness of her being, in her heart, her mind, her emotions, her dispositions, her nature, her character, in the *all* of her."

"I understand nothing of what you are saying," she said.

"I think you do," he said, "and that is why you are frightened."

She put down her head and concealed her eyes in the furs.

"Look at me, slut," he said, sharply.

She looked up, quickly, frightened.

"What are you?" he snapped.

"A slave, a slave," she whispered, "—Master."

"And on Earth?" he asked.

"Not that," she said. "I was free! Free! On Earth there are no slaves!"

"Do not be naive," he said. "And had you been a slave on Earth you might have been better prepared for Gor."

"There are slaves on Earth?" she asked.

"Yes," he said, "and many are kept in superb bondages."

"I did not know," she said.

"How naive you are," he said. "On Earth there are men

and women. Why then should you not expect, too, that there would be masters and slaves?"

She bit on the furs, shaking her head, miserably, frightened.

"But on Earth," he said, "you were not a slave. You were free."

"Yes!" she exclaimed.

"As free, at least," said he, "as any other woman in your unhappy, miserable world, that ludicrous habitat, free to twist and lament, and struggle and perspire, and weep, within the denials, confinements, and strictures, the unseen hobbles and irons, of your culture."

She regarded him, angrily. Her small hands clutched the furs about her throat.

"In a Gorean collar," said he, "you will find yourself more free than ever you dreamed of being on Earth."

"I do not understand," she said.

"In a collar," said he, "a woman is most herself, and thus most free."

"I do not understand," she said.

"On Earth," said he, "you were a college graduate, a member of a sorority, a spoiled brat, and a flirt, and a junior employee in the art department of an advertising agency."

"How could you know about these things," she asked, "that is, the college, the sorority, the advertising agency?"

"Advertising," said he, "is useful in a culture such as yours was, in turning the wheels of frustration and greed, in manufacturing spurious needs, in designing and peddling images, in marketing cosmetics and statesmen, in goading and stirring an insatiable economy to ever greater frenzies of absurdity and vacuity. It is a duplicitous and fraudulent activity. I can see why one as pretty, and as empty, meaningless, and frivolous as you, would be attracted to the endeavor."

"They paid well!" she said.

"Certainly," he said. "Hypocrisy and dishonesty are well rewarded in a meretricious culture."

"No!" she cried. "—Yes," she whimpered.

"You are a shallow, frivolous, meaningless little mercenary slut," he snarled.

"Do not be cruel!" she begged.

"All of you belong on the slaver's necklace," he said. "It is time you sluts were useful. It is time you were good for something. Coffle the lot of you, and put you up for sale. Perhaps someone will be stupid enough to buy you."

She regarded him, aghast.

But," said he, "understand this now. And understand it well, little slut. Earth, and such things, are behind you. They are no longer your reality. Things have radically changed for you. You are on a different world. You have a new reality now, and you have one reality only now—understand that only one that of a Gorean slave girl."

"It is hard for a girl to understand that she is a slave," she whispered.

"A collar and a lashing can sometimes help her to grasp the fact," he said.

She shuddered.

"I am a slave, aren't I?" she said.

"Yes," he said.

"I understood very little of what you were saying before," she said, "about sensings, about love slaves, about men about women."

"It is perhaps too early to talk to you about subtle things," he said. "Later you may recall my words, and understand them. It is not necessary now."

"Is something necessary now?" she asked, uneasily.

"Let me ask you a simple question," he said. "Do you wish to live?"

She regarded him, suddenly terrified. " Yes," she said, "yes!"

"Then something is necessary now," he said.

"What?" she asked.

"This," said he, "remember that you are neither special nor privileged. You must begin to earn your gruel and pellets. We spoke of beauty not being enough, did we not?"

"Yes," she said.

"Do not forget that," he said. "Remember it. It is not enough to be as beautiful as a slave, as though any free woman could be truly as beautiful as a slave. One must know oneself as a slave, and *be* a slave. It is a thing within. It is quite different from being a free woman. Consider your "visitors"."

"Yes?" she said.

"Were you a slave to them?"

"Of course," she said. "I was naked. I was on a chain!"

"So might be a free woman," he said.

She was silent.

"Did you beg to please, did you beg use?" he asked.

"Certainly not," she said.

"Did you gasp, did you cry out, did you moan?" he asked.

"I bit my lip,' she said, "to remain silent, to betray not the smallest feeling, to give them not the least satisfaction."

"But you felt things?"

"One cannot help that," he said.

"And you gave yourself no pleasure, no satisfaction?" he asked.

"Certainly as little as possible,"

"But you did feel things?"

"One cannot help that," she said.

"And, afterwards," he asked, "did you, sincerely and gratefully, and from the bottom of your hot little belly, from the depths of your rejoicing heart, thank them for their attentions to you, thank them for your usage?"

"Certainly not!" she exclaimed, angrily.

"Do you like your brand?" he asked.

She regarded him, startled.

"I see you do," he said. "That is good."

"I do not understand," she said,

"It is pretty, is it not?" he asked.

"I suppose so," she said.

"I wonder if you realize that you welcomed it," he said.

"I do not understand," she said.

"Consider it simply as a mark," he said. "It does enhance your beauty, does it not?"

"Yes," she said, uncertainly. "I suppose it does."

"And you have no objection to that?"

"No," she said.

He found this response encouraging.

"But you understand its meaning, the fullness of its significance?" he asked.

"I fear so," she said.

"And do you further understand that this meaning enhances your beauty in subtle and profound ways a thousandfold?"

She was silent.

"I see that you do," he said.

"I cannot help how I am," she said.

He was certain that she was not inert, not frigid. Not truly, not ultimately. No woman, ultimately, unless anatomically, is frigid. It is almost universally a psychological matter, the result of a crime committed against them, by a mechanistic culture concerned to propagate the ideological sterilities without which it might collapse. The morbidities of culture have their own laws of growth, their own excrescences and foliations, often tended and fructified by strange gardeners who draw their sustenance from the narcotics of its poisonous leaves. Tragic that the dragons of terror must feed upon the souls of the innocent. Such beasts are best crushed in the shell. How deal with them once well fed and aflight?

Few women wish to be frigid. Often little more is required than their understanding that frigidity is not acceptable. That it is not permitted, that it is genuinely not permitted. Sometimes no more than slave bracelets and a chain are required for a woman to understand this. Certainly frigidity is unlikely to survive the impressing of the brand, the affixing of the collar. They then understand themselves to be such that frigidity is no longer an option for them. It is no longer permitted to them. It is a luxury of the free woman.

"Are you frigid?" he asked.

"Certainly," she said.

He saw that she was not frigid, but that she wished to be thought so. It had to do, seemingly, with how she felt she should be seen, or understood. To what tragic abuses had her world subjected her! In the beginning he had perceived her supposed frigidity to be like an armor within which she was naked. Then, as he spoke to her, he thought it more like a brocade beset with hooks, inviting their unlacing. Now, he felt, it was more like a flimsy towel clutched about her, clinging and form-fitting, within which, vulnerable and beautiful, she wished to conceal herself, within which she wished to hide.

He did not think it would be hard to pull that towel away.

"The ice of frigidity," he said, "can be lashed away, at the slave post."

"I do not want to be beaten," she said.

"Perhaps you think you could pretend to be hot," he said.

"Hot?" she said.

"Profoundly aroused, piteously needful, beggingly vital, sexually vulnerable, defenseless, ready, petitioning, reactive, reflexive, helplessly responsive, submissive, and obediently and gratefully to the master's least touch ecstatically orgasmic—hot not as a free woman is hot, that is, warm, or tepid, but hot as a slave is hot, the heat for which men will buy them and have them—*slave hot.*"

She regarded him, fearfully.

"Perhaps you think you might pretend to such?"

"Yes, yes," she said. "I could pretend!"

The mind is interesting, he thought, one can pretend many things, and in the pretense, they can become real.

For such reasons Gorean men were sometimes patient with such as she, permitting them to pretend for a time, until, preferably sooner rather than later, she suddenly discovers, to her fear and astonishment, that unusual transformations have now been wrought in her fair body, and that she has now become the helpless prisoner, to her dismay or delight, of induced, irrepressible raptures, raptures such as she never dreamed could exist, grasping, overwhelming, enthralling, raptures in which she is beside herself with ecstasy, raptures which glorify the collar, raptures which make a mockery of a free woman, raptures which put her forever at a man's mercy, raptures she will seek to regain again and again, raptures for which she will do anything. As it is said, on Gor, the slave fires have been lit in her belly, and they can never be extinguished. Once a slave always a slave. To be sure, the patience of Gorean men is not inexhaustible.

"Gorean men are not fools," he said. "There are infallible signs of true arousal, and yielding. They cannot be faked."

She moaned.

"I would be concerned, if I were you," he said, "that the taverner is not pleased."

"I am concerned," she said.

"He is thinking of making an example of you," he said, "to encourage the other girls to greater efforts."

"I do not understand," she said.

"You have not been much used, as I understand it," he said.

"I think I have been used enough, as you so quaintly put it," she said.

"The word is that you are not much good."

"Oh?"

"That is acceptable for a free woman, perhaps even expected of one, but not for one such as you."

"I am frigid," she said. "I cannot help it! It is the way I am!"

"You are proud of your frigidity, are you not?" he asked.

"I am not a whore!" she said.

"You are far less than that," he said. "You are a slave."

She moved back, trembling.

"Slaves are purchased for many things and purposes," he said, "but surely amongst them, commonly, are the poignancy of their sexual needs, the acuteness of their desires, their ignitabilities, their vulnerability, their readiness, their appetites and heat, their helplessness in the arms of a master, their capacity for sexual ecstasy."

"I cannot help how I am," she said. He thought there were tears in her eyes.

"You are not frigid," he said. "You are only afraid."

"I am afraid," she said.

"That you will discover that you are a slave?"

"I know that I am a slave," she said. "I am branded."

"You are not a slave because you were branded," he said, "but you were branded—*because you are a slave.*"

"I do not understand," she said.

"I think you do," he said. "I do not dispute, of course, that the brand has its performatory aspects, together with its identificatory, social, and commercial purposes, and that it effectively fulfills them, or that its placement makes you a legal slave, a true slave in the fullest sense of the law, literally an animal and totally rightless, subject to sale, to exchange, and such, but I am talking, rather, of something deeper and much more profound, namely, the natural slave, the rightful slave, she who is a slave in the depth of her heart, one who longs to selflessly love and serve, who yearns to submit, to surrender to another, to belong to another, to be owned by another, one whom she will live to serve and please, her master."

In the light of the small lamp, he saw that a tear had coursed down her cheek. She put down her head and wiped it away with a bit of the fur clutched about her neck, and then lifted her head, once again to regard him.

"And, too," said he, "what woman does not want to know herself to be so desired, so lusted for, that nothing but her total possession, her full ownership, yes, *ownership*, will satisfy a man. Is this not what she in her heart longs for, her owner, her master? How could she respect a man who does not so want her, so lust for her, that he will own her? How could she respect a man who is not strong enough to put her naked to his feet, and claim her as his own? Does she not want to be so claimed, so owned?"

Slowly she lowered the furs.

How beautiful she was in the light of the lamp, in the confines of the small alcove!

"Chain me," she whispered.

Slowly, beginning with her wrists, he fastened her hands apart, at the sides of her head. He then fastened her ankles apart.

She pulled a little at the chains. She looked up at him. "I am absolutely helpless, Master," she whispered.

He looked down upon her.

"I beg use, Master," she whispered.

"Are you ready?" he asked.

"Yes, yes, yes!" she said.

He touched her, gently.

She half reared up. "Ohh!" she breathed, softly, breathlessly.

It was true. She was ready.

At such times one must be patient.

She lifted her body, slightly, piteously, timidly, beggingly, to him.

He bent to her, touching her with his lips.

"Yes, Master," she whispered.

Later she again cried out with helpless pleasure.

Doubtless her cry was heard beyond the curtain. Doubtless the taverner would be pleased. There was no mistaking the nature of the cry. It was that of a yielded slave. Other men, too, about the tables, would doubtless have lifted their heads, and glanced toward the tightly closed, tethered leather curtains of the alcove. Perhaps the slaves, too, those on the floor, heard the cry, and smiled, knowing that a new sister, one now not other than they, was amongst them.

"Clearly you are beautiful," he said.

"Thank you, Master," she said.

"It was doubtless that which first attracted the attention of slavers."

"I am grateful," she said. "How tragic had they not seen me! How fortunate I am to have been selected!"

"Few are," he said.

"What will my life be?" she whispered.

"That of a slave," he said.

"Yes, Master," she whispered.

"How will you serve paga?" he asked.

"I will endeavor to serve it beautifully, humbly, deferentially," she said, "hoping that masters will look kindly, approvingly, upon me."

"Or, at least," he said, "that they will not be moved to beat you."

"Yes, Master," she smiled.

"And in the alcoves?"

"Piteously I would beg to be put to their pleasure."

He felt her, as she gasped, and he made his casual assessments. "You need this now," he observed.

"Yes," she said. "Yes, I need this now!"

"You may not explicitly beg on the floor," he said.

"A girl has a thousand ways to beg without speaking," she said, "her expressions, the trembling of a lip, slight movements, of the hand, of turning the palm upward, of the bosom, the pelvis, how she proffers the goblet, how she places her lips upon it, observing the master above its rim—"

"Enough," he said, softly, placing his hand gently over her lovely mouth.

She was thus silenced, and he then again addressed himself to her body, as she gasped and sighed, and pressed against him.

"You will presumably be sold from time to time," he said, "and will know various masters."

"I will do my best to please them," she said.

"I am going to unchain you now," he said.

"Master?" she asked.

In a moment she was freed of all the chains, save that which was on her neck, and fastened her within the alcove.

"Please me," he said.

"I do not know how!" she said, frightened, kneeling beside him. "Teach me, teach me, Master!"

"You beg it?"

"Of course, Master!"

He then, in a preliminary way, taught her something of the use of the lips and tongue, of her fingers and hands, of her hair, of her bared thighs and breasts. It was the beginning of a lovely journey which is never really completed, for the ways of pleasing a master are infinite in number, in touch, in service, in food and drink, in attitude, in speech, in posture, in dress, in cosmetics, in jewelry, in perfume.

Then she was terrified as he cried out.

"Master!" she wept.

"You did well," he gasped, laughing. "You have much to learn, but in you, somewhere, I am sure, is a competent little paga slut."

"Tell me," she begged, "of this world!"

They lay on the furs, side by side. He spoke to her of moons, and fields, and mountains, of the great Vosk, of gleaming Thassa, of long roads, of unusual beasts, of high cities, of the song dramas and the kaissa matches, of fleets at sea and caravans by land, and of customs and practices, and even of Home Stones. And, too, he warned her of free women, and of the terrible dangers they posed to such as she, who wore the collar and bore in their beauty clear evidence of their desirability to men, the trace of the iron's kiss, the slave mark.

"Are there many such as I?" she asked.

"Yes," he said, "and they have much freedom within the city, in their collars and tunics. They are much about, and shop, and do their errands, and meet their friends, and chat and gossip, and such."

"Are they pretty?" she asked, apprehensively.

"Certainly," he said.

"They are not closely confined?"

"All chained in alcoves?" he said.

"Yes," she said.

"Not at all," he said. "And even paga girls are often permitted the freedom of the city when not in service, though sometimes they must carry advertising on their tunics."

"I thought you did not like advertising," she laughed.

"I dislike false advertising," he said. "I see no objection to putting the name of an establishment on a girl's tunic, particularly if the girl is pretty and nicely figured. One of the tavern's delights is right there then, honestly presented, for the perusal of the potential patron. There are, of course, differences in status amongst slaves. For example, girls with private masters, even state slaves, commonly hold themselves superior to paga girls. And some slaves are high slaves, richly gowned, and jeweled, and so on. Sometimes it seems they hold themselves above even free men, though not, of course, free women. They are not so stupid. But, in the end, they are still slaves."

"I see," she said.

"Of course," he said, "I should mention that the paga slaves, if they are not back by the ringing of the appointed bar, will be whipped."

"I understand," she whispered.

"Slave girls are lovely," he said. "They make their aesthetic contributions to our world. Their existence much improves the decor of a city, the attractions of the street, of the parks and fountains, the appeal of a market, such things. On Earth one misses them, at least in public, but then on Earth one misses many things."

"Doubtless it is like beautiful dogs, or beautiful horses," she said.

"But better," he said. "What virile man would choose to live in a world without female slaves?"

"And what slave," she whispered, "would choose to live in a world without masters?"

"It is nearly dawn," he said.

The paga tavern had been quiet beyond the curtain for more than an Ahn.

"Am I to be slain?" she asked.

"It will be decided by the taverner," he said. "He will allow you to rest until evening, and then he will permit you to serve him."

"I do not find him attractive," she said.

"How will you serve him?" he asked.

I will kneel to him. I will press my lips to his feet, and cover them with tears and kisses. I will plead that I may serve his pleasure as the most eager and abject of slaves!"

"Then you will no longer think of yourself as free?" he said.

"No," she said, "only as the slave I am, and now know myself well to be."

"And are you more than a slave?" he asked.

"No, Master,' she said. "I am a slave, and only a slave."

"And will you be responsive to his touch?"

"As I now am, Master," she said, "as you have made me, I cannot resist the touch of a man, any man, nor do I wish to do so. I need these things, these feelings, even if the master despised me, and was cruel to me."

"The taverner," he said, "is a good man, neither contemptuous of his girls, though he recognizes them as mere slaves, nor more cruel or harsh, or perhaps better, firm, than is necessary to maintain the parameters of a perfect discipline."

"He is strict then?"

"Certainly," he said. "You will be kept under absolute and categorical discipline."

"I want that," she said. "I need it. I now hunger for it."

"If you are in the least bit displeasing, you must expect to be lashed."

"I do not want to be lashed," she said. "But I love knowing that I will be lashed if I am not pleasing."

"And perhaps sometime," he said, "you will relish a stroke, if only to remind you, and keenly, that you are a slave."

"Yes," she whispered. "Yes!"

"And when he is done with you?"

"I shall tell him how much I hoped to please him, my master, and, kneeling, head down, thank him, abjectly and piteously, with heartfelt gratitude, for the honor he has shown me, deigning to take one who is only a slave in his arms."

"Good," he said.

We then heard, from somewhere outside, the cry of a tarn, welcoming the sun, rising over the walls of the city.

"It is dawn," he said.

"Hold me," she wept. "Stay. Tarry. Do not release me yet!"

"I must be on my way," he said.

"Let me please you again!" she said.

"How?" he smiled. The oil in the tiny lamp was almost exhausted.

"As what I am," she said, "as a slave, a slave!"

"Very well," he said.

He drew away from her. She reached out for him.

"Position, slut," he snapped.

Instantly she went to position.

"You will leave me here, as I am, chained?' she said.

"An attendant will be here shortly," he said. "And you will be freed, and conducted to your cage."

"Yes, Master," she said. "Master!"

"Yes?"

"May I confess something to you?"

"Yes," he said.

"I have known for a long time," she said, "even from years ago, on Earth, though I have never admitted it to anyone, until now—that men were my masters."

He regarded her.

"All women, in their hearts," she said, "know that men are, and should be, their masters." She looked up at him. "And on Gor," she said, "they are our masters."

"There are free women on Gor," he said.

"Only uncollared slaves," she whispered, "women who have not yet met their masters."

"Perhaps," he said.

He drew on his tunic, and belted it.

"May I inquire your name, Master?" she said, tears in her eyes.

"No," he said.

"I do not even have a name," she said. "They have not given me one."

When one becomes a slave, of course, one's name as a free person is gone. One is then an animal, and animals have no names, not in their own right. They may, of course, be named, and usually are, as is not unusual with animals, particularly pretty animals. The name then, of course, is a slave name, and may be altered, or replaced, or taken away, as the owner wishes.

"You were not given a name," he said, "because it was not clear that you would be kept."

"You know my master?"

"Yes, I have had dealings with him."

"He asked you to see me," she said.

"Yes," he said.

"Will I—will I be permitted to live?"

"Your master will decide," he said. "But I think so, now."

"I think you have saved my life," she said.

"Rather," said he, "if anything, I have helped you to save your own life."

"Thank you," she said.

"It was done when you decided you wanted to live," he said.

"I do want to live!" she said. "Never have I so keenly, so much, wanted to live! And I want to live as what I am, and only am, a slave! It is what I am, and what I want to be! How terrible to be a slave and not be permitted to fulfill one's deepest desires, one's nature, one's bondage! I want to love and serve a man, abjectly and selflessly, with my whole heart and soul, and with the fullness of my being. I want to be owned, and be loved. I want to be obedient and pleasing! I want to be collared and subject to my master's whip! These things were denied to me on Earth, but here I have been rightfully embonded, and here, given no choice whatsoever in the matter, I have found myself become the slave I always was."

He considered her.

She was quite beautiful.

"But now," she said, "for all to see and know!"

This was true. She was now legally, explicitly, and publicly a slave. Nothing could be hidden any longer. All would now see her as such. She was branded. She would be put in a collar. She would have distinctive garments, unthinkable for a free woman. There would be no mistaking such things now. She was now totally different from what she had been; she could now be bought and sold, bargained for, and traded for. She was now no more than a lovely domestic animal. One could make offers to her master for her.

"I feel so free," she said.

"Free?" he smiled.

"In a sense," she laughed. "I feel now I am whole. I am no longer divided. I am no longer in conflict with myself. I have found myself, and where I most feared to search. I knew I was there, but I had been told not to look there, that I must never look there, not there, for there I might find myself! But now I have found myself! No longer now do I need to live a lie. I am no longer a hypocrite. I can now be myself, as I want to be, as I should be, in a man's collar!"

"An abject and shameful slave?" he smiled.

"Yes," she said, "and defiantly so, and gloriously so! I will kiss my fingers and press them to my collar! It is a form of life I desire! It is to be treasured, and sought! I want to kneel, and obey, and please! I want to love and serve. I want a master, a master! Can a free woman even understand that?"

"I think so," he smiled.

"I hope their collars are waiting for them!" she said.

"Perhaps," he said.

He began to untie the straps on the curtains.

"Will I see you again?" she asked.

"I do not think so," he said.

She leaned forward, and tears streamed down her face. He was pleased to see that she did not break position. He would have had to apply the switch to her, had she done so.

He parted the curtains.

One could see the interior of the tavern beyond them, the

tables, the hanging lamps, now extinguished, the dancing place.

He looked down upon her.

"I think you will be given a name," he said.

"Have I seen you before?" she begged.

"I do not think so," he said.

"But you have seen me before?"

"Yes."

"On Earth?"

"Yes," he said. "I saw you several times, on the streets, in restaurants, in your apartment while you slept, I even turning down the covers to better examine your figure, then carefully replacing the covers. I saw you even in the advertising agency, to note how you related to your fellow workers."

"You were thorough," she smiled.

"We are," he said. "It is our business."

"And you decided that I was to be brought here?"

"Yes," he said, "unbeknownst to yourself, you, with others, were entered into the manifests and schedules, your cargoing dates arranged, and so on."

She shuddered. "I knew nothing of this," she said. "I suspected nothing."

"Few do," he said. "I think that is best. Most do not understand what has happened to them until they awaken on Gor, stripped and chained."

"That is how it was with me," she smiled. "I wonder if you arrogant, dominant male beasts can understand what it is to so awaken."

"If we could not," he said, "we would not have you so awaken."

"I see," she said.

"It is good for you," he said, "to find yourself stripped and helpless. It is an excellent introduction to your new reality."

"And then," she said, "a stroke or two of the whip!"

"Such can be helpful, as well," he said. "Do you recall kissing the whip then?"

"Of course," she said, "several times, as I was commanded, and I must, too, thank it plenteously for its stroke, and speak of it repeatedly as 'dear, sweet, beautiful whip'! Then I must lick and kiss the feet of my keeper and thank him for his attentions to one so unworthy as I, for his deigning to attempt to inform, instruct, and improve me."

"Some, of course," he said, "suspect, from some cue or other, perhaps from a careless expression on a man's face, perhaps the glimpse of an ill-concealed master's regard, terrifying to a prey female, but most of these dismiss their fears, however extreme or unsettling, as irrational, as absurd, even preposterous. Later, chained, being vended nude, they realize they were perhaps somewhat hasty in dismissing their apprehensions, that their fears were not as *outré* as they believed. Some others, but very few, act on their fears and try to flee, stupid little beasts, but our surveillance is thorough, and there is no escape for them. They, as the others, will eventually wear the identificatory anklet. It has been decided for them. The pursuits are sometimes amusing, particularly when some of the scurrying, curvaceous little beasts think there may actually be an escape for them."

"I wore such an anklet?"

"Yes," he said. "Numbers on them correlate with our records. Indications are pertinent to different dealers, markets, buyers, and such. They are removed shortly after landing, usually while the merchandise is still unconscious, basic distributions having then been made."

"I was totally unaware." she said.

"That is the usual thing," he said. "Very few suspect, only one, I suppose, in, say, two or three hundred."

"When did you decide on me?" she asked.

"It was one afternoon at the advertising agency," he said. "I observed you haughtily dismissing a young man's invitation, for a luncheon date, as I recall, and there was something about your expression, and the way you turned your body that left him quite abashed. I decided then it might be pleasant to take you to Gor."

"I see," she smiled.

"I thought you might look well in a slave collar, stripped, cringing beneath a man's whip, pleading to serve well, and not be struck."

"I see," she said.

"You had lessons to be learned, at the feet of men."

"I see," she said.

"Was it you who first saw me?" she asked.

"Yes, as it happened," he said.

"And I gather that you found me of some interest?"

"You are a vain little thing, aren't you?" he said.

"Yes, Master," she smiled.

"Good," he said. "A girl should be vain, and think well of herself, and take genuine pleasure in realizing she is special, and precious and desirable, and worth coins, and that she is of interest to men, and of the greatest interest possible to men, of slave interest. What girl does not want to know that men find her so desirable that they contemplate her in terms of collars, slave bracelets, and ropes?"

"You did find me of interest!" she laughed.

"Certainly, I found you of interest," he said. "It was easy to imagine you stripped, and bound hand and foot, on a deep, scarlet rug, at a master's feet."

"Of course!" she said.

How flattering it is to a woman, to know that a man so envisions her, that he sees her in terms of such desire, that he regards her as worthy of binding and having, and perhaps collaring and keeping.

"But understand," said he, "that you were merely one of dozens, by several agents, to be considered, to be appraised, and assessed."

"Only one?" she said,

"Yes," he said.

"I do not like that," she said.

"It does not matter what you like," he said.

"Appraised and assessed!" she said. "It is as though we were dogs, or horses!"

"You were less," said he. "You were slaves."

"Animals!" she protested.

"Of course," he said.

"Gorean men!" she said. "How they see us!"

"They see you as you are," he said.

"As animals, as slave stock?" she said.

"Certainly," he said.

"You think poorly of the women of Earth," she said.

"Not at all," he said. "I think extremely highly of them. Some I would put at even a tarn disk."

"You see us as slaves!" she exclaimed.

"Improperly?" he inquired.

"No, Master," she whispered, lowering her eyes, "—properly."

"But in this," said he, "you are no different from Gorean women."

"We are all women," she said.

"You may break position," he said.

"Master!" she called out.

But he had left the alcove, and drawn the curtains shut behind him. The tharlarion-oil lamp wavered, and went out, leaving her in the darkness. She lay on her side, her legs drawn up.

In a few Ehn the taverner's man, she saw him approaching, visible through the parted curtains, bending down, entered the alcove, at which time she went to first obeisance position, kneeling with her head to the furs, her hands down, beside her head. Shortly thereafter she was freed of her tether and, bent over in common leading position, held tightly, but not cruelly, by the hair, was conducted to her cage.

Perhaps a last remark or two might be in order.

He did not return to the tavern, for she was a mere slave, and, as such, of little interest to a free man, but one hears things. As he had supposed, the taverner found his slave much improved, and was satisfied the next evening with his use of her, though she still had much to learn. She was now piteously solicitous to be pleasing to her master. It would not now be necessary to sell her for sleen feed, nor to make an example of her, before the other girls, casting her alive, bound hand and foot, amongst thirsting, ravenous leech plants. She became eager to be used, and to please, and even began to provoke the jealously, and the antipathy, of her sisters on the floor. They wondered what had been done to her, in so short a time, to turn her into such a slave. Within days men, even some who had been disappointed earlier, were summoning their paga from her. She had learned to move well in silk, and bells, gracefully and seductively, and her eyes, over the rim of the paga goblet, as she knelt and pressed her lips to it, bespoke the deference of a slave, and her needs, and her hope to be found worthy of a master's caress, before she humbly lowered her head between her extended arms, and proffered the goblet. And many was the fellow who fastened her small wrists behind her back with a lace, and sent her hurrying to an alcove, to wait there, however long, upon his pleasure. Rumor has it that she soon became one of her master's most popular girls. "She is an Earth slut!" men laughed, explaining to their satisfaction her helplessness, and her needs. "They are all the same," would say another. "That is why they sell so well," said another. In any event, the small slave survived. One supposes the fellow who had spoken to her at such length had had some role in bringing her to Gor. Perhaps he wished to vindicate his judgment of her worthiness for a Gorean slave block, despite the dismal, unnatural world of her origin. Or perhaps he was merely doing the taverner, his friend, it seems, a favor.

Surely it could not have been a simple act of kindness, merely taking pity on a beautiful, imperiled, frightened slave.

The girl was given a name, and later, another name, a better name. But we do not report the masters' choices in these particulars, in conformity with the intention to obscure the name of the owner, the tavern, the city, the girl.

It could be almost anywhere, couldn't it?

Let the enemy ponder that.

Lastly one might mention that, not unpredictably, the taverner soon received many offers for his luscious Earth-girl slave. Some may think it is cruel to kindle the slave fires in the belly of a woman, thusly so enslaving her and making her so much the victim of her own needs. I do not think so. Too, we must keep in mind that she is only a slave.

It seems but a matter of time until the taverner will part with her, for an excellent offer, and that she will become the slave of a private master.

I think that is best for her.

She is a lovely piece of collar meat.

I wonder if she is unusual amongst the women of Earth. Presumably, as it is a dismal, unnatural world.

But perhaps not.

Perhaps there are many women there, who long for their collars.

But, enough, I turn aside now, to attend to the petitions, and needs, of my charming amanuensis.

She crawls to my feet.

She is pretty on her leash.

She, too, incidentally, was once from Earth.

Confessions of a Polar Bear Impostor

I THOUGHT little of it at first.

It was a coincidence, surely.

Let me introduce myself. However, in order to diminish the likelihood of personal jeopardy, and to minimize the possibility of retaliations on the part of a powerful, arrogant, and unaccountable industry, let me tell you that my name is not really Bill Smith, and that I do not work for a major metropolitan newspaper whose unabashed liberal views and links to vast advertising revenues are unquestioned. Furthermore, I was not born in Peoria, Illinois, in 1981, the fourth son of immigrant parents from Norway. I am, however, an investigative reporter of unusual probity, tenacity, and vigor. I say this not in vanity, but in all candidness, a virtue which in my view might be more assiduously cultivated by others in my profession, for it has a bearing on this article. More than once I received journalism's coveted, though informally conferred, Nuisance of the Year Award, and was thrice voted a certain industry's annually, if secretly, bestowed Annoyance Prize. I dare not supply more detail lest my identity be suspected.

My name is Bill Smith, and I work for a major metropolitan newspaper whose unabashed liberal views and links to vast advertising revenues are unquestioned, save perhaps by benighted conservatives. I was born in Peoria, Illinois, in 1981, the fourth son of immigrant parents, a man and a woman, from Norway. I first committed myself to a career in investigative journalism at the age of nine when I discovered the rewards which might accrue from such inquiries as ascertaining the simultaneous and surprising whereabouts of my missing grade-school principal and our local guidance counselor, Miss, we shall say, X. I soon sensed *in ovo* the promise of a fascinating and lucrative career. My sobriquets are numerous, but I prefer Tiger Mouse, a flattering diminutive first ascribed to me by the disgruntled Mr. Wu Chang of San Francisco, supposedly the notorious blood-thirsty mastermind of a callous, lethal, many-tentacled Tong organization in the area, with at least one tentacle in Berkeley. My investigative work revealed conclusively that he was actually an honest, mild-mannered typewriter salesman near Fisherman's Wharf, not far from the submarine there, with no connections whatsoever to crime, organized, or disorganized. Many Han names, you see, are similar, and the Wu Chang of Tong fame was actually another fellow, seemingly residing at the time in Cleveland, a lead I granted to another reporter, not heard from since. My Mr. Wu Chang, capitalizing on the similar name, had been selling typewriters, an obsolete instrument for printing letters and such on paper, to tourists and locals eager to do business with a supposed criminal mastermind. His business folded shortly after my exposé, and he was forced to found a large chain of retail outlets specializing in more technologically current devices, palmcorders, digital cameras, computers, and such. In deference to Mr. Wu Chang's request I withhold the name of the chain, but it is one which is well known and would be instantly recognized by aficionados of gadgetry, in particular, that of an expensive and technologically advanced nature. He declined to accept the publicity which I was prepared to offer at little or no charge. We remain friends, and exchange gifts on our birthdays. I most recently received a hatchet, with several notches carved on the handle. Tiger Mouse, as he called me, clearly calls attention to my aggressive investigatory prowess, and, I suppose, to my fondness for cheese. But enough of me. What of Olaf? His name, of course, is not really Olaf. I refer to him by that name in order to supply him with all the protection morally compatible with honest reporting, whose chips may fall where they may, and sometimes sink.

Olaf was recruited for his unusual, deceitful, and foul work in Forest Hills, in Queens. a borough of New York City. Forest Hills is, as is privately well-known to various state and federal law-enforcement agencies, a notorious recruiting center for polar bear impostors.

Let me explain how this assignment came about.

"Bill, Tiger Mouse," one day said my editor to me, "our circulation is lagging, and lawsuits abound, for example, this last one, brought by a Mr. Wu Chang. I have spoken to my father-in-law, your uncle, who owns the paper, and we feel you are owed a vacation, at least until the consequences of your recent set of articles blow over."

I knew my uncle owned the paper, and so failed to see the purport of my editor's remark, calling this to my attention. I had not forgotten it. For those of you who might mistakenly and invidiously suspect that my post at the paper was due to sordid nepotism, I must remind you that I began work at the paper before I realized the connection. After ascertaining it, to my consternation, it did not seem fair to Uncle Harold for me to resign, and cost him his finest reporter, Tiger Mouse. We would both have to make the best of this embarrassing coincidence. (Harold, incidentally, like Olaf, are names I am using to protect identities.)

My most recent set of articles constituted a detailed and forceful indictment of the Society of Friends, the Quakers, for their role in brokering deals amongst rogue nations in armaments, in particular, weapons of mass destruction. Earlier articles had revealed the links between the AAA, the American Automobile Association, and concealed chop shops across the nation supplying automotive contraband to intercontinental auto-theft rings, the involvement of Alcoholics Anonymous in bootlegging in Peru and Bolivia, the scandalous relationship of the BSA, the Boy Scouts of America, to Colombian drug trafficking, and so on.

It was not surprising that some fallout might attend such revelations. I had expected as much when the stories went to press. My discoveries were vehemently denied, when noticed, but that was only to be expected in such cases.

An investigative reporter must follow the story and go doggedly where it leads.

Courage is a virtue which I do not lack.

"I am grateful, Chief," I said, "but I do not want to take a vacation. I do not have time to take a vacation. I am working. I am hot on a lead, as usual. Do you know what the Red Cross and the Veterans of Foreign Wars are really up to?"

"That will have to wait, Bill," said he. Then he winked. "You do not think this is a normal vacation, do you?"

"Oh?" I said.

"Not at all," he said, rather conspiratorially, which intrigued me.

"I just had a vacation last month," I said.

"Don't think of this as a vacation," he whispered.

"Where am I going?" I asked.

"To the Arctic Circle," he said.

"That is pretty far away, isn't it?" I asked.

"Far enough," he said, "I think."

"There isn't much up there but ice, is there?" I asked.

"That's what people think," he said.

"I see," I said.

"I have your tickets here," he said. "You are leaving for London tonight."

From London I flew to Oslo, and from Oslo to Longyearbyen. I had mixed feelings about this assignment. Indeed, I did not even know what the assignment was. I began, bitterly, at length, to suspect that my editor had perhaps wished merely to remove me from the vicinity of the paper before the next wave of subpoenas might arrive. Or, perhaps, he thought I had been working too hard, and might profit from a vacation. This solicitude had been manifested several times in the past, even in the recent past.

But an investigative reporter is restless, and alert.

I had been booked on one of the more exotic cruises organized by the fabulous Linkblott line, associated with the great Linkblott magnates of Scandinavia, a polar bear spotting cruise.

That was the main point of the cruise, to spot polar bears, and when the announcements would come over the sound system, at any time of the day or night, we would all rush up on deck, with our cameras, binoculars, and such, to spot the polar bears, who, by that time, would probably have jumped off their ice floes and be submerged. I suspect the bears kept track of the number of ship sightings, and compared and exchanged scores on the matter. There was no problem at spotting the bears at night, of course, given the latitude. Indeed, night would not show up for several months.

We did, of course, spot some polar bears. In fact, we spotted twenty-eight of them. To be sure, they were usually several hundred yards away. One might think that a polar bear sighting would be the occasion for launching the zodiacs and rushing up for a closer view, but landings or close approaches would not be made in the wake of an actual sighting for reasons of safety. The polar bear as you may know is one of the largest and most dangerous predatory animals on the planet. Indeed, when landings were made, no polar bears being about as far as one could tell, our leaders were always armed. Sometimes, you see, seals are scarce. A consequence of this precaution of course, and the bears' seeming concern for privacy, perhaps being miffed at having discovered that large, floating steel objects are not edible, was that we never saw one of these beasts at close range. Indeed, they were usually several hundred yards away. Still, we did have twenty-eight sightings, which, I gathered, was good, even typical. In the thrill of attempting to discern through my binoculars small white dots on ice floes far away, I forgot about investigative reporting. Too, the Linkblott line is famous for its cuisine and wine cellar, or wine hold, I suppose. There were also numerous lectures, mostly about the planet's being doomed, and parties, and fun events on shipboard, by means of which the time was pleasurably whiled away between summons to the decks to attempt to distinguish between polar bears and pieces of ice. The pieces of ice did not scratch themselves.

So I supposed, it was indeed merely a jolly, and perhaps well-earned, vacation, a respite from the ardors of investigative reporting, a welcome and profitable recharging of the batteries of journalistic inquiry, following which one might once again plunge into the exhilarating, invigorating maelstrom of society's iniquity, mismanagement, and deceit.

I might have mentioned, but in rereading this account realize I did not, that when we deplaned in Longyearbyen, another group of tourists, if I may use such an unkind word of polar bear spotters, were waiting to plane, or enplane, or whatever the word of choice might be. In short, they would leave on the same plane on which we had arrived. This arrangement demonstrated the sound thinking, and keen awareness of economics, which abounds amongst European airlines.

"Did you see any polar bears?" we new arrivals asked our predecessors as they filed past, with sweaters, parkas, posters, statuary, models of zodiacs, and such. "Yes," we heard. "We had twenty-eight sightings. We saw twenty-eight polar bears."

We whistled in astonishment, rejoiced in their good fortune, and hoped our efforts in this area would be crowned with similar success.

As a matter of fact, they were.

As our ship returned to the harbor at Longyearbyen, I recalled that intelligence. That was interesting, I thought.

I thought little of it at first.

It was a coincidence, surely.

Still, it was an interesting coincidence.

We, too, had seen twenty-eight polar bears, precisely twenty-eight polar bears.

You must understand, of course, that the travel industry is intensely competitive. Like life, the travel industry seems to flow into any available niche. As life can exist in the stratosphere, in polar ice, in sulfur springs, without oxygen, in the depths of the sea without light, deriving its energy from submerged volcanoes, and such, so, too, the travel industry seems to locate itself in any economically viable habitat. How else explain an interesting voyage with the primary intent of spotting polar bears? To be sure, are there not trips thinking about whales, about exotic birds, about deserts, about jungles, and so on? Once you have seen eight thousand cathedrals and six thousand castles, and eleven thousand aqueducts, bridges, walls and temples, and three pyramids, it is natural, I suppose, to think about polar bears. You are perhaps aware of aardvark expeditions, expeditions with python sightings in mind, and, in the southwest of the United States, gaining in popularity every season, trips for Gila monster spotting, and such.

In such a competitive industry, I thought, would there not be almost irresistible temptations to cut corners, to practice chicanery, perhaps even to admit, where necessary, fraud. Would such an industry not be tempted to guarantee results, and see to it that these results materialized?

I was struck with horror at the ignominy of such a suspicion, and banished it instantly from my mind.

Back, I thought, to the Red Cross and the Veterans of Foreign Wars.

Before taking the plane back to Oslo, and thence to London, and thence to New York, we were to have a farewell lunch at the lovely, local hotel in Longyearbyen. I would certainly, personally, give it several stars, and even a planet or two, or such, and, if you are ever in Longyearbyen, I would recommend it highly. Longyearbyen, incidentally, is itself a small, beautiful city, with the harbor, the mountains, the "watch out for polar bears" signs, and such. It used to mine coal, but, today, I think most of its wealth comes from the tourist trade, or more kindly, the polar bear spotting trade, for it is not only the ships of the redoubtable Linkblott line which venturously ply the icy waters of the north, but those of many other lines, and nations, as well. There seem to be enough polar bears to go around. Many are the shops, and businesses, thriving, too, in this small, lovely city, seemingly muchly dependent on the tourist trade, so to speak, and the polar bears.

During lunch I sat across from, we shall say, X, who was a typically tastefully grizzled professional photographer. He seemed troubled. I did not understand this, for he could doubtless charge this trip off his income tax; yet he seemed troubled. X had had a cabin to himself, in which he had constructed himself a makeshift darkroom. Too, many of us had admired his extensive paraphernalia and supplies. He seemed a veritable human baggage train, as many in his profession. The zoom lens on certain of his cameras might have noted a dropped lens cap in a lunar crater.

"What is wrong?" I asked him.

"I am troubled," he said.

"I have noted that you seemed so," I acknowledged. "Why are you troubled?"

"It is nothing," he said.

I then dismissed the matter, understanding it to be nothing.

Before our plane was to leave, some hours had been set aside for sightseeing, and shopping, mostly shopping, as most of the sights to be seen were shops. This arrangement demonstrated the sound thinking, and keen awareness of economics, which abounds amongst business communities in European municipalities.

Many rifles are available in Longyearbyen.

Shops are full of them.

And ammunition, and much of what you would want to have on hand, if you encounter polar bears. They do wander about, you know, but seldom on the main street, amongst the shops, at crowded hours, perhaps because of the rifles. Those who were once accustomed to do so, if we may believe the neo-Darwinists, may not have managed to replicate their genes. In any event, rifles are common amongst the natives in this area, and it is not unusual to see baby carriages and strollers about, packed with assortments of delightful Norwegian moppets and cherubs, being propelled by attentive fathers with rifles strapped to their backs. Too, Longyearbyen has the only bank in the world, as far as I know, in which fellows frequently enter with ski masks and rifles, and no one thinks twice about it. To enter unarmed and unmasked might, I suppose, instantly attract attention, and provoke suspicion.

"No," I said. "There is something wrong. I am sure of it."

I suspect that this remark was motivated by the unerring instinct of the natural-born investigative reporter. Otherwise it would be inexplicable.

"No," he sobbed. "No!"

I was, of course, prepared to take his word for this. After all, who better than he to know if something was wrong?

Yet the investigative reporter in me remained unconvinced.

As our delightful lunch was concluded, I noted that he left a tip for the waitress. It was something like ten thousand Euros, which, even at the current exchange rates, seemed high for a tip, too, even allowing for beneficent intentions to reduce income inequality.

"You are overtipping," I pointed out to him. "Thus you are attempting to assuage an acute guilt complex. Why do you feel guilty? What have you done?"

Tiger Mouse had pounced, almost as a reflex.

My own tipping, incidentally, leaves nothing in doubt as to my own moral stability and clear conscience.

He flung his head down to the table and began to sob wildly, uncontrollably.

It seemed I had touched a nerve. It is something investigative reporters are good at.

"Come away," I said to him. "Come to the bar. We will find a booth. You must tell me all about it." Many times

I had pretended to be an off-duty bartender, to encourage informants to open up. This charade, in this instance, I was sure would be unnecessary.

Soon we were ensconced in the hotel bar, which, incidentally, I commend to you, if you are ever in Longyearbyen.

Our waiter was a large fellow, young and broad-shouldered, with a large mop of tastefully shaggy blond hair, rather of the sort favored by large, young, broad-shouldered Norwegian males who frequent discos. In an earlier century I speculated he might have broken the hearts of many a rural maid in the land of the Midnight Sun.

I ordered, using five of my forty-one words of Berlitz Norwegian.

He took our order, and withdrew, but, it seemed, not too far away.

I regarded the photographer, sympathetically, encouragingly.

Tears ran down his tastefully grizzled face. "Look!" he said, opening one of his trunks, which he had had at the table and subsequently had dragged behind him to the bar, to the dismay of the clerk on duty at the registration desk, apprehensive as to the effect of this transit on the polished hardwood floors.

As he had bade me I looked into the trunk, but briefly, as it was quickly shut. It was packed with a variety of currencies, of various nations, pounds, pesos, kroners, dinars, zarduks, shells, and such. I noted, amongst these, what appeared to be a large number of bills in U.S. currency, thousand-dollar bills.

We were silent as the waiter brought our order, and then withdrew, but, again, not too far away.

"Dare I ask how you came by these gains, presumably ill gotten?" I inquired.

"I think not ill gotten," said my friend.

"Then why are you overtipping?" I asked.

He twitched, jerking about, his face and body writhing in what I supposed to be the expression of a contorted, semaphoric mass of subconscious conflict.

"Perhaps I am undertipping," he said. "Surely you are aware of the legitimacy of a graduated income tax. Why should a rich man not pay a thousand dollars for a cup of coffee, ten thousand dollars for a bottle of aspirin, a million dollars to see a movie?"

He had me there, so I was silent.

"I sold a photograph," he said.

"That is legal, I suppose," I said, "though it might depend on the nature of the photograph. Did it compromise the queen? Was it the photograph of a secret Norwegian naval base or something?"

"I sold the negative, as well," he said.

I whistled softly. This was apparently serious business.

"I kept one print," he whispered. "For my own protection."

"I see," I said. I recalled hearing earlier, when we had first arrived in Longyearbyen, in a remark seemingly casually dropped by a local travel guide, about a photographer who had been recently run down by a sled-dog team on the highway outside of town. Dog teams in Longyearbyen often draw wheeled sleds, which are more practical on cement surfaces than runners. Too, of course, out of town, on ice and snow, they draw ordinary sleds, vehicles of a sort more familiar to those who have attended movies about the far north. The natives of Longyearbyen tend to be fond of dogs. They are warm, loving, trustworthy, loyal, turn around three times before retiring, and bark at polar bears.

"May I see the retained print?" I asked.

"I would be pleased to show it to you," he said. "In that way it would make it more difficult for them. They would have to kill both of us."

"Maybe you could just tell me about it," I said.

"You are willing to place your life in jeopardy?" he asked.

"I am an investigative reporter," I said. I supposed I was as willing to place my life in jeopardy as much as your average investigative reporter. But, actually, that is not really too much. When it comes right down to it we would rather, however reluctantly, if a choice must be made, place the lives of others in jeopardy, our informants, and such.

"Look!" he cried, whipping out a glossy ten by fourteen photograph.

He had acted too quickly. I had just been preparing, upon reflection, to tell him that though I was an investigative reporter, a certain amount of caution and common sense must temper our inquiries—when it was too late, too late!

I stared, in horror, in disbelief, at the photograph.

"See?" inquired my friend.

"It cannot be what it seems to be," I said.

"Note," said my friend.

"I see, I see," I said.

It was an enormous close up, obviously blown up, of the rump of a large polar bear, as it slipped into the water. It had been taken with one of those cameras to which I have previously alluded, one of those whose zoom lens might have detected a dropped lens cap in a lunar crater, and had then been enlarged, apparently several times.

"It is a zipper," I said.

"Obviously," he said.

As those with some expertise in zoology, particularly polar zoology, would instantly see, and, indeed, as those with no expertise whatsoever in zoology of any sort would instantly see, something was seriously awry.

Polar bears may shed in their summer months, but they certainly do not put on and remove coats, at least not like people, and certainly not with zippers.

Polar bears do not come with zippers.

"Perhaps," said I, "it is not a zipper, but a wrinkle in the film, the result of a fault in the emulsion, a mistake in development of some sort."

"It is a zipper," he said.

"Clearly," I agreed.

"What do you think it means?" he asked.

"Stop hovering," I said to the waiter, who seemed, inadvertently, to have drifted by. He withdrew then, but not too far.

"Clearly there is a simple explanation for this," I said to my friend. "In defiance of laws dedicated to preserving the purity of Arctic wastelands surely some recreant has cast an unwanted coat into the water, from which the zipper became detached, later to be snagged in the fur of that splendid animal."

"Perhaps," said the photographer, "but why then would a mysterious agent, acting on behalf it seems of some powerful group or force, purchase the other prints and negative?"

"As a novelty perhaps," I said. "An eccentric collectible?"

"Perhaps," he granted me.

"Not now," I said to the waiter, using two more items from my Norwegian lexicon.

Soon thereafter I settled our small bar bill, from my expense account, courtesy of a major metropolitan newspaper whose unabashed liberal views and links to vast advertising revenues are unquestioned, at least by most.. Interestingly I settled the bill with a waitress, as the waiter with whom we had earlier dealt was nowhere in evidence, his shift doubtless having been completed. I did not object to his absence, for this lacuna obviated the necessity of leaving a tip. The waitress commented in Norwegian, but her remark did not lie within the compass of my lexicon.

My photographer friend and I parted outside the hotel, each to while away a bit of time in the rifle and parka shops lining Longyearbyen's major thoroughfare, which is about two hundred yards long.

The plane would be boarding in something like a hour or so.

My friend and I went separately, as he was slowed by the necessity of dragging his trunk.

The photograph concerning which we have spoken here had been placed, carefully folded several times, in the left, inside pocket of his coat.

I am afraid that I did not devote the amount of attention they deserved to the parkas, rifles, bullets, compasses, boots, socks, knickknacks, and such, attractively displayed in Longyearbyen's several well-kept emporia. I was dissatisfied with the deft convenience and too obvious plausibility of my explanation of the polar bear's zipper. Another possibility nagged at the edge of my consciousness.

On the way back to the hotel, to gather my luggage and board the bus for the airport, I was distracted by a commotion on the street.

I thought there might be something to investigate here, and, as I was an investigator reporter, I investigated.

Moving politely to the front of a horrified crowd of tourists, intermingled with which were some blasé Norwegians, who seemed to see nothing out of the ordinary in the scene, I beheld, to my consternation, my photographer friend. He was lying beside his opened trunk, which had been forced open. The bunches of currency, however, lay within it unruffled. "He has been beaten senseless," said a fellow, who was with our group. This was not quite true, as my friend was groaning, audibly. Perhaps he had been previously beaten senseless.

Fortunately our local guide was in the crowd.

"What happened?" I asked.

"Polar bear attack," said the man.

"Here?"

"Yes," he said. "It happens sometimes, particularly to photographers. You are not a photographer, are you?"

"No," I assured him.

I bent to the body. I looked to the trunk. Not a dinar or shell was missing.

"Nothing is missing," said the guide.

This is not unusual in polar bear attacks. Commonly not much is missing but half of the victim.

I should also note that neither the tourists nor the locals had touched the exposed riches in the open trunk, no more than the polar bear. Norwegians, as is well known, are an honest folk, even alarmingly so, and unusual people who take long trips to see polar bears, rather than visit a zoo, are very similar in this respect.

"No!" I cried. "Something is missing! A photograph! A photograph is gone!" And the reader has doubtless already surmised that the photograph in question was the very photograph which I had seen in the hotel bar earlier.

The Norwegians in the crowd laughed uneasily. The tourists laughed with less reservation.

"Why would a polar bear take a photograph?" asked the local guide.

"I intend to find out!" I announced.

The Norwegians looked at one another uneasily. The tourists exchanged glances, in a normal manner.

"There are tracks!" I cried, pointing to where an elderly municipal employee was busily sweeping.

I rushed about the municipal employee and hurried from the main street, which takes about four seconds, and found myself in Longyearbyen's wilderness. In a moment or two, guided by heavy paw prints, bloody on some rocks, and by an occasional broken twig, of which there are few in the area of Longyearbyen, and several dislodged pebbles, of which there are many in the area, I followed the trail, away from the city, across the highway, past a small lake filled with very cold water, past several "watch out for polar bears" signs, most of which merely showed the picture of a polar bear and an exclamation point, but that was enough to give one the general idea. The trail led upward, toward a small, dilapidated, apparently abandoned cabin, high on the side of a mountain.

It was to the door of this cabin that the trail led.

The bear had apparently entered the cabin. The cabin, I trusted, was abandoned. Otherwise I would have feared for any occupants.

In a fit of mad, blind investigative zeal, of a pitch and sort understood only by the true investigative reporter on a hot lead, or perhaps by a Viking Berserker, or a marine predator in a blood frenzy, or, say, a chemically enhanced homicidal psychotic, I plunged through the door and found myself face to face with a gigantic, standing polar bear. Moreover, this polar bear was holding a rifle, and it was pointing at my heart!

It was a hunter's nightmare!

"Where is the photograph?" I cried, my Norwegian barely sufficing to enunciate this question.

"There," said the bear, in Norwegian, gesturing with the muzzle of the weapon.

My heart sank, for the muzzle of that lethal device indicated a small pile of ash. "Fiend!" I cried, in English, for I did not know the Norwegian for this word, or had not time to recollect it.

"Do you think you will leave this cabin alive?" asked the bear.

"Your Norwegian is not very good," I said, suddenly. The accent was clearly Berlitz.

"I have twenty-seven words of Norwegian," said the bear, huffily.

"Berlitz?" I asked.

"Yes," he said.

"I have forty-one," I said.

"Berlitz?"

"Yes," I said.

"Obviously," said the bear, "you are more fluent than I. Would you care to speak in some other language, English, perhaps?"

"If you wish," I said. It made little difference to me.

"Do you expect to leave this room alive?" asked the bear, in English.

"Yes," I said.

Actually I do not remember exactly what my response was, but, as I am now writing this, I conjecture that my response must have been something along those lines.

The muzzle of that frightful, dangerous artifact was again trained on my heart.

"Your accent," I said, "is of Queens, New York, perhaps Forest Hills, perhaps Rego Park."

He seemed suddenly shaken.

"I do not think you are actually a polar bear," I said.

The muzzle wavered.

I had him now.

"You are not going to pull that trigger," I said.

At this point we have lost many an investigative reporter.

The bullet blazed past my left ear and knocked a board loose behind me.

"You are not going to pull the trigger again," I informed him.

This time the bullet ripped through the collar of my Linkblott parka, and a panel of the door behind me exploded down the hill.

"You see," I said, "you have missed me twice. Freud has an explanation for this. It is called motivated missing."

I saw that this shook the bear considerably.

"You are not truly a bear," I said, "but a human being disguised as a bear. I would not be surprised if you had a zipper in the back."

I thought I heard a gasp emerge between the fangs in that cavernous maw, and perhaps a choked sob.

"You are living a lie," I informed him, cruelly. Sometimes an investigative reporter must be cruel. We are not trained to pull punches, except in cases where we might thereby annoy our adversary, and risk being pummeled.

"Yes," he said, suddenly, and staggered back, and then sat back on a chair, wearily, behind the table in the room, the rifle lowered, placed on the table, not pointing any longer at me. He put his head in his paws.

"Yes," he said, agonized. "I am not truly a polar bear. I have been living a lie."

"You are clearly suffering from cognitive dissonance," I said, "and are riven with self-conflict." It helps for an investigative reporter to have some awareness of psychology.

The massive, shaggy body shook with dry, throaty sobs. I was touched. My appeal, of course, had been a moral one. Morality is a formidable weapon when applied to the moral. With the immoral it does not work as well.

Suddenly, with his paws, he removed the massive headpiece, which so cunningly resembled the head of one of the Arctic's most fearsome predators.

"You!" I cried.

I beheld the visage of our obtrusive waiter, the large, strong, broad-shouldered youth with the mop of shaggy blond hair, he who looked as though he might easily command the floor of a Norwegian disco.

I suspect he had been chosen in part because of his uncanny resemblance to a large, strong, broad-shouldered, shaggy-haired Norwegian youth, of the sort which might arouse not suspicion, but admiration, in a Norwegian disco. I wondered if he had won the hearts of several of the lusciously gyrating maids of the land of the Midnight Sun. He had but twenty-seven words of Norwegian, but I suspected he could have made them go a long way. Too, Norwegian maids are used to taciturn men, strong silent types who, particularly in the rural areas, are likely to limit themselves to six or seven words a day, most of which have to do with weather and the condition of the stock, but the others commonly expressive of tenderness, regard, and sensitivity.

Norwegian marriages tend to be long-lasting and loving, perhaps in part because harsh words, rather like other words, are seldom spoken.

"My name is Irving, Irving Himmelfarb," he said. "As you suspected, I am from Queens, New York and, indeed, from Forest Hills. I attended Forest Hills High School there, and patronized the Bagel Nosh."

"Go on," I said.

Incidentally, I will now refer to him as Olaf, that in order to protect his true identity.

"Being a reckless youth," he said, "and zealous to pursue adventures, I succumbed to the lure of exotic vistas and ready cash, a good deal of it."

It was an old story, recklessness, a zeal for adventure, the lure of exotic vistas, and wealth.

"And so when the offer of becoming a polar bear impostor offered itself, I leapt at it, naturally"

"That is natural" I granted him, sympathetically.

"Forest Hills, Queens," he said, "incidentally, is a major recruiting center for polar bear impostors."

"I did not know that," I said. I didn't know it at the time.

"Others," he said, "are in Pittsburgh, Cleveland, San Diego, and Los Angeles."

"Certainly the craft is an odd one," I said, hoping to draw him out.

"It is more common than you might think," he said, "that and certain similar or kindred occupations. You must understand, first, that rivalry amongst travel organizations is fierce. Competition for the customer's dollars, or dinars, or shells, or zarduks, is fierce. Economic natural selection, merciless and unforgiving, flourishes. Resources are limited. Economic arms races, so to speak, are rampant. Who will survive? Suppose then, that a travel company forced into exotic niches appealing only to unusual clienteles is on the brink of extinction. What if, for example, a jungle expedition advertising aardvark sightings fails to sight aardvarks?"

"Or a polar marine expedition polar bears," I said, shrewdly

"Yes," he said, "I think you can see that that option is not economically permissible. It would be an invitation to join the economic Dodo birds, Great Auks, and such. Companies will fight to survive, tooth and nail, and they intend to get on with business, if necessary, 'red in tooth and claw.'"

"Naturally," I said. I saw that Olaf was well read. At least he was familiar with Tennyson.

"I did not think of it as wrong, or criminal," he said. "I am not even sure, now, that it is. Is it wrong to try to do what one can to help a brave, desperate, noble, struggling company to survive? Is it wrong to give pleasure to eager polar bear enthusiasts? Do we denounce and castigate actors for donning costumes and presenting plays? For example, we do not really think that Derek Jacoby is Hamlet, at least not most of us. We do not scorn actors for trying to make their living, do we?"

"Not lately," I said. I knew something of the history of the theater.

"Yet fraud," said he, "is clearly involved."

"Yes," I said.

I could almost hear the dark bells of cognitive dissonance clanging in Olaf's subconscious mind.

"The benefits are good," said Olaf, "and one gets vacations twice a year."

"How many polar bear impostors are there?" I asked.

"At any given time, counting days off, the fellows on vacation, and so on, twenty-eight."

"I see," I said.

"But there were things they didn't tell me about," said Olaf, "the loneliness, the ice, the temperature of the water, the lousy raw fish one has to eat, the ridicule of seals who splat their flippers in our very faces, the insolent gulls, many of whom are afflicted with intestinal incontinence, and occasionally the curiosity of real polar bears."

I recalled hearing that one of the earlier expeditions had sighted twenty-nine polar bears.

"That could be dangerous," I said.

"They space themselves out," said Olaf. "It's territorial. The danger is the mating season. It's good to have your vacation then."

"It sounds risky to me," I said.

"We have a shoulder holster inside the suit," he said, patting a bulge near his left foreleg, "and plenty of tranquilizer darts, fifty cc's of fluid in each."

"Still," I said.

"Yes," he said, "it's dangerous."

I shuddered.

"Why don't you quit?" I asked.

He smiled bitterly. "These guys are tough," he said. "Do you think this is the sort of job you can just walk out on? Do you think they let you do that? Do you think they can afford to let you do that? They have too much invested. There's a lot at stake here."

"It sounds like the Mafia," I said.

"The Mafia won't touch these guys," he said. "Too dangerous, too cold, too far from Sicily. Too, the Mafia guys are at least human. They like to eat pizza and spaghetti, and they have a profound respect for family values."

"You can't quit then?" I said.

"I know too much," he said, wearily.

"I see," I said. Surely I had the makings of a great story here. A Pulitzer would be a cinch.

"And so, too, now, do you, Tiger Mouse," said a voice, from behind me.

I spun about to see a middle-aged, pleasant-looking, well-dressed Asian gentleman. I would have thought little of this except that he had behind him several dacoits carrying small hatchets. All were wearing Linkblott parkas.

"I see, Olaf," said the new arrival, "that you are losing your nerve." Actually he used my new friend's name, but I am disguising that name, in order to protect his identity.

"No!" said Olaf, defensively, rising.

"Then perhaps your taste for raw fish?" asked the gentleman.

Olaf looked down, in a surly fashion.

"And you, Tiger Mouse," said the Asian gentleman, pleasantly, "what shall we do with you?"

"How do you know my name?" I inquired.

He smiled.

"You are an agent of Wu Chang!" I cried. "Then his tentacles extend well beyond San Francisco, and Berkeley, even to Forest Hills and Longyearbyen, not to mention Los Angeles, San Diego, Pittsburgh, and Cleveland!"

"And many other places as well," purred the gentleman, in melodious accents suitable for a villain of his particular ethnicity, "Chicago, Seattle, East Orange, New Brunswick, Burlington, Iowa, Bridgewater, South Dakota, and elsewhere."

"Fiend!" I cried.

"It is all a matter of point of view," he said. "Clearly you are not a subjectivist and moral relativist."

"Fiend! Fiend!" I cried.

"Clearly," he said.

"You are all washed up," I said.

He looked at me, puzzled.

"Well lathered" I explained, "and cleansed."

"I see," he said, his eyes clouding.
"Tiger Mouse is prepared to pounce," I informed him.
"You do not recognize me, do you?" he inquired.
"No," I said.
"Perhaps we all look alike," he speculated.
"Not at all!" I exclaimed. I would not fall into that trap! I was not unaware of the requirements of contemporary civility.
"Think hard," he said.

I put my mind to scanning all Asian faces of my acquaintance. Embarrassingly, they did look much alike, all Asian. Fortunately, for my moral self-respect, I realized that to Asians folks like me also looked much alike, and, upon reflection, I supposed we did.

"I thought we were old friends," he said.
"Wu Chang!" I cried.
"You put me out of the obsolete technology business," he said. "Do we not, upon our birthdays, exchange small presents?"
"Yes!" I said. I recalled the small hatchet, with several notches carved into the handle.
"How you have fallen," I cried, "to have become an agent of the notorious Wu Chang!"

Many Han names, as mentioned earlier, are similar.

"I am not an agent of the notorious Wu Chang," he assured me.
"Thank heavens!" I cried.
"I am the notorious Wu Chang," he assured me.

I was certain he was joking. At least the dacoits behind him seemed amused, to the extent permitted by an aspect of sinister severity.

"How else do you think I managed to afford, found, and extend a tentacle into a thousand retail outlets for technologically advanced gadgetry?"

I refrain from mentioning the name of the enterprise, as it would be altogether too familiar to the reader, and might produce disruption and guilt amongst several thousand of its honest, law-abiding, unwitting employees.

"Were it not for your earlier exposé, that brilliant set of articles proving that I could not be, despite seemingly overwhelming evidence to the contrary, the notorious Wu Chang of Tong fame my career might have been tragically terminated, or, at the least, slowed or stunted. The authorities had been closing in on me at the time. I thought that I was through. But thanks to your work, Tiger Mouse, I was saved to thrive in one of the economy's most favored and select niches, that reserved for blood-thirsty criminal masterminds."

"I am pleased to have been of service," I said, "I suppose."

"Still," he said, "you do represent something of an economic drain, birthday presents, and such."

"I am not afraid of you, Wu Chang," I said.

"What of my dacoits, and their hatchets?" he inquired.

"We are talking about you, Wu Chang," I said. "Do not change the subject."

"I admire your courage, Tiger Mouse," said he. "That is certainly your most prominent virtue."

I did not appreciate a subtle innuendo perhaps implicit in his last remark. There seemed something snide in the intonation contour. What of my probity, tenacity, and vigor, my unerring investigative intuition? My keen mind?

"I am going to blow you out of the water, Wu Chang," I said.

"I do not understand," he said.

These cultural barriers!

"It is like a wind machine," I said, "which will lift you up and deposit you on the beach."

"I see," he said, his eyes clouding.

"Tiger Mouse is here," I said. "Your insidious scam is over! I am going to walk out of here right now, right past you, and write the most brilliant, devastating series of exposé articles in the history of brilliant, devastating exposés. You have made the fatal mistake, Mr. Wu Chang, of tangling with Tiger Mouse! You are finished. Step aside!"

I noted that he had failed to step aside.

Once again cultural barriers had intruded.

I saw something like eleven hatchets raised and, if I am not mistaken, a light film of saliva forming about the lips and jaws of several of Wu Chang's dacoits.

Olaf stepped to the side, rather out of the way. I think I might have done so, as well, had I been in his place, which place, in this instance, was directly behind me.

"I am disappointed in you, Tiger Mouse," said Wu Chang. "I had thought you were a true investigative reporter."

"I do not understand," I said.

I had expected to be set upon by eleven dacoits, a hazard such as those which go with the territory I had chosen for myself. Already I was planning on inscribing my exposé on the bloody floor boards of a burning cabin, or the cold pavement leading into Longyearbyen, or, with luck, dictating it from splints and traction in a remote Norwegian hospital.

"It seems to me," said Wu Chang, "that you have not really investigated this matter. What do you truly know of these things? Have you gone undercover?"

"Well, no," I admitted. Candidness is another of my virtues.

"I submit," said Wu Chang, "that you are an outsider here, uninformed and opinionated, that you will write boldly of things you do not understand and know little about."

"That is the way of the investigative reporter," I said, defiantly. I knew my work, my job.

"Olaf," said Wu Chang, "you have lost your nerve. Judging by the bullet holes in the wall and door you have missed Tiger Mouse twice. You are no longer to be trusted on the ice floes. I am not tolerant of failure. I give you the choice of dying a terrible death or taking advantage of an opening in my accounting department. Which will it be?"

"Might I have time off to prepare independently for my CPA degree?" asked Olaf.

"Certainly," said Wu Chang.

"Do you double book?" asked Olaf.

"Yes," said Wu Chang. "The IRS expects it."

"Do I get to keep the first set of books, the phony books, or the real, secret set of books, those that really count?" asked Olaf.

"The second set, of course," said Wu Chang.

"Done!" said Olaf.

He began to remove the polar bear suit. I noted, in an interior pocket, a pocket protector, with various pens and pencils, two erasers, and a high lighter. It occurred to me that Olaf might have originally taken his work with Wu Chang on the very chance of eventually being promoted to a position of such responsibility. I had little doubt that Olaf was an accountant at heart, and would bring zest, brilliance, and, if called for, an astonishing creativity to his work. To be sure, creativity would not be much in demand, given that he was to be in charge of the private records of Wu Chang's diversified and far-flung enterprises.

It crossed my mind, a statistic I had heard long ago, that IRS auditors are almost uniformly fond of fiction, and often drive expensive automobiles. But economics is not my subject. For example, it has always been hard for me, a layman, to grasp how many major firms can lose millions of dollars a year, sometimes billions, year in and year out, and still remain flourishingly in business. This record, one gathers, is to be attributed somehow to advances in the techniques of professional accounting. To be sure, many Renaissance firms, I understand, are still in business, as well.

"And what of you, Tiger Mouse?" inquired Wu Chang. "Are you a true investigative reporter, or not?"

"Give me the suit," I said.

As I donned the suit, I noted that the saliva about the lips and jaws of certain of the dacoits no longer glistened, but now appeared to have dried. Too, a number of them now looked disappointed, at least to the extent permitted by an aspect of sinister severity.

It was thus that I began my tour of duty as a polar bear impostor.

In the beginning it was freezing upon the ice floes. There were problems, too, with jeering seals and marine birds, many of whom suffered from intestinal incontinence. Eventually one develops a taste for raw fish, but, to be honest, not much of a taste. The water, of course, was quite cold, but polar bears manage quite nicely in it, and eventually one learns to do so, as well, thanks largely to the careful engineering of the suit. I was twice approached by amorous she-bears brazenly seeking a mate but I rebuffed their advances, and only twice had to rely on the tranquilizer pistol with which my suit was equipped. My narrowest escapes took place not on the floes but in the vicinity of Longyearbyen, as I was making my way to the harbor. Fortunately one fellow's gun jammed. Another fellow happily entangled his arm in his rifle sling and managed to do no more than blow out a street light. The closest thing was with a father and stroller who was drawing a bead on me, but his infant lost his pacifier, and by the time he had retrieved it for the grieving child I had slipped into the water and was away.

The suit, of course, is equipped with a map, and compass, and global positioning device, and we are furnished with the schedules and routes of the cruise ships. It is important to be seen, but not closely. One look, from far off, and then disappear, seems to be the key to success here. Fur must also be folded over the zipper in the back of the suit, lest another debacle occur with some nature photographer. Once I nearly lost my nerve and leaped up and down on an ice floe, waving my arms about, calling for rescue. But a number of shots fired from the bow of the approaching ship, splintering and gouging the ice about me, reminded me that some on board that ship would be likely to be privy to this little-known and secret side of the travel industry. This close brush with death encouraged me to regain my nerve. I sluggishly returned to the water, with an almost unnoticeable plop, as might a typical gigantic, annoyed, and blasé predator of the north.

Mostly, of course, the game is a lonely one.

One does catch up on one's sleep, which is a plus, and there is little danger of missing a ship, or permitting one to approach too closely. The small radar device, with its alarm located in the vicinity of the left ear of the suit prevents that. A similar device, but sensitive to heat, such as that generated by engines, is located in the vicinity of the right ear. This is also helpful in warning one of the approach of enflamed she-bears.

But on the floes, you see, in the loneliness, and the days between ship sightings, one has a good deal of time to think.

One is much alone with one's thoughts out there.

I remember Wu Chang, who was not such a bad guy, who always remembered my birthday, and I recalled Olaf with fondness. He had missed me twice. I hoped he was happy now, in his cubicle, in some bunker or such, fulfilling his dreams.

Was it so wrong, really, to be a polar bear impostor, I asked myself.

What if the travel industry went under? The effect of that on the international economy would be tragic. Think of the thousands of people working in that industry, who would be thrown out of work, who would be destitute and miserable. And the other thousands who supplied the travel industry, who flew the planes to get people to Longyearbyen, and the folks who raised the grapes for the wine to be kept in the ship's wine hold, or whatever, and the lecturers, and guides, and all the others, and those who depended on them, and so on. It was easy, out there on the ice, to anticipate the domino effect which might plunge the entire planet into anarchy and chaos, precipitate inevitable imperialisms, revolutions and wars.

I thought of the cherubs and moppets in Longyearbyen.

Who would buy their pacifiers if the ships sailed away, never to return? I owed much to one pacifier.

And what of the thousands of naturalists, adventure seekers, photographers, writers of travel memoirs, members of various fraternal organizations, and thousands of others, folks who had wearied of castles and pyramids, and wanted to see the world wild and beautiful as it once was, who wanted to commune with nature, who eagerly hoped to catch at least a glimpse of some fine, brave, proud, defiant life form, pursuing its wild and natural ways with all the menace and regality of old.

Who would deny them this pleasure, this added meaning in their life, these treasured, beautiful moments?

Yes, out on the ice I thought long and deeply.

Perhaps, I thought, there is more to life than harsh truths and investigative reporting. Perhaps, I thought, there are other truths, too, softer truths, more beautiful truths, truths pertaining to what is beautiful, to what gives pleasure, to what can make people happy.

So we polar bear impostors were out on the ice, garrisoned there, sentinels, in a way, keeping our post in a far country, one unspoiled, one beautiful and unpolluted, one much as the Earth once was, and reminding the lovely, wonderful, curious members of our own species, so incredulous and eager, of a world that still exists, albeit in a distant, cold place.

So I thought there are worse things than being a polar bear impostor.

There aren't so many polar bear impostors now, as, interestingly, the polar bears are coming back.

I think that is nice.

During my vacation I had an opportunity to discuss these matters with Mr. Wu Chang, who nodded and smiled, and I understood then why I had been permitted to go out upon the ice, that I might have time to think these things out, in a quiet place.

I am writing the exposé here, of course, but I hope no one believes it.

Too, interestingly, in all my thinking on the ice, I was able to come up with an idea for yet another tentacle for my friend, Mr. Wu Chang. He has now branched out, extending his enterprises into Africa.

On the ice, it is easy to think of warmer places.

We still exchange small gifts on our birthdays.

He will need some lion impostors.

Letters from Gor

I.B.:

Help me! Help me!

I do not understand what has happened, or what has become of me!

They are letting me write this, why I do not know. I do not know what will be done with it. Is it to be sent to you? I do not know. I hope so, I fervently hope so. I am in desperate need of rescue. It is hard to understand them. Two speak some English, and that with a foreign accent, which I cannot place. One seems capable of reading cursive script. I must be careful of what I write. Most here speak no English, or little English, and I do not speak their language, whatever language it may be.

You must help me!

The assignment has turned into madness. You must believe me! The exposé has gone awry! I have not run from you, or deserted the firm! I do not know the date, or how many days it has been. Your informant was more accurate than we had dared dream.

I am writing this literally on my knees, I. B., and I am stripped naked! And there are men here! How casually, how boldly, sometimes how indifferently, they look upon me! They have taken my clothes, completely, even to hairpins and a barrette! My hair is down, about my shoulders. You never saw it thusly. It is long and glossy, I.B., and, I think, has somehow been made more so. I must brush it back, that it not touch the paper, that it not touch the inked lines, still wet. They do not want that to occur. The lines are not to be spoiled, marred or disarranged in any way. They are very strict about such things. Too, the lines must be evenly spaced, and legible, and the letters are to be more rounded than was my wont with the firm. I am to write in a more feminine script. Why? I have not written that way in years, deliberately, forcing myself not to. I suppose you did not know this, but I had tried to disguise my script, to make it more masculine, as I had tried to disguise my body, with straight shirts, high collars, neckties, jackets, slacks and mannish suits. Surely I impressed you with my cool airs and professionalism. Was that not why I earned this assignment, that amazing, remarkable assignment? I am trying to comply with their wishes. Can you imagine that, knowing me, me, trying to comply with the wishes of a *man*? And fearful that they might not find my compliance satisfactory! But these are not ordinary men, I.B. I have no choice. They have given me no choice. I do not think they give women choices, or not women such as I. I do not think I am different. I think any woman would do the same, any woman. Do not blame me! Do not think the worse of me! Kneeling here, naked, it is hard to forget that you are a woman. It would be meaningless to deny it, a senseless, stupid, embarrassing joke, even a blatant effrontery to reason, reality, and truth. Here I cannot doubt that I am a woman. It is something that I am not permitted to deny, ignore or neglect. How silly it would be here to deny that we are different from men, to pretend that we are identical with them. How could I not have understood this before? Did men collude in this deception? Well, they do not do so here. We are so different from them! Our bodies are so small, so soft, so curved, so weak, so vulnerable, compared to their large, virile, vital, powerful, cruel bodies. I find them strangely attractive. How wicked I am! It is so strange here. So different! As you can see, even the paper on which I am writing is unusual, a thick, scraped, smoothed, cream-colored paper of some sort. Holding it to the light, you can see the mesh of the plaited fibers of which it is made. I am kneeling on a soft, deeply piled rug, my knees sunk deeply into it, before a low, small, heavy, sturdy, thickly legged wooden table. The top is of dark, polished wood. To my right is a small bowl filled with black ink. I am writing this with some sort of reed pen. I must try not to blot the writing. Sometimes it is hard. I am afraid of what they might do to me. This place is unbelievably primitive.

Save me from them! You must! I demand it!

L.

Second Letter

Dear I.B.:

I have received no answer to my first letter. I do not know if you received it or not.

Surely I am being held for ransom! Nothing else would make any sense. Surely you have notified the police. Arrange for my release immediately. Pay whatever they ask.

At night they put me in a cage, a cage!

There is not much room in it. I cannot stand up in it. There are bars on all sides, except the top and bottom. They are of steel. I can be seen from all sides. When a man approaches I must kneel and put my head to the floor of the cage, to show deference and respect.

How strange, how infuriating, how humiliating, that I should be expected to show deference and respect, and to men!

They put me in a cage!

I am not an animal!

But they put me in a cage!

I have seen no other women. I do not know what manner of place this is. I do not even know the nature of the building in which I am being kept. I sense that it is a large structure. The only windows in the room in which I am writing this, as before, are narrow, and too high for me to reach. I can see the sky outside. I am beginning to have fearful suspicions about this place, which I scarcely dare communicate to you, lest you think me mad.

If you know what is good for you, and you want your story, you must see to my safe return, and instantly. It is a story which will scarcely be believed!

I do not know where the video camera is, or my notes, but these brutes must return them to me.

Or you can arrange for their return, when you pay my ransom.

I must go now, to be fed. I am to crawl to my food on my hands and knees! I must eat my food, and take my drink, from pans and bowls, set on the floor!

And I am not permitted to use my hands!

Do they think I am an animal!

Are they trying to teach me something? If so, what?

Save me, now!

I demand it!

L.

Third Letter

Dear I. B.:

I have no idea what the date is, so, as with my last letter, I am simply numbering them. This, as you can see, would be the third letter. I have not yet received answers to my first and second letters. Have you received them? Are the police searching for me, though I now fear I am beyond their reach. I am now sure that my suspicions are confirmed, but if I confessed them to you, you would think me mad. Have you arranged for my ransom? Are you negotiating with my abductors? Spare no expense! Get me out of here! Save me! How ironic that I, with my background, attitudes, and values would be asking a man for anything, indeed, begging him for attention, and assistance! But I am begging you now! I never thought I would beg a man for anything, armed with self-serving laws which, like so many others, were engineered to promote particular interests, regardless of their impact on society as a whole. We were to devirilize men, and destroy them, as men, by incessant propaganda, pervasive conditioning, inescapable education, and vague, abundant, menacing law, confusing them, making them self-suspecting, turning them by means of fear and guilt against themselves, in order to seize control of society. But now, I.B., I need you. Save me! Please, I beg of you, save me, save me!

In my last letter I foolishly spoke in a threatening manner, and made demands. Please, forgive me! I spoke thoughtlessly. I trust that you understood that my agitation was accounted for by my anxiety, my predicament. I respect you, and hold you in the highest esteem. I always have! Forgive me attitudes, or words, which, in the past, may have seemed disrespectful, perhaps even haughty, arrogant or insolent. I regret having declined your invitations in the past, for supper, or for evenings at the theater or concerts. If you were to renew your requests, you might find me more amenable now. Surely it would not hurt for you to try!

Save me!

I would be willing to dress in a more appealing manner, one more attractive to men, even to skirts and dresses, to use exciting cosmetics and provocative perfumes, to wear soft, clinging undergarments, lacy things, patterned stockings, high-heeled shoes!

Oh, I.B., can you imagine this? What are they doing to me? I do not know what is becoming of me. I am changing, I fear.

Save me, I beg you, I. B. Save me, please. I beg it! I beg it!

They are beginning to teach me their language. Why, I wonder. The first words I have learned are “La kajira.” I do not know what they mean.

L.

Fourth Letter

Irving:

I was whipped today.

My wrists were taken over my head and cuffed about a ring. Then I was whipped!

Doubtless you cannot even conceive of this.

Can you imagine it, me, whom you know, sophisticated, so severe, professional and cool, stark naked, made utterly helpless, my wrists cuffed about a ring, over my head, being whipped, whipped as though I might be an animal, as though I might be no more than a pretty, ignorant, recalcitrant little animal, one meaningless, a mere nothing, whose behavior was in need of correction!

Can you comprehend it?

All I did was suggest, no more than hint, that I might be rebellious. It was perhaps no more than a fleeting expression of objection, no more than the hint of a thought of possible anger, or defiance, and I was whipped!

I now suddenly begin to suspect that my warders, or keepers, have been patient with me, but that their patience is not endless.

Our plans went muchly awry.

Your informant was correct. Women are taken, enslaved, and sold! I have seen the poor things, collared and chained, frightened, weeping, clutching tiny sheets about themselves, cringing before masters. I was introduced, with the video camera, the material for taking notes, as we had arranged, into a holding area. With what fear the girls, for I could not conceive of them as anything else, regarded me, I amongst them, fully clothed, severely, fashionably, professionally. But I had little time for outrage, or sympathy, for I was at work. Too, frankly, many seemed fit for bondage, cuddly, simple little things, fit to be the possessions, the playthings, of men. Perhaps the best they might hope for would be to obtain a kind, understanding master. Though I suspect that any kindness, and understanding, on the part of such men as I have seen here, would be on their terms, and would not be allowed to compromise in the least the severity, the perfection, of their dominance, their mastery. The males here have not given up their dominance. They have not been conquered, and destroyed, as men.

I videotaped, swiftly, resolutely, yet as carefully, as calmly, as I could, under the incredible circumstances, panning about. Even the tiny, almost inaudible whimpers of the captives were recorded. I am sure of it. It seemed they were terrified to so much as raise their voices. Then, in a bit, too, I took notes. I jotted impressions frenziedly. I wanted to interview some of the girls, but they refused to speak, looking away or putting their heads down, shaking their heads, fearfully.

Why were they afraid to speak to me?

Why?

What was their nature, their condition?

Most were kneeling.

They tried to hide in their tiny sheets, holding them about their bodies, sometimes with manacled wrists.

Why were they frightened?

Why did they not look at me? Why did they look away? Why did they put their heads down? Why did they tremble, fearfully?

Had they been beaten? Had they been taught something of discipline?

Then, angry with them, and hearing the cries of men, I went to a tiny barred window. From there, I could see down into an amphitheater-like room. Several men, some in business suits, some in casual dress, some in uniforms, some in working clothes, were on the tiers. Despite the dissimilarity of attire the men seemed very much alike, virile, powerful, callous, intelligent. It was almost as though some wore disguises, that their nature not be understood. Indeed, it seemed that some wore their clothes uneasily, as though they might be accustomed to a different sort of garments, perhaps freer, less confining. They were unaware of my presence. Their attention was focused on a large wooden block, some seven feet in width, at the foot of the room, in its well, so to speak. I was horrified to see a woman on this block. The sheet was drawn from her. She had had nothing on beneath the sheet. Nothing!. She was made to stand, turn, and pose. There were calls from the block, by a man there, clad in a work shirt and jeans, and calls from the men in the tiers, responding to him.

This was clearly bidding.

She was young, and beautiful, and for sale!

Can you believe it, Irving? A young, beautiful female, naked, and for sale! Literally, Irving, for sale, *for sale*!

How furious I was. Yet, oddly, I felt myself inordinately excited, and profoundly, disturbingly, stimulated. I was muchly aware then that I was a woman, or, more radically, that I was a female. I had never really thought until then what men might do to us—*if they pleased, if they chose.*

I taped this.

Oh, Irving, talk of scoops! This story would have sold out the magazine in an hour. It would have been in all the papers, taken up by the wire services, the radio, television, all the media. When you ransom me you must arrange for the return of my notes, above all the video film!

How did I know that I would be discovered in the holding area!

My presence was to have been undetected. It was to have been secret. And yet, after something like twenty minutes, several men simply entered the area, the chained girls shrinking away from them in fear, hastening to clear a path before them, entered as though fully aware that I was there, and encircled me, on all sides.

I was terrified!

How they smiled!

Did our informant betray us?

The notebook, the camera, were taken. My hands were cuffed behind me. Literally cuffed behind me, in small, sturdy, linked metal circlets of some sort. I heard them snap shut, one, then the other. I was helpless. Something was held over my nose and mouth. I struggled. I could not free myself. I could not escape. It was hard to breathe. The fumes were stifling. I lost consciousness. I awakened naked, later, how much later I do not know, on my side, my legs and arms drawn up against my body, on the steel floor of a small, locked cage. Probably here, wherever this is. Things seem different here, wherever this is. I am frightened.

I trust that you are working to free me as soon as possible.

I will share all the credit for the story with you. Have no fear. I will keep it for the magazine. I will not go elsewhere with it, despite its value. You may have the byline if you wish. My contribution may remain anonymous. The credit is yours, if you like. Or you may even give it to Holly, that meaningless little slut, whom I know is your mistress, if you wish. Have I not seen her fawn on you, and seen how she looks, when she looks upon you?

How I hate her!

Save me! Get me out of here!

I know you like me, or, at least, are attracted to me. A woman can tell such things. If you save me, you will find me more agreeable now, Irving. You see, I am calling you "Irving" now. I have always thought you were attractive. Perhaps you will give me a chance, when I get back, to show you my feelings toward you.

To be sure, you would not find me a Holly! I have pride! Surely you would not want a woman to be yours alone, and not hers, alone. As a true man, you would scorn to have a woman grovel at your feet, in awe of you, desiring to put all she is, and would be, at your feet, desiring more than anything else in the world to serve you, hand and foot, lovingly, helplessly.

As a true man, how disgusting you would find that!

I beg you to free me, Irving!

Yes, I beg it!

Figuratively I am prostrate before you.

Does that please you, Irving, that I should be prostrate before you?

Save me! I beg it!

Linda

Fifth Letter

Dear Irving:

A steel collar has been put on my throat! It is light and narrow, like a band, about a half of an inch in height. It is close fitting. It is attractive. It is not uncomfortable. I am seldom aware that it is even on me, but it is. In the back there is a small, sturdy lock. And the collar is locked! It is locked on me! I cannot remove it. It is literally locked on my neck! Is it a piece of simple jewelry? But I cannot remove it! I do not understand it. What does it mean?

I cannot believe the things they are teaching me!

I have still not been taught the meaning of the first words I was forced to say, "La kajira."

They laugh at me. I dare not evince the least sign of disinclination to obey. They expect, and receive, instant, unquestioning obedience from me! Can you imagine that, knowing me? That I am obeying men? That I must be obedient to men?

And I am obedient to them, Irving. I am obedient to them!

And I am having strange feelings. I can't explain them, but they are sometimes overwhelming. I am finding that it pleases me to obey, that I wish to do so. How strange!

Can you imagine me obeying you, eager to please you, trying desperately to please you?

Wouldn't you like to have me obeying you?

In all things?

In whatever way you might wish?

It is strange, the things they are teaching me. They really seem to be of two sorts. Many are homely tasks, which I am learning for the first time, though with the tools and techniques of this place, things like cooking, cleaning, laundering, and sewing. Perhaps these are skills taught to housewives here, if there are women here. There must be women here. But of the other sorts of things I am taught I scarcely know how to speak. They are teaching me ways to move, and sit, and lie, and rise to my feet, and kneel. They make me kneel with my knees apart, widely, and back on my heels, with my head up, and my hands, palms down, on my thighs, or being held behind my back. In sitting and lying, one must point one's toes in a certain fashion, which curves the calf. One learns to turn the hip out. One learns to lower one's head deferentially. One learns how to crawl, on one's hands and knees, and on one's abdomen. It seems I am being taught gracefulness and submissiveness. Can you imagine that, of me, Irving?

Too, they are teaching me the application of cosmetics, and perfumes. Sometimes they put bells on my collar, and ankles, or wrists. I must learn to walk well in them. When I do poorly I am sometimes struck with a strap.

If you are very nice to me, when I get back, perhaps I will show you some of the things I have learned.

Linda

Sixth Letter

Dearest Irving:

Why have you not answered my letters?

Have you received them?

They still have not taught me the meaning of the words 'La kajira', the first words I was forced to speak in their language.

I have been told that I may be allowed out of the house in a day or two, though I would be accompanied. But first, it seems, something must be done to me. They have not told me what it is. Before it is done, I am told that I must wash and dry my left thigh, high, just under the hip. It must be smooth, and pretty. I do not know what they have in mind. They keep me much in ignorance.

My lessons continue.

I have received instruction in the bathing of men. I do not think they are such lazy beasts that they cannot wash themselves. I think, rather, it pleases them to have this done by a beautiful woman. I am beautiful, Irving. I know that now. What could be the meaning of my beauty? I have received various injections. I do not know their purpose. I was permitted to see myself in a small mirror yesterday. I was startled. I look younger. It is strange.

I have been shown how to crawl to a man and beg him for his touch! How degrading! How shocked and offended you must be, to hear this!

Surely you, as a true man, would not want me crawling naked to your feet, and begging your touch!

How swiftly you would, in consternation, scandalized, looking away, that I not be embarrassed, draw me to my feet, and clothe me!

But I am afraid. Late in the lessons, I had strange feelings, and my voice trembled. Tears ran from my eyes. I tried to control myself, but I could not. I felt my body flushing and shuddering, and felt hot and alive, and moist and running and helpless, and alive, and alive, and so alive, and needful, and felt embarrassing, betraying, uncontrollable, irresistible, undeniable sensations, even secretions, I fear perhaps those of desire, Irving, of sexual heat, of literal sexual heat, Irving, overwhelming me, fierce, piteous sensations, needful and unrequited, emanating from my intimacies, suffusing then my body, my entire body and being! What could be the meaning of these things? But I feared I knew their meaning. What had they done to me? What was I becoming? On my knees, looking up, I discovered I did want the touch of a man. Quickly I put my head down, that they not see this weakness. Then I looked up, piteously. But the lesson was then ended. Unfulfilled, I was herded back, on my hands and knees, poked with a stick, to the cage, and locked within. I grasped the cold bars, and squirmed helplessly. What are they doing to me? What am I becoming?

No, no! You, as a true man, would not want me crawling naked to your feet, helpless, vulnerable, cruelly aroused, in fear of the whip, trembling with need, supplicatory, begging your touch. as piteously as might the most worthless of women, a stripped, needful slave.

Do you know that I found you attractive, my dearest Irving, that I sometimes brought matters to your attention with no other object than to see you, that I sometimes passed your office unnecessarily, to catch a glimpse of you? Did you think it strange that we often encountered one another in the parking lot?

Save me, dearest Irving!

I fear that I am becoming a woman.

Changing,

Linda

Seventh Letter

My dearest Irving, my beloved Irving, my hope:

I have been branded!

They have branded me!

It was done with a small, delicate white-hot iron, pressed into, and held in, for some terrible moments, my flesh. It crackled, and sizzled, and burned, and I could smell my flesh burning, my own flesh, and I screamed and, when it was withdrawn, cleanly, and smoking, I was marked!

This is a different world. I have suspected this for a long time, from the sense of the world, from its air, from certain foods, what I have seen of its culture, but dared not mention this in my letters, lest you think me mad. This is a wild, strange, beautiful world. Where it is I do not know, but there seems a single sun. It seems much like ours, only so different. I have seen no moons. I have surprising energy here, and vitality. My body thrives on the purity, the exhilarating freshness, of the air. I have never felt so alive on Earth. Perhaps this is the way the earth once was.

The foods I have been given are simple, but apparently nutritious. I am sometimes to force my face into a bowl of cereal, or gruel, and finish it, even to the licking of the pan, lest any be wasted. The water, though I must lap it from a pan on the floor, my head down, is wonderfully clear, and refreshing. The vegetables, and fruits, are fresh, and unbelievably tasty. I think they may come fresh from gardens, or farms, to markets in the city, for we are in a city.

As I said, I have been branded. It is a small, tasteful, delicate, but quite unmistakable, mark, high on my left thigh, just under the hip. It is a little hard to describe, but it reminds one of a cursive "k" without the closure of the loop. It is not large. It is about two inches in height and a half of an inch in width. It is clearly placed in my body. I do not know what it means, but it is there, and evident to any who might care to look.

It marks me well, but I do not understand the meaning of the mark.

After my branding, even while I was screaming, overcome with horror and pain, I was taken from the rack in which I had been helplessly bound, and thrown to my belly on the floor. Then a new collar was placed on my neck, and the older one removed. I must then needs kiss the feet of the men who had attended to my branding, and collaring.

There is printing on the new collar, which is much like the old collar, save for the printing. The printing is engraved there. I cannot read the script. I do not know what it says. It is not a matter of having difficulty reading it in a mirror. It is rather that it is in a different script. It must be in their own language. Others can read it, doubtless. But I cannot. It occurs to me that here, on this world, I am illiterate. How strange that seems to me. I do not think they are going to teach me to read. I do not understand.

And so I am in a new collar, and I do not know what the printing on it says. It is a very attractive collar, close-fitting, and such, much like the other, and, as you would suppose, it, too, is locked on me. I cannot remove it. It is not uncomfortable. But it is there. It is a strange feeling, when you think about it, being locked in a collar.

I understand so little!

What sort of woman would be branded?

What sort of woman would be put in a collar, a locked collar?

Are you negotiating with my captors for my release?

Why haven't you written?

Have I offended you? Are you angry with me? At one time I would have laughed at such things, but, now, I am afraid.

This morning, after my branding, and collaring, I was

given my first bit of clothing, if one may call it that, a sleeveless, scandalously brief tunic, with a tie at my left shoulder, which, if tugged, would drop the garment about my ankles. It does cover the brand, though, of course, not the collar. My hands were then cuffed behind me, in light metal restraints, and I was put on a leash, yes, a leash, and led from the house.

Oh, what a marvelous place this is, dearest Irving, how beautiful, dazzling, wonderful, incredible! And there are women here, some tunicked, as I was, and others veiled, and clad in cumbrous robes. There are children here, too, and they are as wild, as unrestrained, as playful, as mischievous, as children anywhere. We went through various streets, and saw more than one market. There are animals here, too, which are unfamiliar to me, some large, lofty, and silken, some massive and hairy, some sinuous and leopardlike. I saw one animal with six legs, in a jeweled collar. I saw no police, as we would know them, to whose attention I might call my predicament. There were some helmeted, armed men, but they seemed so stern, so fierce, and mighty, that a girl, perhaps I should have said a woman, would hesitate to approach them, lest she simply be taken in their arms and utilized for their pleasure. The men here, even peasants, as I suppose them to be, and merchants, and craftsmen, seem sexual and alive. From Earth, I found such virility terrifying. This world is unbelievably primitive, colorful, and sensuous.

Were they just exercising me, as one might walk a dog, or did they wish me to see this world, perhaps that I might better understand my situation? Perhaps both.

I was thrilled!

I did not miss the dense, impatient traffic, the pervasive noise, the gray, choking, sickening air, the rushing about, the crowding, the screaming, of our city.

Earth need not be as it is!

Some of the tunicked girls, let us call them that, for they are girls, given their tunics and collars, yes, they, too, wore collars, lovely, graceful bands upon their necks, closely fitting, collars much like mine, and I do not doubt but what theirs were locked on them as securely as mine on me, looked upon me as though comparing me with themselves, the meaningless sluts! But I straightened my body and returned their haughty gazes. I did not regard myself as inferior to them. I am perhaps trimmer now, and more interestingly curved, than you remember me. It is perhaps the diet, the training, the forced exercises in the house. Perhaps it has to do, too, with the injections, the serums. I do not know. Perhaps these changes are merely in my mind, in my imagination. I do not know.

Three days ago I was permitted to launder for some of the men in the house. I enjoyed this, the tubs, the water, the garments which had been next to their bodies.

We passed more than one girl, sitting, lying, or kneeling, chained by her neck to a ring, placed in the side of the building. There are a number of such rings about, particularly in the business areas, placed there, it seems, as a convenience. Doubtless animals may be fastened to them, too, of course.

The fellow who was my guide in this unusual peregrination spoke some English. When we were in a less frequented district, I addressed him. "May I speak?" I asked, using the formula I had been given early in my stay in the house. It is generally a good idea, I had discovered, sometimes at the end of a strap, before speaking, to learn if speech will be permitted. To be sure, much depends on the fellow, and the context, but, here, on the street, it seemed appropriate to inquire. The leash was a long one, coiled in his hand, and I had no wish, if I could avoid it, of being knelt down, my head to the pavement, and having my calves lashed with the free end of the leash. He seemed a bit taken aback, but said, "Yes." I knew enough, by then, of course, having been several days in the house, to kneel before him, and look up at him. That is commonly how I have been instructed to place myself before men. My hands were fastened behind my back. The leash looped up to his hand.

"Why have I been given this garment to wear?" I asked. It was scarcely modest. It did cover the brand. I thought I was due some explanation for this affront to my dignity. After all, even one being held for ransom must have some rights.

"That you not be naked," he said.

That was not the sort of answer I had anticipated receiving.

"Your body," he said, "is not without interest. If you were stripped, you would be more likely to be stolen."

"Stolen?" I asked.

"Yes," he said.

He had spoken of me as though I were property.

We then returned to the house.

Why haven't you written, why have you not responded to my letters! Have I been too familiar? Have I presumed too much? Have I shown you too little respect?

Desperately,
Linda

Eighth Letter

Dear Mr. Barofsky:

Forgive me for having referred to you as "I. B.," as "Irving," and so on. I was not entitled to be so forward, given our institutional relationships at the magazine. You were my superior. Forgive me, please, for not having accorded you the respect, the deference, you were due. It was wrong that I should have arrogated to myself, without permission, the right to such informality. Perhaps that is why you have not responded to my letters. Perhaps you were offended? I was merely a stupid, presumptuous employee. When you arrange my release, paying whatever ransom is required, you will find me much changed upon my return, deferent, attentive, productive, hard-working, and subservient.

Too, Mr. Barofsky, sir, please forgive me for having spoken boldly in meetings, often essentially in vanity, merely that I might hear myself speak, and often without having received permission, without having been recognized. Perhaps I took this as required, that I might, a modern woman, a liberated woman, impress male colleagues with my malelike decisiveness, my masculinelike strength, my manlike forcefulness, and acumen. How aimless, irrelevant and silly now seem so many of those comments! Some I hope, though, were helpful. The point of the meetings was business, but I tried too often to make them political, to assert myself, rather than deal with the issues before us. I was a child playing a role, and one alien to my nature, as I now understand it. The point of this boorish assertiveness, it seems, was no more than assertiveness itself, that taken as its own justification. How insecure I was! But, perhaps, too, I wanted to call myself to the attention of the men, and to you, sir. I do think that I am highly intelligent, sir, else you would not have hired me. I do not think you were merely interested in my face, and the lineaments of my figure. But I think you suspected their nature, even through the mannish disguises I affected. I sometimes thought you looked at me as though I were naked, and were not wholly displeased with what you saw. Within the severities of that garmenture you suspected, I am sure, that there was a woman, a troubled, unhappy, lonely woman perhaps, but a woman. But you are the sort of a man, I suspected, who would want more than the body of a woman. That would never be enough for you. You would want the totality of her, her body, her emotions, her nature, her mind, the wholeness of her. Perhaps that was why I feared you, and found you attractive, sir. In my dreams I sometimes seemed to think you were the sort of man who would want to literally possess a woman, and that you were strong enough, and powerful enough, to do that, to possess her, and that nothing less than the possession of her, the possession of the whole of her, would content you. When I thought of you I sometimes sensed that my "career," to which I was supposedly completely devoted, was a vapid, prescribed triviality, a marking of time, a distraction from the call of my true nature. I hated my "career," save as a glamorous exercise to convince myself of my own worth, as a means to seek status, a sorry compensation for the vacancies in my life. How I longed for a culture, a simpler, deeper, more natural, more wonderful culture, in which I might fulfill myself as a female in the deepest biological sense, something that would not be a socially constructed artifact, but would bring me to terms with my own deepest reality.

Perhaps you remember when you, at one meeting, in your impatience, suggested I might make a more useful contribution to the meeting by fetching coffee! How angry I was! You may recall that the chairman forced a public apology from you, before us all. How that must have stung, and humiliated, you. The chairman doubtless feared that I would carry the matter into legal precincts, and damage the public image of the company, this perhaps resulting in corporate embarrassment, and perhaps even in financial losses. I now realize, of course, as I realized then, that your remark, however ill-considered it might have been, was, given my behavior, justified. I trust that you are not, sir, allowing me to languish here as a result of that matter, a contretemps, at best. Do not hold it against me, sir. Please, save me! What I never expressed to you was that when you said that my first reaction was a flush of warmth, a sudden sensation of profound pleasure. It was as though I had been told to go into the kitchen, and cook. That is how I really wanted to be treated by men. To be told to go into the kitchen, and cook, so to speak. In that instant I felt deliciously female, and dominated. We long to be put in our place, by men. How can we respect a male who does not understand, and exercise, his dominance? I assure you, sir, the men here understand it, and exercise it. Had I gone to fetch coffee then, I feel I would have done so happily. I would have been pleased to serve, as a woman. I have discovered that there are rewards in service, that there is enormous pleasure and profound happiness in submission. One dominates, one submits. It is not hard to guess what the healthy relationship is, the structure of the ideal complementarity, sanctioned by nature. But, of course, an instant later, flushed, feigning rage, so easy to do, I demanded that the chairman have you apologize to me, to us all, which you, albeit bitterly, and ungraciously, did.

There was another incident, Mr. Barofsky, which may have troubled you. In approved feminist fashion, though these things are not publicized, obviously, we are permitted to use hints, threats, and such, to advance our careers. You may recall that I entered your office, closing the door behind me, and asked for a promotion. This request, at the time, puzzled you, as it seemed to have emerged, unanticipated, out of nowhere. Unbeknownst to you I had informed the receptionist, your secretary, and two colleagues with nearby offices, that I was planning on making such a request. Then, before your desk, I cried out, as though in dismay, tore open the top button of my blouse, smeared my lipstick, and hurried, as though outraged, from the office, certain to be seen, and remarked, as planned, by several others. I fled, seemingly weeping, to my office. The implication would have been clear, in the political environment in which we existed, that you had assaulted, or molested, me, obviously demanding sexual favors in exchange for the promotion. I received the promotion, as you recall, by direct order of the director, to hush up the matter, and avoid a drawn-out inquiry with a hostile sexual-harassment officer. I regret this now, of course. It was not fair of me. It was cruel, I suppose. Nonetheless you must understand that such behavior and threats of that sort are approved, though not publicized, political weapons. After all, I cannot threaten to foment riots, or such. Our blackmail is more personal, and perhaps more ladylike, than that of others capitalizing on invented, or imagined, grievances. As you may recall, "anything is accounted acceptable which furthers the ends of our power, except violence." And I suppose violence would be acceptable to us, as well, if we thought it practical.

Things are so different here, Mr. Barofsky!

I apologize, profoundly, for any unpleasantness I might have caused you in the past, for the incident in the boardroom, for the incident in your office, for all the things, large and small, I might have done to irritate you. I never believed, incidentally, and do not now believe, that you were ever personally intimidated by these things. Weaker men might have been, but you were not.

If only you could see me now, though I would not desire you to do so, as I am unclothed, as I kneel and write this.

Now, collared, and branded, when a man enters the room, I face him, kneel, and do obeisance, with my head to the floor.

And it is so that I would greet you, if you were here.

I would have no choice.

Please note that I am addressing you as "Mr. Barofsky," and "sir," and such. So if my incivility has caused you to hesitate in responding to my letters, or in effecting my release, please hesitate no longer!

Save me from these imperious, uncompromising, magnificent brutes! They treat me as though I might be no more than an animal!

I am learning more words now. I am unfamiliar with the language. I do not recognize it. Sometimes I hear a word which sounds like an Earth word, perhaps from Latin, or English, or German. Interestingly the accents of these men in subtle ways remind me of your accent, at the office. I never did inquire as to your native language.

When you have my ransom paid and I return to work at the magazine you will discover that I have learned my place.

Please hurry with my rescue!

Tomorrow I am to learn the meaning of "La kajira," the first words I was taught to speak on this world.

Once I spoke of myself being prostrate before you, figuratively. I am now going to draw back from the low, writing table and lie before it on my belly, naked, my hands at the sides of my head. Thus when I write the next sentence in this letter, my eighth letter, I will have been prostrate before you, literally, naked.

It has now been done, Mr. Barofsky.

I have been prostrate before you, as a naked supplicant.

Please, sir, expedite my release, please!

Linda

Ninth Letter,

Twelfth Passage Hand, Second Day

Master:

I have now learned the meaning of "La kajira."

It means "I am a slave girl."

You will note that I have addressed you as "Master." That is because slaves, as I have been informed, must address all free men as "Master" and all free women as "Mistress."

How can it be, that I am a slave?

I can't be a slave!

But I discover that I am a slave, truly a slave, literally, actually and legally!

I do not know when, exactly, I became a slave. It may have been when I first uttered the words "La kajira." It may have been when I was put in my first collar. It may have been when I was branded. It may have been when someone signed an order for my acquisition, or perhaps merely put an approval check by my name, I becoming a slave with the affixing of that signature, or that little check mark, on some document, a slave at that time merely not yet collected. Some here on this world, which is called Gor, seem to think that some women are "natural slaves." Some others seem to think that all women are slaves, only that not all of them are in collars. In any event, in my particular case, my nature, condition, and legal status on this world is quite clear. I am property. That is what the keeper meant, it seems, out on the street several days ago, when he informed me that I might be stolen. I gather, for what it is worth, that I might be regarded as worth stealing.

I am owned. I can be bought and sold.

My lessons continue.

I now kneel in the presence of men, when I am addressed by them, when I approach them, and so on. I do this naturally, unquestioningly. It seems the right thing to do. It is not just the conditioning, though we may be beaten if we fail to do what is expected of us, and is proper for us. It is rather that it seems, somehow, fitting, emotionally right, morally appropriate. I would have to fight against the impulse, if I were returned to Earth. Oddly, sometimes, on Earth, I felt an impulse to kneel before certain men, but, of course, one would not do that there. I often felt the impulse to kneel before you, Master. I suppose you did not know that.

Learning that I am a slave has brought a new view of myself into my mind. I am not sure now that I am to be ransomed. That seems to me strange, for I would suppose that my ransom might be considerably more than I could hope to bring displayed on an auction block. Yes, women are often displayed on auction blocks. It is a common way of selling them. Not unusual in this culture. Not all are vended from public cages, cement shelves, or such. And few have the luxury of being exhibited in purple booths. Do I have an enemy? Or is there someone to whom my bondage means more than money? Would someone rather have me in a collar than free? Does someone so lust for me that he will be satisfied with nothing less than owning me? Could anyone desire a woman so much? So much that he will have her as his slave? That he will choose to own her, to make her his, literally *his*? Does money, which is so important on Earth, mean less here? Do they have so much money that they prefer to deal in precious metals, in produce, in animals, in women?

Surely you might buy me, and free me!

I beg to be bought! I beg to be purchased!

I neglected to mention certain aspects of my training. I did not mention them because I thought myself free, and it would have been embarrassing to refer to them, or to acknowledge them, in any way.

Although I remain a virgin, I am being taught how to please men, intimately, profoundly, totally. There is so much to learn, and yet I am sure that I am being shown little more than basic things, expected, as a matter of course, of a woman such I, one in a collar. We exist to please and serve, unquestioningly, immediately, fully; it is what we are for.

Sometimes I think that these things would give me great power over men, and perhaps they do. But then I am again locked in my cage.

I mention these things now because I am informed that one such as I, dare I say, "a slave," is denied privacy. She is to be open to masters. She does not belong to herself, as does a free person, but to others, to masters. For example, she is not permitted to lie. How privileged is the free woman! She is permitted to lie. And, if caught, she need not fear being whipped. How often I lied as a free woman! Now I would fear to be lashed. Do you remember when you asked me, in amusement, if I found you attractive, and I said, "Not at all."? I was lying then, Master. I must now acknowledge it. I did find you attractive, very attractive, more attractive than any man I had ever known. In your intellect, power, and assurance, you seemed so different from all other men. I often wondered how you could be such, so different. Perhaps some men are born that way.

I am also being trained to dance.

The music here, or much of it, at least what I have heard, is bright, intricate, exciting, and sensuous. There are stringed instruments, flutes, drums, such things. The musicians commonly sit on the floor, or on cushions. Doubtless there are chairs here, but, if so, they are perhaps reserved for personages of power and importance.

I have been informed that the form of dance in which I am being trained is called "slave dance."

If you were to buy me, and free me, and return me to Earth, I might show you what I have learned.

Intrigued?

Linda

Tenth Letter,

Fifth Day, the Waiting Hand

Master:

It has been eight days since my last letter. Tomorrow is the New Year here, which is the Spring Equinox. That is interesting. They begin the new year here when nature begins hers.

Forgive me for the conclusion of my last letter. It was clearly intended, and perhaps not very subtly, as bargaining. It was intended to intrigue you, and encourage you to free me, and then hope that I might see fit to repay you with certain favors. A slave does not bargain, of course. She listens, she does what she is told. Her favors are not hers to bestow, but the master's to command.

I was punished for that letter, for they read what I write, of course. I was put to my belly and my ankles were lifted and tied to low bar, some six inches from the floor. The soles of my feet were then beaten.

I have learned my lesson.

Desperately did I beg forgiveness for my stupidity, my foolishness. I beg your pardon, as well, for you are a free man, and I am only a slave girl.

Forgive me, Master.

I sign this letter 'Linda' but that is now a slave name. When I became a slave, I became nameless, as nameless as any other item of livestock. Perhaps it amuses them to continue to call me "Linda," to summon me by that name, to order me about by that name, and so on, but it is a slave name now, put on me by masters, just as you might give a name to any animal, to a dog, a horse, a pig. Still it is a nice name. I always thought you liked it.

Buy me, please! Free me! I do not bargain! I plead!

Linda

Eleventh Letter

En'Kara, Second Day

Master:

They can breed me!

They can hood me, and chain me in a stall, on the straw, to be groped for by, and used by, hooded male slaves. Neither of us is to see the other, that there be no affection formed, that we be unable, each, to later recognize the other. The couplings are arranged by masters, with attention given to traits and speculatively desirable crossings. The couplings are also witnessed and supervised by the masters involved, or their agents. We are also hooded when we give birth, that we not know the child, nor the attendants at the birth. We are livestock! I do not want to be serviced by a stud slave!

How helpless I am!

Buy me! Free me! Save me!

I am told that only a slave begs to be purchased. But I am a slave! Please buy me! Then free me, return me to Earth! Please! Please! Please!

I do not bargain!

I beg, I plead!

You knew me on Earth! You must be horrified at what has become of me! Perhaps we had our differences, but those are behind us now! How absurd that discontented, affluent, free women prattled of "liberation"! Who owned them? Who were their masters? Were their thighs marked, as that of humble, curvaceous, herded female cattle! Where were their collars! Let them belong, if only for a day, to one of these men, men accustomed to own and master women, as thoughtlessly and naturally as they might dogs! Let such women grovel and crawl, and kiss and lick, and beg fearfully, piteously, to please! Then they would dare not speak of "liberation," lest they be punished! Nor, perhaps, would they desire it . But I dare not speak further of this.

Consider my plight! Save me! Please, save me, Master, for I must now, as you are free, address you as "Master."

Have pity, I beg you, on a woman of your world, one whom you knew as the haughty bitch, Linda. I am no longer haughty, Master! I assure you of that! I am now only a confused, desperate, helpless, needful woman! Please, Master!

The bitch has been now been collared, Master.

I wonder why I wrote that line.

Surely you must wish to rescue me from my fate, that of a helpless female slave!

I beg it.

Too, what sort of man are you, if you would not free me? Have you not received the conditioning of Earth, to do what women want, or, perhaps better, what they think they want, or what they are told they should want, or what they feel they should tell you they want? Surely you are not the sort of man who would keep a woman in bondage! Even if the woman were a slave, rightfully so, and deserved to be a slave, fully and in every way, you would surely hasten to free her! You are a gentleman! You would not keep her in a collar, at your feet! Perhaps women should belong to men but you must pretend it is not so. Surely you must "be a man" *by not being a man*! Surely politics must overcome the obvious biology of gender mastery, must overcome blood, and desire. Before contrived social artifacts let nature crumble! But, alas, nature denied is nature poisoned!

What am I saying? What strange thoughts escape me?

But I am not a slave, as you know! That is, I am not the sort of woman who should be a slave! Perhaps other women, lesser women, but not I, not I! But I find myself branded and in a collar! Free me, Master, I beg it!

Surely, if you owned me, you would not keep me as a slave! You are a man of Earth. You would not be serene enough, contented enough, complacent enough, straightforward enough, natural enough, strong enough, powerful enough, man enough, to do *that*. You are not Gorean!

But sometimes I think how fearful it would be to belong to you! I sometimes suspect you would have me well fulfill the requirements of my beauty and collar.

I wonder what it would be like, to be owned by you.

Forgive me, if, above, in playing on the conditioning program to which you must have been subjected, as you are a man of Earth, I have tried to manipulate you. How much of the Earthwoman remains in me!

Forgive me, Masters, too, who may read this letter before it is transmitted, if it is transmitted. Linda, the meaningless slave, is penitent. Linda, the rightfully embonded slut, whom you kindly strive to improve by training, is contrite. She begs forgiveness! Please do not whip her. The whip hurts.

But you, Master, he to whom this letter is addressed, do not forget me. Rescue me! Negotiate with them! Arrange for my liberation! Buy me! Free me!

I beg, beg, beg, Master!

Before you, I beg as a slave, Master, a naked, helpless slave!

Groveling,
"Linda"

Twelfth Letter,

En'Kara, Third Day

Master:

After I wrote to you, only yesterday, I was taken into a tiled chamber, and thrown to the floor before a man in blue and yellow robes, he reclining in a great chair.

Then I was forced to stand, and turn, and pose, and be exhibited before him. I was handled and displayed as might have been an animal. To be sure, as a slave, I am an animal.

Then I was put to my knees and one man held my wrists behind my back, and another pulled my head back, by the hair. By a third, a hideous drink was poured down my throat, my head held back, my nostrils pinched shut, so that, if I would breathe, I must swallow the offensive beverage. But I did not object, and drank it down, eagerly, for I knew it was "slave wine." It was not necessary for them to tie my hands behind my back, as they did later, that I be unable to rid myself of the foul brew, for I welcomed it, but such is routine for them. So for the next Ahn, forgive me, for I am now beginning to think in their units of time, that is something longer than an hour, and there are twenty in the Gorean day, my hands were bound behind me. The meaning of this, of course, is that I cannot now be bred, indefinitely, unless a releasing liquid is administered, which liquid I am told is delicious. So they have no immediate intentions of breeding me. To be sure, the effects of the slave wine are gone but moments after the administration of the "releaser." I am now able to follow much of their conversation. I have been assessed as meeting at least the minimum conditions for a particular category of slave.

I wonder if Master can guess it.

It is called the "pleasure slave."

Doubtless Master is surprised.

Can he conceive of that, that the Linda he knew, with all her insolences, her disdain, her pettinesses and severities, her calculated coldnesses, her seemingly inexplicable, unpredictable hostilities, her cultivated, offensive iciness, her labored political aggressiveness, her suddenly, unexpectedly brandished formalities and reserves, her fear of men, and her hostility toward them, has been categorized as a pleasure slave? *A pleasure slave*! Someone, somehow, it seems, must have found her of interest, for the pleasure slave is seen in terms of the pleasure she can give men! And I think you can understand what is meant by *pleasure*. Perhaps Linda is indeed worth stealing. Who knows? Perhaps he saw a secret Linda, the real Linda, the one she dared not reveal to the world, the one which her world, in its cruelty, refused to permit her to reveal?

But such slaves are said to be helplessly passionate! What do the keepers detect in her, or know of her, latently, the nature of which she, in her fear, scarcely dares suspect?

The pleasure slave is different from a simple breeding slave, or a work slave, such as a laundress or mill worker, or a tower slave, who is utilized usually in domestic service. To be sure, a pleasure slave is a slave, and may be bred, or put in the mills, or put to the floors with brushes, and such.

She may be weight-shackled, and have her head shaved, and be whipped, as easily as any other slave.

A pleasure slave!

Can you imagine that? I, a pleasure slave! Whereas I should doubtless fume with rage at this humiliating degradation, my response was one of elation. Forgive me, but, as a slave, I must speak the truth.

I do think that I have become attractive, and beautiful. It

is nice to know that one is attractive, at least to some men, that one is desirable. I thought myself attractive, beautiful, desirable, even on Earth. I wonder if you thought so. But you should see me now! I am learning to wear silks. They leave little to the imagination. But they are thought appropriate for a pleasure slave, when she is permitted clothing.

One of the men in the tiled chamber said, "She has spirit." Another said, "Splendid, then it will be pleasant for a master to break her to his will."

I wonder what it is, to be broken to the will of a man.

I have little doubt it can be done to me. These men know their work.

So, Master, you know a woman who is now rated as a pleasure slave! To be sure, she would not be likely, now, to bring more than a handful of copper tarsks, a small-denomination coin here, in the market, as others are doubtless more beautiful, and she is not particularly trained. But perhaps she will become even more beautiful, and she may be further trained. Surely, too, a master could train her, to his particular interests and pleasures.

My collar has writing on it, but, of course, I cannot read it.

I am, at the time of this writing, still a virgin. I wonder if you knew I was a virgin. Of course not. How could you have known?

Having had the "slave wine" I do not know how long I will be permitted to retain my virginity. Its disposition, of course, is at the whim of masters. Am I to be soon deflowered? What a ridiculous expression! Virginity here, in a slave, is as meaningless as virginity in a pig. A common way of speaking of the matter here, where slaves are concerned, and sometimes free women, when speaking vulgarly, is "opening for the uses of men." I gather that it is not unusual, after one's deflowering, or opening, and subsequent services to masters, for "slave fires" to begin to burn in one's belly, and, indeed, throughout one's entire body. Already I suspect that, and I must speak the truth, I have some sense of what that means. Although, as yet still a virgin, I have often felt intense, helpless sexual desire. I dare not conjecture the depths, and extents, of such feelings, if I were to find myself subjected to the interests and attentions of masters. One hears of the growth in feeling, and of the varieties of, and tiers of, "slave orgasm." I have little doubt that bondage considerably, remarkably, spectacularly, boosts female orgasm. Perhaps this has to do with the totality of the domination, the differences between the sexes, the complementarity of male and female, the fear, the knowledge that one is choiceless, that one must yield completely, totally. Or, more simply, that one is a slave. The mastery, too, one supposes, has its effect on male desire, and orgasm. How could one be more dominant, more a man, than as a master? That is not politics; that is nature.

I have heard that slave girls, unsatisfied, sometimes cry out with need, piteously, that they can grasp the bars of their cells and cages, pressing tear-stained cheeks against them, imploring guards for their merest touch, that they can furrow the walls of their kennels in frustration. How much then we would be at the mercy of men!

What power they would have over us, we, at their feet, begging!

I wonder if you would like to have me at your feet, your property, your slave, yours to do with as you wished, naked, collared, beseeching, *begging*.

How different from Earth! Yet have we not, even on gray, polluted Earth, wept with loneliness, turned in our beds, and stained many a pillow with the tears of unfulfilled needs?

Where were our masters?

I am afraid of these thoughts, and am intrigued by them. I must admit that, for I am not permitted to lie.

So I am a slave, and, it seems, a "pleasure slave."

I am being taught to be beautiful, and to serve and please men, and in all ways, domestically, sensuously, intimately, fully. It is what I am for, to be owned, and be at the feet of men.

Does that horrify you? Or, I wonder, does it please you?

Sometimes I think that in the heart of every man lurks a master. What man, truly, honestly, does not want to own a beautiful woman? He must be an unimaginative, boorish, simple, piteous sort of fellow.

Perhaps you would have wanted me at your feet. I wonder.

How different from Earth, how different!

Tomorrow they are taking me to a tavern, to dance! I hope to do well. If I do not do well, I will presumably be punished. I might be given the "releaser" and sent to the breeding stalls. I will do my best.

How strange to think of dancing before men, and as a slave!

There will be many girls dancing. I will be only one, and will presumably dance early in the evening. The best are saved for last.

After a virgin has danced she is often hooded and chained in an alcove, for the use of the tavernkeeper's patrons. When next I write to you, if I am permitted to write, I may have been "opened for the uses of men."

Can you imagine the Linda you knew, petty, nasty, manipulative Linda, that superior-acting, smug, haughty, insolently saucy, pretty, nicely curved little bitch hooded, chained in an alcove, and treated, perhaps for the first time, as she so richly deserves?

You may recall, in my last letter, I feared I might be whipped, for my attempt to manipulate you. But I was not whipped. Indeed, the keepers seemed to find that part of my letter amusing. Why I do not know.

They keep us much in ignorance.

Curiosity, I am told, is not becoming in a slave.

A slave,
Linda

Thirteenth Letter,

En'Kara, Fifth Day

Master:

Yesterday I was danced.

I was terrified, but I think I did well, at least considering it was the first time I did such a thing.

I was to dance not only in the square of sand, the musicians to my left, but also in and about the aisles, amongst the low tables, amongst the patrons, who were all strong, sexual men. I was seized several times, by a wrist or ankle, and feared that I might be thrown across one of the small tables, on my back, or stomach, my legs thrust apart, and find myself, in a whirl of silks and a jangle of necklaces, "opened" then and there, instantly. But the tavern men pulled me free, laughing, and, to obscene noises, and raucous shouts, I gathered myself together, and continued. as I could, flustered, frightened, trembling, to dance, to please. At the conclusion of the dance I performed the common obeisance, kneeling in the sand, my head down, the palms of my hands down, on either side of my head, a fitting obeisance for a female slave before masters. I was then taken by an arm, drawn to my feet, and pulled, stumbling, to a tiny, lamp-lit alcove. There I was stripped absolutely naked, save for the collar on my throat. I was then flung down on the deep furs, on my back, and my wrists were chained on either side of my head, and my ankles were chained, apart, to rings. I looked up at the tavernkeeper's man. A heavy leather hood was drawn over my head and buckled shut beneath my chin. I heard the musicians outside, and more shouts. Another girl would dance now. I had danced third. There were to be some twenty dancers. We had been in a side room, waiting to be called to the sand. I tried the chains. I was fastened perfectly, as I knew I would be. These men do not make mistakes about such things. I could see nothing. I supposed that I must now await patrons of the tavern. I believed that I would be "opened" in moments, doubtlessly expertly, casually, callously. In such a situation one does not look for, nor expect, gentleness, sensitivity, compassion or regard from a man. A slave may be used as men please. Soon I heard the leather curtains parted, and, within the hood, foolish as it may seem, I closed my eyes, and gritted my teeth. I was ready. Indeed, in a strange way, I looked forward to my "opening." I knew there might be a bit of pain, though not necessarily. I knew there might be a victorious penetration, an invasive, conquering impalement informing me that I was a woman, and belonged to men, and was "had," and then perhaps a pounding, a thrusting, violent, or persuasive, perhaps brief, perhaps prolonged, perhaps subtle, perhaps crude, a working at, and within, my body, patiently or impatiently, perhaps a working as cruel as a slapping of my face, from side to side, or a working so insidiously seductive that my haunches might suddenly, inadvertently, betray my need, which I wished then to conceal, and would lift themselves piteously, begging, begging for more, and then, one supposed, eventually, sooner or later, helplessly chained, I would feel within myself the sudden claimant flooding of his pleasure. But, rather, to my astonishment, I felt myself turned to my side, and felt two, curved, joined, hinged, heavy metal bands, each perhaps a half inch thick and two inches wide, the left first, and then the right, placed about my waist. The hinge was behind me, at the small of my back. When the bands met at my waist they were close fitting, perhaps too closely, too snugly, fitting. Another such band, fastened to the others, behind me, I think by a chain link, was brought between my legs, and up. The three bands then met at my waist, the second two of them seeming to fit over a staple on the first, the band which had first been put about me, which was at my left. I then heard the snap of a heavy lock, presumably a padlock. I was then put again to my back. The device was fastened on me. One could not think of slipping it, not with a woman's body, not with the narrowness of the waist, the swelling of the bosom, and the width of the hips. No woman could.

Incidentally, Master, my waist is narrower now. I know that because the keepers measure it, I usually standing with my legs widely separated, and my hands clasped behind my neck, which, I am told, is a common inspection position. They also tell me that my bosom is lovely, and that the width of my hips is inviting. I wonder what they mean by that. I think you found me attractive at the office, Doubtless you would find me much more so now, for the contours of my femininity are much more obvious and pronounced now. I wonder if you would object to that. The keepers, the diet, the exercise, and such, have seen to it. Do you know that slaves may be whipped if they do not keep their bodies healthy and attractive? I wonder if that horrifies you, or if you just take it as a matter of course, as might a Gorean.

Please forgive the digression.

I wonder why I should be telling you these things. Have I become so much a slave that I hope that a master might find me "of interest"? Forgive me, you are not a master. You are a man of Earth. How fearful it would have been for me on Earth, being near you, had I realized that you were a master, that you might have looked upon me, and considered me, as a master looks upon, and considers, a woman. How fearful it might have been for a natural slave, to have known herself to have been so close to a master. So close they might almost touch! Yet how amorously overpowering for her would have been even that timid suspicion!

Forgive me.

To continue, Master.

I could feel the sides of a curved metal plate between

my thighs, it held in place by the bands, it attached to the middle band, perhaps welded to it, that between my legs.

When the fellow was finished, he who had fastened the whole tight, heavy, cumbersome device upon me, he slapped it once or twice, familiarly, to show me, I suppose, its nature, and how it was placed. Or perhaps to show me, too, that it was on me, and that I could do nothing about it.

He then left, drawing the curtains closed behind him.

From time to time, as the music continued outside, and other girls danced, one or another man would thrust apart the curtains, look at me, I suppose, and leave. I wonder how I looked to them. I think some of them were angry, to find me so defended, so protected, if only by the narrow, locked, well-placed humiliation of the iron. Sometimes they would mutter to themselves, or exit growling.

So, Master, some men, it seems, desired me.

Yet I am still a virgin.

I wonder if you ever desired me. Here, on this world, girls such as I, in the taverns, in the booths, in the house, in brothels, are rented for as little as a tarsk-bit, the smallest coin, as far as I know, in their currency.

So you see, here, Master, I would be cheap, or I suppose so, if my master, the house, I gather, put me out for rent, say, staked outside, spread for exhibition and pleasure, a copper bowl at my side for the coins. Or perhaps they might send me into the streets as a "coin girl," a bell and a small, locked coin box chained about my neck, over my collar. And woe to the girl who does not bring a jangling coin box back to her master! I am sure you could afford my rent price. But I wonder if you would want me. Perhaps I might do to serve you wine, and fruit, and sweets, while you pleasured yourself with a more beautiful slave.

But let it not be Holly, Master!

I am still a virgin. That must be unusual among slaves. I am, as it is said, "white silk." I am not yet "red silk." I wonder who will "red silk" me. Too, I am, as it is said here, a "pierced-ear girl." For some reason, this seems of interest to these men. Only slaves here, it seems, have their ears pierced, and not all of them. Supposedly the "pierced-ear girl" is the lowest, and most meaningless, of slaves. Yet, they seem to intrigue Gorean men. Reputedly, they bring high prices.

I had had it done to me, the piercing of my ears, some months ago, on Earth, indeed, interestingly, as I think about it now, not long after meeting you. I do not really know why I had it done. It seems so unlike me. Why would I have had it done? Was I aware, I wonder, on some level, of its declarative, amorous portent? Surely, had I realized how revealing and momentous this was to the men of this world, and how clearly, how unmistakably, this would have marked me a certain sort of girl to them, and had I suspected I might sometime find myself amongst them, helplessly so, I assuredly would have never dared to have it done. Or would I have dared, proclaiming myself before them thusly to be what they least respect and most desire? I do not know. With what amusement, and aggression, did they turn my head from side to side, considering these tiny, distinguishing apertures! They mean so little to us, but they seem to mean so much to them! Who is to say what the truths of these things are?

In any event, it is apparently unusual for a pierced-ear girl to be a virgin. I am then, it seems, something of an anomaly. Perhaps I was, too, on Earth, for a "modern woman." I do not know. It is unusual, of course, for any slave girl, or "kajira," to be a virgin. From what I have told you of this world, you will understand that.

Branded,
Linda

Fourteenth Letter,

En'Kara, Seventh Day

Dear Master:

You will note that I have addressed you as "Dear Master."

I know that is not a very Gorean thing to do so, but I wanted to do that.

I must address you as "Master," of course. That is understood. You are a free man and I am a slave, no more than a lowly kajira. But I wanted to use "Dear" in my salutation. At least this once. It reminds me, in a way, of Earth. In a way, it is like writing a letter to a friend. I think I need these letters, and the thought of you. You are, it seems, my only connection with my former world. And, alas, I do not even know if you have received any of them.

Despite my treatment of you, my feelings were actually acutely ambivalent, certainly confused. I resented you, of course, your manhood, and power. Oh, yes, and I hated you, or thought I hated you. And now I find myself writing to you as though you were a friend, my only friend, the only one capable of understanding me. What do these masterful Gorean brutes know of, or care for, an Earthwoman's upbringing and background, the vicious, destructive, denaturalized values leached into her over the years, the conditioned negativities, how her conflicts bound her like wire, how her culture tore her from one side to another, pretending to celebrate her reality while dragging her as far from it as it could? What can they know of, or what do they care for, her torment and pain, her fears, her confusions? Of what interest to them is her astonishment at what has been done to her? Of what interest to them are her feelings, those of a young, haughty, arrogant, affluent, pampered free woman, perhaps even beautiful, who suddenly finds herself no more than a fearful, helpless, rightless, degraded slave on an alien world?

These are things which you can understand.

I am sure of that.

I suppose I hated you. I am not sure. Even as I kneel here, stripped, writing this letter, branded, in a collar, my memories, my feelings, are unclear. Certainly I treated you badly. Certainly I was cruel to you. Certainly I tried to publicly demean you, and to undermine your position at the magazine. I wanted to usurp your position, and authority. I wonder if you knew that. I think perhaps you did. Yes, I am sure you did. In trying to diminish you, and ruin you, perhaps I was using you as a means to compensate for my own loneliness, and unhappiness. I felt great dissatisfaction with the men of Earth, whom I felt were somehow wasting themselves, living like shadows, not men. If they were not men, how could I be a woman? Perhaps I wanted you to stand as hapless proxy for the men of Earth. Perhaps I wanted to ventilate on you my frustration with them, my fury at their feckless incompetence, with their surrender of themselves. Doubtless I wanted to take out this anger, this spite, on you. And yet you frustrated me, muchly. You did not recoil, and cringe, and apologize. You did not accept the antics of the political game. Were the rules strange to you? Did you not understand how it was played? Did you not understand what we could do to you? Were you not aware of the sanctions, the penalties, imposable for intractability, for standing your ground, for defending reality and nature, for refusing to mouth our bromides, for refusing to capitulate to narrow, self-serving, politicized demands? Did you not understand that we can vote, that we can terminate, as it pleases us, the tenure in office of legislators who do not do as we tell them?

A wall of stone might have been more easily moved than you by my stratagems and endeavors. You paid little attention to such things. I could not understand it. You were so different from the others. All my fury, it seems, feigned or genuine, could rise no higher than the soles of your shoes, being barely noted, and when you looked down at me, I felt, to my horror, that before your insolent, measured gaze I was reduced to my essentials, essentials I did not even care to acknowledge. Doubtless you were ignoring my outpourings, my insults, my clever remarks, my ideologically motivated diatribes, and were bemusedly conjecturing my lineaments, and, I suspected, expertly. Do you think a woman does not know when a man's look undresses her? How furious I was, seeing your smile. But I felt, I confess, as vulnerable then as a primitive woman kneeling before huntsmen, as vulnerable as a Spanish lady in a sea-coast town, backed against the far wall of her boudoir, the door broken in by pirates. At such times one learns quickly what one is. Here they teach us to loosen a man's sandals with our teeth. I wonder if I would have been given the privilege of so untying the laces of your shoes?

Yes, I hated you, or thought I did. But, too, I was intrigued by you. You were not like the others. How had you kept the manhood the others had been tricked into relinquishing? Were you more intelligent, or your blood hotter, I wonder?

Then I wondered if my hatred, if that is what it was, was motivated by a subtle fear, a fear of you, a fear of myself.

How attractive, I fear, you were to me!

On some level, I certainly knew that I was a worthless slut. Yes, I chose the words carefully, for a slave may not lie. Perhaps my culture had made me that. I do not know. Could there be no redemption for me? Would I never find myself? In what place lay the secrets of my heart ? Would I never discover them?

I sometimes wanted to remove my clothing before you, and kneel before you, on the rug before your desk. I would have said nothing, but kept my head down. Once you wore boots to the office. I felt an impulse to lie before you, and kiss them.

I was frequently cruel to you, unpleasant, critical, nasty.

I had dreams of you owning me, and uncompromisingly mastering me, treating me with all the authority and contempt I deserved.

The small insults, the petty remarks, the frequent, calculated miseries I inflicted on you, publicly and privately, you bore with patience, with bemused equanimity. It was almost as though you were biding your time, almost as though you were waiting for something, almost as though you knew something I did not.

All that seems long ago.

I wonder if I loved you, Master.

I wonder if you liked me, a little.

The slave is the most vulnerable, helpless, loving, and feminine of all women. It is not surprising then that she commonly lives in love, and for love. How tragic then that she dare not, in her lowly condition, aspire to, or hope for, even the master's liking. It is hers to love; it is his to impose the mastery.

She kneels before him, his.

Collared,
Linda

Fifteenth Letter,

En'Kara, Tenth Day

Dearest Master:

Please forgive me the personal nature of my last missive.

It has little to do with this place, or my current existence. It was doubtless not in order, nor appropriate, for me to refer to our earlier relationship, which had been one often tense, frequently difficult, and, on my part, at least, troublesomely, disturbingly ambivalent.

I wonder if you ever thought of me stripped, and in chains. Really naked, really chained.

Presumably not, for you are doubtless a gentleman.

Forgive my small jest. What man does not want to own a beautiful woman, to possess her, literally? What man has not dreamed of a female, doubtless one of his acquaintance, stripped, bound hand and foot, tightly, gagged, perhaps blindfolded, lying, waiting, on the floor, at the foot of his bed? How inert, how spineless, how boring, how weak, how pathetic, would be the male to whom such pleasantries never occurred.

And how strange would be the female who has never dreamed of writhing in the chains of a master, knowing that he owns her, and that she has no choice but to yield to him completely, succumbing to an ascendant succession of multiple orgasms she is not permitted to resist, lest she be cruelly punished.

There are many slaves in the house. In the last weeks I have met many. And we have trained together.

They are being readied for sale, as might be cattle, or horses. Most seem to look forward, eagerly, to their sale, and tease one another about the comparative prices they will bring. All are eager to escape the gloom and discipline of the house! Surely better to sleep chained to a master's slave ring, than retire to the confines of the small cages in which we are kept. I am, incidentally, no longer kept in an isolated cage. The cages can be tiered. My "apartment" is now on the third level, the second from the left, as one looks toward the cage wall.

I am fed with, and trained with, my group.

I suppose I am to be sold, as well.

I wonder what the men at the office, and other men I knew, would think of me now, and what has become of me. Would they be horrified, really, or would they be rather pleased? I suspect they would think it served me right, and might wish the same fate on various others of their acquaintance.

I think, incidentally, Holly would look well in a collar. I wonder if she realizes that she should be a slave. So she uses her little body to advance herself? On this world she would strive to please a master.

Interestingly I have come to understand that I do deserve to be a slave, that that is what I am, and that that is right for me. I do not know about other women, but I now understand that I am a natural slave, that that is my destiny, and one I welcome. I no longer desire to be free. Or, should I say that the collar has made me freer than ever I could have been as a putatively free woman? In submission I have found joy, in serving fulfillment. I feel I have now begun to fulfill my heritage in a species which is clearly dimorphic, one in which men and women are quite different, radically different, yet beautifully complementary. And this complementarity, at least where slaves are concerned, is recognized in this world and incorporated into its cultural and legal institutions. Here civilization does not contradict nature, but accepts her, and enhances her.

For the first time in my life I have been truly liberated, biologically, psychologically, emotionally.

I think there are many slaves on Earth, waiting for their masters.

A fitting and joyful slave,
Linda

Sixteenth Letter,

En'Kara, Twelfth Day

Master:

Please forgive the forward nature of my last two salutations. I am informed that such expressions as "Dear Master" and "Dearest Master" are presumptuous on the part of a slave, perhaps suggesting some subtle hint of a presumed equality, or intimacy. So, as a slave, I now hasten to address you simply, straightforwardly, as "Master." Even the preferred slave, even the high slave, even the love slave, it seems, would think carefully before daring to address her master as anything other than "Master." Whatever their status, let them remember their place. We are all the same in a very important respect. We are all slaves.

I have discovered, Master, having been permitted the inquiry, while lying on my belly before a trainer, clasping his foot in my hands and pressing my lips to it, that I am not to be sent to one of the emporia for the vending of female slaves, nor even to one of the sales barns in the countryside, beyond the city walls, which might seem more appropriate for me.

It seems I am not to be sold.

I do not understand this.

"Why am I not to be sold, Master?" I asked the trainer.

"Read your collar," said he.

"Alas, Master," I said, "I cannot read."

"Stupid, illiterate slave," said he, and left.

"Yes, Master," I wept.

And so, Master, even if I am not stupid, I am illiterate, here. Gorean women, captured, and enslaved, if of high caste, will be literate, of course. And some lower-caste women can read. Some slaves are doubtless taught to read, that they may be of greater service to their masters. But most, it seems, are not taught to read. I gather that I am not to be taught to read. That will doubtless help to keep me in my place, as a low slave, even a pierced-ear girl! You will remember how literate, how articulate I was! Here I cannot read. Here, commonly, I must ask permission to speak, which permission, of course, may not be granted. Then I must remain silent. You would not find me "assertive" here, Master. No! I have no wish to be punished.

I think of you often, Master. As you are a man, I sometimes wonder if you, in the offices, in the corridors, in the meeting rooms, in the conferences, ever thought of me, perhaps when I was nasty, petulant, petty or troublesome, as your slave, stripped, collared, at your feet. There, at your shoes. That would have changed things, wouldn't it? Then I would have been much different, wouldn't I?

Then I would have been in my place.

And I would have known myself in my place.

As I do now!

Too, I would not want to have been whipped.

I sometimes thought of you as my master, who would see to it that I would be subjected to the delicious domination, even to the threat of, or actuality of, the whip, which would bring my femaleness home to me, without which I could not experience the fullness of my womanhood.

Are we not born to love masters, and to obey and please them, and to serve them, and with our whole hearts and souls?

Is it not what we want to do?

Is it not that which brings us our ultimate fulfillment?

Forgive me, Master. How strange must be these thoughts to you, a man of Earth!

Please do not be offended, or distraught, if a woman

should speak to you the truths of her heart. Doubtless I would never have had the courage to kneel before you and confess such things to you on Earth. And beg of you the collar, yes, the *collar*, and the discipline, without which I could not be whole. But you are not here. You are far away, on a far world, and I am here, wherever this may be. And I am just writing this, and I do not even know if you have ever received, or read, any of my letters. Or if you will receive this one. Perhaps I am only speaking to myself, and not to another. Perhaps these letters are little more than a diary of sorts, the dialogue of a woman, or of a girl, a lonely, frightened owned girl, with her own heart, her considering of hitherto unexplored depths, and new rooms and paths, and surprising perspectives, and, yes, bright, beckoning horizons.

But let us dismiss such thoughts.

Consider them little more than the liabilities and hazards of a slave, one who has now no choice but to speak the truth.

I do not understand why I am not to be put up for sale. Surely these men, businessmen, merchants, are interested in making a profit on me. I cost them nothing. I would try to perform well on the block, stripped, of course, for I am told Gorean men like to see what they are buying, to obey, to pose, to smile, perhaps to writhe, to dance, to petition. I would not want to be publicly lashed. Too, I am curious to know what I might bring. I would surely try to bring a good price. How dreadful to say that, I suppose, but it is true. Perhaps it is not really dreadful at all. Perhaps it is very nice. In any event, you see, Master, how she who was once your colleague at the magazine now understands her true reality, which she, on this world, has been brought to face, accept, and love. Yes, Master—do you find it strange?—*love.*

A low slave,

Linda

Seventeenth Letter,

En'Kara, Eighteenth Day

Master:

I am owned!

It is on my collar! It has been read for me! It says: "*I am Linda. I am the property of Rask of Harfax.*"

I do not know him.

Where is Harfax? This city is called Besnit. Is he of high caste? Is he of low caste? Is he rich? Is he poor? Is he kind, is he cruel? Is he gentle or hard, lax, or severe? Is he handsome and virile? Is he fat or weak? Does he have many women? For some reason, is he fond of Earthwomen?

I know nothing of him.

But that is why I am not being sent out in the deliveries to the markets, chained in the wagons with other girls. I am already owned!

Who is Rask of Harfax?

Has he ever seen me? Why would he want me in his collar? There are many slaves more beautiful, even in the house.

I am owned. Now I am truly afraid. He will hold all power over me! It is to him that I must crawl naked, bringing him the whip in my teeth. Hopefully he will not use it on me! I do not know who he is, but I must try to please him. If only we could choose our own masters! But it is we who are chosen, captured, embonded, trained, displayed, purchased, distributed!

Am I a reward for him, for some service he has rendered?

Am I part of his pay, or a bonus, or given to him as a favor, perhaps the consequence of a mere request, made in passing? Or has he the power to simply designate me, and have me put me to one side, reserving me for himself?

I am a chattel, owned, but I do not even know my master! All I know is his name. Before, I did not know even that. Who is this Rask of Harfax, to whom I belong, as much as a dog, a pig, a sandal?

Who is he?

Who is this Rask of Harfax?

He is my master!

But I do not even know him!

She whom you knew as Linda, once your co-worker, once your fellow employee, is owned by him! She is his slave! He is her master, *literally*.

She must obey him, instantly, and unquestioningly, in all things!

She is a slave, *his slave*!

Can you even conceive of this?

But it is true; Master, it is true!

And please, Masters, my keepers, my trainers, do not strike me, for the tears which have fallen on this page. Forgive me, I beg you. I am sorry, I am sorry, Masters! Please forgive me, Masters!

In consternation,
Linda

Eighteenth Letter,

En'Kara, Twentieth Day

Master:

How cruel they are to me!

No, it is not what you think. No, I was not beaten for the tears which fell upon the pages of my last letter. Indeed, they seemed amused by that hapless indiscretion. It is in another sense that they are cruel to me, which shall shortly become clear.

As you may have discerned, the pleasure slave, branded, collared, trained, dominated, has no doubt as to her *raison d'être*; she is owned for purposes of service and love; that is what she is for, to be a man's loving servant and slave, to be his, humbly, gladly, in all ways.

What may have been more subtle, and perhaps less noted, is that the imperious master understands her as a slave, and treats her accordingly. And she loves him the more for this, as it effectuates the domination, and means that she must strive ever the more fervently, desperately, ingeniously, to please him. She must understand herself as nothing, and the master as all. Without him how could she even be fed?

Does he truly feel the contempt he displays toward her? Does he fear he might grow fond of the vulnerable, cringing, frightened, loving she at his feet? How fearful that would be, to love a slave! And yet I think few "free companions" are as coveted, as desired, as jealously guarded, as uncompromisingly possessed, as the female slave.

They are special to the master. You know how fond men are of what they own, of their properties, their possessions, their toys!

Female slaves. Slave girls.

They are the truest, the most feminine, the most desirable of all women.

But, too, I wonder, Master, if you, a man, could possibly understand the warmth, the radiance, the emotional gratifications the slave derives from her condition. I wonder if you can understand the sensuous, redemptive, meaningful psychological milieu of her existence. Can you imagine the sensuousness of her life, even as she performs small, homely tasks? Can you comprehend the pervasive, profound, irresistible sexual stimulations of her reality, that she is branded, thusly marked as property; collared, thusly demonstrated as slave, the collar commonly bearing identificatory data, the name of the slave, the name of her master, and such; the mode of garmenture accorded to her, when she is permitted clothing, which tends to be brief, and sometimes exotically revealing; certainly she must be clearly, unmistakably distinguished from lofty, superior, exalted free women, whose sandals she is unworthy to tie; too, she must speak, move, kneel, lie, and such, with feminine grace, and so on. She must even wear chains in an aesthetic, graceful, attractive, stimulatory manner.

Did you know that we can be whipped for not being graceful, appealing, and beautiful in our chains?

And how exciting is the clink of the chains when she feels their weight, their obdurate, linked sturdiness, and knows herself perfectly secured, helpless within them, and comprehends their meaning, that she is slave, and at the mercy of the master!

And how exciting, too, is the glimpse of a simple slave tunic, or a swirling drape of diaphanous silk. How exciting the belled wrist or ankle! How exciting a metal anklet, a golden armlet, a silver bracelet, a cheap necklace of slave beads! How exciting a short length of soft cord, a bit of binding fiber, slave wristlets, slave cuffs, a leash, a coil of rope, lying nearby, which one knows may be wrapped again and again about one.

And how frightening the mere sight of the master's whip!

She knows its meaning, and obeys well.

The slave's sexual heat is commonly upon her, and seems to lurk always just below the surface. I have felt receptivity at almost the same instant that I am ordered to my knees.

They light in our bellies "slave fires."

Your critical, nasty, petulant, troublesome Linda, once so arrogant, so haughty, so cold, so superior, is now changed, Master. She is now a fearful, obedient, docile, *amorous* slave!

Yet I remain a virgin, and, it seems, in a way a tortured virgin, for they, of late, have brought me to the very edge of release, and have then denied me the relief I cried out to obtain. Yes, I begged for the relief they denied me! Needfully, shamelessly! How cruel they are! How subtle, how skilled! Then I am often returned to the cage, my wrists tied apart to the bars, and my ankles, too, so that I must writhe there in need, on the steel, unfulfilled. How horrifying must this treatment be then to the "red silk" girl, when I, only a "white silk" girl, am brought by it to a such a pitch of excruciating discomfort. Often the girls are denied to the guards and staff for some days before their sale, that they will appear the more piteous and needful, and will beg on the block all the more pathetically, all the more desperately, for a master!

Master, I want a master! How strange that the Linda you knew, now a slave on a far world, a slave on whom the name "Linda" has been placed by masters, should crave a master, should weep and beg for one.

Yes, Master, I admit it, freely, openly, shamelessly. I want a master!

Who is Rask of Harfax?

A miserable, begging, heated slave,
Linda

Nineteenth Letter,

En'Kara, Twenty-Second Day

Master:

Why do I despise and hate Holly? I do not know. I suppose I was jealous, as she was your mistress. I have wondered, sometimes, how she would look, as a slave. She is certainly a pretty little thing, with those blue eyes and blond hair. Perhaps you thought she was a natural blonde. What would she look like, collared, in a short, simple rep-cloth tunic, kneeling before a master? I think I am younger now than I was, or, at least, seem so. Perhaps it is the diet, the exercise, the serums. I think, now, I would be about the same age as Holly. Perhaps we are both now no more than meaningless "chits." I wonder which of us you would prefer? I would compete with her, for your favor. Yes, she you knew as Linda would compete with her for your favor. And perhaps I could lick your whip more piteously, more lasciviously, more beggingly, than she. You could shift from one of us to the other, of course, as you pleased, as, say, you might tire of one of us or the other, or as you might merely, now and then, desire a change. The other you could send to the kitchen, or put weeping in her cage, or kennel.

A jealous slave,
Linda

Twentieth Letter,

En'Kara, Twenty-third Day

Master:

I have been informed by the keepers that I am "a worthless slave."

It is undoubtedly true.

Certainly I was worthless, as I now understand, on Earth, when I thought myself so special, so estimable, so valuable, so precious, so superior. How well I fulfilled the stereotypes of my ideology, how far I was from my true, deeper self and my heart! Did you know I sometimes slept on the floor, at the foot of, or at the side of, my bed, pretending that a master had put me there, where I might be conveniently at hand, should he want me during the night?

But that was one of the least worthless things about me.

That was one of my few actions which might have been appropriate, and acceptable.

During the day I flourished my politics, my rage, so easy to feign, so useful in garnering attention, my grievances, my power, the law, hints, and threats. But at night I sometimes slept on the floor, at the foot of the bed, or beside it, where something told me I should be, where I belonged.

I wonder if my master, Rask of Harfax, whom I have never met, will one day let me share the surface of his couch. Could I be so esteemed? We are often, I understand, slept at the foot of the couch, chained by the neck or ankle to a slave ring.

It is fitting for us.

Men are dominant, and know how to treat us.

It is for such things that we love them.

I wonder, Master, if you could even recognize me now.

I wonder, if I were with a group of stripped, or tunicked, chained slaves, if you could pick me out. Could you walk amongst us, with a whip, and know which one was I? I think you could recognize me, that you could pick me out. I suspect I might be in some sense special to you. Too, I think that even on Earth, you, not unoften, in your thoughts, saw me as a slave. I suspect you thought of me, at least now and then, perhaps frequently, as stripped and chained, at your feet, yours.

Forgive me, Master. I should not have suggested that such thoughts might have been yours!

Surely not yours!

I have new information for you about Rask of Harfax. Although the keepers are enforcing my virginity, and denying me much, I have striven so hard to learn my lessons well, and to serve them in so many ways, that they are now more willing to speak to me. In sneaking specialties for them from the kitchen, and thereby risking a switching, in pouring their wine rather generously, in well serving their tables, in assiduously washing, ironing, and setting out their clothing, in sedulously sweeping, scrubbing, mopping, and dusting their quarters, in meticulously arranging their furs and setting forth the chains in which, alas, other girls will be clasped, in carefully cleaning their leather and accouterments, in diligently polishing their boots, even when I am not instructed to do so, I have become something of a favorite. I have learned that when a woman genuinely desires to please men, and strives to please them, and does please them, the response of men is likely to be rewarding, one of acceptance, of warmth, fondness, and regard, in my case, of course, regard only insofar as a slave can be held in regard. I think my keepers like me though, of course, I am sometimes treated with great harshness, and am humiliated and struck, perhaps that I be reminded that I am a slave. As though one were ever in any doubt about that!

Some men seem to like me.

I wonder if my master, Rask of Harfax, will like me. I hope that he will like me. If he does not he may sell me, or give me away, or do with me whatever he pleases, as I belong to him. He might throw me bound to fang plants, or leech plants, as they are called here. My left forearm was held near to one, and the flower turned slowly toward me as I watched, fascinated, and then it suddenly struck at me, with its two hollow thorns. The pods began to pump and suck and I screamed as the blood was being drawn into them, darkening the pods. Then the plant was slashed apart with a knife and I was allowed to pull my arm away, and, weeping and screaming, tear the thorns from my flesh. I fear the plants. I will try to be a good slave! He may even give me as feed to hunting animals, six-legged, aggressive, sinuous beasts, called sleen. I do not wish to be torn to pieces, alive, beneath their fangs. They are sometimes used to hunt slaves. Some in the house have been given my scent. So, even if it were not for the chains and bars, the great doors, the keepers with their thongs and whips, I would not try to escape. But, Master, and this is fearful to understand, and will perhaps horrify you, even apart from the security of the house, and the keepers, and the animals, there is no escape for the Gorean slave girl. Even outside the house, this house and others like it, even outside, in the cities, or in the fields, on the long roads, on the winding rivers, even when amongst desert tents or mountain huts, wherever, anywhere, even when she is muchly free, when she can come and go muchly as she pleases, for many are permitted such things, there is no escape for her. Branded, collared, distinctively clad, universally recognized as property, there is no place for her to go, no place to run. She is slave, that and nothing else, and not only in a house, or city, or such, but in a culture, in a society, in a world. The best she might hope for is to fall into the hands of a new master, perhaps far away, who, aware of her indiscretion, will be likely to hold her in a servitude a thousand times more grievous than that from which she fled. So you see, Master, there is no escape from our bondage. It is on us. We are truly in our collars.

Does this horrify you, that there is no escape for us?

Or does it please you, for you are a man?

I wonder if my master will make some allowances for me, at least at first, as I am only an Earthwoman. He will surely know that. If not, I will certainly tell him, if I am given permission to speak. I trust he will not hold me in the bondage of the "silent slave," or, more frighteningly, in that of the abject "she-tarsk." And so I hope he will make some allowances for me. As an Earth female. But I do not think he will. Gorean men tend to be impatient, and demanding, with enslaved women.

But when one's service is diligent, conscientious, humble, and as marvelously pleasing as one can make it, in the kitchen, in the household, in the furs, they tend to be contented. And why not? After all, what more can the master want?

Earthwomen, my keepers inform me, as I kneel branded, naked, and collared before them, make excellent slaves.

That is interesting, is it not?

Perhaps I will not always be "worthless."

Too, it seems we have a reputation for love, and helpless passion. That seems so strange to me, for the women on Earth are praised for their modesty, aloofness, and inhibitions. This Puritanical conditioning, of course, is utilized by, and capitalized upon by, ideologues seeking power. How anxious become the ideologues when a woman finds a man attractive; let her not dare fall in love; let her not dare listen to the whisperings of the natural woman, kneeling outside the "pale of enlightenment." Poor men! Smiling becomes leering; flirting becomes harassment; caressing becomes groping; following a woman around a corner to see more of her, because she is so beautiful, is "stalking," and so on. Earth has become so loveless and sick. All is greed, all is power. How blind I was then, how superficial, how shallow, how narrow!

Must we compete in our frigidity? Is each to be colder,

and harder to bring to heat, than the next? Must we be inert? What is the value of resisting our sex, of using it as a weapon, a dangling tease, to lure unwary males into positions in which we may frustrate, humiliate, threaten, and exploit them? We thrust torches into straw and scold the straw for burning.

But I think there is not really anything wrong with the women of Earth. I think it is only necessary for them to tread beyond that "pale of enlightenment," and find the natural world, which is beautiful.

It is still there.

There is nothing really wrong with the women of Earth. They have just not yet found their collars.

Forgive this disquisition, Master. Such thoughts must, of course, sound strange to you, alien and foreign, you of my old world, Earth.

Perhaps, however, they explain to some extent why Goreans believe Earthwomen make excellent slaves. And why they do make excellent slaves. They have languished too long in a sexless desert. Here they find the rains of Gor, and the verdant fields of a natural world. Let them feel the life-giving rain and run naked through the soaked grass. Here, Master, if they are clasped in the chains of masters, they are at least freed from those of politics. Here they are given no choice but to reveal, under threat of punishment, the sexuality they were forced to deny on Earth; on Earth they hoped to meet men before whom they could be only submissive; here, on Gor, they find men before whom a woman can only be submissive; on Earth they scarcely dared dream of their conquest; here, on Gor, they are conquered; on Earth they toyed with the thought of meeting strong men, so few on Earth, so denounced, so forbidden, perhaps even, in bold, shameless fancy, of granting them favors; here, yielded, capitulated, subjugated, and vanquished, prostrate in capture thongs, they beg for the privilege of being spared, to be accepted as abject slaves.

I told you, Master, that I have learned something of my master, Rask of Harfax. He is a slaver, and the house in

Harfax, with which he is affiliated, has arrangements with this house, in Besnit. They exchange slaves, want lists, and such. Apparently, as one would suppose, there are slave routes plied between this world, Gor, and Earth, and perhaps others, but I do not know. Too, there are apparently intrigues amongst these two, or however many, worlds. Agents are exchanged from time to time. Rask of Harfax, my master, utilizing a different name, and cover, is, or was, working on Earth, in some capacity that I do not even think is clear to my informants. To be sure, he apparently chooses women, as it pleases him, for acquisition and shipment to this world. I say "shipment" for these women are not passengers, but cargo. They are brought here as objects, to be vended in the slave markets. It is a business; they might as well be vegetables or cattle. The slaves I saw on Earth, in my assignment for the magazine, were to be bid upon by various wholesalers, who would then have them delivered to their respective houses. Presumably they are brought to a port here, somewhere, and then distributed as arranged, presumably by wagons and such, in which they would doubtless be chained. Much seems clandestine about these operations, at least with respect to aspects which are subtler than the acquisition of slaves.

Whereas an advanced technology would obviously be required to bring me, and others, to this world, the technology of this world, as a whole, paradoxically, seems primitive, or, perhaps better, classical.

I must, on Earth, have been seen by this Rask of Harfax, or an agent. I do not know where this took place, perhaps in a restaurant, in leaving a cab, on the street, somewhere. Someone must have decided that I was, even then, dare one say, "of interest." Perhaps he thought I had "promise." Perhaps he speculated that I would "do." I suppose I should be flattered that I was assessed worthy to be a Gorean slave girl. Without wishing to sound vain, I suspect few are. Interestingly, many of the girls brought here have natural female bodies, cuddly, juicy, and exciting, short, perhaps a little plump. To be sure, we have our "model" types, as well.

Some women, perhaps at the time a little less beautiful, are apparently selected because of a powerful, latent sexuality. But I think that even they soon become as beautiful as the others, for a woman's beauty blossoms in bondage, as she becomes less inhibited, and more natural, more radiant, freer, happier, more emotionally liberated. Too, interestingly, the men seem keenly interested in the minds of their captives, strange as that may seem to a woman who finds herself stripped and chained. Whereas a master may castigate a slave as "stupid," when she may be merely ignorant, or has made a mistake, or simply because it pleases him, it is clear that we are far from stupid, and the brutes know it. Who wants a stupid slave? Intelligent slaves bring higher prices. They make better slaves. I have met two slaves here who have Ph.D.'s, one in the social sciences, and one in the humanities. But neither, I think it fair to say, seems really more intelligent than her peers in the collar. This may dismay them, but it is true. This is not surprising, of course, as it seems that high intelligence is one of the criteria for selection. And it did not take long, I assure you, for our two young, lovely Ph.D.'s, the first a brunet, from a university, the second a blonde, from a college, to learn that such distinctions, degrees, honors, and such, mean nothing here. They needed look no farther than the shackles on their wrists and ankles, than the bars of their cage, viewed from within, to discern that. Indeed, here, if anything, such distinctions would be a handicap. Here, it only matters how good a slave you are. They learned that quickly. You see, they are intelligent.

Yet it seems to me that, on the whole, the intellect of the masters is greater than that of the slaves, including, of course, mine. The psyches of men here have not been divided, reduced, confused and crippled, riddled with inhibitions and contradictions. Their intellects are whole and free, and allies, not enemies, of their blood.

That is the way we want it.

How wonderful is the mind of the natural man!

Sometimes it infuriates a new slave to learn that her master relishes owning the whole of her, but, soon, she understands that it is, indeed, the whole of her, every corpuscle of her, and the least and most secret of her feelings and thoughts, that is relished, prized, and owned.

But sometimes, too, the brutes put us to our knees and treat us as though we were nothing, no more than the dust beneath their feet, and we, then, kneeling, heads bowed, knowing ourselves no more than the dust beneath their feet, better know our collars, and better understand what we are, to our joy, slaves.

So, Rask of Harfax, or someone, it seems, saw me, and arranged, perhaps for his amusement, that I should be introduced into a slaving area, under the pretext of investigative reporting, an area in which, of course, I soon found myself taken in hand, back-cuffed, and rendered unconscious.

But I am not sorry to be here, though here I am only a meaningless slave.

I know little more than this of my master, Rask of Harfax.

It gives me comfort to be allowed to write to you. I wonder if you have ever received any of these letters.

I wonder if I am really a worthless slave.

Doubtless it is true, but that really means, I suspect, merely that the keepers are not yet fully satisfied with me. Surely I have seen their eyes glint, as they have looked upon me, as I, fearing the whip, was forced to move lasciviously, provocatively before them in my training.

But a master might improve me, I am told, training me to his tastes. I wonder if you would like to train me to your tastes, Master, teaching me your tastes in drinks and food, how you wish your shirts ironed, how you would like your bed turned down, and such, and how, of course, I should perform in the bedroom, or elsewhere, perhaps in the living room, or on a porch, or in a garden. I wonder if you would keep me chained at the foot of your bed, in the Gorean fashion. I wonder, if you kept me as your slave, on Earth, say, in your penthouse, in Manhattan, or on that estate on

Long Island to which it seems you have access, if you would let others know, that I might be shamed, revealed there, though on Earth, as no more than a degraded slave. Or if you would keep my bondage secret, choosing to conceal my abject servitude from the world, keeping it a secret known only to two, the slave and her master.

But even a worthless slave, I take it, would bring a few coppers in the market. Some might buy her, for example, on speculation, whip-training her, and then putting her up for a profit.

I wonder if you would bid on me, and, if your bid was successful, what you would do with me. You would promptly free me, doubtless. But I wonder. Seeing what I have become, I think you might not free me. You might like the way I am now. You might keep me. At least, if you found me pleasing. I wonder if you would find me pleasing. I do not wish to shock you, Master, but I would try to be pleasing.

I would try desperately to be pleasing to you. If I were not pleasing to you, fully, and in all ways, I trust that you would see to it that I became so.

To the master belongs the whip. There is no slave who does not fear its stroke. If she is not pleasing, she knows it will be used on her.

I sensed you were the sort of man who could whip a slave, and would whip her, if she were not pleasing.

I sensed that you were the sort of man who could whip me, and would whip me, if I were not pleasing.

I wonder if this is true.

Please do not be offended.

It is just a thought.

Were you to come for me in the house tonight, carrying a lamp, you would find me in Room Twenty-Seven. There are many such rooms, it seems. I did not know that before. Climb the steel steps and stand on the narrow, steel walkway. I will be on tier three, in cage two. You need not worry about not finding me there. I will be locked within. In the light of your lamp, I would awaken, and perform obeisance before you. If I do not immediately awaken, strike the bars, or prod me. That is what the guards would do.

Am I a worthless slave?

I suppose it is true.

But how could I, from my world and background, my warpings and distortions, my terrible Puritanical conditionings, my negativities, compete with exuberant, sexually liberated, sexually free, collared beauties native to this world?

But I must try, Master.

I am told that Earthwomen make good slaves. I shall strive desperately to be such.

A worthless slave,
Linda

Twenty-First Letter,

En'Kara, Twenty-Fifth Day

Master:

I am longing for a master, I am longing for my master, who is Rask of Harfax. I hope he will be kind to me, but firm, as well. I know I need discipline. And Gorean men, I am certain, will supply it. Some masters are doubtless harsh, and some perhaps excessively severe. That makes me afraid. That is a frightening thought. We, as slaves, are so vulnerable!

I wonder what my master will be like.

One wonders, one is afraid.

It is my hope that he will not be too harsh, or too severe. But I would prefer him to be terribly harsh, or even terribly severe, to being weak. I want him to be firm, categorical, uncompromising, *absolutely uncompromising*, and strong. I want to be in no doubt that I am truly his slave. We want to fear our masters, as well as love them. How else can we be their slaves? We wish to know that we have no alternative other than to obey instantly and unquestioningly, and with perfection.

How else could we so fully serve them, and so fully love them, and so helplessly and joyfully yield to them—with the unmitigated rapture of the totally conquered, totally owned, helplessly ravished slave?

I am the sort of girl who needs someone to keep her in line. I must toe the mark, if necessary, fearfully.

And, I am informed by the men of this house, my keepers and trainers, that I need have no fear on this count, that no Gorean master will leave that matter to chance!

I entertain that intelligence with apprehension, but anticipation.

I long to cry out, to moan, to gasp, to scream, to weep my submission to my master!

Who is this Rask of Harfax?

Some of the keepers know this Rask of Harfax. Perhaps they have worked with him. They assure me that he will make me "crawl well." His discipline is apparently strict, and uncompromising. I hope I will not be punished frequently. I will surely try to please him, with the all of me, with my body, my hands, my fingers, my lips, my tongue, my hair—and with my mind, my imagination, my emotions, and my heart, and my soul, all of me! After all, I am his. He owns me.

As a female slave, I would be less than his dog.

I will try to serve him well.

Surely he does not know me personally, and will have no reason to "pay me back" for anything, no reason to exact any revenge upon me, now that I am a vulnerable, helpless, defenseless slave.

I will be a stranger to him, and he will know nothing of me other than my appearance. Presumably he will have passed on that, somewhere, personally or from photographs, perhaps from video film. He may not even remember approving my acquisition, perhaps by no more than putting a check by my name on a collection order.

How fearful it would be, if he had known me! How much I would have to pay for! If a great deal were known about me, the things I did and said, and tried to do, at the magazine, and elsewhere, I fear that I would be in considerable jeopardy, and would be due for, as well as would richly deserve, much punishment. Hopefully he will know nothing of such things. Hopefully he will seldom beat me. Perhaps I must be beaten at times, if only to remind me that I am a slave, but I hope, on the whole, as I shall serve him to the best of my ability, doing all I can to please him, that he will be an understanding and tolerant master, and will not hurt me.

I do not want to be hurt.

I want to be owned, and to love. I want to love him with the helpless, vulnerable, glorious wonders of a slave's love.

I long to meet my master, my beloved master, he who owns me, wholly, he whose I am. It is my hope he will soon come for me, or that I will be hooded, and taken to him. I long for his chains. I want to kiss his whip. I would beg to do so. I want him to use it on me, if he wishes. I am totally his. I want him to strip me, to lock my hands behind my back in slave bracelets. I want to kneel before him, and serve him.

I see that a tear has fallen on the page. I hope that I will not be punished for that. I do not think I shall be. If I am, I must accept the punishment unquestioningly, making no objection, for I am a female slave.

That is appropriate for a female slave. To go fearfully, weepingly, tremblingly, unquestioningly, to the cuffs. Does that shock you?

Let me shock you further.

Linda embraces her bondage. Looking upon her branded thigh she rejoices. She treasures her brand. She loves her collar. She now respects men, and knows them as the master sex. She desires that they be so, for without that she cannot fulfill her womanhood. She takes pleasure in submission, in kneeling and serving.

She has been made a slave. It is right for her. Her bondage is precious to her. She wants it. She loves it!

How you, of Earth, must scorn her for that!

But what can you know of these things, you, a man, and one of Earth?

Ah, yes, you are a man of Earth!

You have been informed as to what a woman must be, as I was, as well. Who decided that, I wonder, and with what purpose in mind.

How disappointed then you must be in me. What has become of that proud, privileged, independent, free female, I do not say "woman," you were supposed to esteem, respect, and, too, hurriedly advance? She has surely fallen far short of the political criteria of your culture.

No longer does she conform to external criteria, imposed from without, but rather, now, to the internal songs of her awakened heart.

You are a man of Earth!

So despise me, hold me in contempt, scorn me as you might "the dust beneath your feet"! All these things, if you wish. I do not object. And it would not matter if I did. Too, I accept it. It is fitting. I am a slave.

I am content now to be what I am. And I love being what I am. It is what I want, for the first time in my life not what someone else wants, that I may be enlisted as an ally to further unnatural and hateful ends.

Let no one else tell me what I am to be. Let me be what I want to be.

I am content.

I wonder if you would know me now, Master. Physically perhaps, but inwardly, psychologically?

She whom you knew as an unpleasant, outspoken, ill-tempered, officious, beautiful, slyly conniving colleague is now quite different, very different; you cannot expect a woman to be the same in bondage, as out of it; she is now only a slave, his, her master's, and humbly begs to serve him. As you can see now, Master, the Linda you knew is indeed now "worthless," not only from an impatient, chiding keeper's point of view, given her impoverishments, her ignorances and naiveties as a slave, that she has not yet fully satisfied them, but, surely, too, from an Earth point of view, from the currently required political point of view, so denaturalized and superficial, and doubtless, man of Earth, from your point of view. Surely you can no longer respect me, for what I have become, if you ever did. So rejoice, the nasty, troublesome Linda you knew is now worthy of no more than your contempt. Despise her.

Despise her, for she is now only a worthless, meaningless, embonded slut. Yet, Master, she is happier now than ever she was on Earth.

Desiring to serve her master,
Linda

Twenty-Second Letter,

En'Kara, Twenty-Eighth Day

Master:

I shall miss writing to you.

I have been informed that this is the last letter I am to write to you.

I am informed that my master, Rask of Harfax, is soon returning from Earth. In several days, he should be here, in Besnit. Then I am to be hooded, and taken before his curule chair, and knelt there. It seems he is an important personage. Naturally I am diffident, nay, even fearful, to belong to someone so important.

How unworthy I am to be the slave of such a man!

Then I am to be unhooded, and look for the first time upon the face of my master, he who owns me, who can treat me as he wishes, who can do with me as he pleases.

I am afraid, but eager.

Who is Rask of Harfax?

I wonder if you have ever received any of these letters.

If you have received them, or any of them, and read them, I am grateful. Thank you, Master.

I do not know if I told you this, and I hope the observation does not insult you, or trouble you, but you seem much as these Gorean men, Master. They remind me of you. You remind me of them. I think that you are strong enough, demanding enough, possessive enough, jealous enough, aggressive enough, ambitious enough, all the forbidden, outlawed virtues of manhood on Earth, to be Gorean. How rare for a man of Earth! So few of the males of Earth are men. Thus, so few of the females of Earth are women. I wonder if Nature designed the sexes to supplement one another, to achieve a wholeness of species, rather than to conflict with, and contradict, one another. How grotesque is the prescribed masculinization of women, the prescribed feminization of men, the spiritual spaying and neutering. Of what value is that to a gene pool, or species? How can it prove of benefit to any but the haters, and the failed and frustrated?

Forgive me for these thoughts.

I am lonely. I await my master. I am his to claim, his to serve. Yesterday they again brought me helplessly to the verge, and would not permit me the fulfillment, of the yielded slave girl. I am told that that moment, that conclusive, crucial, decisive victory over me, which would convince me of my bondage as nothing else, though I am piteously desperate to yield it, now to anyone, belongs to my master. He will apparently have it so. Thus it will be so. I long to lie in his arms, branded, in his collar, his by custom, by nature, by law, by might.

Farewell, Master.

I am she whom you once knew as Linda, now a Gorean slave girl.

Do not think badly of me.

I am happy.

I wish you well,
Linda

The Old Man and the Sprinkling Can

THE old man was not sure what to do about the sprinkling can. He was a painter. Perhaps you have seen samples of his work.

The can was in the studio, against the wall, below one of the horizontal bars, of the sort utilized by the dancers in their exercises.

A large mirror was on the other side of the room.

It is not really clear what the sprinkling can was doing there, but one supposes that there were plants about the studio, and it doubtless had its humble horticultural role.

He was very fond of the dancers, and often painted them. To be sure, who would not be fond of the dancers, such lively, exquisite, graceful young women.

Sometimes I think it is only an old man who truly understands how beautiful women are. One sees them when young, of course, naively, almost innocently, through the frames and flames of delight and desire. How blessed and precious is that vision! How unpredictable, and different, and marvelous they are! Now when one is old, or even middle-aged, one understands the wings of summer and the finite tracks of the morning, and the unrelenting parabolas and meridians of time, the ineluctable trajectory of seasons, the imminence of cold winds, readying themselves in their factories and burrows beneath the horizon, understands the messages of falling leaves, of the shortening of days, the coming of winter, of the ineluctable desolation.

Understanding these things the older man, or perhaps even the middle-aged man, sees young women in a very special way. He is no less aware, of course, of their beauty and desirability than the newest creatures, rising even now to the crest of the turning wheel, young creatures vigorous and curious, startled and enraptured, hearing for the first time the pipes of Pan. But he sees their beauty not only with the eyes of youth, but, too, beyond that, with the wondering poignancy of an aware, condemned creature, one frailly and briefly, for so short a time, ensouled.

Surely wisdom is a treacherous, venomous gift, one arriving in its own time, not always welcome, and surely uninvited, but, too, it is one not without its pleasures.

It is through the eyes of wisdom that one sees time, and bodies, and souls, like falling leaves.

And thus the old man, or I suppose even the middle-aged man, sees women in a special way, sees them not simply in their flowering but also in their journey, in their passage, sees them even now against the onset of winter, and, thus, in this way, he not only sees them, but knows them, cares for them, and loves them.

In this way he can understand them, in a way the young man doesn't, and, in my view, shouldn't.

The dancers painted by the old man are still with us. Don't we wish we knew them as he did, as they fussed with their costumes and shoes? They are still there, alive in their way, thanks to his work, and love, alive and busy, oblivious to us, as we look on, in the paint and canvas. I suppose they are not immortal, even there, no more than mountains or pyramids, but we still have them with us, thanks to him, at least for now. We would have liked to see them perform.

So what has this to do with the sprinkling can?

A great deal, actually.

You see, the old man had painted this picture, of these young dancers, at their work, and exercises, just one of many pictures, and they, as usual, not even noticing him really, or not muchly so. And he had the sprinkling can in the picture.

That is where the problem comes up.

Should that sprinkling can be in the picture or not? What is the point of a sprinkling can in a picture of dancers? Surely it does not belong there. So he paints it out. But now he is troubled. This is supposed to be a realistic picture, as honest to sprinkling cans as dancers, and art should be truthful, and the can, after all, was there. And so he paints the can back in. There it is again now, right there, in the picture. But who is master, the painter, or the sprinkling can? Is he to be a naive naturalist, a mindless realist, at the mercy of accidents, of posters, cracks in walls, of furniture, wherever it might be located, and sprinkling cans? Certainly not. An artist is not one of those new-fangled, obnoxious machines that can't even hold a brush, a mere device, a mechanism, that routinely, dispassionately, docilely reproduces an image of whatever it happens to find in front of it. So the can is painted out. Good riddance! Or pretty good riddance! The artist is master. And does not a true artist inevitably, as the saying is, dip his brush in his own heart's blood? And in what richer color could he paint? Is he a spineless employee of reality, one of its minor clerks, or is he to be its reshaper, a demiurge molding worlds to his own pleasure? Certainly. So the sprinkling can does not have to be there! He agrees with that. It does not have to be there, and he has painted it out. But now he must ask himself a serious question, one quite compatible with his own emboldened, volitional sovereignty. To be sure, the decision is his. The question, of course, is now: Should the sprinkling can be there?

In the end it is there, because he wants it there, because it is right that it should be there. In its way, it had an aesthetic obligation to be there. It has an artistic duty to discharge, and will discharge it.

He paints the sprinkling can back in.

Why should he have done that?

Remember the girls, and the world, and darkness and light, and spring and summer, and fall and winter. Remember the barracuda, the leopard, the smile of a baby, the stain of rain on a brick wall, the sun behind clouds, the snort of a horse, and its pawing, the growl of the lion, voicing its warning, the hawk in flight, high, so beautiful, so terrible, the shadow of a tree on rocks, the rodents of time, so patient; recall night and day, and the absurdity of it all, and the infinite, transient preciousness of it all. And the sprinkling can is a part of this. It is a mundane artifact, perhaps, but does one effect anything critical on that score? Is it not beautiful in its simple, complacent way, humble and unassuming, and is it not very real, as real as moons and stars, and pebbles and molecules, in its metal and shaping, and surely it hints of plants, and flowers, and growing things, and their joy and doom, and it is there, after all, somehow, in the studio. And does it not, as it happens, have something to say, somehow, in its own way, about dancers, and differences, and the ways of the world, about the large and the small, and the important and the unimportant, which is so important, and about life? We think so. Not only the girls are beautiful but small things, as well, the sound of the shoe on the smooth wood, the rain splashed on the window, the piano, not in such good tune, the sharp reprimand of the *régisseur.*

And so I think, all in all, the old man was right.

And the sprinkling can remains in the picture.